"TARGET ACQUISITION!"

"Cool it, man!" Stratton warned. "We don't have release yet!"

The MiG ahead leveled out two thousand feet above the jungle. Bayerly followed the target onto the deck. Green mountains flashed past on either side as the fleeing aircraft wound its way up the Nam Mae Taeng Valley. He'd heard Tombstone's warning and knew the MiG's wingman was somewhere behind him but decided to hang on for a few more seconds. There was still time . . .

"Come on," Bayerly muttered, willing the carrier to give him permission to fire. "Come on, you bastards."

The target circle jittered back and forth on his HUD, but Bayerly kept the F-14 pressing in on the MiG's tail. A brilliant pinpoint of light broke free from the target, then a second and a third, all trailing smoke in graceful arcs toward the jungle. The bandit was popping flares, trying to break Bayerly's lock.

"Made It!" Stratton yelled. "I see him! The other bandit's all over us!"

"Hold on, Kid! I'm on this one. . . ."

"Oh, shit! He's goin' for a lock, man!"

"Cowboy Leader, this is Homeplate. Your request for weapons release is denied. Repeat, denied. Standard ROEs apply. Fire only if fired upon."

"Come on . . . come on . . ."

CARRIER

Book Two
VIPER STRIKE

Keith Douglass

J
JOVE BOOKS, NEW YORK

CARRIER 2: VIPER STRIKE

A Jove Book / published by arrangement with
the author

PRINTING HISTORY
Jove edition / December 1991

ISBN: 0-515-10729-8

Jove Books are published by The Berkley Publishing Group,
200 Madison Avenue, New York, New York 10016.
The name "JOVE" and the "J" logo
are trademarks belonging to Jove Publications, Inc.

PRINTED IN THE UNITED STATES OF AMERICA

10 9 8 7 6 5 4 3 2 1

PROLOGUE

General Hsiao Kuoping stooped beneath the still-turning blades of the helicopter as he strode across the tarmac toward the group waiting to receive him. It had rained the night before, and the runway was slick with pools of water on which the helo's prop wash etched churning patterns.

The long flight northeast from Rangoon had only added to Hsiao's anger. Twenty-four hours before he had been in Bangkok. Travel from the Thai capital to this remote corner of Burma was dangerous, and the chance of discovery became greater each time he risked travel between the two countries.

Hsiao was not in uniform, but the Burmese honor guard snapped to attention and the officers saluted. One of the three officers present wore the austere uniform of a general of the Chinese People's Army. The other officer, a ponderously fat man, wore the gaudy uniform trappings of a Burmese army general.

With his glasses, short stature, and graying hair, Hsiao Kuoping looked more like a college professor than a military officer, but the attitude of his reception committee was one of deference. Once, he had been director of the foreign service branch of China's intelligence directorate. Theoretically, he still was. Beijing did not yet know that he was now working not for them, but for himself.

1

Thunder rolled through the sky, and Hsiao looked up. A pair of Chinese fighters, Shenyang J-7s, dropped below the overcast and overflew the field, the tops of their swept-back wings trailing white contrails in the wet, morning air.

"This is indeed an honor," one of the Chinese officers said. A small, waspish man, General Xiang Xu was Hsiao's commander of the PRC forces covertly based in Burma. "We thought you were remaining in Bangkok until the end of the week."

"That was my plan, yes," Hsiao replied, his voice low and dangerous. Xiang and the Chinese colonel at his side shifted uncomfortably under his stare. The fat Burmese officer, who did not speak Mandarin, just looked confused. "Unfortunately, events seem to have dictated a change of that plan. What cretin ordered the suspension of flights from Fuhsingchen?"

Xiang swallowed. "I . . . I gave the order, Comrade General."

Hsiao stared down at the smaller man until Xiang dropped his gaze. "And your reason?"

"We received word here two days ago that an American aircraft carrier battle group was entering the Gulf of Thailand, possibly in support of the Bangkok regime. I thought it would be best if we suspended the flights from Fuhsingchen, rather than risk being detected by the Americans."

"And are the Americans so formidable that everything I have planned, everything I have worked for must be suspended simply because a few of their ships approach the Thai coast?"

"Sir . . . *comrade* . . . we tried to notify you. But communications between our base here and Bangkok are slow and uncertain."

"I sent the message alerting you to the situation yesterday, General," Colonel Wu Ying added quietly. He gave Xiang a sideways glance. "I thought you should be apprised of the situation."

"Quite right, Colonel." Thunder echoed again as the two fighters approached the airfield once more. Their landing gear were down, their flaps deployed as they settled toward the end of the jungle runway. "I see the transfers have been resumed."

"Only this morning, yes, sir," Wu said. "Eighteen have arrived already, counting those two. Those still at Fuhsingchen should all be here within the next twenty hours. I ordered the flights resumed as soon as your message reached us this morning."

Hsiao watched in silence as the two J-7s touched down and shrieked past the spot where the group stood. Drogue chutes popped from their tails, slowing them.

This operation had been years in the making. It was complex and far-reaching, and the most insignificant of incidents could unravel everything. Xiang's interference could have destroyed the timetable completely.

Hsiao arrived at a decision. "Colonel Wu, place General Xiang under arrest."

Wu stiffened to attention. "Sir!" Two of the soldiers nearby stepped forward, flanking Xiang. One pulled the pistol from the general's holster.

"I protest!" Xiang exploded. "I have friends on the Central Committee!"

Hsiao ignored the man. "Colonel Wu, you are in command here now."

"Comrade General," the colonel said, drawing himself up taller and squaring his shoulders with pride. "You honor me!"

Hsiao knew exactly what thoughts were going through Wu's mind—recognition, advancement, promotion . . . It was a shame that so capable an officer was doomed to disappointment. As far as the fighter squadron commander knew, he was here with his command in Burma on the orders of Beijing, part of a covert program sanctioned by the Central Committee.

Colonel Wu would have been shocked to learn that the Chinese aircraft now based at Mong-koi had been diverted from other duties by Hsiao's own intelligence apparatus, that Beijing knew nothing of this operation. The planes were being assembled at Mong-koi using the same arms pipelines that had funneled Chinese arms to revolutionary governments around the world for decades.

But the requisitions and the approvals had been Hsiao's, not the Party's.

Wu would be lucky not to be shot once his part in this affair was known. As for Xiang and his friends in Beijing, he would never have a chance to communicate with them. Their fates, however, did not concern Hsiao, except for the need to keep the colonel's suspicions allayed until after *Sheng li* was fully under way.

Sheng li. The phrase, Mandarin for *victory*, sang in Hsiao's brain like the theme of a people's triumphal march. Soon, soon . . .

"You will maintain the timetable as I have written it," Hsiao told Wu. "Events in Thailand have reached the point where nothing must interfere with the timing of this operation. Nothing!"

"Understood, Comrade General. And General Xiang?"

Hsiao spared the general a single glance. The man stood between his two guards, half supported by them. His eyes were glassy, and he looked as though he were in shock.

Hsiao had known Xiang was a fool from the beginning. The man's sole virtue lay in the ease with which Hsiao had been able to manipulate him, and the former intelligence officer had needed a high-ranking puppet at Fuhsingchen airbase in south China in order to divert the stolen aircraft.

But he was no longer needed, and his weakness made him a liability now.

"Shoot him," Hsiao said.

"No! I am a loyal general officer of the People's Republic! You cannot do this!" Xiang struggled in the grip of his captors, but he was helpless. His screams and shouted protests and threats dwindled away as the guards frog-marched him away.

"I insist you tell me what is going on!" the Burmese general said, speaking Burmese. General Nung Kol's round and florid face gave the impression that he was sweltering in the braid-heavy coat with its row upon row of medals.

"Nothing that need concern you, General," Hsiao said, easily slipping into Burmese himself. "A breach in discipline is being corrected."

The sharp crack of a gunshot rang from around the corner of the air operations building punctuating Hsiao's bland statement.

Kol's eyes widened at the sound and he licked his fat lips. "I warned General Xiang that the shipments of fighters from China should not be interrupted. I warned him that—"

"*Sheng li* will continue as planned," Hsiao said quietly, interrupting him.

General Kol cast a brow-furrowed glance toward the sky. As commander of the new military base at Mong-koi, he was continually worried about the Chinese presence here, unsanctioned by his superiors in Rangoon. He, in his way, was as much a traitor to his own people as was Hsiao. "You are certain, General Hsiao, that the Americans cannot detect these aircraft with their satellites? I have heard that they can see in the dark, that they can read newspapers from space—"

"Calm yourself, General. Not even the Americans can watch everything that happens everywhere in the world! And if they do see them, so what? Your government does not even know these planes are here, true? The Americans may protest to Rangoon, and Rangoon will deny everything, and there the matter shall rest, for the Americans will be unwilling to pursue it. I assure you, General Kol, that they will have no idea of the true situation until it is far too late."

"The Americans could still pose a serious problem," the Burmese general insisted. "The Thais have been their pets for years. And an American *carrier* . . ."

Hsiao kept his face a smiling mask. Kol was as stupid as he was corrupt, a useful tool within the Burmese military structure who also happened to be in the pay of the various drug syndicates ruling the Golden Triangle. Hsiao had been able to control him easily enough so far simply by threatening to expose those financial connections, but soon the time would come when he could dispense with the Burmese warlord entirely. In the meantime, he had no idea that *Sheng li* was designed not to destabilize the Thai government—though that, too, was part of it—but to bring Thailand and Burma to the brink of war.

"I know about the U.S.S. *Thomas Jefferson*, General," Hsiao said. "But their so-called supercarriers are not as

invulnerable as they would have you believe. You may leave
them to me."

Kol watched the aircraft slowing at the far end of the
runway, then turning in line to make their way toward
camouflaged hangers. "Are these planes sufficient to deal with
the American carrier, then?" he asked.

"Twenty-five Shenyang J-7s once they've all arrived,"
Hsiao said. "Ten Nanchang Q-5 ground attack planes. An
American nuclear carrier like the *Jefferson* carries ninety
aircraft. In fighters alone they outnumber us. But it will not
come to that."

"You seem quite sure of yourself," Kol said stiffly.

"You must trust me on this, my dear General Kol. When the
time comes, *your* people will deal with the Royal Thai Army,
Colonel Wu here will deal with their air force." He paused and
allowed himself a smile. "And I will deal with the *Jefferson*!"

Colonel Wu grinned. "That will be a tremendous victory,
Comrade General," he said in Burmese. "The Central Committee will make you a Hero of the People."

Hsiao watched the last of the J-7s vanish into a hangar at the
far end of the airfield. The irony of Wu's patriotic sentiment
was amusing. If Beijing found out too early what he was doing,
it would mean disgrace . . . then death. The rewards, however, made any risk worthwhile. Riches and power far beyond
anything possible in the service of the State would soon be
his . . . and his alone.

Hsiao smiled. "Yes," he agreed. "It will be a victory such as
the world has never known."

CHAPTER 1

The U.S.S. *Thomas Jefferson*, CVN-74, surged ahead through gentle seas. Her flight deck was a confusion of urgent motion as men in bright color-coded jerseys made ready to hurl two forty-million-dollar aircraft into the sky.

In the cockpit of an F-14D Tomcat perched on the carrier's Number One catapult, Lieutenant Commander Matthew Magruder, call sign "Tombstone," made a final check of his aircraft's systems, his eyes sweeping the gauges and dials of the F-14D's instrument console for any sign of failure or malfunction. Turning in his ejection seat and glancing back over his shoulder, he could see the ready light showing yellow high on the island superstructure of the carrier.

Off the starboard side of his aircraft, he could see the bow catapult officer, wearing a yellow jersey and the bulbous radio headgear known as Mickey Mouse ears, cycling his hand vigorously over his head. Tombstone pushed the twin throttles under his left hand forward, feeling the Tomcat shudder under the twin-engine onslaught of raw noise and power. Glancing aft once more, he saw the air above the deck shimmering with the heat of his jet wash boiling up from the erect shield of Catapult One's Jet Blast Deflector.

The island's ready light winked to green. They were cleared for launch.

7

"All set back there?" he asked.

"Ready to go, Mr. Magruder," his RIO said over the Tomcat's intercom. Lieutenant j.g. Jerry "Dixie" Dixon was Tombstone's Radar Intercept Officer, his backseater for this flight.

To port and aft, a second pale gray Tomcat crouched on Catapult Three, trembling as its pilot throttled up. The modex numbers stenciled on the plane's nose read 232, while the tail displayed the red snake device of Squadron VF-95, the Vipers. The two aircraft would be launching together.

Tombstone faced starboard again and casually tossed a two-fingered salute to the bow catapult officer, informing the deck crew that he was ready for launch. The cat officer looked left and right, checking first with the bow safety observer, who was standing at his station, arm out, thumb extended into the air, then with the sailor at the bow catapult control console, and finally checking for one last time that the Tomcat and the catapult slot running forward were both clear. Only then did he return Tombstone's salute, twist gracefully to the side with his right hand pointing forward off the bow, then drop to one knee and touch the deck.

Below the flight deck, steam exploded against the catapult pistons, and the cat shuttle attached to the aircraft's nosewheel whipped forward, dragging the F-14 with it in billowing clouds of white vapor.

The jolt flattened Tombstone against his seat. Acceleration pressed his eyes back in his head and squeezed the breath from his body. There was a sharp rattle of steel wheels and a rushing blur of motion as the plane hurtled forward, passing 180 miles per hour in less than three seconds. For one instant the F-14 hung suspended in midair, just off the carrier's bow, and then the wings bit air. Tombstone's left hand punched the gear handle, then he trimmed the ship and brought the stick back, pulling the Tomcat up in a ten-degree climb.

"Tomcat Two-oh-one, good shot," he said, letting the carrier know the cat had delivered power enough to get him safely airborne.

"Two-three-two, good shot," said a voice a moment later.

The second plane was aloft as well. Tombstone pulled back on the throttle until his wingman could catch up. Side by side now, the two aircraft continued to climb, angling toward a patchy ceiling of broken clouds against blue sky.

"We copy, Sharpshooter," the voice of the carrier's Air Boss said over Tombstone's earphones. "Have a good one."

"Rog." Tombstone clicked frequencies on his comm select panel. "Sharpshooter Two, this is Leader. How do you read, over?"

"Loud and clear, Stoney." His wingman was Lieutenant E. E. Wayne, better known as Batman to the rest of Squadron VF-95. "Looks like we're CAVU clear to Bangkok."

Tombstone looked to port. Tomcat 232 was holding position just off his left wing. He saw the helmeted heads of Batman and his RIO, Lieutenant Ken "Malibu" Blake, facing him. Batman gave him a cocky thumbs-up.

"Ay-firmative," Tombstone agreed. Ceiling and visibility unlimited. It was a glorious day for flying. "Next stop, ladies and gentlemen, exotic Thailand . . ."

The two F-14s continued to climb until they reached twenty thousand feet. Scattered clouds spread out below them, cast into sharp relief by their own shadows against the ocean. At three hundred knots—about three hundred forty-five miles per hour—the Tomcat's variable-sweep wings automatically swung back until the aircraft looked like a pair of broad, gray arrowheads hurtling through the blue glory of the sky. The *Thomas Jefferson,* a floating combination of airport and city with six thousand men living under her four-acre roof, dwindled astern until she was lost against the endless sea.

"Sharpshooter Leader, this is Homeplate." Tombstone recognized the voice in his headphones as that of Commander Stephen Marusko, known as CAG for Commander Air Group. "Homeplate" was the call sign designation for the *Jefferson.*

"Sharpshooter. Go ahead, Homeplate."

"Just a reminder, people," CAG said. "Mind the ROEs."

ROEs stood for Rules of Engagement, and these had been meticulously listed and discussed during the preflight briefing that morning. *Jefferson*'s air wing was flying in support of the

Royal Thai Air Force, a mission which would carry them over
a combat zone. They'd been emphatically warned, however,
not to become involved in combat. The ROEs for the op
established a hard deck of ten thousand feet, a lower limit
below which they were not allowed to fly, and established a
shoot-only-when-shot-at protocol that required an order from
the carrier for weapons release.

That would hardly be a problem. So far, the guerrilla forces
fighting the Thai army and air units were armed with nothing
more threatening to aircraft than SA-7 Grails, the shoulder-
launched missiles which explained the hard deck rule. Sharpshooter's op plan called for a rendezvous with one of *Jefferson*'s
KA-6D tankers north of Bangkok for refueling, after which they
were to proceed to the area north of Chiang Mai. Two of
Jefferson's Tomcats were already flying cover for Thai aircraft,
though they'd been ordered to stay out of any actual combat. It
was thought that the mere presence of American carrier aircraft
would reassure the Thais of U.S. commitment to their ally.

So far, everything had gone smoothly since the first patrol
had been launched at 0600 that morning.

"Copy, Homeplate," Tombstone said. "We'll be good."

"Uh . . . Commander?" Dixie's voice was harsh over the
ICS. "We're getting some kind of radar sweep. Intermittent
like."

Tombstone could hear the pulse over his headset, a deep-
throated twang like the plucked string on a bass, repeated every
few seconds. "Search radar," he said. "Probably the airport at
Phu Quoc."

"Jeez, that's creepy."

"No big deal, Dixie." He looked through the canopy to the
right. The coastline of Vietnam lay a hundred miles in that
direction, lost in clouds and distance. He could see a smear to
the northeast which might be Cambodia's Koh Tang Islands.
Vietnam. He thought of his father, shot down in a raid over
Hanoi. "They're keeping an eye on us, that's all."

"Yessir." He heard the hiss of his RIO's rapid breathing over
the intercom. "I guess this stuff is old hat to you, huh, Mr.
Magruder? I mean, after Wonsan and all . . ."

Tombstone wasn't sure how to answer. Dixon was a newbie. He'd come aboard at Yokosuka, *Jefferson*'s last port of call, only three months earlier, one of the nuggets flown into Japan to replace the men lost during the raid into North Korea. He was eager, brash, and excited by the prospect of flying backseat for Tombstone Magruder, but at times the youngster's hero worship could be a bit much.

Hero. The word tasted sour. He'd never wanted it applied to him, never asked for all the fuss. . . .

Matthew Magruder had seen nothing particularly heroic about his actions over Korea three months before. They'd just . . . happened. He'd led the Combat Air Patrol which covered Navy helos ferrying the crew of a U.S. intelligence ship captured by North Korea to safety. There'd been a ferocious dogfight with North Korean MiG-21s. During the turning and burning in the skies above Wonsan, Tombstone's Tomcat had been hit, his RIO badly wounded. Refusing to eject and lose his backseater, he'd somehow limped back to the *Jefferson* on one faltering engine, sliding the crippled F-14 into a flight deck barricade in a shower of sparks.

For Tombstone, there'd been no heroism at the time, no question of bravery . . . only a job to be done and his determination not to drop his unconscious RIO into the gray seas off Wonsan.

The medal they'd given him was a pretty thing, a gold Maltese cross set against a sunburst with the image of a sailing ship in the center. The ribbon was dark blue, bisected by a single vertical white stripe. The commendation that went with it declared that Lieutenant Commander Matthew Magruder had, during the period from 26 September to 30 September of that year, "distinguished himself by extraordinary heroism in military operations against an armed enemy." It went on to mention his six combat kills and the rescue of the wounded Naval Flight Officer in his aircraft.

The Navy Cross was the highest decoration possible short of the Congressional Medal of Honor, and the CMH was awarded only for actions against a nation actually at war with the United

States. The Wonsan strike had not been part of a war, not in the traditional sense; it was typical instead of this new era of international politics, when nations threatened and maneuvered, when ships and aircraft clashed . . . but when the victories were won or lost by politicians.

Men were wounded or killed for the sake of those victories, though, just as in a real war. That was the tragedy, one which no medal could relieve.

He pushed the thought from his mind. Tombstone decided that his father would have been proud of him. Sam Magruder had racked up an impressive display of fruit salad during his short career, including both the Silver Star and the Distinguished Flying Cross.

But the Silver Star had been posthumous, and the expression on his mother's face when she received it along with the word of Sam Magruder's death haunted Tombstone still. He'd gone on to make Navy flying his life, but he tended to be cynical about the medals that came with it. Personally, he was far prouder of the "battle E" Viper Squadron had won for its part at Wonsan.

He shook himself free of the dark mood which threatened to close in on him. "Leader to Sharpshooter Two," he said. "You there, Batman?"

"I'm with you, Stoney."

"Pull out the stoppers. I feel the need for speed."

"Affirm. Let's do it."

"Going to burner. On my mark, three, two, one . . . punch it!"

Tombstone rammed the throttles forward to full military power. The added boost kicked the F-14 forward with a shuddering jolt. As the Tomcat's speed crept up the scale toward Mach 1, the shudder increased . . . then suddenly vanished as the plane broke the sound barrier. Batman's 232 aircraft kept pace.

Behind them, the search radar at Phu Quoc continued to thrum its lonely, monotonous tune.

1358 hours, 14 January
Tomcat 101, near the Thai-Burmese border

Lieutenant Commander John "Made It" Bayerly, CO of the VF-97 War Eagles, banked his Tomcat for a better view of the action on the valley floor below. The terrain here was mountainous, forest-shrouded peaks rising in steep folds and humps above the meandering clefts of valleys. The tree canopy ten thousand feet below was unbroken save for the flash of sunlight from a twisting stretch of river.

To the south, Bayerly could see white contrails drawing themselves across the dark foliage covering the ground. Four Royal Thai Air Force Falcons were making an attack run on suspected guerrilla positions on the banks of the Taeng River—the Nam Mae Taeng, as it appeared on Thai maps. Roads in this area were virtually nonexistent, muddy, twin-rut smugglers' tracks for the most part, but the Thai CIA had reported what might be a truck park and military camp down there. If the rebels *were* getting help from the socialist Burmese government, they would be stockpiled and distributed from such a camp.

In any case, it was the perfect opportunity for the RTAF to practice with their new purchase. The American F-16 Falcons had been delivered to the Thai government only recently. The nimble, dual-purpose aircraft could carry over ten thousand pounds of ordnance for ground attack. Their load on this afternoon was considerably less. Each plane carried four Rockeye II CBU-59s, cluster bombs designed to scatter hundreds of tiny bomblets in a broad footprint across the jungle. Against unarmored troops, their effect would be devastating.

From this high up, Bayerly could not see the attack well, but he could make out the sparkles of detonating bomblets among the trees, saw the surface of the river thrash as the Falcons rocketed up the valley. A contrail stabbed up from the shore, describing an odd, corkscrew path as it chased the Thai Falcons. An SA-7, Made It thought. The reason the ROEs were keeping him stuck uselessly almost two miles above the action.

So far as Bayerly was concerned, the ROEs for this op were nonsense. What good would a show of American support for the Thai government do when the U.S. aircraft were so far above the jungle the guerrillas didn't even know they were there?

Below, the Grail's smoke trail gave out as its fuel was expended, and the warhead dropped unseen back into the trees. The Falcons pulled up and clawed for altitude, their pass complete, their contrails sharp as the planes bored through the humid air above the jungle.

He eased back on his Tomcat's throttles, glancing first at the RPM meter on the panel just above his left knee, then at his airspeed indicator. The thunder of the twin GE F110 engines dropped to a smooth growl as the aircraft, its swing wings extended to their full-forward position, cruised above the rolling green carpet of jungle. His wingman, Lieutenant j.g. Peter Costello, call sign "Hitman," parked his F-14 off Bayerly's starboard wing.

"Hey, Made It," Bayerly's RIO said over the ICS. "Word from Sierra Bravo Four-six. Sharpshooter is refueled and on the way."

"About damn time," Made It replied. "Only danger we're likely to face is being bored to death."

Lieutenant "Kid" Stratton, his backseater, chuckled. "So we'll give the hero his turn on the boonie patrol. I could use a shower and a cup of coffee."

Bayerly didn't answer. Tombstone Magruder and the fuss that had been made over him since Wonsan was rapidly becoming a sore point with Made It. Where the *Jefferson*'s other aviators joked and bantered about Magruder's name in the headlines, the press conferences, and all the rest, for Bayerly it was all simply a bitter reminder that his own career was nearly at an end.

"Magruder can go—"

"Hold it," Kid interrupted. "Something from Sierra Bravo."

"Let's hear it."

There was a click as the RIO piped the radio call through to Bayerly. Sierra Bravo Four-six was one of *Jefferson's* E-2C Hawkeye radar surveillance planes. A so-called "force multiplier," a Hawkeye increased the efficiency of American Naval aircraft by detecting targets at ranges far beyond the reach of the Tomcat's own AWG-9 radar, and by coordinating widely scattered warplanes both on routine patrol and during combat.

"Cowboy, this is Sierra Bravo Four-six," the Hawkeye observer's voice was saying. "We have unidentified bogie, bearing three-five-zero from your position, range five-two miles. Can you confirm sighting, over?"

There was an anxious moment's silence. "Can't find 'em, Made It," Stratton said. "They're lost in the clutter. Must be pretty low."

Made It opened the radio channel. "Sierra Bravo, this is Cowboy Leader. No joy on your sighting. Repeat, no joy. Over." This was ridiculous. If the Hawkeye wanted them to sort targets from the reflected returns off the mountains, they'd have to grant permission to go below the hard deck. At this rate, they wouldn't spot any bogies until the targets were right on top of them.

"Cowboy, Sierra Bravo. Bogie may be Burmese incursion Thai air space. Homeplate requests visual confirmation, repeat, visual. Come to new course, three-four-five. Over."

"We copy, Sierra Bravo." He brought the stick over, watching the compass heading slip through the numbers until the Tomcat was on the indicated bearing. His left hand nudged the throttle forward and the F-14 picked up speed. Hitman Costello's aircraft paced him.

"Yo! Got them," Stratton said. "Two bogies, bearing three-five-one, range forty. Shit, that's across the green line, Made It. You think they're Burmese?"

The green line was shorthand for the Thai-Burmese border. "Probably a couple of Thai recon planes that got lost," Made It replied. "Sierra Bravo Four-six, this is Cowboy. We have the bogies and are going to buster."

Together, the Tomcats surged forward, closing rapidly now with the two unknowns. Bayerly eyed the jungle unrolling beneath the belly of his F-14. They were flying over Thai territory now, but farther north, somewhere among those ravines and jungle-covered hills, lay the Shan District of eastern Burma. The green line was clear enough on the map, but political realities were less obvious in the real world. At ten thousand feet there was nothing to distinguish country from country.

Bayerly opened the tactical channel. "Cowboy Leader to Cowboy Two," he said. "You've got overwatch, Hitman. Hang back."

"Affirm, Made It. Watch your hard deck."

Costello's F-14 broke right and cut power. In seconds, Bayerly's aircraft was far ahead.

"Bogies still coming," Stratton said. "Hey, Made It? They're not squawking. I've got IFF on a couple of Thai F-5s down on the deck, but not a beep from the bogies."

"We'll be able to get our primaries on 'em pretty quick," Bayerly replied. "Primaries" was aviator's slang for eyes and instincts. "We should be in eyeball range any time now."

"There are the friendlies. Ten o'clock low."

Bayerly looked in the indicated direction. Two Thai F-5 Freedom Fighters were flying parallel to the Tomcat's northerly course three thousand feet below and half a mile ahead, lean, dagger-slim, and deadly.

"Got 'em." He searched ahead, toward the north. Movement caught his eye, a pair of black specks just above the forest canopy. "Tally-ho!" he called over the radio. "We have bogies in sight."

The specks grew, closing with the Thai F-5s at better than Mach 1. They flashed past so quickly that reaction was impossible, *identification* was all but impossible . . . but Bayerly had an instant's glimpse of delta wings centered on a blunt, tube-shaped fuselage.

"Sierra Bravo," he yelled into the microphone in his oxygen mask. "This is Cowboy Leader! MiGs! MiGs!"

Bayerly pulled back and left on the stick, dragging the Tomcat into a steep turn to port.

"Cowboy Leader, Sierra Bravo." The Hawkeye operator's

voice sounded remote and unhurried. "Homeplate requests verification of bandit sighting."

Bayerly wondered if they believed the report. He wasn't sure he believed it himself. There weren't supposed to be any MiGs here.

"Verified, damn it!" he yelled. "Two MiGs. Two MiGs! Coming in fast!"

CHAPTER 2

Carrier Air Traffic Control Center, pronounced *cat-see* by *Jefferson*'s officers and crew, was a suite of darkened compartments on the 0-3 deck directly beneath the "roof," the carrier's flight deck. Lit by the green and amber glows of numerous radar screens and the illumination from the large, transparent status boards, it was an eerie place where men spoke in urgent but subdued tones, where petty officers paced the decks behind the operators as they listened to air traffic through headsets trailing wires.

Commander Marusko slumped into one of the elevated command chairs normally reserved for the ship Captain or the admiral when they were in CATCC and rested his coffee mug against the chair's arm. "MiGs? *Whose* MiGs?"

"No ID yet, CAG," a senior chief said, pressing a headset earphone to one ear. "Sierra Bravo Four-six says they may have come across from Burma, but they didn't get a solid track. Ground clutter."

"Somebody check *World's* for me." *World's Air Forces* was one of the standard references for the air inventories of other countries. A third-class radarman checked the entry. "Socialist Republic of the Union of Burma," he said, reading. "They've got twenty-two combat aircraft, sir. PC-7s and AT-33s." He looked up. "Nothing in here about MiGs, CAG."

This is damned strange, Marusko thought. If the Burmese didn't have MiGs, who did? Cowboy was a long way from Laos, and China was separated from Thailand by a hundred miles of Burmese territory. "Get the admiral on the batphone," he said, referring to the special phone system which gave a direct line to every important person and department on the ship. "Let him know we could have a situation here."

"The MiGs are closing with the Thai F-5s," the chief announced. "We're getting the feed straight through Sierra Bravo now."

"Pipe it over the speaker, Chief."

There was a hiss of static from the loudspeaker, a burst of noise as a cockpit microphone was opened. "They're closing with the Thai F-5s now." The voice sounded like Bayerly's RIO. "Holy shit! Launch! Launch!"

"Who's shooting at who?" CAG asked.

"Blue bandit launch on one of the F-5s," Stratton said. "Missile in the air!"

There was another burst of static, followed by Bayerly's voice. "Sierra Bravo, this is Cowboy Leader." He didn't know yet that his words were being relayed directly to *Jefferson*'s CATCC. "Request weapons release. Repeat, request weapons release."

"Wait one, Cowboy. Homeplate, Homeplate, this is Sierra Bravo Four-six. Do you copy Cowboy's request, over?"

"Have him wait," CAG snapped. He turned to one of his staff nearby. "Did you get the admiral yet?"

"On his way, CAG."

The situation was exploding out of control with horrifying speed. If one of those MiGs launched on an American aircraft, the Tomcats would return fire. An international incident was in the making here, and Marusko didn't even know who the enemy was.

He looked at one of the transparent plot boards, where sailors practiced at writing backwards were filling in data on two other airborne Tomcats. "Sharpshooter," he said. "Where's Sharpshooter?"

"Due to rendezvous with Cowboy in five minutes."

"Tell 'em to pour on the coal. Get them in there!"

"Aye, sir."

"And scramble the alert fifteen," CAG added, referring to pilots standing by for a launch with fifteen minutes' warning. "I want another flight up ASAP."

1406 hours, 14 January
Tomcat 101, near the Thai-Burmese border

The pair of Thai F-5s had split left and right when the MiGs streaked past. The bandits had hauled around in a high-G turn, side by side in the familiar "welded wing" formation, dropping onto a Freedom Fighter's six—off his tail and following— before loosing the missile. Bayerly had seen the flash, had watched with disbelief as the white contrail unraveled through the sky, tracking the Thai plane.

And *Jefferson*'s only response had been the order to "Wait one." The delay grated at him worse with each passing second. How long was it going to take *Jefferson*'s command staff to debate the issue?

"Homeplate, this is Cowboy Leader!" he called. "We have two MiGs on two RTAF F-5s. Request permission to intervene. Over."

"Cowboy, Homeplate," the reply came back a moment later, scratchy as it was relayed by the far-circling Hawkeye. "Negative your last. Wait one."

The missile was turning now, following one of the F-5s. The Freedom Fighter twisted hard to port, its pilot pulling eight Gs at least as he tried to evade the oncoming air-to-air killer. The contrail swung onto the F-5's tail, still closing, and vanished into the engine exhaust. There was a brilliant flash, followed an instant later by a fireball that ate its way through the Thai plane, scattering fragments of burning debris across the sky. Bayerly watched a stubby wing and a portion of the fuselage tumble as they trailed smoke into the jungle below.

"Homeplate! One Thai plane has been killed. Request weapons release!"

"Copy, Cowboy. Wait one."

"Kid!" Bayerly snapped. "Arm Sidewinders! We'll get a lock while we're waiting for those bastards."

"Weapons armed." The F-14 carried eight of the deadly air-to-air AIM-9L missiles slung beneath its wings.

Bayerly pushed the stick over, putting the Tomcat into a dive. One of the MiGs was cutting across his bow from right to left a mile ahead. He concentrated on the computer-generated images on his heads-up display, willing the targeting pipper to connect with the rapidly moving target symbol.

"Watch the hard deck," Stratton warned. "Watch your altitude, man!"

"Screw the hard deck!" He tightened up on the turn, feeling the Gs press him down against his ejection seat until he dropped in on the other plane's tail, half a mile behind. The MiG was at nine thousand feet and still descending, heading north.

Bayerly followed.

1408 hours, 14 January
Tomcat 201

"I have him!" Tombstone said. "One o'clock and low!"

"Tally-ho!" Batman replied, announcing that he too had the other plane in sight.

"Homeplate, this is Sharpshooter Leader. We have visual on Cowboy Leader and one bandit." He checked his altitude and realized with a jolt that Bayerly was well below the ten-thousand-foot hard deck. "Cowboy is in hot pursuit."

"Copy, Sharpshooter. Stand by."

"Tombstone!" Dixie called from the backseat. "MiG, bearing two-seven-five. He's going for Made It's six!"

Tombstone looked to the left, searching the sky. He saw the second MiG, a thousand feet below and already lining up on Bayerly's tail.

"Cowboy Leader, this is Sharpshooter," Tombstone called. "Wake up, Made It! Watch your six! Bandit coming in hard!"

But he knew it was already too late to stop the MiG from lining up the shot.

1408 hours, 14 January
Tomcat 101

Bayerly heard the warbling growl in his headphones that told
him he had a heat-seeker lock on the plane ahead. The target
pipper on his HUD turned from a square to a circle, with the
letters ACQ flashing beside it. "Target acquisition!"

"Cool it, man!" Stratton warned. "We don't have release
yet!"

The MiG ahead leveled out two thousand feet above the
jungle. Bayerly followed the target onto the deck. Green
mountains flashed past on either side as the fleeing aircraft
wound its way up the Nam Mae Taeng Valley. He'd heard
Tombstone's warning and knew the MiG's wingman was
somewhere behind him, but decided to hang on for a few more
seconds. There was still time. . . .

"Come on," Bayerly muttered, willing the carrier to give
him permission to fire. "Come on, you bastards."

The target circle jittered back and forth on his HUD, but
Bayerly kept the F-14 pressing in on the MiG's tail. A brilliant
pinpoint of light broke free from the target, then a second and
a third, all trailing smoke in graceful arcs toward the jungle.
The bandit was popping flares, trying to break Bayerly's lock.

"Made It!" Stratton yelled. "I see him! The other bandit's all
over us!"

"Hold on, Kid! I'm on this one. . . ."

"Oh, shit! He's goin' for a lock, man!"

"Cowboy Leader, this is Homeplate. Your request for
weapons release is denied. Repeat, denied. Standard ROEs
apply. Fire only if fired upon."

"Kid! Where's our tail?"

"On our six, range one mile! He's got a lock! Made it, he's
got lock!"

Bayerly could hear a second tone over his headset. The
Tomcat was being targeted by the second MiG. "Tell me when
he launches!"

"He's closing, Made It! Still no launch."

"Come on . . . come on . . ."

1409 hours, 14 January
Tomcat 201

Tombstone saw the second MiG lining up on Bayerly's Tomcat. He'd heard the order relayed from Homeplate, but he couldn't wait and do nothing while the enemy plane took a shot at Made It and Kid. He dropped the Tomcat's right wing and slipped into a steep dive. "Hang back, Batman," he called. "We're going in."

"That'll violate the hard deck, Tombstone," Batman replied.

"We'll discuss my fitness report later." He saw three aircraft symbols on his HUD now, Bayerly sandwiched between two MiGs. "Dixie! Tickle that guy with a radar lock."

He lined up on the trailing aircraft, waiting for the warble that told him he had a lock. If he couldn't fire the missile, at least he could startle the MiG's pilot, who would hear the radar lock as a tone in his own headset and know an American plane had him in its sights.

"Tone," Dixie called.

The target MiG did not waver. Either he wasn't aware of Tombstone's weapons lock, or he was gambling that the Americans would not fire first.

"He's not going for it," Tombstone said. "Going to buster." He rammed the throttles full forward, cutting in the Tomcat's afterburners. Acceleration slammed him against his seat.

With startling swiftness, the trailing MiG swelled to fill his HUD. Tombstone cut the burners, then finessed the stick to starboard, angling the F-14 so that it would pass the MiG on its right side with a few yards to spare. At close range, Tombstone could see details of the other plane's construction down to the individual rivets along the fuselage. It was not a Soviet export aircraft, he saw, but a Shenyang J-7, a Chinese copy of the MiG-21 built under license. He'd faced them before over Korea. It was silver with red control surfaces, and he could read the numbers on the nose. There were no national markings or unit ID, however. Was it Chinese, Burmese, or something else?

The pilot looked back at Tombstone across the narrow gap between the aircraft, eyes wide above his oxygen mask. Tombstone brought his stick back to the left, closing the gap slowly, drawing closer . . . closer . . .

The J-7 pilot needed no further urging. As Tombstone brought the F-14 tight across the Shenyang's bow, the other pilot cut his aircraft sharply to the left, breaking contact with Bayerly's plane and angling away from Tombstone with his own afterburner blazing. Tombstone held the turn, pulling a full circle as he began climbing once more.

"Cowboy Leader, this is Sierra Bravo." Tombstone could hear the Hawkeye calling Bayerly. "Cowboy Leader, be advised you are entering Burmese airspace. Come to course one-eight-zero, execute immediate."

Tombstone leveled off at ten thousand feet, searching the northern horizon. Dixie spotted Bayerly's plane first on radar and gave him the bearing. Tombstone could see him then, the second of two contrails flitting across the jungle, two miles to the north and down on the deck.

The border was invisible, but Tombstone knew that Bayerly had already crossed the line and was plunging deeper into Burmese territory with every second.

1409 hours, 14 January
Tomcat 101

Bayerly's thumb caressed the trigger as the MiG grew large in his HUD.

"Cowboy Leader, this is Sharpshooter Leader," Magruder's voice called over the radio. "Break off, Made It. Break off!"

"Cowboy Leader, this is Homeplate," a second voice added. "Terminate pursuit. Repeat, break off and RTB."

Return to base? Bayerly shook himself. He was sorely tempted to fire. But no, his career was in a tailspin already. A stunt like that would make him crash and burn for sure.

"Shit!" Bayerly snapped. Savagely, he yanked back on the

stick, hauling the F-14 vertical as he cut in his afterburners and clawed for the sky. The MiG continued to race toward the north, dwindling into the haze on the horizon. At ten thousand feet Bayerly leveled off, bringing the Tomcat around to a southerly heading. He could see Magruder's plane loitering in the distance, Wayne and Costello circling beyond that. The realization that he'd pursued the enemy MiG miles into Burmese territory hit him like an icy wave.

Quickly, he checked the sky around his Tomcat, but it was empty of hostile aircraft.

"Where's the guy on our tail?"

"Tombstone brushed him off, man," Stratton said. The RIO sounded shaken. "That bandit's heading out of Dodge at Mach 1."

Bayerly groaned inwardly. Magruder again. That made it worse. He pushed the throttles forward, going to buster.

The air battle, such as it was, had ended.

1411 hours, 14 January
Tomcat 201

"Cowboy Leader, Sharpshooter." Tombstone was angry. Bayerly had deliberately violated the ROEs on two points . . . three if you counted mixing it up with the intruder aircraft in the first place. "What the hell were you playing at?"

"Get off my six, Magruder," Bayerly's voice replied. "I'm not in the mood." A short string of profanity followed, harsh and biting.

"Whoa there, don't go ballistic on us, Made It," Tombstone said. "You're way out of line!"

"Tell it to your damned uncle, *hero*," Bayerly snapped. The words carried suppressed fury, and his voice nearly broke. "I've had it with all of you bastards!"

Tombstone opened his mouth to deliver a burning reply, then stopped. Something was riding the other aviator, and until Tombstone knew what it was, he wasn't going to push. He didn't know Bayerly that well, but he could tell that the man was on edge, more than could be explained by post-combat jitters. The CO of the VF-97 War Eagles was a big, bluff man given to occasional bursts of temper, but he was a competent pilot. He wouldn't have been given a squadron skipper's slot if he wasn't.

In any case, the other skipper was not under his command, and the tactical frequency was not the place to chew out another pilot. The whole matter would have to rest until they got back to the carrier.

Then the voice of the Air Officer back aboard *Jefferson* broke in on the tactical net. "This is Homeplate. Ninety-nine aircraft, RTB. I say again, ninety-nine aircraft, RTB."

The radio call "ninety-nine aircraft" referred to all of the carrier's airborne planes. "That's it," Batman said. "They're calling us back to the bird farm."

That wasn't surprising, Tombstone thought. Not after the incident he'd just witnessed, an incident tracked on the Hawkeye's long-range radar. Bayerly was not going to need *his* report to get himself hung.

But the man's attitude still puzzled Tombstone. Crossing a border in hot pursuit of a MiG he could understand. In combat, nothing existed save your plane and your opponent's plane, and the adrenaline rush of battle could wipe everything else from your mind.

It was the acid . . . the *pain* in Bayerly's voice that bothered him, that and the crack about his uncle. Made It had seemed withdrawn for the past few weeks, worried presumably, by something he'd not shared with the other men in the wing. For the first time, Tombstone wondered if the other aviator's personal problems were interfering with his flying.

Navy aviators joked about *living on the edge,* referring to that wild mix of speed, bravado, and arrogance which characterized the life of the typical fighter pilot . . . at least in the perceptions of Hollywood and the public. They did not talk about going *past* the edge, about losing the self-assurance which alone let them put their lives on the line day after day, week after week.

Had Bayerly just lost it? With a trap coming up, they might all be about to find out.

1515 hours, 14 December
Tomcat 101, Marshall stack

Bayerly was still seething as he held his aircraft at two
thousand feet, maintaining his position several miles astern of
the U.S.S. *Jefferson*. The holding pattern, called a Marshall
stack, was primarily used in rough weather or at night, but with
all of the carrier's far-flung aircraft lining up for their traps,
several low on fuel, the Air Marshall had shuffled them into the
stack, giving each its own priority on the big green board in
Ops which kept track of aircraft status.

From fifteen miles out, the *Nimitz*-class nuclear carrier
looked tiny, a sliver of a gray rectangle almost lost on the wide,
gray sea. The other ships of CBG-14, *Jefferson*'s Carrier Battle
Group, were scattered across the ocean in all directions.
Bayerly could make out the lean shape of the U.S.S. *Vicksburg*, the group's Aegis cruiser, trailing the carrier astern; the
DDG *Lawrence Kearny* and the DD *John A. Winslow*
were positioned well out on either flank. Farther out still, mere
specks on the western horizon, were the CBG's two ASW
frigates, *Gridley* and *Biddle*.

"Tomcat One-oh-one," *Jefferson*'s Air Marshall said over
Bayerly's headphones. "Charlie now." That was the signal to
leave the Marshall and begin his approach to the carrier.

"One-oh-one, roger." He banked the F-14, descending to
eight hundred feet and going into the final turn which would
bring the aircraft in above the *Jefferson*'s wake. Pulling out of
the 4-G turn, Bayerly cut the throttles back to idle and popped
the speed brakes. As the F-14 dropped below three hundred
knots, the Tomcat's wings began to slide forward. Bayerly
overrode the wings with the manual control, keeping the
Tomcat looking clean and sleek as it went into the break.

Don't go ballistic on us, Magruder had said. Bayerly
reached up to wipe the sweat from his eyes and found his hand
blocked by his helmet visor. Magruder's words still burned.

Bayerly's discontent had been gnawing at him, ever since
the drama of Operation Righteous Thunder had played itself

out in the skies over Wonsan three months earlier. He was hard
pressed to even identify the emotion, but he knew it was
connected with Tombstone Magruder and the lionization which
had been directed at him ever since the Korean raid.

They'd been treating the guy like a genuine grade-A
hero . . . press interviews, TV, the Navy Cross from the
Secretary of Defense, the works! What Bayerly felt was not
jealousy, exactly, but it was closely akin . . . a sense that
blind luck had once again shown a vicious prejudice. As if the
nephew of the carrier group's admiral needed any *more* luck!

His speed dropped quickly. At two hundred eighty knots
Bayerly let the wings slide forward, providing extra lift and
control at low speed, then lowered the landing gear. At two
hundred thirty knots he lowered the flaps, still slowing, still
descending, now at six hundred feet above the waves and a
mile abeam of the *Jefferson*.

The carrier looked bigger now, but she still carried the
impression of being an impossibly small target on a very large
ocean. The *Jefferson*'s island rose along the starboard side of
her flight deck in a tangle of radar antennæ and masts, of
catwalks and windscreens. From off her port side, he could see
the aircraft arrayed on her deck, appearing tiny and white
against the dark surface of her "roof."

Passing the carrier's stern, Bayerly set his rate of descent at
six hundred feet per minute and initiated a twenty-two degree
bank to the left. Sweeping across *Jefferson*'s wake some three
quarters of a mile behind her, he worked the controls to line up
for his approach to the deck. From here, he could see the
Fresnel lens system on the port side, across the flight deck from
the island. The Fresnel lens, or "meatball," an arrangement of
lights which changed their relative positions as he changed his,
showed him whether or not he was aligned properly with the
carrier's deck. It was time now to "call the ball."

"One-oh-one," he said, identifying his aircraft. "Tomcat
ball. Six point one." The number gave his fuel state, sixty-one
hundred pounds.

"Roger ball," the voice of *Jefferson*'s Air Boss replied from
the carrier's Primary Flight Control, "Pri-Fly" in popular

jargon. The acknowledgment had just passed from the Air Boss to the Landing Signals Officer, or LSO, standing at his station just below the Fresnel lens. Bayerly was half a mile astern of the *Jefferson* now, seconds away from the roundoff of her flight deck.

Damn Tombstone Magruder, anyway! Him and his Top Gun airs. He never boasted about having been through the Navy Fighter Weapons School at Miramar, but he managed to let you know without saying it. There was an arrogance about the man, an assumed superiority.

"Power up!"

Damn! He'd let his speed fall too fast. His Tomcat was dropping too quickly down the glide path. He pulled back on the stick and nudged the throttles forward. The F-14 rose . . . too much, damn it!

"Wave off!" the LSO sang in his ear. "Wave off!"

His wheels touched the deck, but too far forward, missing all four of the arrestor cables stretched across the aft end of the flight deck in his path. He was already jamming the throttles to full forward, building enough thrust to get the F-14 back in the air.

"Bolter! Bolter! Bolter!" The LSO's call was an embarrassing litany as the Tomcat raced down the deck, the island a gray blur off his starboard wingtip. Then he was airborne once more.

CHAPTER 3

1525 hours, 14 January
Flight deck, U.S.S. *Thomas Jefferson*

Tombstone watched the *Jefferson*'s stern spread out before and below his F-14 as he held the aircraft's angle of attack steady. He spared one final glance for the ball, noted that he was square on target, then let the Tomcat slip over the roundoff and down to the deck. His wheels touched with a jolt; at the same moment he rammed the throttles to full military power, just in case his tailhook failed to engage one of the arrestor cables.

He felt the reassuring forward surge of deceleration and dragged the throttles back to idle as the hook snagged the number-three wire. After checking his instruments for fire or warning lights, Tombstone let the F-14 roll backwards slightly to "spit out the wire," then followed the hand signals of a yellow-shirted deck director.

In the sky, a Tomcat is the epitome of grace and maneuverability; on a carrier deck it has all of the delicate grace of a beached walrus, especially when the flight deck is wet or rolling in heavy seas. Carefully, he folded the Tomcat's wings, then nudged the throttles up slightly, using his feet to control brakes and rudder pedals for the turn into his designated parking space.

Chief Bob Smith, crew chief for Tomcat 201, was already unfolding the ladder on the port side beneath the cockpit when Tombstone cracked the canopy. "Smooth mission, Commander?"

"Not bad, Chief." He was still worried about Made It. He'd heard the LSO call the bolter for 101 over the radio, knew that Bayerly would have been directed out and around for another pass. He decided to make his way across the deck to the LSO's platform aft of the meatball.

Batman's Tomcat 232 swept in across the stern for a graceful trap on the number-three wire. Tombstone waited for an opening, then trotted across the open flight deck, past the small army of deck crewmen and handlers who were working on the recoveries.

Lieutenant Commander Ted "Burner" Craig stood with a cluster of other officers behind the collapsible windscreen mounted at his console on the LSO platform. Burner was VF-95's LSO, a tall, blond man from Indianapolis who was dividing his attention between the incoming planes themselves and their TV images on the Pilot Landing Aid Television screen on his console. In one hand he held the "pickle," a handle with a guarded switch which triggered the red wave-off lights bracketing the meatball at his back like the rings around a target's bullseye. In his other hand he gripped a telephone handset for communicating with the Air Boss up in Pri-Fly, as well as with the incoming pilots.

"Ho, Stoney," Burner said as Tombstone jumped off the flight deck and into the well behind the windscreen. "With you in a sec."

Tombstone watched the next Tomcat, the number 203 prominent on the nose, line up for a trap. While Tombstone and Batman had been over northern Thailand, other aircraft from their squadron had been patrolling the skies closer to the *Jefferson*. Lieutenant Ron "Price" Taggart's 203 ship had been one of these.

Burner spoke into his handset. "You're a little left, Price," he said. "Come right a bit." Taggart's F-14 corrected. "Good . . . good . . . not too much. Deck's coming up. . . ."

The Tomcat shrieked onto the deck, engines revving as the wheels clattered across steel. The arrestor hook caught the number-four wire, dragging the F-14 to a halt.

"I'll give him a 'fair,' " Burner said, making a notation on a clipboard in front of him. As squadron LSO, it was Burner's job to grade every landing each pilot made. The possible marks were "okay," the best possible; "fair," which was average and indicated the aviator had made the proper corrections on time; "no grade," which meant that there'd been danger to the plane, the crew, or other personnel; and "cut," meaning a real screw-up, one which could have ended in disaster. The LSO's grades were a source of intense competition among the aviators, with each week's ratings posted on the greenie board off the hangar deck for everyone to see.

Burner looked at Tombstone. "That's it for your squadron, Tombstone. You come to watch Made It?"

"Is he the last one up?"

"Yup, Air Boss charlied him again a couple of minutes ago. He's coming around next."

Lieutenant Commander "Di Di" Roberts stood at Burner's side. He was VF-97's LSO this afternoon and responsible for getting Made It down on the deck. As Burner handed him the pickle, he was already speaking into his handset. "A little high." Light glinted from his sunglasses as he spoke. "Power down . . ."

Tombstone couldn't hear Bayerly's reply, but the incoming Tomcat responded, power dropping, nose rising. Not enough . . . "Shit-fire, he's afraid of the deck now," someone said behind Tombstone's back.

"Still high," Roberts said. He glanced quickly at the PLAT screen, then back at the F-14. "Power back, just a tad more . . ."

Bayerly's aircraft swept in across the roundoff, chasing its own shadow across the deck, its dangling tailhook sweeping just above the taut arrestor cables. Roberts triggered the pickle in his hand, and the bullseye lit up red behind him. "Wave off! Bolter! Bolter! Bolter!"

The Tomcat's wheels touched with a grating squeal, and then the noise was lost in thunder as Bayerly's engines opened up full. The blue-gray Tomcat flashed past the LSO platform, setting the air above the deck shimmering with the heat of its jet wash. Then the aircraft was dwindling into the sky ahead of the carrier, banking to port.

"That's okay, Commander," Roberts said calmly into his radio. "Happens to us all. Bring her around again. Third time's the charm, old buddy." He released the transmit switch on the handset and looked Craig in the eye. "He doesn't sound good, Burner."

"Rattled?"

"Something."

A telephone buzzed on the console, and another officer picked it up. "Air Boss, Di Di," he said, holding the receiver. "Captain wants to know if there's a problem."

"No goddamn problem," Roberts replied. "Just a two-time bolter. He'll make it next go-round."

Tombstone crossed to the deck railing and looked across the waves. Bayerly's Tomcat was a tiny silver speck now, gleaming in the sun far beyond the rescue helo, which was maintaining its position two miles off *Jefferson*'s port beam. Each time an aviator pulled a bolter, it shook his confidence in himself and in his aircraft that much more . . . making the next attempt harder. It had happened to Tombstone more than once, and the feeling was not a good one. He'd known aviators who had pulled ten or twelve bolters in a row before finally making a trap. One had passed out cold minutes after climbing out of his plane; another had walked straight down to the CAG's office and turned in his wings. Of all the operations expected of a Navy fighter pilot, none was more difficult, more stressful, more out-and-out *scary* than landing an aircraft on a carrier's flight deck.

"Right, Made It," Roberts was saying into handset. "You're lining up fine. Captain says if he can assist by maneuvering the boat, just say so. Say again? Okay . . . roger that. Bring her on in. Soft and smooth . . . just like you were sticking your best girl . . ."

Bayerly's Tomcat pulled into its final break three quarters of a mile behind the *Jefferson*. Even at that distance, Tombstone caught the signs of nervousness, the slight flutter to the wings as Bayerly overcompensated, corrected, then corrected too far. He was fighting his Tomcat, wrestling it toward the trap.

Not good . . .

"You're lined up fine." Roberts's voice was a soothing balm. "Still a bit high. Slack off some. More . . ."

"Shit!" someone behind them snapped. "He's still too high!"

Roberts grimaced, shaking his head. Tombstone saw the same thing, felt the same worry; Bayerly was still afraid of the deck after his first two close calls. He was going to bolter again.

"Wave off!" Roberts pressed the pickle switch. "Wave off!"

1529 hours, 14 January
Tomcat 101

Bayerly saw the red wave-off signal and bit off an obscenity. What happened next passed too quickly for the luxury of decision or reason. He *had* to get down on deck, had to land before his already shaken nerve went completely and he made a fool of himself in front of every man in the squadron, in front of the wing, in front of *Magruder*. . . .

The thought of death didn't even enter into the equation. With a savage yank on the throttles, he cut back the engines until they were barely idling, and brought the nose up . . . up . . . ! He heard Di Di Roberts shouting at him, but he was already committed. His F-14 plummeted.

The tactic, known as "diving for the deck," was not an approved technique for carrier landing. Screw that, Bayerly thought. Any port in a storm . . .

As the deck rushed up to meet him, he throttled up. His tailhook snagged the number-four wire just as his landing gear slammed into the deck with a jolt that slammed Bayerly's tailbone and elicited a yelp of surprise or pain out of Stratton. He cut back the engine, then sat there, unable for a moment to move. The sheer shock and . . . not *joy*, precisely, but surprise of being down and in one piece were overwhelming.

He pulled his oxygen mask away from his face and ran his hand over his eyes. His glove came away slick with sweat.

But he was down!

1705 hours, 14 January
CAG's office, O–3 Deck, U.S.S. *Thomas Jefferson*

Commander Marusko leaned back in the chair with a squeak of casters. Tombstone and Made It stood at attention side by side, facing him across his cluttered desk. He ran one hand across his balding scalp and burned the two of them with his blackest scowl.

"So, are you hotdogs going to tell me what the hell that was all about up there, or just stand there looking at me shit-faced?"

Both of the aviators avoided his eyes, focusing on some point behind his shoulder. They'd changed out of their flight suits and wore their khakis.

The office was small and cramped, as were most such spaces on board the *Jefferson*. This one reflected the man who occupied it: framed commendations and degrees adorned the bulkheads . . . those not taken up by book shelves or filing cabinets. A plastic model of an F/A-18 perched on a shelf above the IBM Selectric on its typing stand. Books on engineering and flight avionics were interspersed with quarterly fitness reports. A color photograph of an attractive woman and a pretty teenaged girl rested atop a ship's library copy of *Moby Dick*.

The title CAG—Commander Air Group—was a holdover from the days when a carrier fielded an air *group* rather than an air wing; Navy tradition being what it was, the older term was still in use, like the word "head" in a Navy where the enlisted men no longer went to the "head" of the ship to relieve themselves.

More and more, the carrier Navy was coming to use the concept known as "SuperCAG," where the wing commander acted strictly as an administrator and never, as in Vietnam days, actually flew. That, Marusko had long since decided, was his real problem. He still found time to get in his qualifying hours in the air, but he no longer flew on a regular basis with the rest of the aviators. For someone who loved flying as much as Marusko did, that was a constant, gnawing pain.

"I don't know what you mean, sir," Bayerly said. He kept his eyes straight ahead, his middle fingers correctly aligned with the crease in his uniform pants.

"We'll start with you, mister," Marusko said. "You violated the Rules of Engagement for your mission on at least three points. You went below the hard deck, you crossed the border into Burma . . . and don't give me that hot-pursuit shit. And you engaged in close combat with unknown forces in everything but the shooting. God damn it, you were this close . . ." He held up thumb and forefinger a fraction of an inch apart. "*This* close to getting into a shooting match with those people. What do you have to say for yourself?"

"Sir, we . . . I mean, our orders indicated we were to fly cover for our Thai allies. I understood that to mean protecting them from hostile aircraft. I had to go below ten thousand feet to position myself in case I had to engage. Sir."

"Mmm. And your little joyride into the Shan District of Burma?"

"I was on the bandit's tail, sir. I . . . uh . . . was escorting him to the border. And with the other bandit on my six, I couldn't get clear without exposing myself to possible hostile fire."

"Bull," Marusko snapped. "You were gambling that you could get a shot off if the bandit on your tail launched." He looked hard at Tombstone. "And you. What's your excuse, Magruder? You went below the hard deck, engaged in violation of standing ROEs, and came within a few feet of scattering a very expensive aircraft across the mountains in a midair collision with a foreign national."

"There's not a whole lot to say about it, CAG," Tombstone said slowly. "It was pretty tight up there. I thought Commander Bayerly might need assistance. The bandit didn't react when I got a lock on him. Shaving him off was the only way I could think of to do it without opening fire."

"And if that bandit had pulled something as stupid as your stunt, you wouldn't be here right now. And your uncle would be trying to explain the loss of you and forty million of the taxpayers' dollars to CINCPAC and the Pentagon and the CNO and for all I know the goddamned White House too."

Marusko stared at him a moment longer, then at Bayerly. When he spoke again, it was with quiet deliberation. "You gentlemen are expected to practice your career calling aboard this vessel in a professional and workmanlike manner. I needn't remind either of you that the Navy has invested a great deal of time, effort, and money in those careers, and it expects you to take them seriously. We're not out here to play games, but to carry out our orders precisely as they are given to us. We do not play tag with unidentified aircraft. We do not let ourselves get suckered across international boundaries. And we do not engage in aerial games of chicken that could result in nasty international incidents! Do I make myself clear?"

Their response was a lopsided chorus. "Clear, sir." "Yes, sir."

"The two of you are fine aviators with excellent records, both squadron commanders entrusted with grave and far-reaching responsibilities. You, Magruder, should have known better. I think your uncle would expect better of you. I know damn well that I do! Understood?"

"Yes, sir."

Marusko slumped back into his chair, toying with a pen scooped off his desk. He could tell he'd touched a raw nerve with Tombstone. He'd probably gone too far there, he decided, with the crack about the guy's uncle. "I understand your motivations, Magruder. You saw a buddy in trouble and went to bail him out. If this were combat, I'd have to commend you for quick thinking." He slammed the pen down on the desktop before him. "But damn it, this wasn't combat today. Your orders were to support Royal Thai Air Force operations over the Nam Mae Taeng."

"Begging the CAG's pardon," Tombstone said, the words

clipped and tight. "But what the hell does *support* mean if we can't engage the enemy?"

"It means, in this case, that you were up there to show the flag, to demonstrate U.S. support for the Thai government . . . not fight their damned war for them!"

Marusko sighed. In all probability, everyone from the admiral clear up to the President would love to see this whole thing covered over. That simply wasn't possible, though. The incident had been seen by too many people, from the pilot of the surviving Thai aircraft to radar operators on board the circling Hawkeye and the Aegis cruiser *Vicksburg*. And God knew how many others had been watching, across the border in Burma, or even farther north, in the People's Republic of China. It was getting increasingly difficult to keep such things private anymore.

"Okay," he continued at last. "Like I said, Magruder, I understand what made you do it. This time we'll leave it at an ass-chewing. Next time . . ." He made a sour face. "You had better make goddamn sure there *isn't* another time. Get me?"

"Yes, sir."

"Interpreting your orders to suit yourself is a damned raggedy-assed sea lawyer's stunt. Pull it again and your ass is mine. Got it?"

"Yes, sir!"

"Get the hell out of here."

"Aye aye, sir."

"Bayerly, you stand fast."

Tombstone wheeled and hurried out the door. Bayerly remained standing at attention. Marusko considered the man for another moment. He had on the desk before him the report from VF-97's LSO. He wasn't concerned about the bolters—every aviator ran up a string of those at one time or another—but the no-grade mark was serious. Bayerly had endangered himself and his shipmates by that juvenile dive for the deck, and that couldn't be allowed to pass unpunished.

"Bayerly," Marusko said slowly. "You and me have a problem. If it was just the ROEs, I'd kick you out of this office like I just did Tombstone. But your little trick up on the roof this afternoon worries me. You dived for the deck . . . and you came damned close to wiping yourself out, along with your RIO and half the guys on duty up there." He waited for a response. "Well? Anything to say?"

"No, sir. I guess . . . I guess it was a bad call on my part, CAG."

" 'A bad call.' How about bad judgment?"

"Yes, sir."

Marusko studied the big aviator for a moment. "Son, you've been moody as hell for weeks now. Ever since Wonsan, in fact. Am I right?"

"If you say so, CAG."

"Want to talk about it?"

"Nothing to talk about, sir." He shrugged. "I screwed up today, that's all."

Marusko shook his head. "I'm taking you off flight duty, Made It. You're in hack until I tell you otherwise."

Bayerly looked stricken. "But, CAG—"

"Save it." He tapped the reports on his desk. "You're grounded, pending further investigation."

"Yes, sir." Bayerly's face was emotionless once more.

"Dismissed."

"Aye, aye, sir." Bayerly spun smartly and departed.

Marusko stared at the closed door for a long moment after Bayerly had left. He didn't like doing what he'd been forced to do, but there was no alternative that he could see. Bayerly's attitude had verged on sullenness since Wonsan. That was always a bad sign, and when an avaitor's emotions began affecting his performance, it was only a matter of time before there was an accident.

In the meantime, Marusko had to figure out how he was going to word his report. He didn't want to see Bayerly's career endangered, but the guy was skating close to having his flight status jerked for good.

Sometimes, Marusko did not like his job.

1712 hours, 14 January
0–3 Deck, U.S.S. *Thomas Jefferson*

Tombstone was waiting with Kid and Dixie in the passageway outside the CAG department suite. They turned when Bayerly stepped out of CAG's office. He looked pale.

"What happened?" Tombstone asked.

"Yeah, Made It. We heard some shouting."

"Nothing." Bayerly rubbed his mustache with a stubby finger, and frowned. "Listen, Magruder. I can get on just fine without your covering for me." He pressed past Tombstone in the narrow corridor. "Get out of my way!"

"Whoa, there, buddy!" Tombstone felt a flash of anger at Bayerly's rebuff, but he contained it. Something was bothering Made It and now was the time to have it out. "You've been running ballistic for weeks now, and today you just missed buying the farm! What the hell is with you anyway?"

Bayerly scowled. "Forget it, Magruder. Your fancy medal doesn't cut it with me." He turned and continued down the passageway.

"Shee-it," Dixie said wonderingly. "What gives with Made It, Tombstone?"

"I don't know, Dixie." Worse, he didn't know how to find out. The problem was something personal, but what? Bayerly's mention of the medal suggested jealousy, but such petty motivation seemed totally out of keeping with the man's solid record for professionalism. Tombstone watched Bayerly's stocky form retreating down the seemingly endless succession of cross-passageway frames and wondered how he could clear the air between them.

Probably, what Bayerly needed most was time. Tombstone decided to approach him again, but later, after things had settled out a bit.

Maybe after the *Jefferson* reached Thailand . . .

CHAPTER 4

"Gooooood evening, Jeffersons!" Master Chief Raymond C. Buckley, Jr., beamed into the camera and delivered his best Pat Sajak imitation from the lectern set up as his number-one prop in the television broadcast he made twice each day to the carrier's crew. The room, called CVIC—pronounced "civic"—for Carrier (CV) Information Center, also served as one of *Jefferson*'s television studios. Banks of lights glared at him from three directions as he launched into the familiar patter. "This is the Chief of the Boat, comin' at you with another edition of *What's the Gouge.* . . ."

The master chief of a modern supercarrier was the one direct link between the enlisted crew and the ship's officers, known by all, respected by all, likely to turn up almost anywhere within *Jefferson*'s two-thousand-plus compartments and passageways with a friendly word or good advice. Captain James Fitzgerald, the ship's Commanding Officer, and Captain Vincent C. Glover, the ship's Exec, depended on Buckley to know how the crew was feeling, could count on him for an honest assessment of a man up for captain's mast on some minor charge . . . or for word about unpleasant racial tensions in the engine room. On the other side of the tracks, enlisted men depended on Buckley for the straight word, the "gouge" as it was known, on what was happening in a world where

individual crewmen had very little control over their own lives
and destinies.

More often than not, the sheer, overwhelming *uncertainty* of
a deployment at sea was the worst part of the cruise. Would
there be liberty at the next port? Would families be allowed to
visit next time the ship was in Japan? That was one of the
reasons for *What's the Gouge*. The ship's closed-circuit television programming was one of the best ways there was to keep
the crew informed.

"There's been a lot of wild scuttlebutt going around about
our next port of call," Buckley said, leaning against the lectern
and staring into the camera's eye. "And there have been even
wilder stories going around about just what it is we're supposed
to *do* there!"

The red light on the camera winked off as a second camera
picked up the scene. A TV monitor to one side faded from an
image of Buckley's smiling face to a map of Southeast Asia.

"You all know where we're bound for, of course," Buckley
said. "Some of you old hands out there know our next port of
call real well. Bangkok!"

He grinned as he heard a distant, low-voiced murmur,
almost a rumble which echoed down *Jefferson*'s steel passageways. A few hundred men were cheering and whooping in the
TV lounge a deck down and several frames aft . . . and that
cheer was being repeated throughout the ship. Bangkok had a
certain reputation. . . .

"The rumors have been flying though as to whether or not
there's going to be liberty in Thailand. The insurrection in the
northern part of the country has been getting worse, and in the
past few weeks there have been student riots and uprisings in
Bangkok itself.

"Well, I'm here to give you the word straight from the
Captain. There's going to be liberty. Things are quiet in
Bangkok right now. Order has been restored in the streets, and
the way things are shaping up we're going to be visiting the
jewel of Southeast Asia for ten days—" The distant thunder
redoubled, and several of the men standing off-camera in the

CVIC provided appropriate sound effects by applauding and whistling.

It took several seconds more to restore order in CVIC. Liberty was always a subject of keen interest on board ship, a break in the shipboard routine at sea where day followed day with a mind-numbing sameness. The average sailor in *Jefferson*'s crew was nineteen years old; for him, a taste of the exotic eased the bite of homesickness.

The noise in the room subsided, and Buckley laughed. "I can tell a lot of you already know something about where we're going. If I can get your one-track minds off girls for a moment, though, let me tell you something about the place."

He began giving a travelogue-style presentation about the country, referring occasionally to note cards on the podium in front of him. Buckley had been fascinated by the fact that Thailand, alone of the nations in Southeast Asia, had never been a colony of a European power, that even the *name* Thai meant "free." *Muang Thai*, "Land of the Free," was fiercely proud of that heritage.

"You all know the capital of the country is Bangkok," he said. "But don't forget that the Thais themselves call it *Pra Nakhorn*, the 'Heavenly Capital,' or better yet *Krung Thep*, the 'City of Angels.' You guys from Los Angeles ought to appreciate that."

He went on to explain how important Thailand was to American interests in the region. Its neighbors on three sides included Laos and Cambodia—both communist—and Burma. The Socialist Union of Burma had been under one Marxist military dictatorship or another since 1962. Recent free elections had carried with them the promise for democratic reform, but for the present the military continued to rule that impoverished country.

"Thailand is a member of both SEATO and ASEAN," he said, "and is one of the United States' very few strong, democratic, and pro-Western allies in the region.

"Of course, most of you old hands remember how important Thailand was back during Vietnam. After the war, we turned our bases over to the Thais, packed up our gear, and went back to the World. The political know-it-alls predicted that Thailand would go the way of Cambodia and Laos in a few months. It didn't. Thai politics are unique in that everyone in the country loves and respects the King.

"Thailand is a constitutional monarchy." Buckley paused to perch his glasses on his nose and look down at what he had written on an index card before him. "The King's name . . . I'd better read this to get it right . . . The King's name is Bhumibol Adulyadej. He provides a tremendously stabilizing influence that keeps the lid on Thai politics. During a crisis, by constitutional law, he remains neutral . . . so even during a coup you have the rebels swearing loyalty to the Crown. The ordinary Thai people take respect of their monarch very, very seriously. No revolutionary would get very far if he didn't revere the King as much as they did.

"Back in 1981, for instance, there was a coup attempt by a group of army officers who called themselves the Young Turks. They were strong, well-armed, and commanded a fair percentage of the country's military forces . . . but as soon as it became clear that they did not have the King's blessing—despite his official neutrality—support for their movement fell apart and they were crushed.

"Under the King, the Thai government is a weird mix of democracy and military rule. It's based on the English system, with a prime minister and a two-house parliament consisting of the Senate and the National Assembly, but both tend to be dominated by military officers. In Thailand, it works out, military officers can work in the business sector, run banks, own hotels, or serve in government . . . and still have an active military career. They rule according to the Thai constitution, so the government cannot fairly be called a junta or a dictatorship. King Bhumibol, incidentally, is also head of the armed forces."

Buckley continued to talk, explaining that documentaries, travelogues, informational pieces, and VD films would be broadcast over the closed-circuit channel for the next several days, but he was certain that most of the crew were no longer listening. He'd been on the other end of such broadcasts more than once, going all the way back to his days in Nam, and he knew that by now the sailors would be more interested in the stories being told by the old hands who'd been to Bangkok before. Those stories would have less to do with Thailand or its culture than with favorite bars and sexual exploits. Bangkok's rep as a sin city where anything could be had for a price made it one of the Navy's all-time favorite liberty ports, and nothing he or any DOD instructional film had to say about it would change that one bit.

He glanced at the clock on the wall and saw that he was down to his last few minutes of scheduled broadcast time.

"That brings me to *Jefferson*'s mission in these waters, men. Our ship has been ordered to the Gulf of Thailand to show American support for the present government in Bangkok. The insurrection in the northern part of the country has been getting worse in recent weeks, and there have been rumors, unsubstantiated, of a possible coup—like the one by the Young Turks in '81—by officers who feel the government should be reacting more decisively to the rebel threat.

"As most of you know by now, our operations with Thai military forces began this morning, when we started flying joint missions with them over northern Thailand. By this time you've heard the rumors that some of our planes tangled with unknown aircraft this afternoon, up near the Burmese border. I can tell you categorically that, while strange planes were intercepted, they were turned back at the border and no shots were fired at or by American aircraft.

"Our intervention in Thailand is intended as a gesture only, a show of support for the Bangkok government.

"So tomorrow, Jeffersons, we will be anchoring at the Thai naval base at Sattahip. If conditions ashore remain peaceful, liberty should commence for all hands on a rotating basis, beginning at 1700 hours tomorrow evening."

The director signaled with a slashing motion across his throat, and the camera dollied in for a parting close-up. "Well, men, I see my time is up. A reminder that water conservation is in effect, so remember your proper Navy shower technique.

This is Master Chief Buckley, signing off for *What's the Gouge?*"

The battery of lights dimmed and the director stepped past the camera. "Good show, Master Chief."

"Thanks, Pete. You think anybody was listening?"

The other chief laughed. "They heard 'ten days in Bangkok.' I think the ship gave a little shudder just then. Hey, you ever get a real, honest-to-goodness Patpong massage?"

He grinned. "Many times, Chief. Very relaxing."

"So what do you think, Master Chief? What are the chances for things to stay quiet for the whole ten days?"

Buckley smiled as he unclipped the microphone from around his neck. Every man aboard was probably wondering the same thing. If the students started throwing rocks again, liberty would be canceled so fast it would make the collective heads of the *Jefferson*'s crew spin. "I don't know, Pete. The word is the Thai army has things in hand."

He hoped it would stay that way.

He wondered about those Chinese fighters. Every man aboard knew that the Burmese didn't have Shenyang J-7s. So where had they come from? And why? There was no way in hell that anyone could convince him that those planes had been flown by Communist Thai rebels!

Master Chief Buckley was a naturally optimistic man, but he had a bad feeling about this one. Too much was unknown . . . including the identity of the enemy.

He just hoped the *Jefferson* wasn't sailing into something she couldn't handle.

2010 hours, 14 January
Crew's lounge, U.S.S. *Thomas Jefferson*

Most of *Jefferson*'s crew had heard Master Chief Buckley's broadcast. Those who hadn't, quickly heard from their shipmates. Bangkok indisputably was a *great* liberty port, and throughout the evening every bull session on board had but a single topic.

Four off-duty sailors sat at one of the round-topped tables in the crew's lounge. They weren't the only ones in the room. Other small groups were scattered about the area, reading, watching TV, or playing war games. A gentle rumble rose from the deck, more felt than heard. The lounge was located far aft, almost directly above *Jefferson's* four massive, twenty-two-foot-wide propellors, and the room pulsed with their throbbing strokes. No one noticed, however. The ship's pulse was part of the background, long since accepted and forgotten.

Seaman Apprentice David Howard had enlisted in the Navy in April, three days after his eighteenth birthday. After twelve weeks of boot training at the Recruit Training Center in San Diego and two dreary weeks in a holding company, he'd been given his orders for sea duty and his first ship: the U.S.S. *Thomas Jefferson.*

He'd been at sea for five months now, less two weeks in Yokosuka. After all that time, he still wasn't certain whether his luck at drawing the *Jeff* had been good or bad. Most seamen hated carrier duty, where the ship was big enough to get lost in, quarters were as cramped as in a holding barracks ashore, and twelve- and even fourteen-hour workdays were the norm rather than the exception. Howard didn't mind the hard work, and there was an undeniable romance in the air each time one of *Jefferson's* aircraft was hurled aloft in steam and raw noise. His hardest adjustment was in his social life.

Howard was quiet, even shy, and had never made friends easily. His shipmates seemed a decent enough bunch, if a bit loud and profane, but Howard still hadn't learned how to let down his own inner barriers with them. He found himself drawn to their conversations, though, *wanting* to belong.

"Aw *shit*, man!" Signalman Third Class Charles Bentley leaned back, hands clasped behind his short-cropped blond head. "Ten fuckin' days in bee-*you*-tiful shit-hot Bangkok! Gentlemen, we have got it *made*!"

"You been there before, Bentley, right?" Radarman Third Fred Paterowski chugged the last of his Coke and crumpled the can. "Tell, man! Tell!"

"Hey, man, it was fuckin' A-numbah-one! That was . . . lessee, '88, I guess. When I was on the *Arkansas.*"

Howard sipped his Coke, listening. He didn't know how to take Bentley, who seemed bright but who was only a third class after eight years in the service. He'd probably been busted, since most ratings could make second class before their four years' enlistment was up. Howard couldn't help wondering what the guy had done . . . or did he simply not care?

The lounge was a large room, with paintings drawn from Navy history, with comfortable tables and chairs under fluorescent lights and a wooden lectern at one end. Howard remembered sitting in this room five months before, listening as Captain Fitzgerald stood behind that lectern and talked about responsibility, about *making* something of their time aboard the *Jefferson*.

In five months, Howard had done his best to be a good sailor and fit in with the routine . . . doing what he was told and staying out of trouble. As a seaman in the deck division, he was one of hundreds of enlisted men available for general duties which ran from standing lookout, serving as roving fire and security patrol, participating in FODs and field days, and keeping lines and gear up on the roof shipshape. His previous daily assignment had been a dull but undemanding one: cleaning and stowing the dozens of wire-frame Stokes stretchers which the medical department kept ready along the starboard side of the island on the flight deck. A week ago, though, he'd been transferred to Air Ops, where he stood by as a message runner.

"Runner," in this day of radio and satellite communications, meant that he fetched coffee for officers and chiefs, but he enjoyed being in what he thought of as the carrier's heart, a huge room where earnest ratings bent over radar screens in semi-darkness, murmuring into radio headsets as they talked with aircraft hundreds of miles away. It gave him a feeling of importance to be there, even if he didn't know exactly what was going on. He'd met Paterowski in Ops, and was finding himself drawn into the radarman's circle of friends.

"I hear Bangkok's plenty hot," Seaman Ernesto Rodriguez said. He also worked in Ops, where he was striking for

Radarman. He shook his head, and his teeth flashed brilliantly against his dark face. *"Ai-ai-ai!"*

"Shit, man," Bentley said, grinning. He was in his favorite element now, telling tales of past exploits. "These ain't your average T-town *putas,* Ernie! In Bangkok, you can get anything, and I mean *anything*! I remember me and a coupla buddies going to this place in Patpong. That's Bangkok's Sin Central, kiddies. Aw, *shit*!" He rolled the word, savoring it. "You shoulda seen this place! Red curtains, glass beads. They had this specialty, see, where six girls take you into this room, see? And they all strip down, you know, an' then they strip you down and lay you out on this table. And, I swear to God, they gather around and start *licking* you, all over . . . toes, fingers, *every*where!"

The circle exploded in a chorus of hoots, groans, and table-pounding. Paterowski held his white hat in his lap and vigorously pumped his fist underneath, pretending to masturbate.

"An' after about a year of this, one of the girls climbs up and kind of lowers herself down on top of you, see, real nice and easy? And while the rest of them keep with the licking and sucking she . . ."

Howard looked away, feeling his face burn with embarrassment . . . embarrassed all the more by the fact that he *was* embarrassed. He had seen exactly one liberty port during *Jefferson*'s deployment—Yokosuka, "Yokuska" as the others insisted on calling it—for the two weeks the carrier had anchored there after Wonsan. During that time, he'd managed two trips into Tokyo. He'd seen the Imperial Palace from the jogging path outside the private grounds, the Outer Garden with its giant fountain, and a hodgepodge collection of shrines, government buildings, and department stores that were now completely jumbled in his mind. He'd not been sure that he'd *seen* Tokyo at all, and the stories traded by his shipmates when they'd left port increased his doubts.

"How 'bout it, Howie?"

"Huh?" Howard blinked, feeling foolish. "Sorry. What'd you say?"

"Reveille, son!" Paterowski said. "Wake up! Your betters are trying to instruct you in the finer points of life here, but you ain't tuned in!"

"You know what Howie needs?" Rodriguez said. "We oughta treat him to a night in the Patpong!"

"Yeah, man! He can dip his dong in the ol' Patpong!"

"Whatcha say, cherry?" Bentley demanded. "Wanna lose your cherry?"

"I . . . I don't know, guys. I mean, I'll have to think about—"

"Hey, why think, man, when you could be gettin' your clock cleaned?" Rodriguez laughed. "Holy shit, man! Bang-fuckin'-cock! What a break!"

Howard felt a small, secret thrill. It would be okay, wouldn't it? If the other guys made him go along? He didn't want them to think he didn't like them or anything, or that he thought he was better than them. . . .

He didn't know if he was looking forward to liberty in Bangkok or not. He was already feeling both embarrassed and guilty . . . but this might be the chance to find out what there was to feel guilty about. A kind of initiation into the mysterious inner circle of the Experienced Sailor. Bangkok might be the best thing that had ever happened to him.

Just so long as Charlene, his girlfriend back home in Colorado, never found out.

CHAPTER 5

The convoy of black government limousines had been waiting for them when *Jefferson*'s launch pulled up to Sattahip's docks. The drive up the coast to Bangkok took almost ninety minutes, most of it in the express lane of the four-lane highway designated Route 3.

Several army trucks and armed jeeps accompanied the convoy, but the escort was more for show than for defense. They'd passed a small demonstration gathered outside Sattahip's north gate, twenty or thirty unhappy-looking locals holding up banners and placards and chanting something in Thai. One sign in English declared "Yankee Imperialists out of Asia," while another rather enigmatically read "Blood Atrocity on Wonsan." A number of Thais who seemed not to be part of the demonstration simply stood by and watched, most smiling, some waving at the convoy as it raced past.

Rear Admiral Thomas J. Magruder, immaculate in his dress whites, turned in the limo's seat as the convoy accelerated onto Route 3, looking through the back window. The commanding officer of Carrier Battle Group 14 assured himself that the limos following with several of his staff personnel and aides were still with the convoy. There had been time only for a brief reception with the Thai military officers at Sattahip. The real business of the day was scheduled for later, in Bangkok, and he didn't want to lose half his staff in the traffic.

"Well, CAG," he said, settling back in his seat. "We're past the demonstrators."

Commander Marusko looked up from the briefing papers he was reading. "Yes, sir. Not that it amounted to much. That was a pretty laid-back group of radicals back there."

"Someone probably paid them to walk around with those signs." Magruder grinned. "A dirty job, but someone has to do it."

"Yeah. You know, Admiral, somehow Thailand seems an unlikely place for a communist revolution."

Magruder had to agree. Bangkok was one of those strange Oriental blends of East and West, a city like Tokyo, Singapore, or Hong Kong. Everywhere, the strangely canted, peaked roofs and golden spires of *wats*—the local Buddhist temple— rose and mingled with the glass-and-concrete monoliths of modern architecture. In many ways, it had more in common with the West. A communist insurrection had sputtered on in the more remote parts of the country since the 1970s. Only in the past few months had the situation become unstable.

That was why *Jefferson* had been ordered into these waters.

Chaos was the word that came to Magruder's mind as they left the main highway and followed the Sukhumvit Road past upper-class residential side streets, then plunged into the city's heart. The city streets were a teeming, endless jam of cars, trucks, buses, carts, pedestrians, and the curious three-wheeled passenger-carrying scooters called *tuk-tuks*. Everywhere, signs advertising "Rolex" and "Pepsi" coexisted with signs covered with the buttonhook loops of Thai writing and the blocky ideographs of Chinese. A gigantic billboard featuring a dark-eyed Thai movie actress, her bare breasts almost modestly covered by a stripe of advertising copy, towered across the street from the gleaming and tranquil spires of a *wat*, a green Buddha, standing three stories tall, looming in a niche between two glass skyscrapers.

People clogged the sidewalks and streets with complete disregard for the traffic. Thais and foreigners alike in Western dress mingled with shaven-headed monks in yellow robes; with farmers selling food from egg-crate stalls; with merchants hawking souvenir Buddhas, gemstones, watches, and grass-hoppers from rickety stalls; with white-helmeted police and Thai soldiers in khaki uniforms; with tourists from a dozen countries all carrying Japanese cameras. Within the space of seconds, Magruder saw Western business suits, Philippine *barongs*, Indian *saris*, Japanese *kimonos*, Indonesian *sarongs*, Sikh beards and turbans, traditional Chinese robes, miniskirts, cutoffs, T-shirts, and everywhere, *everywhere*, American blue jeans. The limousine was air-conditioned and the windows rolled up, but the bawling cacophony of the streets still filtered through; shouted pleas, screamed invectives, shrill sales pitches and greetings in a dozen languages; braying horns; clashing gears and thundering vehicle engines in earsplitting need of mufflers.

The convoy was slowed to a crawl by the traffic, but with horns blaring it continued to make headway against the tide. Several blocks past the landscaped magnificence of the Thai Intercontinental Hotel and the sprawl of a four-story shopping mall, the limo turned right and began making its way along the colorful turbulence of one of the dirty, crowded *klongs*, or canals, which had given Bangkok its reputation as the Venice of the Orient.

The seat of Thailand's government was located on the north bank of the Klong Phadung. Magruder had expected a colorful and ornate palace of some kind and was surprised to learn that the government carried out its business in a complex of modern, air-conditioned skyscrapers several blocks from the old National Assembly building, the King's palace, and the zoo. The convoy plunged into the cool semi-darkness of an underground garage. Thai naval officers in dress whites and army officers in ribbon-heavy khakis led them through fluorescent-lit, air-conditioned passageways that seemed light years removed from the steamy, crowded streets outside.

In a comfortable conference room, a navy captain bowed formally to the Americans, his hands pressed together as though in prayer in the salutation known as a *wai*. "Sirs, may I present Major General Duong Rangsit of the Royal Thai senior staff," he said formally as the door at the far end of the room opened and a squat, ponderously overweight Thai officer walked in.

"*Savahtdi!*" the general said warmly. He gave a perfunctory *wai*, then extended his hand to Magruder for a cordial Western handshake. "I have been instructed personally by His Majesty the King to welcome you to our City of Angels!"

"The pleasure is mine, General Duong."

A second officer, a lean, dark-eyed man, followed the general into the room. "This is my chief aide, Colonel Kriangsak Vajiravudh," Duong said. "He has been assigned as liaison officer between your command and mine while you are in our country."

A half hour of pleasantries followed, and a discussion of subjects ranging from the raid at Wonsan to a recent coup attempt in the Philippines. As tea was served by white-jacketed attendants, Magruder leaned back in his chair.

"I suppose we should touch on the main reason we're here," he said, gesturing. An aide handed him a copy of CBG-14's orders which he slid across the table to Duong. "As you can read there, we have been directed to assist your government in every way possible short of actually participating in combat. It is the belief of the Joint Chiefs that combat operations which resulted in Americans flying missions against Thai nationals would not be productive for either government."

Duong gave a wry smile as he flipped through the pages. "I tend to agree, Admiral. Especially given the curiously anti-American flavor of the demonstrators lately." He shook his head sadly. "I've not seen anything like this in Thailand before. I wonder sometimes if the rumors of foreign leadership among the insurrectionists are not true. Most Thais *like* Americans!"

"This is a somewhat awkward situation, actually," Magruder said. "On the one hand, we're supposed to demonstrate our support for your government. On the other, we're to keep a low profile and try not to get shot at. Sometimes our orders can be a little . . . contradictory."

Duong laughed. "The very essence of bureaucracy! In any case, there should be no problem. Our people will take heart with the knowledge that one of America's supercarriers is anchored at Sattahip. Our aviators will be inspired flying alongside yours. But we certainly do not envision a combat role for your people."

"So what is the military situation?" Magruder asked. "Our sources haven't been very informative on that point."

Duong gave a massive shrug. "The Thai CIA believes the insurrection in the northern districts is simply a renewal of the old communist guerrilla offensive. The Communist Party of Thailand was never able to secure a strong power base among the people they pretended to represent. We've had very little trouble out of them since we beat them in the Chong Charn Mountains in 1982.

"This . . . this new movement appears to have begun about six months ago. If it is the old CPT, then it has been reborn, with new leaders, new sources of supplies and arms, everything. They are elusive, well-armed, and well-supplied. Their leadership and discipline appears to be quite good. On an individual level, their soldiers are not as good as ours, not as well-trained."

"Have there been many major engagements? How bad is it up there now?"

Duong pursed his lips, then made a so-so gesture with his hand. "Militarily, the insurrection is not a serious problem, though obviously we are concerned. So far, most of what we have seen are skirmishes and raids, coupled with attempts to extort rice and other supplies from the local villages. The greater danger is less direct." He exchanged glances with Colonel Kriangsak.

"I would have to agree," Kriangsak said in a low, cultured voice. "Some of our officers feel that the government's current policy is too lenient, too soft on communism. This has raised the possibility of a coup."

"Toss out the old guard so that we can do things right," Magruder said.

"We have been responding to the threat in strength," Duong continued. "A number of army units have already been transferred to the border, and others are scheduled for move-

ment within the next few days. Air groups have been reposi-
tioned north to both Chiang Mai and Chiang Rai."

"What about the possibility that the rebels are being supplied
from Burma?" Marusko asked. "I'm still worried about those
MiGs."

"There is some evidence that the rebels are being supplied
across the border," Duong said. "But there is no *proof*."

"Those MiGs look like pretty good proof to me," Marusko
said. "Your average jungle-fighting guerrilla doesn't normally
pack MiG-21s as part of his personal armament!"

"Burmese support is a possibility, yes," Duong admitted.

"Actually," Kriangsak said, "we haven't yet been able to
confirm that they *have* MiGs. Rangoon has denied the incident."

"But there seems to be no other reasonable explanation."
Duong shrugged. "I suppose the MiGs *could* have been
Chinese aircraft, though what reason the PRC would have had
to cross several hundred kilometers of Burmese territory to
attack one of our planes . . ." He waved one hand helplessly
in the air. "It makes no sense."

"Burma is still the most likely enemy," Colonel Kriangsak
added. "They have been Thailand's traditional enemies for
centuries, and there is little doubt that it is they who are
supplying the rebels in the northern provinces."

"We also have to know whether our air operations can
continue over your territory," Magruder said. He paused to
take a sip of tea from the cup at his elbow. "We grounded all
ops yesterday except for routine CAPs. I don't want my
command to blunder into a combat situation before we know
what the score is."

"We will be strengthening our own air patrols along the
border, of course," Duong said. "I should think there would be
no problem for you to continue your flights as well. My
government is especially anxious to make use of your Hawkeye
early-warning aircraft."

Magruder nodded. "No problem there. Also, we will be in
a position to pass on satellite reconnaissance photos of the
border. That might help make the situation up there clearer.

And something more . . ." He handed another set of papers across the table to the general. "My staff and I have been discussing the possibility of loaning you a TARPS aircraft and crew for a few days."

"Excuse me," Duong said. "TARPS?"

"Stands for Tactical Aerial Reconnaissance Pod System," Marusko explained. "It's a strap-on pod carrying special cameras and infrared imaging scanners. We sling it from the belly of a Tomcat, and it gets us close-up pictures . . . better and faster than we can usually manage from a satellite."

"We thought that might be useful for locating guerrilla trails and camps," Magruder added.

Duong examined the written proposal for a series of TARPS flights over northern Thailand, then passed it over to Kriangsak. "That could be of enormous benefit," he said. "Your orders, however, are to avoid combat. If those MiGs reappear . . ."

Magruder grinned. "If that happens, General, maybe you'll have your confirmation of Burmese involvement."

"That might not be wise, General," Kriangsak said softly. "With all due respect to our American friends, the risk of an incident involving them is great. Next time the Burmese intruders could well try to down an American plane instead of one of ours. That could precipitate an unfortunate incident."

Duong's pudgy fingers drummed on the tabletop for a moment. "Point taken, Colonel."

"There is a further difficulty," Kriangsak continued. "So far as the dissident officers are concerned, too much reliance on American help might be as bad as inaction against the communists. We must be seen to be handling this ourselves, without *farang* involvement."

Magruder smiled. "I think we can manage to stay inconspicuous, Colonel. Here's what we can do . . ."

They continued to work out the details of the joint Thai-American operation.

Thailand had been winning her long fight against Communism, but for many years Bangkok had been losing another war, the war against the drug lords of the Golden Triangle in the northern part of the country, and now the drug war was high on the agenda of the White House. Washington was concerned that the resurgence of guerrilla activity in northern Thailand might somehow be connected with the Golden Triangle's deadly trade, in the same way that Marxist rebels in South and Central America funded their operations with cocaine. For years, heroin traffic in the region had been controlled by various warlords in the area who, in turn, answered to a cartel—mostly Chinese—based in Hong Kong.

With the U.S. Navy helping the Thai army in its operations against guerrillas, the CIA, the DEA, and other organizations with an interest in the region could get a good look at the area's drug trade as well. Guerrillas and drug smugglers would be using the same trails, even the same camps. The fact that communist insurgents were operating within the Golden Triangle at all meant that they were somehow linked with the local drug lords. No one, including the Thai army, moved through some parts of Thailand's north hill country without their approval.

None of this was discussed openly with Duong, of course. TARPS reconnaissance of the border region would assist the Thai army in putting down the insurrection; whether or not the U.S. Navy pulled copies of the data for other purposes was, of course, up to them.

After almost an hour of discussion, Duong leaned forward, steepling his fingers. "I am inclined to accept your offer, Admiral," he said at last. "Particularly if the RTAF has the primary responsibility for protecting your people. Your . . . your TARPS aircraft could be based at an airfield in the area where we could provide ground security as well."

"That would be satisfactory," Magruder said. "I would suggest that we provide you with two aircraft, though, one to carry the TARPS, one as wingman." Flying wingman formations was basic to U.S. air tactics, and Magruder didn't want the entire responsibility for protecting the TARPS plane to rest with their Thai hosts.

Duong nodded. "Two aircraft could hardly be interpreted

as major American assistance," he said. "And the air base I have in mind is somewhat remote."

"Where is it?"

"North of Chiang Mai. It's a small military base called U Feng, about twenty kilometers from the border." He turned to face his aide. "Colonel, you were just stationed there, were you not?"

Kriangsak nodded. "Yes, sir. Headquarters staff for almost two years."

"Then you will have all the information these gentlemen need. I'll leave that to you."

Whom to send? Magruder wondered. Properly, this should have been a volunteers-only mission, since whoever went would be missing out on liberty in Bangkok. That alone could qualify U Feng as hardship duty.

For a recon flight like this, though, he wanted someone with plenty of experience flying the electronics-laden pod. Most Tomcat drivers were familiar with TARPS, but some had more experience than others. The name of Lieutenant Commander Matthew Magruder came to mind.

Magruder smiled. Simply ordering his nephew to take the U Feng mission might solve several problems at once. He'd heard the rumors and jokes about VF-95's skipper, winner of the Navy Cross, the fair-haired admiral's nephew. It was impossible to avoid the ugly specter of favoritism in a situation like this, and ever since Wonsan, Magruder had been wondering if it wouldn't be a good idea to have Tombstone transferred to another command. Maybe the rumors could be scotched if it was Tombstone who was ordered to fly up to U Feng for fun and games in the jungles of the Golden Triangle.

So, Tombstone and his RIO, plus one other Tomcat and crew. A week at U Feng should be sufficient to map most of the threatened border area.

He hoped Tombstone would understand. A week at U Feng wouldn't exactly be a pleasant break from shipboard routine.

Tombstone, Batman, Nightmare Marinaro and Price Taggart all sat in the synthetic leather chairs of the Ready Room, sipping Cokes and swapping stories. They were on Alert 15, but it had been a quiet night so far and only twenty minutes remained in the watch. The atmosphere was relaxed, full of joking and good-natured banter.

They laughed as Tombstone wrinkled his nose. "Come off it, Batman, you don't know what the hell you're talking about! You've never even been there!"

"Hey! Trust me, man! Trust me! I used to go out with this blonde back Stateside, y'know? An airline stewardess for TWA! Tits like you would not believe! And she *told* me that the Airport Hotel was where the stews hang out whenever they're in town."

"Bull!" Nightmare said, grinning. "You're saying your girlfriend told you where to pick up Western girls when you were here?"

"Hey, she didn't know I was going to be in Bangkok when she told me! We were in bed at the time, as I recall . . . and she was kind of under my spell, know what I mean?"

Tombstone shook his head. "Maybe you'll run into her when you're there."

"Not likely. She quit and married a lawyer from Duluth. Great tits, though. The Batman flies first class, all the way!"

"Delirious again, poor boy," Price said sadly. He picked up an empty soft drink can by Batman's elbow and shook it lightly. "Too much sugar. Makes 'em hallucinate."

"Must be," Tombstone agreed.

"Shit," Batman said agreeably. "You two clods are just jealous! There you'll be, off on the frontier with gomers and alligators for playmates . . ."

"Right on," Nightmare said. "Ol' Batman and me are gonna be making the rounds in Patpong while you two are slapping mosquitos out in the jungle! Don't worry, though. We'll remember you to the girls . . ."

"You want to kill them or shall I?" Price asked Tombstone.

"Aw, let them live. They both had deprived childhoods."

"Deprived of nookie," Batman agreed. "We're making up for lost time."

Tombstone snorted. "Perhaps I should remind you that you guys are still going to be working. That's *work-ing* . . ." He dragged the word out cruelly. "You know . . . flying? With an airplane? Working with the Thais?"

"That's it, man!" Nightmare said. "Working with 'em by day and playing with 'em by night! Some of those Thai babes—"

"Uh uh," Batman said, shaking his head. "Not me. None of this here local gook poon for yours truly! That's why I'm for the Airport Hotel!"

"So what's wrong with local girls?" Price asked. "You prejudiced or something?"

"Nah. I just want a gal in my league, is all. You know how stews just *love* fighter jocks . . ."

"You'd be a natural with your medal, Stoney," Nightmare said. "You go into the bar, see? You sidle up alongside a lonely-looking lovely, and you quietly let slip that you are a genuine American Naval hero, winner of the Navy Cross . . ."

". . . and all of a sudden you've got twenty gorgeous girls," Batman finished for him. "All rubbing up against you in their low-cut gowns, just *begging* you to take them back to their room!"

"Sounds crowded."

"That, my friend, is the true and deep tragedy of the American hero. Alone . . . unloved . . . unappreciated, he nevertheless must bear the slings and arrows of misfortune—"

"That's 'outrageous fortune.' "

"Y'know, Stoney, now that I think about it, maybe you should let me borrow that fancy ribbon of yours. I could put it to real good use!"

"Yeah!" Nightmare snickered. "It's gonna be wasted up in that jungle!"

Tombstone laughed, but the reminder about the medal brought a small stab of guilt. He still felt uncomfortable with the whole hero idea and wished the others would drop the subject.

"Well, Stoney," Batman said slowly. "I'll tell you. I will be thinking of you while you're up at that remote, jungle outpost. I truly will. And the first stew I get in the sack, I'll slip in the old salami and say, 'Stoney, this screw's for you!'"

"Your generosity is overwhelming."

He looked away from the group, toward a large, mounted photograph on one paneled bulkhead. Taken from another aircraft, it showed ten aircraft from VF-95 flying in formation toward the camera, with the bow-on *Jefferson* astern and below.

The squadron.

Despite the banter, Tombstone had been looking forward to his assignment at U Feng ever since CAG had told him about it that afternoon. He was not one for nightlife, and he didn't feel the driving need to bed and boast that seemed to animate the others. Batman, perhaps, was more typical in that respect. At least he followed the aviator's party line.

Well, he could have his stewardesses, and welcome. Tombstone was eager to see something of a mystic land that was more fairy tale than fact.

One thing was certain. His assignment to U Feng was going to give him a week away from the ship. A week away from Batman. Tombstone liked the guy, but he could certainly get on a fellow's nerves with his super fighter jock routine.

Tombstone leaned far back in his chair and scratched himself comfortably. Yes, Batman could bang his stews until he was blue in the face . . . or wherever. For Tombstone, the jungles of the exotic Golden Triangle might be just the vacation he needed.

CHAPTER 6

"Now hear this! Now hear this! Lieutenant Commander Magruder, report to the admiral's office on the double!"

Tombstone turned as the voice blared from the 5-MC speaker mounted high on the island about the flight deck. "Now what the hell . . . ?"

Chief Bob Smith looked up from the maintenance reports he'd been reviewing with Tombstone. "What the shit you been up to, Commander?"

"Beats me, Smitty," Tombstone said, handing another stack of maintenance forms to the bearded senior chief. "But it sounds like I'd better find out."

He started down the line of aircraft parked along the edge of the flight deck, their tails hanging out over the water like gigantic, roosting birds. Across the deck, green-jerseyed handlers were working around an SH-3D Sea King helicopter which had arrived on board *Jefferson* twenty minutes earlier. Tombstone had seen the landing but not the passengers. He wondered if the helo's arrival had something to do with his summons to see his uncle.

At a doorway leading into the island he nearly collided with Batman, who was just coming out onto the roof. "Hey, Stoney! You hear?"

"I heard."

"You up for a lecture from your uncle or what?"

Tombstone pulled off his cranial and his floater—the helmet and life jacket worn while working on the flight deck—and shoved them at Batman's gut. "Whatever it is, it'll beat the hell out of listening to any more of your stories!"

Batman laughed. "Aw, you're just jealous, Stoney!" Breakfast in the Dirty Shirt Wardroom that morning had been made entertaining by Batman's tales of his rendezvous in Bangkok the night before with a gorgeous blond stewardess named Becky. "You oughta come into town with me tonight! Becky's bringing a friend!"

"Not tonight," Tombstone said, grinning. "Too much paperwork to do."

He made his way down gray steel corridors, then trotted up a succession of zigzagging ship's ladders up through the heart of the island. Minutes later, he arrived at the admiral's outer office on the 0–9 deck level and opened the door. A yeoman first class looked up from a steel desk and nodded. "Mr. Magruder! You're to go right in, sir."

The inner sanctum looked more like an executive's office than something on board ship, with wood-paneled bulkheads and oil paintings of sailing ships and Navy aircraft. The deck was carpeted, and the furniture would not have been out of place in a men's club. Only the round, steel-framed portholes along one bulkhead proved that they were still aboard ship.

Tombstone had always been troubled by the protocol of having a two-star admiral for an uncle. Navy custom and common sense both dictated that he play it conservatively and pretend he didn't know the guy . . . at least until they were alone and discussing nonmilitary subjects. It was easier this time, though. The admiral was not alone. Captain Fitzgerald stood by the bulkhead, looking out a porthole, and there were three civilians seated in chairs in front of the admiral's desk.

He realized that these must have been the passengers who had arrived earlier aboard the Sea King. Two were men, one small with owlish-looking glasses and a crumpled suit, the second taller and brawnier and wearing a loud print shirt and a handlebar mustache. The third civilian was a woman.

She was lovely, wearing a conservative gray skirt and jacket which seemed out of place with the disarray of her blond hair—the result, Tombstone decided, of the cranial she'd worn during the helo flight to the carrier. Her eyes were a pale, ice blue.

"I'm Pamela Drake, Commander," she said in a crisp, businesslike tone as she rose. It was clear immediately that she was the one in charge of the trio. "American Cable Network. This is my cameraman, Bob Griffith. My soundman, Hugh Baughman."

He shook hands with the two in turn. Griffith was the tall, mustached man, Baughman the one with glasses.

Tombstone exchanged a brief glance with the admiral. "Welcome to our boat, Miss Drake," he said.

"Pleased to meet you, Commander." She raised one perfectly arched eyebrow at the admiral. "But I don't care to be patronized. I may be a civilian, but I know you call something this large a 'ship,' not a 'boat'!"

"Actually, he's quite correct, ma'am," Fitzgerald said. "Aviators always call their carrier a 'boat,' God knows why. Even when you get too old to fly, like me or the admiral here."

"Mind your manners, Captain," the admiral said. As Pamela resumed her seat, he turned to Tombstone. "It seems that you're something of a celebrity, son. Miss Drake here has come out to the *Jefferson* to get some film clips for a news program special she's doing. When she found out you were aboard, well . . ."

"I don't understand."

"Ever hear of a news program called *World Focus*?"

"Yes, sir." *World Focus* was a popular nightly program Stateside, with a news-magazine format and aired by ACN. Mildly liberal, sharply critical of the current administration and its foreign policy, the show had never appealed enough to Tombstone for him to follow it much when he was in the States. "I haven't seen it since we were Stateside last, of course."

"It's a one-hour program," Pamela said. "Five nights a week, covering current news topics. The closing fifteen-minute slot each evening is a segment we call *Up Close*. Generally, we run with a single topic five nights in a row, examining it from every side, featuring in-depth interviews, that sort of thing."

"But what does that have to do with me?" Tombstone asked. He felt uneasy. Pamela Drake's direct manner, her no-nonsense tone of voice made him feel like she had him on camera.

She pursed her lips. "Next week we will be presenting an *Up Close* series on Navy carriers, whether they're necessary in today's world. We'll be linking it to the *World Focus* pieces we'll be airing at the same time on the trouble in Thailand . . . whether we should be here, what danger there might be in our getting involved in Thailand, that sort of thing."

"And you want Tombstone here for an interview," Fitzgerald said.

"That's right." She gave Tombstone a sidelong look. " 'The Hero of Wonsan,' the press was calling him a few weeks back. I think we should feature him in an interview which we'll work into the carrier piece. Who is he? What was it like shooting down six North Koreans? What did he feel about that?"

"Just a damn minute," Tombstone said. "I didn't do it for fun . . ."

"No one said you did, Commander. But now you're here in Thailand, presumably carrying out our government's foreign policy. What are you doing? How do you see the situation?" She smiled suddenly. "I think you'd have a lot to contribute, Commander."

"Our instructions are to cooperate with you, Miss Drake," the admiral said. "You can make arrangements with the Captain here for any shooting you want to do on board the *Jefferson*."

"I'll do that, thank you. As long as my crew and I are here now, can we begin with a tour of your ship?" She smiled again, a dazzling display of perfectly white teeth. "I mean your *boat*!"

"I don't see why not," Fitzgerald said. "Tombstone? Would you care to show the lady and her people around?"

He did not care to, but one did not tell the Captain that. "Of course, sir."

"You'll have dinner with us this evening, Miss Drake?" The admiral was trying to be charming, but somehow it wasn't coming off well. He seemed ruffled by her challenging approach toward Tombstone.

"Sorry, we can't. We'll need to get back to our hotel. In fact, if we can arrange it, it would probably be easiest if we could conduct most of our interviews with the commander in Bangkok instead of out here. Possibly at our hotel?"

"As you wish. How long will you need him?"

"Oh, two or three sessions will be enough. I imagine we could fit him in for an hour or two these next few evenings."

Tombstone groaned to himself. "May I remind the admiral," he said, picking with care the words he could use in front of the press, "that I've been assigned to temporary duty ashore."

"I don't think that will be a problem, Stoney. We can find someone to take your place. 'Full cooperation,' remember?"

It appeared that there would be no escape.

Twenty minutes later he was leading Pamela and her crew through the twisting bowels of *Jefferson,* taking them down the island deck by deck until they were in the maze of passageways beneath the flight deck. The experience of walking down one of *Jefferson*'s long interior corridors never failed to amaze a first-time visitor. The passageways ran straight for hundreds of feet; every thirty feet or so they were interrupted by a cross frame with an oval-shaped door called a "knee-knocker" because they forced a tall person to simultaneously stoop and step high to go through. Watching someone approach down a passageway was like watching one's own reflection in an endlessly reflected series of arched mirrors.

"My God," Baughman said breathlessly as they turned a sudden corner and confronted another infinite regression of knee-knockers. "How many miles of tunnels do you have in this thing?"

Tombstone grinned. "Never counted 'em. It might give you an idea of her size, though, if you think of *Jefferson* as an eighty-story building lying on her side. In some ways, she's a self-contained city. We've got a population of over six thousand, with one radio station and two television stations, a barber shop, a hospital complete with OR, a dentist's office, a ship's exchange which passes for our own shopping mall, a newspaper and printing office, laundry service, a hobby shop. . . ."

"Anybody ever get lost down here?" Pamela asked. She stepped back against a gray-painted bulkhead as three dungaree-clad sailors squeezed past, going the other way.

"All the time," Tombstone replied. "Everybody carries maps the first few days they're aboard. After that, well . . . I know I'd get lost trying to find my way around down in snipe country, and I've been aboard six months."

"Snipe country?"

"Engineering spaces, below and aft. Don't worry. That's not where we're going."

"Do you *know* where we're going?" Griffith said. He was out of breath, lugging the bulky camera he balanced on his shoulder. He'd taken a number of shots of various parts of the ship at Pamela's direction, but he looked as though he'd be a lot happier taping congressmen in a shore-based studio.

"Sure thing, Mr. Griffith. This way."

They took another turn into a blind corner with a ladder zigzagging precipitously into the depths of the ship. He led them down three levels. Pamela seemed to be bearing up well under the indignities of navigating the steep ladders in her skirt; more than once, though, Tombstone had to lead the way with a bellowed "make a hole" to clear the sightseeing sailors who had gathered near the base of the next ladder down. It seemed that *Jefferson*'s grapevine was working at full efficiency, alerting sailors to the fact that a woman was making a tour of the vessel.

"We were on the 0–3 deck," he explained as they left the ladder and doubled back in an unexpected direction. "That's the level immediately under the 'roof,' or flight deck. Now we're on the 0–1 level, coming up on the hangar deck."

"Does that mean we're as far down in the ship as we can go?"

"Hardly. It means the decks below this one are numbered differently . . . one, two, three, and so on down to the keel. Counting the island, *Jefferson* is twenty stories tall."

They made one last turn and emerged into a vast, steel-lined cavern.

A visitor's first look at *Jefferson*'s hangar deck never failed to raise the same emotions: surprise and awe. Thirty feet deep, two thirds the length of the carrier and covering two acres, the vast chamber looked like the inside of some immense shoreside warehouse. The glimpses of sunlight and blue sea caught through the huge, oval elevator bays were so restricted that they might as well have been views overlooking a river from a storage building back home. The air rang and echoed with shouted orders, the roar of tractors, the clatter of tools and metal on metal.

Most of the deck space was occupied by aircraft, each with wings folded in a characteristic way depending on its type: F-14s with their variable-sweep wings angled back along their flanks, A-6 Intruders with the wings broken in the middle and folded across their spines, a lone Hawkeye with wings twisted at right angles and rotated back to avoid the dish-shaped radome on its back. Space not occupied by aircraft was made hazardous by yellow-painted tractors, called mules, which busied about in a strange blend of geometry and ballet.

"It's enormous!" Pamela said.

"Yup," Tombstone agreed. "Follow me."

"What's that smell?" Baughman asked.

Tombstone sniffed the air. Curiously, he was aware of Pamela's perfume, a subtle hint of roses and vanilla, but nothing more. "Probably a mix of oil and JP5," he said. "That's what we use for jet fuel. After you've been aboard awhile, you don't even notice it."

"You carry a lot of jet fuel on board?" Pamela asked.

"About two million gallons."

"My God!" Griffith said. "That stuff's pretty explosive, isn't it?"

"Yeah. We have to be pretty careful with it."

Pamela gave him a searching, sideways look. "Why do you carry so much?"

Tombstone laughed. "Actually, it's not enough. We have fifty or sixty active aircraft at any given time. Each one flies twice a day, and burns two, maybe three thousand gallons each time up. At that rate, two million gallons doesn't least nearly long enough! We need to take on more fuel just about every week."

"I thought nuclear carriers didn't need replenishment."

"To run the engines, no. *Jefferson*'s nuclear fuel supply will keep her cruising sixty thousand miles a year for fifteen years, sure, and uranium takes up only a tiny fraction of the space a load of fuel oil would. In fact, because of that, we can carry more avgas than conventional carriers do. But we still have to take on fresh supplies pretty often. Not just avgas either, but food, stores of all kinds. One operation like Wonsan pretty much wipes us out on munitions too. That's why we put in at Japan afterwards, to stock up."

As he talked, he led them across the tangled maze of the hangar deck toward one of the huge, oval cutaway openings in the side of the ship.

"This is one of the elevators?" Griffith asked.

"That's right. Port side aft. Actually, it's a section of the flight deck which moves up and down on those rails along the outside of the hull. We have four of them, and they can lift sixty-five tons at a time. We use them to transfer aircraft back and forth between the hangar deck and the roof."

As they stepped across the yellow-and-orange painted warning stripes which marked the joint between deck and elevator, Pamela stopped and looked at the opening, large enough to pass an aircraft with its wings folded. "You know, Commander, a big question being debated back on Capitol Hill these days is whether aircraft carriers are too vulnerable to be worthwhile in a modern war. And now that I've seen one, I have to wonder if your critics aren't right."

"What do you mean?" He led the group to a railing, out of the way of a mule and a team of yellow-jacketed deck handlers maneuvering an F-14 Tomcat onto the elevator. The dark waters of Sattahip Bay lapped at the ship's side twenty feet below.

"What did you say . . . two million gallons of aviation fuel? What happens if an enemy missile flies through this big hole in the ship's side?"

Tombstone grinned. "That debate has been going on since the Falklands War. That's when the Navy suddenly realized that a cheap missile could do big-time damage to a very expensive ship."

"And there was the *Stark* in the Persian Gulf," Pamela pointed out. "Can you really justify spending billions of dollars on something that can be blown out of the water by a single Exocet costing, oh, say a few hundred thousand dollars?"

"In the first place," Tombstone said slowly, "the *Jefferson* is not the *Sheffield*."

"Sheffield?"

"A British DDG, a guided-missile destroyer, sunk by air-launched Exocet missiles during the Falklands War," Tombstone explained. "Look at it this way. *Jefferson* has over two thousand separate watertight compartments. Sinking her . . . well, you might as well try to sink a piece of styrofoam."

"That sounds ominously like the argument they used for the unsinkable *Titanic*," Pamela said. Her eyes twinkled. She seemed to enjoy sparring with him. "In a war, you'd have quite a time hiding a ship this big from Russian satellites. One nuclear cruise missile and . . . where would your styrofoam be then?"

Tombstone crossed his arms. "Look, if Russia and us start tossing nukes at each other, we're going to be losing a hell of a lot more than carriers! *Jefferson* can fight a nuclear war all by herself if she has to, but her main purpose is as a deterrent . . . and to give the President some non-nuclear options in a crisis."

"Like Wonsan."

"That's right."

"Okay, what about conventional weapons then? You're still vulnerable. An Exocet could slip right through this big doorway here, explode in there among all those airplanes and . . . whoosh!"

"In combat, these openings are closed off by sliding armor panels. We keep them open in fair weather and in port to keep the hangar deck aired out, but we can seal her up tight when we need to. So we won't have SSMs bouncing around on our hangar deck.

"Now, look over there." He pointed aft toward a railed sponson extending from the hull along the ship's port quarter. "See that grouping of six tubes, like mortars? That's Super RBOC." He pronounced it "are-bock." "For Rapid-Bloom Offboard Chaff. Antiship missiles like Exocet are guided to their target by radar. When CIC—that's the ship's combat information center—picks up incoming missiles, those tubes fire off clouds of radar-reflecting fibers called chaff, just like the chaff dispensers on my Tomcat. The missiles home on the chaff and miss the ship.

"Now, look up there." He turned around and pointed forward, far up along the curve of the ship's hull. "Up there on that forward sponson . . . see something that looks like a big, white, dome-topped garbage can? That's one of our Mark 15 Phalanx systems, or CIWS." He pronounced the acronym "sea-whizz." "That's for Close-In Weapons System. It's a big Gatling gun, computer-controlled and radar-directed, which can rattle off 20-mm depleted uranium rounds at the rate of fifty per *second*. Each slug is two and a half times denser than steel and is moving at something like seven hundred miles per hour when it hits. The control and aiming is precise enough to target an incoming missile and blow it right out of the air. We have three Mark 15s aboard *Jefferson*: that one port side forward, one to starboard below the island, and one aft on the port side of the fantail."

The deck handlers had completed maneuvering the Tomcat onto the elevator. A klaxon blasted warning, and then the elevator gave a hard jolt and began crawling upwards.

"Phalanx," Pamela said thoughtfully. "Wasn't that the defense system on the *Stark* that was turned off at the wrong time?"

Tombstone met her cool gaze evenly. "Yes, ma'am. It was."

"But of course, that can't happen aboard the *Jefferson*."

"No ma'am, it can't."

The elevator rose level with the flight deck and shuddered to a halt. From here, it was like standing on a dry land airfield, with the control tower island rising far across a very large stretch of dark-colored runway. The aircraft parked along the edge of the four-acre flight deck, the helo still resting in front of the island, the tiny figures of deck handlers going about their duties—all served to emphasize the overwhelming size of the *Jefferson*. With no flight operations going on, the flight deck was unusually quiet.

"You still haven't convinced me, Commander," Pamela said as they stepped off the elevator and started across the flight deck. She stopped Tombstone with a hand on his shoulder and turned, facing west. Three of the other ships of *Jefferson*'s battle group were visible scattered at widely spaced intervals across the Sattahip anchorage. Closest was the shark-gray shape of the *Vicksburg*, the CBG's Aegis cruiser. Astern was the DDG *Kearny*, and farther off still, the frigate *Biddle*. *Winslow* and *Gridley*, the remaining two vessels of CBG-14, were still at sea, patrolling in the Gulf of Thailand. "Look," she continued. "You have a nine-billion-dollar aircraft carrier . . . and you still need all those ships just to protect her!"

Tombstone laughed.

"What's so funny?"

"Excuse me, ma'am, but that's a pretty common misconception."

"Those other ships don't protect the carrier?"

"Oh, to a certain extent, sure. The frigates are mostly for ASW—that's anti-submarine work—and they act as a screen to keep enemy subs from getting too close. But *Jefferson*'s aircraft are her whole reason for being. Look . . . think of a map of the United States. Now imagine the *Jefferson* sitting in Washington, D.C., okay?"

"Okay."

"Her frigate escorts would be deployed as far apart as, oh,

say, Pennsylvania and parts of North Carolina. But her F-14 Tomcats would be on patrol over Maine, South Carolina, Tennessee, and Michigan."

"My God . . ."

"Her S-3 Vikings would be sub-hunting in Ohio. If there was need for a bombing run, her A-6 Intruders could hit Chicago."

"Good Lord! I had no idea you guys covered so much territory," Baughman said. He sounded impressed.

"Put that same battle group in the Med," Tombstone continued. "With the *Jeff* off Greece, our planes could cover places as far apart as northern Italy and Syria, Odessa on the Black Sea and the deserts of Libya." He paused, suddenly self-conscious, then smiled and gestured at the *Vicksburg*. "You see, as far as we're concerned, it's *us* who protects *them*!"

She laughed, a warm sound, and she reached out and touched his arm. "I must say, Commander, that I admire your love for your ship. *Boat*," she corrected herself. "It certainly shows when you talk about her!"

He smiled in reply. "If you think that's bad, wait until you get me talking about flying. That's my real love."

Suddenly she turned serious. "Yes, I imagine it would be." She looked at Tombstone for a moment, then, abruptly, turned away. "Okay, boys. You got what we need?"

"That should do it," Griffith said, patting his camera. "We've got five—ten good minutes' worth."

"We could get you back on board in the next day or two while we're conducting flight ops," Tombstone offered. "You could get some great shots of catapult launches . . . or recovery operations aft. It's a lot more exciting than miles and miles of gray steel passageways!"

"We may take you up on that," Pamela said. "For now, though, I think we should set up a time to meet you in Bangkok. I'll want to get some of what you said today on tape. You can be quite persuasive when you want to be, Commander."

"I guess that's why they made me tour guide," he replied. "To keep your show from getting too one-sided!"

She smiled. "We'll see. I'll take up your schedule with your admiral. By the way . . . Admiral Magruder is your uncle, isn't he?"

That again. "Yes, ma'am, he is."

She laughed. "Well, that must be convenient!"

"I don't know what you mean." He couldn't tell from Pamela's bantering tone whether she was serious or not. Back at Yokuska, after the fight at Wonsan, the press had had a field day with the fact that he was the nephew of the battle group commander. Tombstone kept his face impassive and turned away. "This way, if you please."

As he led the civilians across the flight deck, Tombstone couldn't help connecting Pamela's seemingly offhand comment with their quiet, unstated hostility to the very idea of the *Jefferson*. To them, the carrier represented billions of misspent dollars, and he could tell they were looking for ways to attack her.

And now it felt as though they were attacking *him*.

CHAPTER 7

"You're at attention, Mister!"

Batman gave up any thought of keeping this discussion on a friendly, personal level and held himself ramrod stiff, keeping his eyes focused on a point on the bulkhead behind CAG Marusko's left shoulder. "Yes, sir!"

Marusko examined the Shore Patrol report in his hand and shook his head slowly, as if he couldn't quite believe what he saw written there. "One ornamental hedge. Two rows of flowers. Tire marks across the landscaped lawn. A rock garden, complete with a decorative Buddhist shrine. A god-damned *palm* tree." CAG looked up, peering over the top of his reading glasses. "Just how the hell did you manage to park the car in the hotel tennis court? It was fenced in!"

"Well, it *was*. Sort of. Sir."

"Rental car."

"Yes, sir. You see, the brakes were kind of bad, and—"

"How much did you have to drink?"

"Gee, I'm not real sure, CAG. We'd stopped at the Oriental first. Then we went to the Thai Intercontinental. The girls were showing me around, you see. . . ."

"Driving under the influence. Property damage. This is serious, Mister. *Damned* serious!"

"Yes, sir."

"Next there's this . . . this complaint from the same hotel. An unidentified man wearing boxer shorts, and two . . . ah . . . partly dressed young ladies, ran through the lobby, startling a number of the hotel's guests. That wouldn't be you and your 'friends' again, would it?"

"Uh, probably not, CAG. I mean, I don't remember too much after the—"

"The man in boxer shorts was screaming, 'Viper Squadron, launch when ready!' at the top of his lungs. Ring any bells?"

"No, sir."

"And then the finale. This same man and his female companions removed the rest of their clothes and went swimming in the hotel pool."

"I really wouldn't know anything about that, sir."

"It seems one of the restaurant lounges in this hotel has a large picture window, which looks out into the pool. *Under*-water. Very atmospheric, I understand."

"I'm sure it is, sir."

"The man proceeded to grapple with one of the women in the water, apparently in an attempt to copulate with her. In front of approximately fifty of the hotel's guests who happened to be in the lounge at the time."

"I'm sure if he'd known they were watching, he wouldn't have done it, sir."

"Responding to a call by the hotel, the Shore Patrol finally found you behind the pool house, apparently hiding from the establishment's security people, stark naked and sopping wet." CAG looked up again. "It doesn't say what became of your skinny-dipping companions."

"Oh, that was their hotel. I imagine they made it back to their room."

"You sorry son of a bitch! In one night you have managed to disgrace your uniform, your squadron—"

"Well, actually, I wasn't wearing the uniform at the time—"

"*Damn* it, Wayne, don't you play games with me!" He slapped the report down on his desk. "I could have your ass out of here with this! Do you understand me? I could have your wings handed to me on a platter!"

Batman swallowed. This was worse than he possibly could have imagined. "Yes, sir."

"Now, you have a choice, mister. We can handle this right here, just you and me. Or we can go to the Captain with it. What's it going to be?"

"I'll be glad to . . . to work it out with you, sir."

"Good." Marusko nodded. "Good! The skipper wouldn't want to be bothered with shit like this. Now for the good news. Somehow you managed to luck out on one part of this sorry story, Wayne. The hotel has agreed not to press charges so long as you pay them . . ." He consulted the report again. "Right. Two thousand, nine hundred fifty dollars for damage to their landscaping. Apparently they haven't been able to connect you with the swimming pool incident, because that wasn't mentioned in their claim. Or maybe they've decided to start featuring X-rated sex shows for their clientele."

"Three . . . three thousand dollars, sir?"

CAG picked up another paper. "Add to that an estimated eight hundred dollars for the rent-a-car people. The collision with the palm tree and the tennis court fence didn't do that Datsun's bodywork any good." Marusko removed his glasses. When he spoke again, it was with a low, almost quiet voice, the voice which CAG Marusko used when he was in his most dangerous mood. "So, four grand will settle things with the civilians and you luck out, but by God you still have to settle with me, Wayne. I'm not letting you off the hook that easily! Do we understand each other?"

"Yes, sir. Perfectly, sir." Almost four thousand dollars! As a Navy lieutenant, Batman received $2,596 this month, a figure which included both flight pay and the temporary bonus of hostile fire pay for his service in Korea, but he was still going to have to take out a Credit Union loan to raise that much cash all at once. He'd be paying this one off for quite a while.

"It occurs to me, Mr. Wayne, that a change of scenery would be beneficial for both of us. It will remove you from the temptations of exotic Bangkok . . . and it will get you out of my sight. It happens I have an empty slot for a special duty assignment. How does U Feng sound to you?"

Batman's jaw dropped. "U Feng? But that's . . . oh, *shit*!"

"You have a problem with that, Mister?" Marusko's voice was whipcrack tight again.

"No, sir. No problem, sir." U Feng!

And the worst of it was, he hadn't even made it with Becky or Arlene. His attempt in the pool had been just that . . . and a dismal failure after all that he'd had to drink. And Becky had promised him another chance tonight. . . .

"It is now 0914 hours. I want you and your RIO in the Ready Room, suited up and ready to go, by 1430 hours this afternoon. I'll have your orders cut by then. Launch is at 1500."

"Yes, sir." There was nothing more to be said.

"Get out of here!"

"Aye, aye, sir!" He fled.

Behind him, Marusko picked up the Shore Patrol report again and began re-reading it. His reserve broke at last, and he collapsed back in his chair, laughing helplessly.

1445 hours, 16 January
CATCC, U.S.S. *Thomas Jefferson*

Made It Bayerly crossed his arms and surreptitiously leaned against the bulkhead of the darkened room.

"Air Boss says they're ready to go on Cats One and Three," a third class radarman at one of the consoles said.

"Okay, Paterowski," Senior Chief Hansen said. He looked bored, sitting back in the room's command chair with a mug of coffee in his hand, his headset perched at an angle to uncover one ear. "Tell 'em we're ready to pick up."

"They're going to launch the helo first."

"Makes sense."

Bayerly glanced over at the status board, where a young third class was writing backwards on the transparent plastic. The Sea King's mission was listed as Bangkok, a run to the Thai Airlines helipad in the city and back.

That would be Tombstone Magruder's helo.

Damn the man, anyway. Bayerly's thought was raw pain and

anger. The word had quickly spread throughout the ship that the three civilian visitors to the carrier the day before had been from a high-powered Stateside news program, and that one of them, a real looker of a woman, had asked specially to interview Commander Bigshot Magruder. So now the lucky bastard was on his way to Bangkok.

Bayerly glanced to his left. Several other naval flight officers from various squadrons were there, standing in various attitudes of relaxation or boredom. It was standard practice for NFOs to stand stretches of duty in Air Ops, where they could be asked for advice during a crisis, especially one involving a man in their unit. Since he'd been relieved of flight duty, it was natural that Bayerly put in more than the usual duty time for VF-97. He didn't like it, though. He didn't like it one bit.

The other officers had been all but shunning him since his suspension, almost as if he'd already lost his wings. Even now, McConnell, Rostenkowski, and the others seemed to be avoiding his eyes, and he could imagine their pointed comments behind his back.

The pain burning in Bayerly's gut felt like jealousy, though he knew it wasn't. It was despair for a career slowly but surely closing down. He'd known it, felt it for months. Back during the Wonsan operations three months ago, it hadn't been coincidence which had led CAG to assign the hotshot missions to Tombstone Magruder while posting Bayerly to routine CAP flights over the carrier.

Magruder had downed six MiGs and won the Navy Cross. Bayerly had sat it out on the sidelines. And all because of what had happened over a year ago . . .

"Helo away," a radarman said. Several television monitors about CATCC showed the gray bulk of the Sea King lift off the middeck, hover for a moment, then dip its blunt bow and angle off toward the north. Other monitors showed the view forward. Aft of two of the four catapults, JBD shields rose slowly behind the two Tomcats readying for launch. A deck officer gave the hand signal to bring the engines up to full power.

Bayerly wondered how Batman Wayne felt about being

snagged to cover for Magruder. The rumors about *his* escapade last night had been spreading about the ship as well.

He sighed. There had to be a way to change things . . . *had* to be! If he couldn't turn things around, his next posting was going to be to Adak, Alaska . . . and then it would be retirement as a lieutenant commander, with precious little to show for twelve years of service.

Twelve years!

The cat officer on the Cat One monitor dropped to one knee and touched the deck. Tomcat 232 lurched forward in a billowing cloud of steam as the catapult slung it off the *Jefferson*'s bow. Almost simultaneously, Tomcat 203 hurtled off the carrier's waist. Together, the two planes grabbed for altitude, afterburners flaring orange.

Bayerly watched them turn toward the north, still climbing, and his fists clenched in anger.

2000 hours, 16 January
The Dusit Thani Hotel, Bangkok

"I don't know," Tombstone said. "I've never thought much about it, I guess."

He was perched on the edge of a comfortable settee, feeling very much out of place. The room, part of a walnut-paneled, richly furnished suite, had been provided by the hotel as an impromptu studio for Pamela Drake and her film crew. Tombstone had tried to suggest that there were plenty of studio facilities aboard the *Jefferson*, but she'd replied that the carrier's surroundings were too cold, too formal to come across well on American television.

Pamela was seated on a divan opposite him and slightly to his left, and a low, wooden coffee table had been pulled between them. Griffith stood several feet away, squinting into the eyepiece of his camcorder, while Baughman bent over the dials and wavering needles of his sound equipment across the room. Several other people in Pamela's film crew hovered in the background, hidden behind the bright, standing lights which bathed him in a hot, white glare. Tombstone could hear

the whir of the camera as he tried to gather his thoughts, and
he was painfully conscious of the small microphone dangling
against the breast of his dress white shirt.

"Surely you've *thought* about it, Commander," Pamela said.
She had a rich, seductive voice. It would have been sexy,
Tombstone thought, if he hadn't been convinced that she was
using it to set him up for the kill. "All those press conferences,
your name in the headlines back home . . ."

She'd just asked him what he thought about being a national
hero.

"I can't really say that I was a hero," he said. "I certainly
wasn't any more of a hero than several thousand other guys
who were there."

The subject of the discussion was the Wonsan raid three
months before. He hesitated, finding his thoughts cluttered by
memories. He remembered Commander Marty French, killed
while trying to land his damaged F/A-18 on the *Jefferson*'s
flight deck. And his good friend Coyote Grant, who'd been
captured by the North Koreans, escaped, and ended up helping
the Marines and a Navy SEAL team accomplish their mission
behind enemy lines. And Batman, who had shot down three
KorCom fighter-bombers before they could attack the fleet.

But how could he put across everything that he felt in a few
words?

"The point is," he continued, "that all of us were just doing
our jobs. That's not very exciting or romantic, I know, but
that's the way it was. An American ship and its crew had been
captured on the high seas in an act of piracy, and the President
sent us in to bring them out. We did."

"You are entirely too modest, Commander." She leaned
forward, and Tombstone caught a whiff of perfume as she
lightly touched one of the ribbons on the top row of his award
display above his left shirt pocket. "Is this the Navy Cross?"

She'd indicated the blue ribbon with its single white stripe.
"Yes, it is."

"And that's only the second highest decoration the U.S.
Navy can award its people. Why do you think your superiors
singled *you* out of all those thousands?"

He grinned uneasily. "If you figure that out, let me know."

"According to the official report," she said, "you refused to eject from your damaged aircraft because your copilot was wounded and would not have survived if you'd left the plane."

"RIO."

"Pardon?"

"He was my RIO, my Radar Intercept Officer, not my copilot."

"And you don't think you should have gotten a medal for that?"

"I think the guys on the carrier should have won a medal. Let me tell you, it took real guts deciding to let me bring my shot-up Tomcat down on the deck! If I'd crashed and burned, I could have done real damage."

"The report also says you managed the battle above the city of Wonsan and were personally responsible for downing six Korean aircraft."

"Yes."

"Doesn't that make you a hero?"

"I'm proud of the job our boys did. It was a job that had to be done. I'm not particularly proud of shooting down those other aircraft, no."

As he said the words, Tombstone knew that he was lying. He was immensely proud of his ACM victories. That was the sort of achievement that every Navy pilot strove for, proof that his training and long hours of flying and practice had paid off, proof that he had the ultimate "right stuff" in a one-on-one contest with the enemy.

But at the same time, Tombstone hated to be reminded that those victories represented six dead men. Never mind that they'd been trying to kill him or his comrades at the time. Those had been *men* in those MiGs, all of them pilots like him, probably with families, wives, kids. . . .

It was not something to dwell on, and he bitterly wished he knew how to steer this interview in another direction.

Pamela seemed to sense his discomfort, and turned away. "Cut!" she said. "Okay, people, let's take a break. Save the lights."

"Looked good," Griffith said, lowering the camcorder. "Why'd you quit?"

She stood and stretched with a smooth, sinuous movement of arms and shoulders. "I'm tired. We need to regroup." She turned and smiled at Tombstone, her golden hair swirling just above her shoulders. "You're coming across *very* well, Matt. Was something bothering you about that last line of questioning?"

He smiled. "It showed, huh?"

"Only to someone who's interviewed as many guilty congressmen as I have." She sat down again and laid one perfectly manicured hand on his knee. "You're doing *splendidly*!"

"I was a bit uncomfortable with where things were going," he confessed. "I *really* don't like talking about this hero stuff."

She laughed. "Not only handsome, but modest too! How are we going to get you to open up about yourself, Matt?"

He could sense that she was trying to build him up, to put him at ease, and he felt a vague displeasure at the attempt to manipulate his feelings at the same time that he admired the way she was pulling it off.

"Miss Drake, I—"

"Please!" she said. "It's Pamela!"

"Pamela. Can't I convince you that being a hero doesn't really have anything to do with just doing my job?"

"You might convince me, but I doubt that our viewers would understand. You're an air ace, a Top Gun. You've gone into single combat with the enemy in a silver steed with magic weapons that Buck Rogers would envy. That's the stuff heroes are made of, Matt."

"But I thought you wanted this series of yours to be about how expensive aircraft carriers are!"

She laughed again. "We'll get to that, don't worry!" She turned serious again. "What I really want to do is show the whole story, the men as well as the machines. You can't have one without the other."

"I agree. But you know, us aviator types tend to steal the show. Maybe you should show something about the ordinary guys who make *Jefferson* run. Most of them are kids, nineteen . . . twenty. They work sixteen-hour days, and that's routine. When the pressure's on, I've seen them go all out for forty-eight hours straight. Down in engineering they're working in hundred-ten-degree heat. Up on the flight deck there's not a single man among them who hasn't come close one time or another to getting blasted over the side by jet wash, or sucked into an engine intake, or decapitated by a snapped arrestor cable. You know, the deck of an aircraft carrier may be the most dangerous work place in the world, but those kids do it, day after day. *They're* the heroes, not hotdogs like me."

"Can there really be such a thing as a modest fighter pilot?" Her lips quirked up in a thoughtful smile. "I thought all fighter jocks were supposed to be so arrogant and cocky!"

He grinned. "I guess it helps. Nowadays, though, you're better off if you have the temperament of an engineer."

"Well, I don't think I would have believed it if I hadn't seen one with my own eyes." She looked at her watch. "I'd say we've done enough for today. Boys? Let's wrap it."

Tombstone studied her profile for a moment. Despite their differences, he felt himself attracted to her. She seemed to feel his eyes on her and turned suddenly, their eyes meeting.

"I tell you what," he said. "It's late and I haven't had dinner yet. Know someplace in Bangkok where we could have some authentic Thai food?"

She pursed his lips. "I should warn you, Commander, that I don't get involved with my . . . subjects."

"That makes you sound like a lab technician. What am I, a rare specimen?"

"Okay, I'll tell you what. There are several restaurants right here in the Dusit Thani. There's the Mayflower . . . that's Chinese. Or the Shogun for Japanese food. Or the Hamilton for French cuisine. We'll have dinner, but only if it's on my expense account."

"Hey, how could any self-respecting hotdog refuse an offer like that? Let's go!"

They settled on the Mayflower. The food was good, but Tombstone scarcely noticed it.

CHAPTER 8

Located across the Chao Phraya River from the capital, Thonburi was supposed to be Bangkok's sister city, but so far as Pamela could see, the area was simply a continuation of the buildings and shanties, Buddhist *wats* and tourist traps, dark-watered *klongs* and waterfront piers making up the low, oriental urban sprawl that was Bangkok.

The district's Klong Dao Kanong carried a special reputation, however, a place where visitors to Thailand could glimpse a fragment of a largely vanished way of life, the floating markets of Thonburi.

She stole a sideways glance at her companion. During much of the interview the night before, Matthew Magruder had seemed reserved, even shy. Now he displayed an animated, almost boyish exuberance as he studied a guide booklet and pointed out landmarks and sights along the waterway. Pamela was not a morning person, and she wondered if Tombstone's Navy hours were responsible for his break-of-day brightness.

Still, she had to admit she was enjoying herself . . . and enjoying his company. This expedition had been rather hastily planned, and she'd not been entirely certain at the time that it was a good idea.

It had been late enough the previous evening when Tombstone had decided to stay in the city overnight. Today was

Saturday and the aviator had this weekend off, so there was no need for him to get back to the ship until Monday.

Almost . . . *almost* she'd suggested that he spend the night with her, but a final professional reserve within herself, the knowledge that mixing business and pleasure like that would only lead to trouble, had decided her against it. He had arranged for a room for himself and not even suggested that they share her bed. Pamela felt a mild disappointment at that which bordered on regret. It wasn't that she *wanted* the guy to make a pass at her . . . but she wasn't used to such gentlemanly discretion—or patience—and it left her wondering if the man even found her attractive.

She pushed the thought aside. What Tombstone had suggested instead had turned into a delightful excursion that left her feeling far closer to the man than a recreational romp in bed would have. They'd left requests for wake-up calls at the ungodly hour of five thirty A.M.—zero-dark-thirty, as Tombstone had called it—met in the hotel coffee shop for a thoroughly American breakfast of coffee and Danish, then made it to the Oriental Docks in time to catch a tour boat by six forty-five.

The boat had brought them to Thonburi, navigating through a *klong* crowded from shore to shore with native craft of all descriptions, heavily laden with tropical produce. Here, two pretty Thai girls in enormous lampshade hats, obviously sisters, jostled their skiff close to the shore to display a bountiful pile of dry fish; there an ancient man with white whiskers spread woven mats on the dockside piled high with fried bananas and noodles. Perhaps most surprising were the tourists. *Farangs*—the Thai word for foreigners—outnumbered the locals by a considerable margin, and most of the shops along the *klong* appeared to be selling souvenirs, cameras, and native crafts aimed at Western tourists. The air was thick with the sharp tang of Thai spices and foodstuffs. The crowd noise was loud enough that she had to lean close to Tombstone's shoulder and raise her voice to be heard.

"What are you so serious about?" she called. He'd grown

quiet in the last few minutes, and she wondered what had triggered the change.

He flashed her a shy smile. "Just wondering if my dad ever came here. He would've liked this place. He liked *people*."

Tombstone had told her about his father earlier that morning, about Sam Magruder's death while attacking a bridge in Hanoi. "Lots of servicemen came here for R&R back then, didn't they?" she asked.

"That's probably when Bangkok got its reputation as sin city." He stopped next to the spot where a black-eyed girl who couldn't have been more than twelve was selling custard-like sweets wrapped in banana leaves. "Here! Let's try some of these."

Tombstone indicated he wanted two, and fished in his pocket for several *baht* to pay for them. "*Kawpkun!*" Tombstone said as she handed the bundles up from her boat.

The girl burst out laughing, though whether at Tombstone's pronunciation or in pleasure at the tall *farang*'s attempt at her language, Pamela couldn't tell. "You are welcome!" The Thai girl replied in perfect, somewhat stilted English.

"I didn't know you spoke Thai, Tombstone," Pamela said, trying one of the custards. It was at once sweet and tart, reminiscent of butterscotch. When had she started using his call sign? she wondered. Last night sometime. It seemed so . . . natural.

"Oh, was that Thai?" He feigned innocence, then sobered. "Actually, a wise man once said that you need to learn two words in any language in order to get along in another culture."

"Oh? And what are those?"

"*Please* and *thank you*."

"And who was the wise man?"

"My father." He shrugged. "It really helps a lot if you at least *try* a bit of their language. It is their country, after all."

"Matthew Magruder, the more I know you, the less likely you seem as a Navy aviator. You're supposed to be arrogant!"

"Sorry. You want to see my Tom Cruise *Top Gun* imitation?"

"No, the Navy has enough Tom Cruises. I kind of like you the way you are."

He shook his head. "What is it about the Navy? During the interview you were going after the Navy's carrier program like nobody's business."

She thought back to the questions she'd asked on camera, and saw what he meant. Much of the thrust for her series called into question the whole issue of the Navy, of the government spending tens of billions of dollars for a fifteen-carrier fleet it no longer needed. While drawing out Tombstone and getting him to talk about himself, Pamela had argued that carriers were too expensive and too vulnerable, useless high-tech toys in an age when nuclear confrontation with the Soviets was no longer a likely possibility, and when Third World banana republics no longer knuckled under to gunboat diplomacy.

Pamela knew she'd done a damned good job putting her message across, too. Still, she'd liked the way Tombstone had kept the ball coming back into her court. He believed in carriers as an extension of Presidential foreign policy with an almost passionate conviction. He'd not convinced her of his side of the argument, not by a long shot, but she admired the way he stood up to her.

Maybe that was what she found most fascinating about the guy.

They finished the custards and disposed of the banana leaf wrappings in a streetside waste container.

"It's *waste* I don't like, Tombstone," she said after a long silence. "We don't need multibillion-dollar floating airfields anymore. Maybe back in the days when we were toe-to-toe with the Soviets, but . . ."

"The Russians aren't the only bad boys on the block," he said. "Besides, they're preoccupied with their own troubles right now . . . but there's nothing that says they might not come out of their hole sometime soon meaner and scrappier than ever."

"Nonsense." Her tone was harsher, more sarcastic than she'd intended. "The Cold War is over, or hadn't you heard?"

He looked at her, his gray eyes like ice. "You know,

Pamela, I've had the distinct impression all along that you had it in for us service pukes."

The accusation hit her in the pit of the stomach like a blow. She stopped in mid-stride, turning on Tombstone, unable to keep the fury out of her face and voice. "Don't you say that! Don't you *ever* say that!"

Tombstone's expression showed first confusion, then concern. "Pamela? What's wrong?"

Slowly, she forced herself to relax, unclenching her fists, and looking away from the Navy officer to study the crowd surrounding them. As many people as there were, the surroundings felt strangely private.

Pamela took a deep breath. "Sorry, Commander," she said. "It's . . . what you said."

"What did I say?"

She was silent a long moment. "I'll tell you something. Something I . . . don't like to talk about." She looked away, catching her lower lip between her teeth before she continued. "I had a brother once."

He gave her a hard look. " 'Had'?"

Pamela nodded. The pain was still sharp. "His name was Bobby and he was three years younger than me. I was a journalism major at Pitt when he graduated from high school. Our . . . our family was all set to pack him off to college, but he wouldn't have any of it. You talk about conservatives! He figured the colleges were all liberal hotbeds—this was the dawn of the Reagan Era, you understand—and that there were better ways of getting an education without spending forty thousand dollars for a piece of paper to hang on a wall."

"What happened?"

"He joined the Marines." She sniffled once, surprised that the memory still brought tears. "He went to boot camp at Paris Island, then got assigned to a rifle platoon going overseas. Beirut."

"Oh, God . . ."

"October, 1983. Some crazy drove a truck bomb into his barracks one floor below where he was sleeping. They never even found enough of him afterward to send home in a body bag."

"I'm . . . sorry . . ."

"So, Commander, I *do* care for . . . for 'service pukes,' as you call them. And that's why. As a journalist, yes, damn it, as a *liberal* journalist, I take great pleasure in putting the spotlight on waste in the military, especially on fat, braid-heavy Washington S.O.B.'s who ship young men like Bobby off into impossible situations, places where they aren't even allowed to defend themselves, places where they can get killed, *killed* just because . . . because . . ."

Pamela wasn't sure just how she got into Tombstone's arms. It hadn't been *her* idea, but she made no move to break away.

"I'm sorry, Pamela," he said. "I had no idea . . ."

"How could you?" She took a step back and looked up into his face, searching. "Tombstone, I . . . I really was interested in *you* during the interview. Not as a hero. Not as some kind of target in a campaign against government waste. As a person. I can disagree with a national policy and still see you as a . . . as a person, can't I?" She'd almost said "friend," and wasn't sure why she'd changed the word at the last instant. Pamela had not felt this confused in a long time, and it embarrassed her.

"I wish you would," Tombstone said. He grinned. "Why do you think I went to all this trouble to be with you someplace where we didn't have a camera staring at us?"

She looked around and was suddenly aware that several Thais nearby were casting dark looks in their direction. "Speaking of staring . . ."

Tombstone followed her glance and smiled. "Thai custom," he said. "They disapprove of public displays of affection between the sexes. Even holding hands." He was still holding hers.

"Hey! I've seen *guys* holding hands in public here."

"That's different. Friends are a lot more demonstrative with each other in public here than back Stateside. But boys and girls have to watch their step."

She pulled her hand free. "Maybe we should watch ours,

then." She looked at her watch. "I should get back," she said. Why did the words hurt so? "They'll think I got kidnapped or something."

"We can catch a water taxi over here." He pointed along the pier. There were fewer boats now, and the remaining waterside vendors were starting to pack up their wares. Western tourists continued to wander along the street, though, wandering in and out of the shops and store fronts facing the *klong* like brightly-colored ants on an anthill. "Come on."

She didn't want to go back to the hotel.

1245 hours, 17 January
Tomcat 232, over the border thirty miles northwest of U Feng

Batman sat back in his ejection seat, shaking his helmeted head sadly. "C'mon, Malibu. Give me a break. You think I *like* being out here in the boonies? Playing tag with crawlies as long as my arm?" He shuddered. That tropical centipede he'd seen legging it across the floor in his barracks at U Feng the night before hadn't been quite *that* big, but . . .

"Hey, dude," his RIO said over the ICS. "All I know is I was enjoying liberty call in the big B, and then I find out there's been this here change in orders. If they want to punish you by sending you to Siberia, fine, but what did *I* do to deserve this?"

"Guilt by association, my man. You hang out with the wrong people."

"Next time I'll know better. Watch it. Coming up on the first TARPS run. Switch on . . . cameras running."

To Batman's eyes, the jungle canopy below remained unbroken, mysterious and secret. To the high-tech eyes of the camera pod slung beneath his aircraft, however, the trees were far more transparent.

The TARPS pod consisted of a flattened, streamlined canister attached to one of the F-14's weapons mounts and tied in with the aircraft's navigational computer. TARPS could be fitted to a Tomcat in a matter of hours and was used by the Navy to convert standard F-14 fighters to the reconnaissance role as necessary. The pod contained a KS-87 high-speed frame camera, a KA-99 panoramic camera, and perhaps most useful of all, an AAD-4 infrared line scanner.

Fitted with TARPS, an F-14 could overfly suspected enemy positions and take high-resolution recon photos which, more than once, had caught the surprised expressions of antiaircraft gun crews as the Tomcat flew overhead. The lateral panoramic camera could photograph in telescopic detail broad stretches of terrain clear to the horizon in a format which allowed extreme enhancement and enlargement.

The AAD-5 created a line-by-line heat image of the terrain unfolding in a continuous strip with photographic clarity, revealing everything in the aircraft's path within a swath which ran very nearly from horizon to horizon. Infrared photography was an especially valuable tool for intelligence work. Batman had examined IR photos which showed the heat shadows of aircraft, identifiable traces marking where planes had been parked on an airfield, hours after they'd been moved; he'd seen infrared shots of oil storage tanks which revealed the level of oil inside as though the tanks themselves were transparent; he'd seen shots of hot vehicle engines gleaming like bonfires through layers of foliage or camouflage netting.

IR scans of the Thai jungle would reveal hidden trails just as clearly. The cleared, hard-packed ground of foot trails or roads gave off different levels of heat than the loose humus around it, and the jungle could not entirely conceal the patterns of temperature differentials. Jungle roads were clearer still, and vehicles would show up like burning flares.

Batman glanced out the canopy. To starboard, toward the north, lay Burma. There was an air base off that way, fifty kilometers distant. Mong-koi, it was called. He remembered the MiGs that had come across the line four days earlier. He could see nothing but jungle mountains, partly masked by clots of drifting cloud.

To the south, Price Taggart's Tomcat drifted lazily off the starboard wing. "Two-oh-three, this is Two-three-two," he said over the radio. "You with me, Price? We're starting our run."

"With you, Batman," Taggart's voice replied in his helmet. "Lead the way."

"We have signal lock," Malibu said, "Beginning run . . . now . . ."

Images picked up by TARPS could be stored or beamed back to a base for immediate processing. This time around, the images would be held for analysis on board *Jefferson*.

"Smile down there," Batman said. "You're on *Candid Camera*. . . ."

The minutes dragged on. Though TARPS technology allowed the reconnaissance aircraft to move at a reasonably high speed—Batman was cruising at nearly five hundred knots—the need to stick to a particular course was irksome to any fighter pilot. It made him feel predictable, and therefore vulnerable. Not that there was evidence of anything more hostile in that green maze than cobras and malaria. Now if there'd been a SAM site or two down there . . .

Becky was supposed to be in town for a few more days. He wondered if CAG would relent and bring him back in time to enjoy another run into Bangkok.

"Hey, Batman? You see something there?"

Malibu's voice over the ICS snapped Batman's attention back to his VDI. The camera feed from the TARPS pod showed the IR line scan on the screen, a shifting picture in black and white. Odd. There were dazzling points of light down there. Cooking fires?

"I think we have stumbled across one of those quaint and charming tribes of native hill people you've heard tell about," he said. It seemed strange, though. There were a *lot* of fires down there.

He held the Tomcat in straight, level flight, throttling back to less than four hundred knots at an altitude of three thousand feet. He dismissed the idea that he'd caught a band of smugglers. If that was a camp of some kind hidden beneath the jungle canopy, it had a population numbering in the thousands. He could see the engine flares of trucks now, too. It looked like he'd stumbled across some sort of army. . . .

An army. Those weren't Thai troops down there, not that many, not in this area.

Batman's eyes strayed to the northern horizon, encountering unrelieved green. That whole region was a regular breeding ground for armies, most of them the personal guards of drug lords. No doubt some of them were operating on this side of the border as well.

Whatever it was down there, it was damned big. "I wonder what they're going to make of this back at U Feng," he said to Malibu.

"Damned if I know. Want me to call it in?"

"Let's finish the run first. Good God! There's no end to them! Just what the hell have we found anyway?"

1248 hours, 17 January
Mong-koi, Burma

"General Hsiao! Major Sai is calling! The Burmese radio operator pressed the telephone handset against his ear. Around him, other men in Burmese army uniforms sat at the radar consoles which filled the Mong-koi control tower. Through the large, inward-slanting windows of the tower, the Mong-koi runways could be seen, flat, straight-lined slashes through the jungle. "He reports two American aircraft over his position!"

"American aircraft? What kind?"

The radio operator spoke briefly into the radio before turning again. "Sir! He doesn't know."

Peasants, Hsiao thought. Peasants who could scarcely tell the difference between a jet interceptor and a helicopter. Most of the soldiers in the People's Army now fighting in northern Thailand had been recruited from the ranks of militias formerly in the service of the various warlords of the Golden Triangle. Major Sai had, until recently, been working for the notorious Khun Sah, a Burmese drug lord widely known as the Prince of Death. His United Shan Army still dominated much of eastern Burma.

That would not be the case for very much longer. Once

Hsiao's agents controlled Thailand, he would be able to dictate his own terms to the likes of Khun Sah.

"American reconnaissance aircraft," Hsiao said. "From the carrier at Sattahip."

"Major Sai requests instructions, General," the operator said. "Shall he open fire?"

SA-7 missiles might down one of the planes, but killing two was unlikely. More probably the planes would flee, bearing precise coordinates for the point at which they'd been fired upon. "Tell him to do nothing. Support will be there in a few minutes."

"Yes, sir."

Hsiao sensed the ponderous bulk of General Kol coming up beside him. "General Hsiao?" The Burmese sounded worried. "What are you planning?"

Hsiao looked past the fat general, his eyes seeking the shadowed forms of several MiGs parked beneath the patchwork cover of layered camouflage netting. Ignoring Kol, he snapped an order. "Colonel Wu!"

"Sir!"

"Do we have a patrol ready to go?"

"Yes, general. Four aircraft are fueled and standing by."

"Scramble them."

"At once, General!"

"General Hsiao—" Kol began, but he stopped when the former Chinese intelligence officer turned a cold gaze on him. He swallowed, then made himself continue. "General Hsiao, perhaps it is not wise to antagonize the Americans. After all, a plan so broad, so complex. To shoot down American fighters here, now . . ."

"Your concern, General," Hsiao said quietly, "is this base and the Burmese forces we have in the field. The Americans are *my* concern."

"But if attention should be called to this air base—"

"It does not matter, Kol," he replied, omitting the formal use of the Burmese general's rank as a reminder of who was in charge. "After tonight it will not matter what the Americans know . . . or their Thai puppets!"

Kol lowered his gaze. "Of course, General."

The mournful wail of a siren could be heard faintly through the windows of the control tower. Across the tarmac, Chinese aircrews were wheeling the first of four J-7 fighters onto the runway. Hsiao could see four pilots, already wearing their green form-fitting pressure suits, dogtrotting toward their planes with their helmets under their arms.

"In any case," Hsiao continued, "there is nothing to worry about. So far as anyone else is concerned, this will simply be one more minor border incident."

The first Chinese pilot clambered up a ladder and slid into his cockpit. Crewmen detached power lines and wheeled the starter cart out of the way as the engine coughed into life, the whine rising above the moan of the siren. The canopy came down as the Chinese MiG started to roll.

Hsiao nodded to Wu, who was pressing a headset against one ear. "Have them stay at treetop level all the way to the target, Colonel. Perhaps we can surprise our American friends."

Moments later, the first two J-7s shrieked off the runway.

1249 hours, 17 January
Tomcat 232

"How about one more run?" Batman asked. He pulled the Tomcat into a sharp, banking turn to port. They had turned to cross the greatest concentration of heat sources, crossing the area from south to north. This had taken them close to the Burmese border, though they were still south of that invisible line.

"Fine by me," Malibu replied. "I don't really fancy visiting Burma anyway."

"Two-three-two!" Taggart's voice exploded over Batman's headset. "Bogies incoming, bearing three-four-oh at one-four miles!"

That put the targets across the line, well into Burma. "Rog," he said. "How many?"

"Two bogies," Taggart replied. "Repeat, two bogies. I think they're low. Keep losing them in the ground clutter."

"Stay on 'em. Malibu! You have them?"

"No joy, Batman . . . no! Got 'em! Two bogies, range now one-zero miles. Shit, Batman! They're coming straight in!"

Batman hauled back on the stick, clawing for sky. Whatever was about to happen, he wanted some room to maneuver.

The bogies kept coming.

CHAPTER 9

"Let's split up and see if we can get a better look at these guys," Batman said. He kept the F-14 in a sharp, twisting climb. The jungle fell away beneath the Tomcat as sunlight flooded the interior of the cockpit.

"Roger that," Taggart replied. "Not too far, though. Don't want to lose you."

American aircraft did not generally use tight-knit wingman formations but preferred the system known as "loose deuce." Having one of the two planes well out in front of the other, and a mile higher or lower, improved the chances of spotting the enemy, as well as giving two sets of aircraft radars a better look at the target.

"Range eight miles," Malibu called from the backseat. Batman leveled off at nine thousand feet, already searching the northwestern horizon for some visual sign of the approaching planes. "Still coming, speed six hundred knots."

"Okay. Call up the *Jeff* and tell them we have a situation here. I think we'd—"

"Shit!" Malibu exploded. "We have four bogies now, repeat, four bogies!" They must have been flying wingtip to wingtip and hard on the deck to confuse the Tomcats' radars.

"Homeplate, Homeplate, this is Tomcat Two-three-two," Batman radioed. "Do you copy, over?"

"Two-three-two, Homeplate," a voice answered moments later. Radio communications with the *Jefferson* were being relayed through a Hawkeye circling near Bangkok. "We copy."

"Homeplate, we have four, repeat, four bogies closing from three-four-oh at six hundred. They're coming in over the line."

"Copy, Two-three-two. Break off and RTB."

"Rog," Batman said. "You copy that, Price? Time to get out of Dodge."

"I don't think they're going to let us, Batman," Taggart said. "Tell you what. Get down on the deck while I run interference."

Batman thought about it for a brief moment. Taggart's suggestion made sense. Tomcat 232 was carrying two Sidewinder missiles in addition to the TARPS pod, not enough for a sustained dogfight if it came to that. Taggart was carrying eight missiles, and had greater maneuverability as well.

"Where the hell are our escorts anyway?" he snapped.

"We have six Thai F-5s at one-five-nine," Malibu replied. "Range thirty miles."

"Great." By the time they arrived, the fight would be over. He made his decision. "Right you are, Price Tag," he said. "Have fun and mind the ROEs."

He banked left into a sideslip dive which took the F-14 hurtling toward the jungle canopy. Tree-clad mountains rushed up to meet him, growing larger until he was so close that the ground became a featureless green blur. Taggart's aircraft dropped astern, taking up a position between the bogies and Batman's plane. The Rules of Engagement still applied. They couldn't fire until they were fired upon, but Taggart's maneuver would give Batman the chance to get clear whatever happened.

Batman leveled off at two thousand feet above the treetops, heading south. He cut back on the throttles, cutting the Tomcat's speed until the wings slid forward. He didn't want to get too far ahead of Taggart. A river flashed into view, winding through a valley between emerald hilltops.

Batman saw the flash in the same instant as Malibu.

"SAM! SAM!" his RIO yelled. "Seven o'clock!"

"Got it!" Batman hauled the stick left instinctively, turning into the missile in an attempt to make it overshoot. He recognized that corkscrewing white trail at once, the signature of a shoulder-launched SA-7, called "Grail" by NATO. Some bastard down there had lobbed it at them as they cleared the treeline along the river.

"It's closing!"

"Hang on, Malibu!" he yelled. "Pop flares!"

But he already knew they weren't going to make it. . . .

1250 hours, 17 January
Tomcat 203

"There they are!" Taggart's RIO called. "They're coming in behind us!"

"Hang on, Zig! I'm goosin' it!" He rammed the throttles full forward, cutting in the Tomcat's afterburners as he stood the aircraft on its tail. He heard Zig-Zag Ziegler grunt over the ICS as the acceleration slammed them into their ejection seats.

"We got two splittin' off!" Zig-Zag reported, his voice crackling over the ICS with excitement and tension. "Two splittin' off! They're comin' after us, man!"

The Tomcat continued to climb, pursued now by a pair of Chinese-copied MiGs, while the two remaining MiGs stayed on the deck, streaking south. Taggart caught a glimpse of sun flashing from silver wings, of arrowing white contrails in the humid air.

He pulled the stick over sharply, breaking out of his climb and dropping toward the jungle. If the MiGs going after Batman got too far ahead . . .

"Tone!" Ziegler yelled. "Price! They got lock-on!"

He heard the warble of missile lock over his headphones. Someone was lining him up for a radar-targeted launch.

"Keep cool, Zig," he yelled. "They're messing with our minds, that's all!"

The MiG launched an instant later.

1250 hours, 17 January
Tomcat 232

There was no time to think as the SAM clawed toward the
Tomcat. Tactical doctrine claimed that it was easy to shake a
Grail's infrared lock; often all that was necessary was to
throttle back until its electronic concentration on the plane's
engines was broken.

The problem was they were already flying low and slow.
He'd have to goose it hard just to get enough speed for
maneuver . . . and he was rapidly running out of sky.

He dropped the Tomcat's left wing, sharpening his turn. He
could see the Grail's twisting white tail bending to follow. It
was ignoring the flares, homing unerringly on the heat from the
F-14's engines, and Batman remembered learning that Grails
were fitted with filters which screened out decoy flares. He had
to pick up speed *now*. . . .

Trading precious altitude for more speed, Batman plunged
toward the jungle canopy, watching as the rapidly sweeping hands of his altimeter ticked off the feet. The missile
followed. . . .

1250 hours, 17 January
Tomcat 203

Taggart pulled the Tomcat into a seven-G turn, standing on the
port wing as he tried to outrace the missile. "Chaff!" he yelled.
"Dump chaff!"

Packets of aluminum-coated mylar strips burst one after
another from the Tomcat's tail, dispersing in a cloud behind
and below the aircraft. Taggart caught a glimpse of the two
MiGs following him, a tight-knit pair of specks low on the
horizon. The radar-homer twisted toward him.

"Homeplate! Homeplate!" he called. "This is Two-oh-three.
We have launch. Repeat, confirm bandit launch!" Switching to
the intercom again, he added, "Arm missiles!"

"Hot and armed."

The missile curved through the sky toward them. . . .

1251 hours, 17 January
Tomcat 232

Batman kicked in the Tomcat's afterburners, and six Gs molded him to the hard frame of his ejection seat. "Keep . . . popping . . . flares . . . !" he grunted against the pressure. The treetops clutched at his left wingtip, seemingly only a few yards below as he hauled back on the stick. He glanced back over his shoulder as he pulled out of the dive, estimating the Grail's angle of attack. Adrenaline surged, sharpening every sense, every perception.

The missile flew up the F-14's port engine.

Batman both heard and felt the explosion, a solid *whump* which transmitted itself through the aircraft's frame. His instrument panel exploded with red warning lights. His left fuel pump was gone . . . trim control . . . left rudder . . . The engine fire warning lit up and Batman hurriedly shut down the fuel flow to the port engine and initiated a shutdown. God! They'd been savaged!

"Malibu! You still with me?"

"I'm okay! I'm not sure the plane is!"

Smoke boiled from the Tomcat's port engine. The left wing dropped low, and the aircraft began shuddering as Batman struggled to bring it under control. "Mayday! Mayday!" He could hear Malibu in the backseat reciting the litany of an aircraft in distress. "This is Tomcat Two-three-two declaring an emergency! We have been hit by hostile ground fire and are going down. Mayday! Mayday . . . . !"

1251 hours, 17 January
Tomcat 203

Taggart kept the F-14 turning as the radar homer closed. The missile was visible as a minute flare of light on the end of a growing trail of white smoke as it came closer . . .

closer . . . then plunged through the invisible cloud of chaff and flashed past the Tomcat a hundred yards away.

"We did it!" Zig-Zag yelled. "We're clear!"

The homer's radar lock was broken. "Now let's give 'em one back!" Taggart said. He brought the Tomcat around smoothly, pulling out of the turn above and behind the pair of MiGs which had fired at him. They were jinking now, aware that the American had escaped them, aware that he was closing in on their six.

In targeting mode now, he selected a target on his HUD display. The square graphic of the targeting pipper turned to a circle and he heard the growl of the Sidewinder in his headphones: lock-on!

He closed in for the kill.

1251 hours, 17 January
Tomcat 232

"Batman!" Malibu called. "I'm getting dead air on the radio. I don't think we're getting through!"

A chunk of shrapnel might have sheared an antenna lead. Batman checked his compass. They were on a bearing of three-four-nine . . . almost straight north, heading smack for the Burmese border if they hadn't crossed it already. He tried to turn again and felt the Tomcat buck wildly in response. Damn! That missile must have torn half the portside stabilizer away!

Using flaps and the aircraft's tendency to sag to the left as it hung from the starboard engine, he began working to bring the Tomcat around in a slow, sweeping turn. There was no way he was going to land this baby back at U Feng, but at least he might make it back over Thai territory. Batman had no desire to sample the hospitality of the current military regime in the Socialist Union of Burma.

"How bad is it?" Malibu called from the back seat.

"Bad . . . but we'll manage!" Batman replied. He checked the altimeter. They were holding their own, anyway, still level at five hundred feet. "Remember the briefings on the Grail?

We still have a good chance of getting back." In the '72 war in the Middle East, something like sixty percent of the Israeli warplanes hit by Grails had still managed to make it back to friendly airfields. The SA-7 was nasty because it was small, portable, cheap, and could be fielded in great numbers, but the warhead together with its fragmentation casing only weighed about four pounds . . . too small to do serious danger to an aircraft as heavy as the Tomcat.

More red lights came on. That warhead might be small, but it was vicious . . . and modern jet fighters were relatively fragile things, vulnerable to a high-velocity spray of shrapnel. They were losing hydraulic pressure now. They still might make it, though, if . . .

"Batman!" the RIO called. "Bandits, one o'clock! Watch it . . . *watch it!*"

1252 hours, 17 January
Tomcat 203

Taggart squeezed the trigger on his stick. "Fox two! Fox two!" The call gave warning to friendly planes that a heat-seeker was in the air. The target MiG broke to the right, wildly trying to lose the Sidewinder which was closing with its engine flare with relentless persistence. Flares broke from the MiG's tail, tumbling away to either side like roman candles at a fireworks display.

The Sidewinder caught up with the fleeing MiG, ignoring the flares for the far hotter and more inviting target of the J-7's tailpipe flare. There was a flash, and black smoke boiled from the plane's engine. Taggart could see the wings flutter as the pilot struggled to regain control. . . .

Aflame now, the J-7 hit the treetops a second later. An orange fireball boiled up through the trees, uncoiling like the head of some gigantic, hooded snake.

"*Score . . . !*" Ziegler yelled. "Splash one MiG!"

1252 hours, 17 January
Tomcat 232

The two incoming MiGs flashed past the damaged Tomcat, hurtling toward the south before beginning a broad, sweeping turn which would bring them in behind Batman and Malibu.

"Where's Taggart?" Batman asked. "Malibu! Do you see Taggart?" If Tomcat 203 was close by they had a chance. Unfortunately, the failed attempt to cut the MiGs off from the TARPS plane, followed by a brief dogfight, had separated the two American planes by a number of miles.

"Negative! I've got nothing on the scope! Shit, Batman, I'm dead back here!"

Batman tried again to turn the stricken F-14, to bring the nose up in a bid for altitude, to do anything. Slowly, the Tomcat began to respond. The aircraft was still bucking and kicking, but he managed to drag it into a slow, rising turn to starboard.

Then he heard the telltale warble of a radar lock in his headset.

"Batman!" Malibu yelled. "They're locking on!"

"I hear it! I hear it!" *Damn* the controls! The Tomcat kept bucking as he coaxed the ship into a tighter turn.

"Launch! We've got launch! Coming in hard on our six!"

They were still turning, but it wasn't going to be enough.

A moment later something hard slammed into the Tomcat's tail, filling the sky with flames.

1252 hours, 17 January
Tomcat 203

"Price!" Zig-Zag yelled. "I've lost the Batman!"

"What do you mean, lost him!"

"He's dropped off the screen, man! I don't see him!"

"Shit . . . !" The terrain here was rugged. "Keep watching! He may pop up again!"

"We got two more targets at two-eight-three," Zig-Zag

announced. "Range seven miles, heading north at six hundred."

"Where's the green line, Zig-Zag?"

"Shit, man, I don't know! We could be in Burma now for all I know!"

"You'd better hope we're not. If those bastards nailed Batman, I *want* them!"

"Too late, Price. They're scooting north like nobody's business. I think they've had enough."

The dogfight was over. Taggart forced himself to relax, almost muscle by muscle. It was over, and they were still alive!

But where were Batman and Malibu?

1253 hours, 17 January
Tomcat 232

The Tomcat was coming apart around them as they plummeted toward the rugged terrain. Batman saw jungle rushing past his canopy as they skimmed a towering hill, falling into the valley beyond. "That's all she wrote," he told Malibu. There was nothing else to be done. "We're punching out!"

"Rog!"

Altitude eight hundred. It was now or never. He grabbed the bright, yellow-and-black painted ejection loop between his knees and yanked back.

There was an explosion, and the Tomcat's canopy broke away. Then Malibu's ejection seat slid up the rails and into the sky with a shrill roar, followed an instant later by a slamming kick in the butt as his own escape system fired.

Wind smacked him in the face and chest, clawing at him, snapping and whipping like a living thing, and for a horrible moment, Batman thought he was going to be torn in two . . . that the force would break his neck, that . . .

The parachute deployed above him, checking his tumbling fall with a rush that felt as though he were rocketing once more into the sky. Quickly, he looked around, hoping for a glimpse of Malibu, but he couldn't see him. He did spot the F-14, still falling toward the jungle, upside down now with its empty cockpit like a blind eye. Flame boiled from the shattered tail, unfolding in a trail of smoke all the way down.

He looked down, suddenly aware of the jungle. The unbroken green beneath his flight boots was taking on more and more shape and texture as it swept up to meet him from below. At close range, he was aware of folds in the terrain he'd not seen before; he was dropping into a steep-sided valley which had been all but invisible from the sky, but which now was taking on the proportions of the Grand Canyon.

And there was no way he could avoid those trees.

CHAPTER 10

"Homeplate, Homeplate, this is Tomcat Two-oh-three."

"Go ahead, Two-oh-three."

"Homeplate, we are declaring an emergency," Taggart said. He continued to scan the hills and jungle below as he sent in the message. "Tomcat Two-three-two is down, repeat, down."

"Copy, Two-oh-three. Do you have chutes in sight? Over."

"Negative chutes, Homeplate. We didn't even see where they went down. They were out of visual when they were hit. Over."

There was a long, static-filled silence. Finally, the voice of *Jefferson*'s Air Ops controller came on the air again. "Tomcat Two-oh-three, RTB. Please confirm."

"Negative, Homeplate. I have fuel to orbit until a SAR can arrive." They would need help from a Texaco if they stayed up that long, but they could extend their stay over the border by two or three hours at least.

"Tomcat Two-oh-three, Homeplate. Negative on SAR. You are directed to RTB. That is, Romeo—Tango—Bravo, execute immediate. Do you confirm, over?"

Taggart sighed. If he circled long enough, he might pick up their radio, but the terrain here was so rugged they would have to be mighty lucky to fly over the right spot at the right time. Another possibility was to spot the flyers' chutes from the air,

109

but with so much jungle, that was an even longer shot than the radio.

Homeplate was right. No doubt they'd be coordinating a rescue with the Thais. "Affirmative, Homeplate. We copy. Two-oh-three, coming home."

He brought the stick over, swinging Tomcat 203 onto a southern heading.

1254 hours, 17 January
Over the Thai-Burmese border

Batman remembered reading once about British SAS tree jumpers, an elite airborne unit trained to parachute into the jungles of Malaysia. The idea had finally been abandoned. There was simply no way that jumping into a jungle canopy could be made *safe*. . . .

He watched the treetops growing closer, reaching for him. The gruesome image of hitting an upthrust branch inserted itself in his mind and would not go away; he could be skewered as neatly as a shish kebob.

As he lost altitude, though, he realized that he was being blown sideways. The risers on his parachute were not designed for aerobatics, but they did give him some control. He began tugging at them to spill some of the chute's captured air, letting him slip sideways at a faster rate. The sun-glint from a river at the bottom of the valley beckoned to him. Landing in the river or in the mud along its bank seemed far more attractive to Batman at the moment than crashing down through that solid-looking deck of treetops.

The last of the forest giants whipped past his boots, and then he was over water. The river looked shallow, more mud flat than water, with steep clay banks to either side.

Then the river too was passing beneath him. He was being blown across the river's cut and into the opposite bank. Trees rushed at him like a gray-green wall.

He struck, smashing full-length into a sheer dirt wall. The blow stunned him and he slid helplessly down the bank, landing in a heap in the mud at the bottom. After what felt like a long time, he managed to unhook his parachute harness and slowly stand up on legs suddenly gone shaky. Leaning against the embankment, he began stripping off his life preserver, then decided to keep it. The vest was designed to carry his survival gear—knife, first-aid kit, compass, SAR radio—and its bright yellow color might attract attention from the rescue boys.

And there would be a rescue, he was certain. Price and Zig-Zag would be looking for him. Hurriedly, he pulled the SAR radio from his vest and thumbed it on.

"Mayday! Mayday! This is Batman, Tomcat Two-three-two, requesting assistance. Does anybody read me? Over!" He waited, then repeated the message.

And again.

And again.

There was no answer but static, and Batman wondered if the jungle-covered slopes around him were blocking the signal. He wasn't certain of his exact location, but U Feng was at least thirty miles to the southeast, well out of range.

Shifting tactics, he held the radio to his mouth again. "Malibu, Malibu, this is Batman! Do you copy? Over?"

Again there was only the whisper of static, harsh above the softer sounds of the jungle around him. Batman felt a stab of worry. Malibu should certainly be in the same valley and well within range. Helplessly, he shook the SAR unit, wondering if it was the transmitter which was damaged, or Malibu who was unconscious, hurt . . . or worse.

And there were the people who had fired those SAMs. He wondered if they might have the equipment to pick up his SAR broadcast and home on it. Now *there* was a pleasant thought!

The jungle seemed to close in on Batman then, an ominous green shroud which threatened to smother him. He was alone, lost, on his own without even a pistol to defend himself. Malibu might need him, and he didn't know which way to go.

Somewhere close by, a monkey or bird cut loose with a shrill, hooting screech that sounded eerily like human laughter.

To Batman, it seemed as though the hostile jungle was laughing at *him*.

1320 hours, 17 January
Control Tower, U Feng Airfield

Major Lin Thuribhopal of the Royal Thai Air Force looked up
from the map spread across the table, meeting the eyes of the
helicopter pilots facing him. All wore olive-drab flight suits
and carried their helmets. Their helos, UH-1 Huey "Slicks"
purchased from the Americans during the final days of the war
in Vietnam, were warming up on the tarmac outside.

"The Americans have agreed to pull out and leave search-
and-rescue operations to us," he told them. "It is important to
find the crew of the downed plane quickly, if they are still
alive. There are reports of guerrilla activity throughout the
region."

"Will we have fighter cover?" one of the pilots asked.

"Yes. We are already diverting six F-5s into the area. It is
unlikely that the Burmese will risk such odds to cross the
border again." His finger traced along a region south of the
Thai-Burmese border, well beyond the north-south course of
the Nam Mae Taeng Valley from U Feng. "Here," he said.
"Sector one-seven. Reports from the second American plane
suggest that the first aircraft went down here."

"Rugged country," one of the pilots commented.

"Then you'd better get started," Major Lin said. "We have
only another five hours or so before dark."

The pilots departed, leaving Lin alone to contemplate
the map. The ghost of a smile played at his lips. Sector
one-seven . . . that was at least fifty miles from where the
plane had actually gone down. If the Americans *had* survived,
they would not be walking out of that jungle soon.

And if they didn't make it by tonight, they would be too late.

He rolled up the map and returned it to its metal tube.
Outside, the chatter of helicopter rotors rose in pitch as the
SAR choppers prepared to depart.

General Hsiao would be pleased that there would be no
interference from the Americans on this critical day. The
general's coded radio message moments ago had been most

insistent about that. If the Americans were found and rescued, it would be difficult to keep their comrades from coming to U Feng to pick them up, to search the area where they'd been shot down.

That could not be allowed. Not *now*.

Major Lin put the map container in its storage rack and returned to his duties in the air operations tower.

1830 hours, 17 January
Fantail, U.S.S. *Thomas Jefferson*

Jefferson's liberty boat was kept in almost constant operation, especially during the weekend when duty schedules were adjusted to allow more of her crew to go ashore. It was a forty-minute round trip from ship to shore to ship, with the stubby-looking, open landing craft—called a mike boat—tying up at a Sattahip dock only long enough to put another liberty party ashore and to take aboard any officers and men waiting to get back to the ship.

Tombstone had caught the gray government shuttle bus out of Bangkok for the ride back to Sattahip, arriving at the wharf well after dark. At the waterfront, he could clearly see the *Jefferson* riding at anchor out in the bay. The elevator doors were open, and light from the hangar deck spilled out into the night, casting long shimmers of reflected light into the water below the ship. The island too was brightly lit, and from this angle, Tombstone could even make out the lights on the carrier's drop-line, the string of lights hanging down her stern from the flight deck roundoff as a perspective aid for night traps.

The dark waters of the bay were crowded with other vessels. He could make out the anticollision lights of *Vicksburg* and *Gridley,* swinging on their hooks almost a mile astern. The other ships of the CVBG were still at sea but would have their chance at Sattahip's facilities later. Elsewhere, civilian craft motored back and forth closer inshore, respecting the moored warning marker buoys which preserved *Jefferson*'s close-in security zone.

This early in the evening, there was no one waiting at the pier for a ride back to the carrier. Tombstone accepted a life jacket from the chief boatswain's mate in charge of the craft and stepped aboard as the man at the wheel gunned the diesel engines as if he were revving up a motorcycle. Line handlers cast off from the bollards, and the mike boat pulled away from the pier, angling out across the dark water toward the *Jefferson*.

Tombstone was in a decidedly confused state of mind. He'd gone into Bangkok the afternoon before, convinced that Pamela Drake would prove to be an enemy, someone determined to twist his words in such a way that he—and the Navy—would look foolish. The interview had been a surprise in that Pamela had gone out of her way to make him feel comfortable . . . and she'd been far more interested in his role as a hero than in the waste and mismanagement of the United States Navy.

And then there'd been dinner . . . and this morning's stroll in Thonburi. It was strange. If he was any judge of women at all, she'd been as reluctant to part as he.

There was a stiff breeze over the water, and by the time the mike boat approached the *Jefferson*, his uniform shirt was damp where it wasn't covered by the life jacket. A float had been rigged at the ship's stern, a temporary pier resting on the water and secured to the ship's hull lines. The boat's coxswain steered the craft alongside with practiced ease as a sailor in dungarees caught the line tossed by a man standing in the bows. The diesels throttled back to a low, rumbling idle, and the mike boat bumped gently against the float.

The ladder between the float and the fantail twenty feet above had wheels which allowed its lower end to roll freely with the movements of the water. Waves generated by passing boats in Sattahip Bay set the wheels to squeaking madly from time to time, the sound interspersed with the hollow thump of the tires secured to the floating pier as bumpers colliding with *Jefferson*'s hull. Tombstone trotted up the nearly vertical ladder and swung onto the fantail. He saluted the colors, then turned and saluted the officer of the deck. "Request permission to come aboard."

"Granted," the OOD replied, returning the salute. "Welcome aboard, sir."

The head of a line of men in civilian clothing and orange life jackets stood nearby, the line itself extending back into the long passageway which connected the fantail with the hangar deck. A chief was addressing them in fatherly tones, warning them that the district known as Klong Toey, famous as a rough waterfront strip in Bangkok, was strictly off-limits to all Navy personnel. Tombstone started to move past them and into the passageway when someone called him.

"Stoney! Hey, Tombstone!"

He turned and saw Fred Garrison. The aviator had been off to one side of the fantail deck, apparently chatting with the camo-clad Marine at the .50 caliber machine gun which was mounted on the railing as a security measure when the *Jefferson* was in port. "Army!" Tombstone said, using Garrison's running name. "How's it going?"

Garrison removed his aviator's sunglasses and jerked his head toward the passageway. "C'mon inside, Skipper. I gotta talk to you."

Past the machine shops, the passageway opened into the hangar deck. A number of *Jefferson*'s boats and small craft were stored on cradles at the aft end of the two-acre cavern. Garrison led Tombstone to an out-of-the-way corner of clear deck space next to the Captain's launch.

"I had to talk to you before you heard it on the bush," he said. The bush telegraph was slang for the unofficial lines of shipboard rumor and information and was widely regarded as faster and more authoritative than official channels.

"What is it?" Tombstone didn't like the expression on Garrison's face. That look, mingled worry and sadness, generally meant bad news.

"It's Batman and Malibu," Garrison said. "They're down. Shot down by MiGs."

Tombstone's eyes widened. "Oh, God! Were there chutes?"

He shrugged. "Price and Zig-Zag made it back and trapped a few hours ago. They're still getting debriefed. The word is that the Batman and Malibu were out of sight when they went in. No sign of chutes, no SAR radio contact . . . but that could just mean they were too far away." He hesitated before adding, "There's a hold on SAR ops up there. Something about problems coordinating with the Thais. I'm sorry, Tombstone. But I thought you'd want to hear it straight."

"Yeah." Tombstone nodded. "Yeah, thanks."

Batman and Malibu down . . . attacked while flying the mission Tombstone was *supposed* to have been on.

"You okay, Skipper?" Army was watching him closely.

"I'm fine." Tombstone kept his voice level. "No problem. Where's CAG?"

"Ashore."

"What? Where, Sattahip?"

"Better than that. Bangkok. With the admiral and most of both staffs. They flew in by helo with their war paint on."

Coordinating with the Thai military over what to do about the incident, no doubt. Would there be a rescue effort, he wondered, or were Batman and Malibu going to be left on their own?

Garrison seemed to sense the fire in Tombstone's eye. "Look," he added. "I'm sure everything possible's being done for our guys. . . ."

"Yeah," Tombstone said. He turned to leave. "Right. I'll grab CAG when he's back aboard."

"Where you heading, Skipper?"

"Up to the ready room. After that I'll be in my quarters if you need me."

He walked away without another word.

1900 hours, 22 December
Klong Toey, Bangkok

General Hsiao entered the warehouse as his chauffeur held the door wide. The building was located in a run-down section of Bangkok's waterfront district, a dilapidated, rust-streaked collection of warehouses and storage sheds off At Narang Road.

Hsiao strode down passageways formed by stacked crates

and wooden pallets. A Thai shipping company, itself owned by Hsiao's agents, had bought the warehouse the year before, and it served well as headquarters and meeting place, out of the public eye.

His office was a plasterboard cubicle in the back, equipped with desk, telephone, and a single chair. It was illuminated by a single bulb hanging on its cord from the ceiling. A teenager armed with an AK-47 performed a crude approximation of snapping to attention as Hsiao opened the door and went inside.

"Phreng!" Hsiao called. "Phreng, where are you?"

A dark-skinned Thai civilian with a jagged white scar down the left side of his face appeared in the doorway moments later. "General Hsiao," he said without expression. "We were not expecting you to return so soon."

Hsiao stared back at the man, assessing him. Phreng Kitikachorn had been a minor gangster, one of Bangkok's medium-level providers of heroin and raw opium, until Hsiao had taken him into his growing organization. Never much more than a petty thug, Phreng and the criminal contacts he maintained throughout the city nonetheless had proven useful as Hsiao assembled the intricacies of *Sheng li*. There were times when Hsiao needed such contacts, times such as this, which was why he'd kept Phreng on the payroll.

"Things are moving more quickly than we anticipated," Hsiao said. "It appears that the Americans will soon be involved."

"Yes, sir."

"I need several American sailors, men off the carrier now at Sattahip. Bangkok should be full of them tonight . . . especially Patpong."

"Yes, sir." There was the faintest tug at the corner of the Thai's mouth. "My girls have been busy already."

"Yes." Among his other enterprises, Hsiao knew, Phreng ran a string of girls in the sex and sin district called Patpong. He shifted to English, which Phreng understood. "Perhaps you can put them to good use tonight. I need two or three men from that carrier. They should work in radar, in flight operations, or in the carrier's air traffic control center." He pronounced the words carefully, and made Phreng repeat them back before shifting back to Thai. "Tell your people, quickly."

"There is urgency in this, sir?"

Hsiao nodded. "There is. I am not sure what the Americans' reaction to the loss of one of their planes will be. It is possible that they will recall their people in Bangkok back to the ship. We must capture the men I need before that happens."

"It will be done, sir. Where do you want them?"

"Here. We will use the rooms downstairs. Go, now."

Phreng gave a perfunctory *wai* and departed.

Hsiao thought for a moment. It was late, well past normal office hours, but Sword might well be at his desk despite the hour. With things about to break at U Feng, the agent would be working to prepare things for his role in the coming drama. Hsiao picked up the phone. Dialing a number, he asked to be connected with a particular extension. "Is Den Phitsanuk there, please?" he asked when a familiar voice answered.

There was a long silence. "Den is visiting family in Chiang Mai," the man at the other end replied. Question and response were code phrases, identifying each speaker to the other and verifying that there were no eavesdroppers on either end.

"Perhaps I can reach him there," Hsiao said. "In one hour."

He was about to hang up the phone. The message, that he needed to meet personally with the agent known as Sword at a particular rendezvous in an hour, had been delivered. But he heard Sword's sharp intake of breath over the phone. "Please! Wait," the man said. "This line is clean. We can talk."

Hsiao frowned. This was a flagrant violation of the security rules he'd laid down at the very beginning of this operation. Sword should have known better. "We will talk," he said sharply. "In an hour."

"No. *Now*." Sword was persistent. "There is trouble . . . an American naval aircraft lost near U Feng. The Americans have scheduled a meeting with members of the government. They are demanding permission to mount search-and-rescue operations in the area. I may not be able to put them off much longer."

Hsiao glanced at his watch. "It is already past seven," he said. "It is rather a late hour for government meetings, is it not?"

"The Americans are . . . upset."

"You will be at this meeting?"

"Of course, sir. General . . . our people fear what the Americans may do!" The voice sounded desperate. "We could lose *everything*!"

Hsiao forced himself to remain calm. Sword could jeopardize much more than the Americans would if the man lost his nerve now.

"We have lost nothing," Hsiao said gently. Now, he judged, was the time for soft words and assurances. He needed Sword to guide upcoming events within the government, especially once word of U Feng reached Bangkok sometime later this night. "We shall use the Americans, not avoid them."

"Are you saying we will confront the Americans directly? Your MiGs will never get within a hundred miles of their carrier!"

Hsiao laughed. "You talk about the *Jefferson* as though it were magic! She is a large warship, to be sure, but she is not invulnerable!"

"You have a battleship or two hidden in reserve, perhaps? Or a cruise missile?"

"We have something much better, my friend. Surprise . . . and the Americans' own feelings of safety within a friendly port!"

"I fail to see how that can help us."

"You, my friend, are the key. You can make everything work. Remember! I chose you because you can make the bureaucracy *work* for us! Reports can be mislaid, orders delayed, decisions postponed or deferred."

"That doesn't help us with the Yankee carrier. If they should decide to openly side with the government—"

"They will have other things to worry about."

"What, General?" The voice carried almost open scorn. "Suicide motor boats? An armada of hang gliders? This is a nuclear-powered aircraft carrier we face!"

"A nuclear-powered aircraft carrier, yes. A ship which is enormously vulnerable." He chuckled. "You know many today claim that the aircraft carrier is already obsolete. That its vulnerability, its total dependence on the other ships of its battle group, would actually make it a liability in a war."

"You have an idea." It was a statement of fact, not a question. "What is it?"

Hsiao laughed gently. "Not over the phone, Sword. Attend the meeting and report to me afterward. Then I will tell you what I have in mind."

CHAPTER 11

Liberty in Bangkok was proving to be memorable, but not at all what David Howard had expected. It had started on the mike boat, when Bentley, Paterowski and Rodriguez had closed in on him like predators, escorting him ashore, standing in line with him waiting for the bus, then regaling him with improbable stories of sexual athletics for almost two hours as the ancient vehicle rattled its way up Route 3 into Bangkok.

They'd spent an hour simply wandering the streets, gawking at the sights and discussing what to do next. Bentley was in favor of visiting a bar he'd heard about in Klong Toey, an idea that terrified Howard since the waterfront district was strictly off-limits to American military personnel. The others preferred a trip to the infamous Patpong Road which they'd heard so much about from Bentley. Howard wasn't much happier with that idea, but he didn't want to be the one to argue about it.

Patpong won out in the end. Patpong Road had been pretty much like Bentley had said it would be, a glittering, tawdry, neon-bright strip of bars, nightclubs, sex theaters and cheap-looking hotels. The villainous-looking taxi driver dropped them off beneath a towering, red-lit sign flashing five repetitions of the word "topless." A sign across the street proclaimed the most sensual massage in Bangkok. Nightclubs abounded, and bars were everywhere, each with its own gimmick: nude dancers, dart contests, old movies, and special shows that promised "Sex! Live Girls! On Stage!"

According to Bentley, Patpong was just another street by day, but at night it became the sex and sin center of the city. Traffic crowded the narrow road, mingling freely with bands of laughing, jostling Thai men and small groups of foreigners. The street smelled, a mixture of spice, garbage and raw sewage. Howie fought to control his stomach. He didn't belong here, and he felt out of place and embarrassed.

They had dinner first at a Japanese restaurant called Mizu's Kitchen, then spent another hour roaming the street before choosing a bar called the Golden Coast. It was dark inside, and crowded. The very air throbbed to the beat of hard rock. They were met as soon as they stepped inside by four dazzling Thai girls, each wearing high heels and three wisps of golden silk and string which with considerably generosity might have been called bikinis. There were numbers on small badges pinned to their bras. Paterowski explained to Howie with a wink and an elbow nudge that the numbers allowed the bar's patrons to ask for a particular girl, just in case there was further business they wanted to transact with her later.

There seemed to be a scantily clad, numbered girl for every male in the bar, drinking with the customers, laughing and talking. Howie's girl wore the number 21. She had a sweet smile, and Howie thought she was the prettiest girl he'd ever seen except, possibly, for Charlene back home.

But Charlene had never worn a bathing suit like *that*. When Number 21 turned around to lead the way to a table, it looked like she was wearing nothing but a couple of pieces of gold string, and Howard didn't know how to react to the sight of her bare buttocks. How did you talk to a girl who walked around like that in public? He felt a fiery, stiffening urgency in his loins he'd not known since Charlene had let him kiss her in her father's car, and was immediately ashamed of the comparison.

"C'mon, guys and gals!" Bentley cried, sitting down at the table. "What'll it be?"

They ordered something fiery and potent the English-speaking bartender called Mekong Wine and Bentley called

"Patpong panther piss." Howie's head was swimming after the first couple of sips, though whether that was from the drink, excitement, or fear he couldn't tell.

"Boy oh boy," Paterowski said, leaning back in his chair and rubbing his hands together. He was looking toward a brightly-lit stage at the back of the room. "Get a load of that!"

If Howard was surprised by the brief attire of the hostesses, the floor show nearly finished him. The girl was stark naked, dancing with rhythmic, sensuous gyrations. Howie stared, unable to take his eyes off her.

"*¡Ai!*" Rodriguez exclaimed. "*¡Tal tetas!*"

"I'll stick with this one here," Bentley said, leering as he pulled his girl closer and toyed with her bra. "She's got class! You can tell . . ."

Paterowski's girl grinned as she rubbed her hand down his shirt front toward his crotch. "And you horny sailor men," she said. "We know!"

"Right you are, babe," Bentley said. He took another swallow of Mekong. "Best in the fleet!"

Howard wondered how she'd known the four of them were sailors. They were all wearing civies and looked like typical tourists, as far as he could tell.

"You all *Jefferson* men?" one of the girls wanted to know.

"Sure are," Paterowski said. "You heard of us?"

"I think we want find out!" The girls giggled, as though sharing a secret.

Number 21 pressed herself close to Howard, nuzzling his ear. Her perfume threatened to overwhelm him. "So what you do, sailor?" She laughed. "On ship, I mean."

"Uh . . . actually, I'm a message runner," Howie said. Number 21's breast was rubbing against his arm, each movement threatening to dislodge the scrap of material covering it. "I . . . uh . . . run messages."

"Hey, don't be so modest, Howie!" Rodriguez said. "Don't let him fool you, *chica*. He's right up there in CATCC with the rest of us."

"This cat-see," Bentley's girl said. Her number was 15. "Is what?"

"The heart of the carrier, babe. The center of the whole damned show."

"Like radar? We know radar. Very important on ship."

"Right you are, honey," Paterowski said. "We run the radar. The flyboys couldn't even land without us there to help 'em. But hey, we didn't come here to talk shop!"

"We like big, important guys," Bentley's girl said. "For you, very, very special treatment! *Sanuk!*"

"What's *sanuk*?"

The girls laughed and Howard's girl explained. "Is fun!"

"Hey, I like the sound of that!" Rodriguez said.

"Yeah," Paterowski said. "What say we go someplace where we can enjoy some *sanuk* in private?"

"You wait." Number 15 pulled away from Bentley. "Wait here minute. I call, get special place. We go have fun."

"Whoa!" Paterowski said, watching her go. "We got some hot numbers here, hey, Bent?"

"Told you Patpong was a great place. Wonder what she has in mind?"

Number 15 didn't return for nearly fifteen minutes. When she reappeared, she was wearing a leather miniskirt and a fire-red silk blouse and carried a pocketbook. She snapped something at the other girls in Thai.

Howard's girl replied with a machinegunlike barrage in the same language. He felt her stiffen next to him and sensed that she was angry though he couldn't tell what the argument was about. The first girl spoke again, her tone imperious as she gestured toward the front of the bar. The others seemed to give in, then. All three stood up gracefully and walked away, not even looking back or saying good-bye.

"Hey," Rodriguez demanded. "Where're they going?"

"You think they go on street dressed like that?" She held out her hand for Bentley. "They meet us at *special* place. I call friend, all fix. You see!"

"What do you say, guys?" Bentley said, smirking. "Let's party!"

"I'm with you, man!" Paterowski said, rising.

The drinks already paid for, they trooped out of the Golden

Coast, following the girl. Howie wondered what her name was. The number seemed so . . . degrading, somehow.

On the street, Bentley's girl led the way along the crowded sidewalk. "Hey, where we goin', *chica*?" Rodriguez asked.

"Not far. You see!"

"What about the other girls?" Rodriguez asked.

"They come. You see!"

She led them across the street, then turned a corner into a narrow alley between a topless bar and an establishment which billed itself as a short-time hotel.

Howard pulled back. He didn't like the tawdry feel to the whole scene, didn't like the numbers, the open advances. It made him feel dirty. "This isn't for me, guys," he said suddenly. "You all go on without me."

"Howie!" Rodriguez said. "Shit, don't lose it now, man! I mean, these girls are *hot*!"

"Uh-uh." Fear . . . and denial turned to resolve. This was *wrong*. "You guys go ahead, Ernesto. I'll be over there." He pointed to another bar across the street next to a massage parlor. He could hear a thumping beat which sounded like country rock, and its neon sign promised American food. There was nothing on its marquis about girls or sex. He turned and started across the street, threading his way through the traffic before the others could stop him. "Get me when you're ready to go, okay?"

"Right, man, if that's what you want." He checked his watch. "Shouldn't be more'n a couple of hours, okay?"

"Fine." He turned and started walking away, resisting the urge to run as he dodged cars, taxis, and speeding *tuk-tuks*.

He didn't look back.

2325 hours, 17 January
U Feng

Major Lin Thuribhopal took the stairs silently, two at a time. He held in his hand a Type 67 automatic pistol, a Chinese design with a built-in silencer which gave it a heavy-barreled, clumsy look. Slung across his shoulder was more substantive firepower, an Israeli Uzi, also silenced. Lin had heard that Hsiao had acquired the weapon from a drug lord in the Golden Triangle.

Nothing Hsiao did could surprise Lin now. The man who claimed to be a high-ranking member of the Chinese intelligence service had an organization which extended into three countries at least, and reached into the highest levels of the governments of both Rangoon and Bangkok.

But now, Lin took a special pride knowing that tonight, at this moment, the entire plan known as *Sheng li* rested upon *him*.

He reached the floor directly beneath the control tower booth, a windowless area partitioned into small offices where flight plans and weather advisories were filed. A bored-looking air force sergeant sat at the reception desk, feet up, a paperback novel in his hands. He saw that he had a visitor and started to rise. "Yes, Major? What can I—"

The Type 67 in Lin's hand gave one loud, harsh *chuff,* then another, the weapon bucking in his hand. The sergeant's eyes widened as twin stains of blood appeared high on the front of his uniform shirt, spread, and merged. He groped for the revolver strapped to his hip and Lin fired a third time, this time tearing away part of the man's throat and knocking him back against his chair.

Lin was appalled at the sound. He'd thought the silencer would eliminate the pistol's noise, the way they did in the movies, but the shots had been as loud as someone smashing the desktop with a baseball bat.

"Sergeant Pho?" someone called from the next office. "What's going on out there?"

Lin's hands were shaking now, but he was ready when the duty officer walked out of his office. He fired again before the air force lieutenant had even seen him. The officer staggered back against the door frame, hands clenched across his stomach, eyes bugging out in shock and pain and surprise. The next shot caught him high in the forehead, shattering his skull and spraying the wall with bits of scalp, hair, bone, and splatters of blood.

The assassin waited for a long moment, listening for any further movement. The guard on the floor below was already dead, his throat slit when Lin came up on him from behind. The only people left in the building should be the duty traffic controlman and one or two assistants manning the tower consoles on the floor upstairs. Had they heard? Lin held his breath, waiting for some response.

Nothing.

Moving quickly now, Lin dragged the two bodies back into the lieutenant's office and closed the door on them. There was no time now to mop the streaks of blood on the wall or the linoleum floor, but with luck, no one else would be coming up those stairs until it was too late.

Since he didn't know for sure how many people there were in the tower gallery, Li tucked the pistol into his waistband and unslung the Uzi, yanking back the charging handle to chamber the first round. Quietly, he walked to the door to the stairs going up, opened it, and went through.

The stairwell was kept closed off at both ends and darkened to keep light from spilling through from below and ruining the night vision of duty personnel in the tower. He reached the top of the stairs, paused on the landing outside the closed door, then tapped lightly with the muzzle of the Uzi's heavy suppressor.

The door swung open seconds later. Lin glimpsed dim red lighting, the amber glow of radar screens, a young private's expression of horror as he saw the Uzi in Lin's hands. The private tried to slam the door shut, but Lin squeezed the Uzi's trigger. Firing full auto, the SMG sent 9-mm slugs chopping through door and private alike, the sound somewhat quieter than the earlier suppressed pistol shots.

Lin rammed his way past the splintered door and burst into the room. A railed walkway circled the tower chamber above the level of the door, with stairways leading up at two points. Another private sat at a radar console, already turning in his swivel chair as Lin fired again. The private staggered to his feet, then pitched forward over the railing as Lin extended the burst, sweeping across a corporal who was rising from his chair at another console nearby. Glass popped and crazed as bullets smashed through window panels.

A fourth man, the duty officer, was lunging toward an alarm button when Lin's deadly scythe of gunfire cut his legs out from under him and sent him tumbling to the floor.

The Uzi's slide locked open, the magazine empty. Drawing the pistol, Lin climbed the stairs, then paced about the walkway. The lieutenant and the corporal were both still alive. He killed each of them with a single shot through the head. Both privates were already dead.

From the control tower's upper deck, he could look through the huge, slanted windows which gave a view out across the jungle in all directions. A half-moon illuminating scattered clouds low in the west gave light enough to distinguish the jungle's edge. Nearer, but still a couple of hundred meters off, floodlights bathed a portion of the tarmac off the main runway where a maintenance crew was working late on a Thai F-5 down for repairs. Lin studied the workers through a large pair of binoculars sitting on the console. There was no sign of alarm, no indication that they'd heard the gunfire. Fortunately, the windows were still intact save for a chain of white-starred bullet holes. If one of those panels had shattered completely, he could have had the whole base coming out to investigate.

So far, then, so good. Lin went to the tower radio and turned the channel selector to a carefully memorized frequency, then picked up the microphone and began speaking. "Victory, this is Arrow. Victory, this is Arrow. Do you copy?"

There was a nerve-grating delay filled with the hiss of static. Then a voice replied, "Arrow, this is Victory. We receive you. Go ahead."

"Victory, Arrow. Execute. Repeat, execute."

The voice on the other end acknowledged and the channel went dead. Lin picked up his Uzi, dropped his empty magazine, and replaced it with a loaded one from the pouch riding on his hip. He rolled the corporal's body out of its chair and sat down, facing the sunken doorway through which he'd just come. All he had to do now was wait.

0038 hours, January 18
Hawkeye Victor Kilo Two, over Central Thailand

The E-2C Hawkeye was an ungainly-looking aircraft, driven by twin turboprops and mounting a twenty-four-foot-wide, saucer-shaped radome above its spine. The saucer, rotating at the rate of six revolutions per minute, was the housing for the aircraft's powerful APS-125 UHF radar. Despite its strange appearance, the E-2C was widely regarded as the single most capable radar-warning and air-traffic-control aircraft in service, able to track more than two hundred and fifty air targets at a time, and to control as many as thirty friendly interceptors. On board were five men, the two pilots, a CIC officer, an air controller, and a radar operator. *Jefferson* routinely kept at least one of her four Hawkeyes airborne at all times, where they served as the long-range eyes of the carrier battle group.

The CIC officer was Lieutenant Dave Dunning. He braced himself against the overhead as he leaned over the shoulder of the radarman first class for a closer look at the bogies.

"There they are, sir," the radarman said. "They come and go. I think they're hedgehopping."

The amber screen showed a confusing tangle of blips, most identified by their IFF transponders as commercial flights or Thai military aircraft. Clear at the top of the screen, though, was a tiny cluster of lights. They showed no ID, and they appeared to be moving southeast.

"Keep on 'em, son." Dunning opened a channel and began speaking into his helmet mike. "Homeplate, Homeplate, this is Victor Kilo Two."

"Victor Kilo, Homeplate. We copy."

"Homeplate, we have multiple unidentified targets, bearing three-four-four, range approximately two-three-zero. They appear to be inbound, relative bearing one-three-zero, speed three-five-zero, over."

"Roger that, Victor Kilo. How many contacts, over?"

"Homeplate, hard to call it." The targets were at the extreme limit of the Hawkeye's radar range. "Estimate eight to ten bogies. They . . . Homeplate, they appear to be coming across the border, probably at extreme low altitude."

"Copy that, Victor Kilo. Stand by." There was a long silence. Then; "Victor Kilo, come to three-five-zero. CIC wants a continuous track of your targets."

"Rog." Dunning stared at the blips on the amber screen for a moment longer. Like everyone else in the carrier air wing that day, he'd heard about the MiG attack, knew that Batman Wayne and his RIO had been shot down up there. "Someone back there better pass this on to the Thais," he added. "It looks to me like they're about to get dumped on."

"Roger that."

He listened as the Hawkeye's pilot confirmed the course change instructions. *Jefferson* was sending Victor Kilo Two farther north, hoping for a better look at those intruders. As he watched, one of the small blips in the cluster split as the E-2C's radar got a better look at it, then merged once more. There were at least eleven of the bastards . . . probably a lot more.

What the hell were they doing up there?

0150 hours, 18 January
U Feng

The alert telephone was buzzing, and Major Lin ignored it. Thai air defense radars had probably detected Victory and someone in Bangkok was passing on the warning, but it was too late now. Already he could hear the clatter of the approaching helicopters. They were clearly visible on the radar, a triangular formation of blips coming in from the northwest. Other blips circled more quickly in the distance. Those would be the MiGs providing air cover.

"Arrow, this is Victory," a voice said over the headphones Lin was wearing. "Commencing final approach."

"Victory, Arrow," he said. "All clear. You have complete surprise."

On the field, several of the RTAF personnel working on the down-checked F-5 had stopped and were staring into the night. The rotor noise was much louder now.

A dazzling beam of light stabbed out of the sky, casting an oval circle of illumination across the tarmac. Lin could just barely make out the dark mass of the helicopter behind the searchlight as it drifted down out of the night. Behind it a second helo approached . . . and a third. As they moved into the illumination cast by the worklights on the field, their hulls became more distinct . . . the familiar shapes of UH-1 Hueys, RTAF roundels prominent on their tails. Several air force men began walking toward the first helo to help secure it, stooping as they moved to avoid being caught by the rotors.

The lead Huey's cargo bay hatch slid back. Soldiers began piling out. Gunfire stuttered from a pintel-mounted machine gun, the muzzle flash a jagged flicker in the darkness. The air force men began dropping, mowed down by the sweep of an invisible blade. Small-arms fire was added to the machine gun's chatter. Someone screamed.

More helicopters were touching down all over the base, their cargo doors sliding open, troops jumping out. Overhead, the first escorting MiG shrieked low across the airfield. There was a sudden flash, then the dull *whump* of an explosion. Flame boiled into the sky, illuminating the field as a dozen Thais scattered in every direction. The F-5 burned furiously.

Lin turned when he heard the pounding of boots coming up the control tower steps. "Lieutenant!" a shaky voice screamed in Thai. "Lieutenant! It's an attack!"

The soldier stumbled through the door and into the tower chamber. He saw the bodies on the floor and gaped. Lin's burst of fire caught him an instant later, slamming him backward into a wall in a splatter of blood.

More explosions thumped in the night, these from the direction of the barracks. Already, the volume of fire was dwindling. The attack had been so sudden, so unexpected, that only the handful of soldiers actually on guard had been able to respond, and those few had been quickly overwhelmed.

The alert phone continued to buzz.

"Victory!" a new voice called from the door. "Victory!"

"Arrow!" Lin replied, giving his code name as countersign. He stood up as a trio of soldiers cautiously entered the control tower room. The leader wore the green uniform and collar device of a Burmese army lieutenant. The two soldiers were more raggedly clad in a mix of uniforms. Drug army conscripts, Lin decided. One held an AK-47, the other an American M-16.

The officer smiled. "Major Lin?"

"I am Lin." He lowered his Uzi. "Welcome!"

The lieutenant turned away. "Do it."

Both soldiers opened fire at the same time, the bullets punching through Lin's body, sending him sprawling back across the tower radar console.

Lieutenant Bhan Sun had carried out his orders. There'd been a grave risk that the Thais might learn just how thoroughly their military was penetrated by Hsiao's people.

That could not be allowed to happen. He made certain that Lin was dead before leaving the tower. Outside, the last of the Thai soldiers and airmen were being rounded up and shot.

There would be no enemy witnesses to what had happened at U Feng.

CHAPTER 12

0705 hours, January 18
The Nam Mae Taeng Valley

The night had been miserable. A heavy rain during the hours before dawn had soaked Batman to the skin. Swarms of mosquitos had descended on him from the nearby river, bringing with them glowing memories of countless films and lectures on the dangers of malaria in the tropics. He'd swallowed a couple of Dapsone pills as preventative and smeared insect repellent from his survival kit on his face and hands . . . not that the stuff seemed to have much effect. Between the rain and the insects, he'd gotten little sleep during the night.

Throughout those hours, Batman's SAR radio had remained silent, though he checked it periodically and broadcast his Mayday message as frequently as he dared. He was still afraid of being tracked down by whoever had launched on him, but the need to contact the Thai Air Force or his own people far outweighed the need for radio silence. That faceless enemy out there in the jungle *might* home on his transmission and run him down, sure, *if* they had the equipment, *if* they had the trained personnel, and *if* they had the desire; on the other hand, friendly forces would never find him if he remained silent.

So he kept calling . . . but he was more certain than ever that the valley walls were blocking his signals. He would have to climb higher to have an unrestricted line of sight. The problem with that idea was that he would be leaving Malibu. He was sure his RIO must be in the same valley somewhere. They'd ejected at almost the same instant. The fact that Batman had not seen his partner's chute meant little. He'd had other things on his mind at the time.

Batman didn't let himself think about the possibility that Malibu's chute had failed to open at all.

He'd spent most of the previous afternoon and evening quartering as much of the valley as he could reach, which, he was forced to admit, hadn't been much. Visibility in the jungle was less than thirty feet. It was possible he'd passed within ten yards of his RIO and never known he was there.

He'd felt more hopeful as he searched along the riverbank and found tracks . . . dozens of them, like bulldozer tread marks in the mud, but narrower. It looked as though someone had been driving construction vehicles back and forth along the river. They seemed relatively fresh, which suggested that someone—loggers, possibly—were working the area, that this stretch of jungle was not as isolated as he'd thought.

But after several more hours of searching, Batman was forced to admit that he couldn't tell which direction the vehicles had been moving, north or south, and while they weren't old, they still might have been several days old.

And he still needed to find Malibu.

Finally, as the unseen sun began warming the jungle floor, burning off the mist which had lingered there since the rain, Batman decided that his best bet was to get to the top of a hill where he could signal an aircraft if it passed overhead.

The river ran north-south, which meant Thailand—assuming he *had* strayed over the border—lay *that* way. To the left, the valley's east slope gave him the quickest access to an unrestricted hilltop.

And possibly from up there he could look down on the valley's treetop canopy and spot Malibu's chute.

He started climbing.

0930 hours, 18 January
CAG's office, U.S.S. *Thomas Jefferson*

"Thanks for seeing me, CAG," Tombstone said as he stepped into the cramped office. He'd not had much sleep the night before, and he was feeling the effects this morning.

"No problem, Stoney." CAG looked drawn and tired as well. "Pull up a chair and sit yourself."

He sat. "I'd like to know what's being done for Batman and Malibu," he said without preamble.

Marusko signed. "Not a hell of a lot, Stoney. Not yet, anyway. Half the brass on this boat were up in Bangkok last night. You must have heard."

Tombstone nodded. "A little."

"The admiral was pushing for a full-scale SAR effort, but the Thais turned us down."

"But why?" The Thais had a fair-sized air force, but most of their planes were old and dated, Vietnam-era stuff like Broncos and F-5s, plus a single squadron of F-16 Falcons. "We could make a TARPS run, and—"

"It was a TARPS mission that got us in this mess, remember?" Marusko shook his head. "Things could be getting hot up there. After our meeting last night, something had the Thais stirred up. And the Hawkeyes we had on station over central Thailand picked up what might have been an invasion."

"An invasion! Who? The Burmese?"

Marusko fingered a ballpoint pen on his desk. "That's the working theory for the moment. The Burmese are denying it, of course." He shrugged. "The . . . ah . . . historical animosity between Thailand and Burma goes back a long way. Sometimes the Burmese shell the Thai side of the border just for the hell of it, it seems."

"Still, that shouldn't stop *us* from sending in a search and rescue. Those are our people up there, CAG."

"I know that." Marusko's voice was hard. "But we're not running a SAR. That's being left to the Thais."

"No SAR! Shit, CAG! We can't just leave them up there!"

For Tombstone, the situation had an eerie sense of déjà vu. When his wingman—another friend—had been shot down off Korea three months before, distance and political consider- ations had prevented an immediate search-and-rescue effort. The look on Marusko's face told him that this situation was very much the same.

"Tombstone, you have to understand that the Thai govern- ment is very sensitive about their northern border. They've had trouble with the Burmese for centuries . . . and there are constant charges of corruption and connivance on their part regarding the drugs that come through that region out of the Golden Triangle. They agreed to have our two planes come into the area to help with recon the other day . . . but inviting our whole SAR force is something else entirely."

"Oh, come on, CAG! We could manage with just a couple of planes—"

"Tombstone, we don't even know if Batman and Malibu are still alive. Two-oh-three didn't sight their chutes, remember."

"Damn it, we've got to *know*!"

"Look, it's out of our hands, okay? I just got off the phone with Colonel Kriangsak just before you walked in here."

"Kriangsak?"

"Our liaison with the Thai armed forces. I was on him at the meeting last night, and again this morning. He says his government is afraid large numbers of aircraft would be misinterpreted by the Burmese, maybe trigger a war."

"If that's what it takes—"

"Knock it off, Commander. We're not at war with Burma, okay? And the Thais don't need that kind of pressure right now. Not with an all-out insurrection going on up there, not with all the rumors floating around about a possible coup attempt. I'm afraid we're going to have to let them handle this their way."

"Their way. What's that . . . sit back and wait for Batman and Malibu to walk out of the jungle on foot? Good God, they could be lying up in those hills hurt, or dangling from their harnesses in a tree!" Tombstone licked his lips. "Look, CAG. Maybe we can't send the wing up there, but how about just a couple planes? A sneak-and-peak TARPS. I'd like to—"

"Negative." Marusko's voice was flat. "The word is to wait, let Bangkok handle it." He folded his hands on the desk. "Look, Stoney, I know how you feel." Marusko's usual casual warmth returned. He ran a hand through his hair and leaned back in his seat. "Why don't you take the rest of the day off? Catch the bus into Bangkok, get your mind off it."

Tombstone considered it. He'd enjoyed the day he'd spent in Bangkok with Pamela and had been entertaining hopes of seeing her again. Now, though, knowing Batman was down . . . maybe dead . . . the prospect felt like torture.

"If it's all the same, CAG, I have some paperwork to catch up with." He stood, and the chair's legs scraped the deck like nails on a blackboard.

"I'd scuttle that paperwork if I were you, Stoney. I suggest you—"

"Will that be all, sir?"

CAG scowled. "That's all."

"Thank you, sir." He turned and strode through the door, his thoughts whirling. He found himself thinking again about Pamela. It was strange. He very much wanted to share his grief and worry with someone . . . but not with Pamela, not when he was still trying to puzzle out the newly awakened feelings for her which he had only just discovered. Talking with her about Batman right now would feel too much like a play for sympathy.

Besides, how could she know what losing a friend like Batman was really like? That special camaraderie among combat aviators was something not shared with outsiders, mostly because they simply were not expected to understand it, *couldn't* understand it without having been part of the fraternity themselves.

Briefly, Pamela's words about the death of her brother returned to him, but Tombstone dismissed them. It didn't really matter whether she could understand or not.

Bitterly he strode down the passageway toward his quarters.

1015 hours, 18 January
CATCC, U.S.S. *Thomas Jefferson*

The darkened chamber of CATCC seemed quieter than usual this morning, and Howard felt as though every one of the men in the room was waiting, listening to hear what he had to say. Somehow, he forced himself to walk across the deck to the raised swivel chair where Chief Paulsen sat sipping a mug of coffee while reading the morning report.

It was the hardest thing Howard had ever tried to do in his life. "Chief?" he said.

Paulsen did not look up. "Yeah, kid?"

"Chief, I gotta talk to you." He glanced around the room. "Alone . . . please?"

His section chief considered for a moment, then heaved himself out of the chair. Setting the mug down, he jerked his head toward the passageway. "Okay. C'mon."

Howard sighed and followed.

He'd waited at the bar for two and a half hours after leaving the others, wondering if Bentley and the others were ever going to come back for him. He'd been half afraid his desertion had made them mad enough to leave him there.

Then he'd started getting worried. Bentley might pull a trick like that on a raw nugget, but Howard thought that Rodriguez and Paterowski actually liked him. They'd have come back for him.

It was nearly midnight when Howard decided he *had* to leave. The last bus to Sattahip left from in front of Lumpini Park on Rama Four Road at 0100, and if he missed it, he'd be marked AWOL—absent without leave—on the morning muster. That could lead to a captain's mast and disciplinary action.

First though, he'd returned to the Golden Coast. Something about the setup had not seemed right. That one girl, Number 15, had gotten rid of the other girls . . . but then explained they'd all meet later. Something was wrong there. Howard had heard stories of sailors getting rolled in strange cities while on liberty. Once Bentley had told the story of a friend of his who'd woken up in Tijuana to find his companion of the previous night gone . . . along with his wallet, shoes, and every stitch of clothing.

Suppose something had happened to them.

He'd felt embarrassed going into the Golden Coast the first time; it had felt a thousand times worse going in again later, alone. A smiling Thai girl had come up to him, and he'd stuttered as he asked if she knew Number 21.

"Sure," the girl said. "She's on duty now. I get her."

Howie had felt his blood turn cold. Number 21 was supposed to have gone after the others. What was she doing here? Quickly, Howard had scanned the other people in the bar, searching faces. He didn't see Bentley or the others, but . . .

Then he saw Number 15. For a moment, he'd thought perhaps it was a different girl with the same number, but there was no doubt. Even in the near darkness, he could see enough to know it was her. She was wearing the skimpy G-string and bra again and was sitting in the lap of a customer. A moment later, she turned slightly and her eyes met his, widening in recognition. Howard had turned and fled then, certain that something was wrong.

On the street outside, though, he'd changed his mind again. The likeliest explanation was that Bentley and the others were having some fun with him. They'd met with 15 and 21 and the others, had their *sanuk,* then decided it would be a great gag to go off and leave Howie waiting in Patpong. They'd probably boarded the midnight bus and were already halfway back to the ship.

So Howard had caught his bus and made it back to Sattahip, boarded the mike boat, and motored back to the *Jefferson* with a mob of drunken, story-swapping sailors. It was after 0300 when an exhausted Howard had tumbled into his rack, promising himself he would have words with the others when he saw them at breakfast.

But they'd not been at breakfast. At morning department muster they'd been marked down as AWOL.

Chief Paulsen led Howard into the passageway. "Okay, kid," he said. "What's on your mind?"

Howard swallowed. He was still embarrassed by the events of last evening, didn't even want to admit that he'd been to Patpong, but he was worried about his friends. "Chief? I think Bentley, Rodriguez, and Paterowski might be in trouble."

"Damned straight they're in trouble. When they go up before the Old Man, I'll lay you odds Bentley and Paterowski lose their crows. That's trouble, all right."

"No, Chief. Something worse." And he began to explain what had happened.

1040 hours, 18 January
Near the Thai-Burmese border

Batman had nearly reached the top of the ridge when he heard the clatter of a helicopter in the distance. The sound brought new strength to legs aching from the long climb and he quickened his pace. He could see patches of sky just ahead. There might be a clearing at the top.

He emerged into full sunlight. The crest of the hill was strewn with house-sized limestone boulders rising from the clay and soft earth of the slope, and the rock was holding the surrounding forest at bay. Panting, holding his side where a painful stitch burned with each breath, Batman stumbled onto the flat surface of one of the rocks. He fumbled for his SAR radio. "Mayday! Mayday!" he called. "This is Batman! Does anybody read me?"

The view from the limestone cliff looked out across mile upon green mile of jungle to the north and west. He could see the helicopters now, two of them, flying side by side far to the north.

North? He checked the position of the sun at his back. Yes, north. And far enough away that they had to be over Burma even if he was on the Thai side of the border. At this distance, he could see no markings. Were they Thai helicopters intruding over Burmese airspace as they searched for him, or did they belong in Burma's air force? They looked like UH-1 Hueys, and he remembered hearing somewhere that the Socialist Union of Burma had a few Slicks left over from Vietnam days. Now that he thought about it, those two were moving too fast to be part of a search pattern.

Hell, at this point it didn't matter *who* they were. "Mayday! Mayday!" He was shouting now. "Calling two military helicopters approximately two miles north of my position! Please respond!"

He kept at it until the helos were out of sight. They hadn't even slowed down.

Batman raised the SAR radio to his ear and gave it a shake. If the helos weren't part of a search, they wouldn't be listening on the SAR channel. Still, he was beginning to wonder if the damned thing had been damaged by his collision with the riverbank. That would explain . . .

He froze, aware—without knowing how—of movement directly behind him. He'd heard nothing, but something, a movement of air or shadows, had alerted him. Very, very slowly, keeping his hands in view, he turned around.

The girl was standing ten feet away at the edge of the jungle. She was young, no more than twenty, with dark skin and eyes as black as her hair. Batman thought she looked Filipino or even Latino; she didn't have the obviously Oriental features of most of the Thais Batman had met so far. She wore a green bush hat and ragged camo fatigues with a tiger-stripe pattern. A red triangular badge with a gold star was pinned to the hat's front, and she carried an AK-47 with the muzzle leveled at Batman's chest.

"Yah klihyun vahi!"

Batman didn't know what the girl was saying, but the tone was unmistakable. The language sounded like Thai, but he couldn't tell if she was Burmese, Thai, or a hill bandit. It seemed best not to antagonize her, however. Making no sudden movements, he dropped the SAR radio and raised his hands. "I don't understand you," he said.

The girl's eyes widened. "American?"

There was no point in denying it. "That's right."

The AK's muzzle didn't waver. "You come. *Reeb kao!* Hurry!"

At gunpoint, Batman was led back into the jungle.

CHAPTER 13

The girl with the AK led Batman north along a jungle trail which followed the ridge for almost a mile, then descended the east face of the slope in a series of sharp switchbacks which left the American completely disoriented. In a steep-walled pocket of a valley shrouded by towering, murk-shadowed trees they reached the camp.

Batman saw only twenty or thirty people in the encampment, though he suspected there were many more. Most were young men, wearing army fatigues or camouflage uniforms, but he saw other women like his captor, and there were children as well, most carrying weapons. One boy who could not have been older than eleven watched him with solemn, black eyes, his grubby hands clutching a folding-stock M2 carbine which must have been left over from World War II.

It was a strange mix of old and new. The hootches were constructed of bamboo and leaves, but a Toyota pickup truck was parked just off the dirt road which wound up to the pocket valley from the deeper valley below. The youngest children were naked, riding slings on their mothers' hips; everyone else wore military uniforms, though many were ragged or mismatched items from several different armies. The weapons in view included U.S. M-16s, M-79 grenade launchers, the ubiquitous AK-47, and an RPG-2 with its bulbous snout. One ancient, toothless man, however, carried what looked like a muzzle-loading cap-and-ball rifle from another age.

Batman's escort led him past a silent row of armed children and gestured, indicating that he should wait beside a tree. "You stay here," she said in her accented, singsong voice. "Wait."

"Fine by me, love," Batman replied easily. She turned her back on him and walked off toward one of the hootches.

Batman was not sure how to read the situation. Was he a prisoner or not? The militarization of the camp suggested that these people were rebels or, possibly, the private army of some local drug lord. As the girl walked away he realized that he could make a run for it.

But those kids watching him might be more proficient with their motley collection of weapons than they looked. Besides, the girl had let him keep his survival knife, which was riding in plain view in its scabbard clipped to his life vest.

It would be better to wait, he decided. Things might not be as grim as they seemed.

Looking around curiously, he noticed an odd decoration in the tree trunk, a backwards C and what looked like the letter J, picked out in spent brass cartridges hammered into the bark. Some sort of memorial perhaps? A grave marker? He assumed that the letter C had been reversed out of ignorance, as in a child's attempts at writing.

"Batman, you son of a bitch! You're alive!"

He turned at the yell and saw Malibu leaning on a forked-branch crutch and making his way out of a hootch. Except for a bandaged left ankle, the RIO appeared fit and well. "Malibu! Here I thought you were wandering around lost in that jungle! I might've known you'd be the one to find civilization first!"

"Hey, dude, wasn't me! Civilization, like, found *me*!"

Quickly, his RIO explained that he'd come down near the top of the ridge, and even managed to steer for a relatively open spot and avoid the bigger trees. His landing had been less than textbook, however. He'd hit hard, spraining his ankle and smashing his SAR radio against a rock with a blow that might have cracked a rib or two. He'd lain there stunned for several hours.

Then the Karens had found him.

"Karens?" Batman asked.

"Yeah, compadre," Malibu said. "And they're the good guys. Seems like you and me, old buddy, are way inside the Socialist Union of Burma. They say they've been fighting the Burmese since 1949. From the sound of things it's lucky they found us, and not the other guys."

Batman grinned. "I was wondering there for a while. The one who found me doesn't seem to care much for Americans!"

"Americans are something of an unknown here, Lieutenant," a new voice said at his back. "Trust does not come easily to some of us."

Turning, Batman saw a black-haired man of perhaps fifty, wearing American combat web gear and holding an AK-47. An unfamiliar rank device of some kind was pinned to his fatigue cap. The young woman stood behind him, her face an unreadable mask.

"Batman, this is Colonel Htai of the 12th Brigade, Karen National Liberation Army."

"Welcome, Lieutenant Wayne," the colonel said in perfect English. "We have been looking for you since we found your comrade yesterday."

"Thank you, Colonel. I'm real glad to be here."

"Come to my headquarters, and we will talk."

Htai's headquarters was a hootch raised on stilts, with a single sentry outside. Malibu, unable to navigate the spindly ladder up to the entrance on his bad foot, remained outside.

Inside there was no furniture but a kind of low, foot-tall desk on the split bamboo floor. Tacked to one wall was a British Army topological map dated 1952. A number of weapons leaned against another wall—M-16s, AK-47s, and several RPGs—beneath a faded color print of Jesus.

Htai seemed to note Batman's surprise at the picture. "Most Karens are Christian, Lieutenant," he said. "Does that surprise you?"

Batman admitted that it did.

"We are also anti-Communist, and we forbid our people to deal in opium. We fight to have our own nation . . . one where . . . what is it you say? There is liberty and justice for all." He squatted cross-legged on the floor behind the desk and gave Batman a hard look. "You Americans do not seem to know much about our struggle here."

Batman remembered having heard something about the Karens in a briefing about the Thai-Burmese border, but beyond the fact of their existence, he knew nothing. He accepted the man's wordless invitation and sat down. "I'm afraid not, sir."

Htai shook his head slowly. "We do not understand the American attitude. Burma is ruled by a vicious socialist military dictatorship, by communists in all but name, yet your country and many others send them money and weapons, have done so for years . . . hoping to buy their friendship." He gestured toward the weapons against the wall. "Still, we manage to provide for ourselves. We survive."

"What are you fighting for?"

"For our *country,* Lieutenant. For the land we call Katoo-lie." Htai leaned over and spat, expertly directing a stream of red betel nut juice between two bamboo slats in the floor. "Year after year, the bastard Ne Win tries to exterminate us. Always he loses."

Ne Win, Batman remembered from his briefings, had been the military dictator of Burma for many years. He'd been replaced by a coup several years before, and the colonels who ruled that unhappy country now had promised democracy and a new constitution, but most analysts felt that he was still the real power in Rangoon.

Batman heard a step behind him and looked around. The girl who had brought him here stood in the door. The colonel said something in an unintelligible language, and she replied in a rapid-fire barrage of singsong words.

That red patch pinned to her boonie hat . . . When Batman had first seen the gold-star-on-red device, he'd assume it meant his captor was Communist. He saw now that it had been cut from a uniform.

Probably a Burmese uniform. The device was a war trophy. It spoke of this people's abilities . . . as warriors, and as survivors. If he and Malibu were going to survive, they needed the Karens' help.

The soldier left, and the colonel turned to face Batman again. "You seem to have attracted some attention here, Lieutenant. An enemy column is approaching our valley. They search for you and your friend."

Batman licked his lips. There'd been ice in Htai's voice when he spoke of not understanding American foreign policy, as though he might hold Batman responsible. He plunged ahead, speaking quickly. "We need your help, sir. Somehow, my friend and I have to get to Thailand. I know you don't have any special love for my government, but I can promise that you will be rewarded."

Htai looked away, his black eyes going to the picture on the wall. "Rewarded how?"

"I don't know. Money perhaps. Gold. Something can be worked out. At the least your help will generate sympathy for your cause back in—"

"We do not need sympathy, Lieutenant. We need mortars. Assault rifles. Ammunition. Grenades." The colonel's lips quirked back in what might have been a smile. "With a thousand 81-mm mortars we could drive the Burmese from our land once and for all."

He was tempted to promise the colonel anything, but sadly, Batman shook his head. "I can't promise you anything like *that*, Colonel." If the U.S. government was trying to buy Rangoon's friendship, Batman doubted that military aid for the Karens would be forthcoming.

Htai appeared to consider the question for another moment. "At least you are honest," he said at last. "We will help you. Money we need too . . . for we must buy rice from the Thais to feed those of our people who live in camps along the border."

Batman let out his breath. "Thank you, sir."

"You may not thank me later. The Burmese have been in this area in great numbers lately. The trip will be hard and dangerous." He nodded toward the open door. "The woman who brought you here is Sergeant Phya Nin. She is waiting

with your friend. Have her get the two of you something to eat,
then make ready. We leave in one hour."

Batman left the hootch wondering if he and Malibu could
trust these people. The colonel seemed willing enough . . .
but if the Burmese were closing in, the Karens would be a lot
better off without having to look after a pair of tenderfeet on an
overland trek through the jungle.

It would be so much easier to dispose of the Americans
quietly . . . or sell them to someone who might be interested
in them . . . like the Burmese or the drug lords.

But as Batman stepped back into the filtered green light of
the jungle floor, he saw the armed Karens gathering outside
and knew that he and Malibu had very little choice in the
matter.

1300 hours, 18 January
Dirty Shirt Wardroom, U.S.S. *Thomas Jefferson*

Tombstone leaned back from the table, his mind racing
furiously. He was unaware of the clatter of silverware and
dishes in the mess, or the low murmur of conversation among
the other officers around him. The submarine sandwich he'd
bought lay untouched on his tray. He'd been chewing on the
problem of Batman and Malibu for three hours now, and he
could think of little else.

CAG had said there would be no SAR flights off the
Jefferson, that the Thais were insisting on handling the search
for Batman and Malibu themselves. It was possible that
the other problems breaking loose—rumors of invasion in the
north and an impending coup in the city—were enough to make
them sidestep the whole issue. The two Americans could easily
get lost in the cracks.

But there were many ways to address the problem. The
Thais didn't want massive U.S. intervention, and Tombstone
could appreciate that . . . but what about a single plane on
TARPS recon? Sure, it had been a TARPS aircraft which had
been shot down the first time, but that didn't mean it would
happen again. Perhaps a flight of RTAF planes in the area

could be diverted as escort. They were supposed to be up there looking for Batman anyway, weren't they?

CAG had mentioned that Batman and Malibu might have gone down on the Burmese side of the line . . . but what if they hadn't? Or what if they were close to the line, a few miles to the north, close enough that a friendly plane making a sweep could pick up their SAR broadcast? At least *Jefferson* would know then that they were alive, and could work out a decent plan for bringing them out.

And maybe the Thais, with all of their political problems, would actually be glad to be rid of this one extra problem. If he played his cards right on this one, maybe the Thais would wind up *asking* for his help. . . .

What was the Thai liaison officer's name? Kriangsak. Maybe there was someone in his office he could talk to. Hell, CAG had told him yesterday to take an evening off. He wasn't scheduled for duty this night . . . so why not? He could check out with CAG after chow and catch a bus into Bangkok.

The chances were that no one in the Thai bureaucracy would be able to help, but at least, Tombstone thought, he'd be trying to *do* something. It was better than moping in the wardroom, picking at his food and feeling sorry for himself.

And besides, he might get lucky. . . .

1015 hours, 18 January
Admiral's office, U.S.S. *Thomas Jefferson*

"Come in." Admiral Magruder looked up from his desk as Captain Fitzgerald and Vince Glover, the ship's Exec, walked in. He knew there was trouble by the look on their faces, before they even said a word. "Let's have it."

"We've got a strange report, Admiral," Fitzgerald said. "Tell him, Vince."

"There's a kid down in CATCC, Admiral. SA Howard. I just got a call from his chief. Seems he thinks three of his shipmates were kidnapped."

"Kidnapped? That's a new one."

"The guys he's named are AWOL, sir," the Exec said. "The

chief said he figured it was a . . . uh . . . rather imagina-
tive attempt by Howard to keep his buddies out of trouble. But
if they did just miss the last bus, they could've caught the first
one this morning. It kind of lends credence to the story."

"How sure is Howard of his facts?"

"Hell, Admiral, this is an eighteen-year-old. He's not sure
of anything. I think he's still freaked out by his first time ashore
in Bangkok."

Magruder chuckled. "The city has that effect."

"But he's sure enough to be pretty excited about it," the
Captain added. "He insists that if it was all a joke, his buddies
would've been back aboard before he was. I've reviewed these
men's records. They're all steady. No reason to think they
might desert."

"Who were the victims?"

"Radarman Third Paterowski. Signalman Third Bentley.
Seaman Rodriguez."

"We're doing some more checking on them," Glover said.
His frown deepened. "But Admiral, there's something more. It
may be nothing. . . ."

"Spit it out."

"One of the men is a radarman working in CATCC.
Another's an RD striker . . . also in CATCC. And this kid
Howard was assigned as CATCC message runner."

Magruder understood what Glover was saying. "Three out
of four of these guys from CATCC." he said, rubbing his chin.
"Doesn't necessarily mean it was deliberate. Three buddies, all
from the same department, all hit the beach together. Get into
trouble together . . ."

"Yes, sir. But we can't ignore the possibility that there was
more to it than that."

Magruder sighed. "Agreed." He looked at Fitzgerald.
"What do you think, Captain?"

Fitzgerald shrugged. "Could just be a case of grabbing three
guys off the street at random. They could've gotten rolled and
be laying in an alley someplace."

"But . . . ?" Magruder prompted.

"We ought to proceed dead slow, Admiral. There have been

anti-American demonstrations . . . and according to our
Thai sources, the communists have been cheering the downing
of our Tomcat yesterday. I'd say we should treat this seriously."

Magruder sighed. "Agreed." He was worried, more worried
than he wanted to show.

When addressing the men of his carrier battle group, the
admiral liked to stress the fact that no man's job on board the
Jefferson was less important than any other, that everyone had
a part to play. In the sense that the ship was a seagoing city
with each department supporting all of the rest that was true.

But he would have felt a lot less worried had the missing
men been from the ship's laundry. Men assigned to CATCC
knew a hell of a lot about how things worked on a carrier, about
call signs and radio frequencies for regular air traffic, about
daily schedules for carrier ops and exercises. . . .

"It's probably nothing," he said again. "Nothing worse than
some of our boys getting rolled, that is. But we won't take the
chance. Vince, put out the word through the SPs. Liberty is
cancelled for all personnel."

"Aye, aye, sir."

"Have Intel debrief Howard. Maybe he can tell us something more, something we've missed."

"Yes, sir." The Exec paused, then scowled. "Damn . . ."

"What is it, Mr. Glover?"

"I just remembered, Admiral. CAG just showed me a list of
senior personnel ashore. Your nephew . . . uh . . . Commander Magruder, sir. He's on it."

"Tombstone? Why?"

"CAG said he was under some stress, and he'd told him to
take some time off."

"We have any other squadron COs ashore?"

"Yes, sir. Bayerly, VF-97."

"Thank you for telling me." He felt a sharp disquiet. Three
men from CATCC missing . . . and now both Tomcat skip-
pers were ashore as well. Bayerly had been temporarily
replaced as squadron CO, of course, but it still didn't seem to
be a good idea to have both men off the ship *now*.

Fitzgerald interrupted his bleak thoughts. "Do you really think there's a connection, Admiral? Between the kidnapping and the attack at U Feng, I mean."

"Hell, I don't know. We *can't* know. But if we wait until we get the facts straight, it may be too late."

Fitzgerald nodded. "Agreed. Problem is, if I don't have the facts I get to feeling a bit paranoid."

"Sometimes, Captain," Magruder said evenly, "that's the best way to be."

1250 hours, 18 January
Warehouse District, Klong Toey

The unconscious man's hands had been shackled together, then slung over a meathook suspended from the warehouse ceiling. His head lolled forward against his bare chest. Silently Hsiao went through papers and IDs found in the man's wallet. "A third class petty officer," he said. "Not a man of high rank."

"They were not wearing uniforms," Phreng said. They were gathered at the edge of the harsh circle of light which illuminated the naked prisoner. His personal effects, together with certain tools, were spread out on a nearby table.

"Never mind, Phreng," Hsiao said. "You did well. If these men work in air traffic control, as you say, they will have information we can use."

"Thank you, General!"

"You know what we are looking for." Hsiao nodded at a bucket of water standing on the floor nearby. "Revive him and proceed with the questioning. You know where to reach me when you're through."

"Yes, sir!"

Hsiao turned, his eyes meeting those of a man who stood in the shadows outside the circle of light. The agent known as Sword had arrived only moments earlier. "Come with me."

"This is insane, General," the man said as they walked away. "Kidnapping American naval personnel was never part of the plan!"

The stacked crates rose like canyon walls around them,

creating privacy, and Hsiao allowed the challenge to pass without rebuke. Sword was tense, on edge . . . and would have to be handled with great care.

"It would be better if we had officers for questioning as well," Hsiao said softly.

"Officers! No! Impossible!"

"Flight officers would be best," Hsiao continued as though he'd not heard Sword's words. "They are certain to know the procedures we are interested in. These low-ranking seamen"— he jerked his head back over his shoulder to indicate the prisoner—"may not be sufficiently trained for our purposes."

Behind him he heard Phreng's voice questioning . . . demanding.

"You do not understand, General!" The man was almost frantic now. "It is far more dangerous to kidnap officers. . . ."

"I fail to see how." He walked several more steps, then added, "There will probably be a number of *Jefferson*'s pilots in Bangkok tonight."

"Yes, sir." Sword stopped.

Hsiao paused, waiting for him to go on. "You know where such officers could be found, do you not? You are in a position to know, certainly."

"I want no part of this, General Hsiao. I never anticipated this. My position in the government could be—"

"Your position, Colonel, is with me!"

The words seemed to shock the other man.

Hsiao was aware that his entire plan could never have been carried off without this man . . . senior aide to the Thai Army's General Duong . . . and liaison officer with the visiting American naval forces. Colonel Kriangsak had been invaluable already, but his greatest service was yet to be carried out.

"An American officer has been calling my office all day," Kriangsak said reluctantly. "One of their pilots. He's talked to several of my people . . . says he wishes to discuss the possibility of his helping out in the search for the Americans who vanished the other day near U Feng."

Hsiao nodded. "Excellent. Excellent! Call him. Set up a

place and time to discuss it with him. And you will take some of my people with you."

"Sir, I don't—"

"This may be the best opportunity we have for capturing one of their people. Two would be better if you can manage it. We can use one against the other that way."

"But General—"

He was interrupted by a long, shuddering, drawn-out scream from behind them. The scream went on and on and on before lapsing into a throaty gurgle. Then Phreng's voice could be heard once more, harsh and insistent.

Hsiao kept his face impassive. Perhaps Kriangsak simply needed to be reminded of the stakes in this game.

"Yes, General," Kriangsak said slowly. They reached the door, where a guard saluted. "I will see what can be done."

As the door closed behind them, the screaming started again.

CHAPTER 14

They'd left the camp in the late morning, traveling not on the road which descended down the valley, but up the forest-clad slope to the north, following a maze of nearly invisible paths which zigzagged among the trees toward the crest. The girl, Phya Nin, had been put in charge of the Americans. Two teenage boys under her command were detailed to carry Malibu in a bamboo litter. This made for slow going . . . but it was faster than if Malibu had tried to negotiate the climb on his crutch. From time to time the way grew too steep for the litter bearers, however, and Malibu had to get off and walk, helped along by Batman and one of the Karen boys.

They walked for three hours, negotiating one forested ridge after another. As nearly as Batman could tell, judging by the sun and his compass, they kept heading north, deeper into Burma. His fears that the natives were going to double-cross them somehow grew sharper.

While they were inside Burmese territory, control of this section of the country was still an open question. The Golden Triangle was the private preserve of various warlords. If the Karens somehow suspected that he and Malibu had come to this remote corner of the globe as part of the ongoing war against the drug producers, they might reason that those warlords would pay handsomely for their capture.

155

The thought made Batman shiver. If Malibu had been able to travel freely on foot, Batman would have urged an immediate escape. But he couldn't abandon his RIO, and it seemed certain that the Karens would run them down in minutes if they tried to E&E together.

No, they would just have to wait and see what happened.

In mid-afternoon, the group stopped for a twenty-minute rest. When they set out again, it was toward the east. By the time the sun was setting that evening and the group stopped again, Batman was certain that they were now heading in a generally southeasterly direction.

Toward U Feng.

His second night in the jungle was more comfortable than the first. The Karens built small, closely guarded fires, and Batman gratefully accepted a bowl of hot rice mixed with chunks of some unidentifiable meat, the origins of which he refused to question. He ate the meal with his fingers, sitting by the fire between Malibu and Phya. The night sounds of the jungle surrounded them, a cacophonous symphony of shrieks, chirps, and insect twitterings. The air smelled of wet earth and rain. Mosquitoes swarmed from the darkness, and the shadows of huge bats darted and swooped beyond the circle of the fire's light.

As Batman ate, he watched the girl. He wanted to talk, to make conversation . . . but he was at a loss as to how to begin with this young woman, barely out of her teens but wearing fatigues and carrying an assault rifle. Her conversation during the long day had been limited to phrases like "Hurry up," and "More quiet! Don't thrash in leaves so much!"

"I understand your people have been fighting for a long time, Phya," he said at last. He slapped at the mosquitoes gathering on the backs of his hands despite the repellent coating them. "Why do you do it?"

"For Katoolie," she said, echoing what Colonel Htai had said that morning. Somewhere in the darkness, near another fire, a child laughed. The ghost of a smile played at Phya's lips. "Children see country perhaps. Someday."

"No, I mean *you*. Why are you a soldier, Phya?"

"I kill Burmese." Her eyes glittered. "Kill Burmese forever."

He heard the ice in her voice. "Why do you hate them so much? I mean, you've been fighting them for forty years! You can't hope to win!"

"We win. Someday. Or we die. Mostly we win."

"Against the Burmese Army?"

She bristled. "You no believe?" She paused. "When I bring you to camp today, leave you by tree. You remember tree?"

The tree with the letters made of empty brass cartridges hammered into the bark. Batman felt cold. "CJ," he said. "Initials?"

"Not letters. Numbers," she said. "Burmese way write number twelve."

"Twelve?"

"For the 12th KNLA Brigade. Is way we mark victories. We take place from Burmese, we mark. That camp, we take from Burmese two months ago. Kill one hundred fifty enemy." She fingered the red triangular patch on her hat. "Take this from Burmese soldier."

The matter-of-fact way she said it sent a shiver down Batman's spine. She might have just admitted stepping on a spider. He swallowed. "You sound like you enjoy killing them."

"Not enjoy, no." Her dark eyes watched him from beneath the brim of her boonie hat. "Is not much choice. Either fight . . . or die. Burmese want kill all Karen. Wipe out forever."

Her words had a cold finality about them. Mass genocide? Surely Rangoon wasn't bent on exterminating these people.

"You not believe?" she said.

"It's a little hard to accept," Batman admitted.

"Americans help Burmese . . . not know they want kill Karen?"

Batman didn't like the way the conversation was going. Did she blame the United States for helping the Rangoon government? More to the point, did she hold him and Malibu responsible? "Believe me, Phya, I don't know anything about the Burmese! I certainly don't know about them trying to wipe out your people."

"Hell, Phya," Malibu added. "We didn't know anything about this war until we landed in it!"

"War last many year," she said, staring into the fire. "Burmese not beat Karen, until they start killing villages."

Batman exchanged glances with Malibu. His RIO shrugged. "Sorry. Killing villages?"

She gestured toward the dark jungle around them. "This place, this part jungle not our home. Not Katoolie. Karen live . . . far southwest. One hundred . . . two hundred mile. Mawchi. Pa-an. My village near Mawchi, on Salween River.

"Burmese come my village six . . . maybe seven month ago. Their . . . how you say? Sky machines, make noise like thunder."

"Helicopters?" Malibu volunteered.

"Exact. Hel-copters. Kill my people. Kill my *village*."

"They shot your people?" Batman asked. "From helicopters?"

She nodded. "Sky machines hang above village. Use rocket. Use machine gun. Kill people, cows, goats. All die. They land then, burn whole town." She raised her head. Firelight glowed red against her skin, illuminating the curve of her jaw, her eyes. "My . . . my husband there. He die. All die."

"How did you get away?"

"I washing clothes in Salween, with other village women. See machines, hide. See smoke of village in sky. Karen soldiers come, tell me. Later, when safe, I see. Then I join Twelfth Brigade, KNLA." A sad pride touched her voice. "I join. Kill Burmese who want kill all us!"

"They wiped out your village. . . ." Horror pricked at the nape of Batman's neck.

"Not just my village, but others. Many others. You want know why I fight? I fight for children, for place they can live."

"War to the knife, compadre," Malibu said quietly.

Batman nodded. His mental image of the typical revolutionary guerrilla was of a ragged character fighting for some political goal, supplied by one superpower or the other. The Karens were literally fighting for their survival as a people, were carrying out that fight with virtually no outside support . . . and they'd been doing it for over four decades.

Batman shivered at the thought. "Good God . . ."

"Yes," she said. "God good. He give strength. We kill many Burmese."

He watched her for a long moment as she leaned forward, arms around her knees, rocking slightly back and forth. The top two or three buttons of her tunic were undone, and he could see a small, gold cross on a chain, resting on the smooth, dark skin above her bosom. It caught firelight as she moved.

Batman remembered Htai telling him that most Karens were Christians. He felt an overwhelming sadness. The Burmese did not have the greatest army in the world, not by a long shot . . . but they had an army many, many times larger than the scattered tribesmen living in the jungles along the borders of their country. The Karens were a tiny minority . . . among the Burmese, and among the other religions in an area overwhelmingly Buddhist, Hindu, or spirit-worshipping animist.

"You're fighting against such terrible odds," he said. Somehow he wanted to help, but didn't know the words, didn't know what he could do. He wanted to reach out and take Phya in his arms, but knew that so familiar a gesture would be wrong. Like Htai, she was not looking for sympathy.

She looked at him quizzically. "Odds? What mean odds?"

"Uh . . . there are so many of the enemy. So few of you. Your enemy outnumbers you terribly."

To Batman's surprise, she laughed. "No, Lieutenant." She stopped, laughed again.

"What's the matter, Phya?" Malibu asked. "What's so funny?"

"Nothing matter, Lieutenant," she said. "But you not understand. You see, God with Karens, make us outnumber *them*!"

1930 hours, 18 January
Americana Hotel, Bangkok

The Americana Hotel was a survivor of Bangkok's Vietnam-era economic boom, when the Americans on leave found the city the ideal spot for R&R. The boom had ended in the early seventies when the Americans pulled out of Nam, turned their bases in Thailand over to the Royal Thai Air Force, and went home. Many of the businesses, from cheap brothels to deluxe hotels, had failed, but the Americana, and others, had struggled on.

The Thais were a resourceful and resilient people, however. Somehow, they'd managed to turn their surplus of hotels, resorts, and places of entertainment into what amounted to a natural resource; Thailand, as it turned out, was one of the very few countries in the area where Westerners felt either comfortable or welcome. It was the burgeoning tourist industry which kept hotels like the Americana going.

This establishment's economic recovery, Tombstone noted as he entered the hotel's lounge, was not yet complete. The dirt was well-hidden by dark colors and the dim light, but the paint on the walls was chipped and cracked in places, and water stains marred both the expensive-looking teak floor and the plaster ceiling.

A Thai waiter approached, his hands folded before his chest as he bowed in a traditional *wai*. "Commander Magruder? Your party is waiting for you. Please follow me."

Tombstone followed the waiter past tables and booths, past potted tropical plants and softly bubbling aquariums. A large American flag was dimly visible in the poor and smoky light, draped across one wall. At a table near the back of the room, a small, dark man with a neat mustache rose to greet him as he approached.

"Commander Magruder?"

"That's right. You must be Colonel Kriangsak."

The colonel gave Tombstone a polite *wai*. "At your service, sir." He gestured to the seat across the table from him. "Do me the honor of joining me!"

"Thank you, sir." He sat down. "I certainly appreciate your seeing me. I was surprised to get your call this afternoon."

"Not at all. Can I order you a drink?"

Tombstone glanced at the glass by Kriangsak's elbow, and recognized the heavy fragrance of the Thai drink known as Mekong wine. "A rum-and-coke'd be fine."

Kriangsak signaled a waitress, then folded his hands before him on the table. "My people tell me you wish to take part in the search for your missing comrades."

"If possible, yes, sir." Tombstone felt a new thrill of hope. Colonel Kriangsak, certainly, had some pull with the various Thai military bureaus and bureaucracies. As liaison between the Thai and American forces, he might at least know who Tombstone could talk to.

"I fear that will be difficult, Commander. At least until the area is secured from rebel forces."

Tombstone tried to mask his disappointment. "Rebel forces, Colonel?"

Kriangsak smiled and held one hand up. "Nothing I'm really at liberty to discuss. I shouldn't have spoken of it, even. But . . ." He leaned forward over the table, dropping his voice conspiratorially. "You have heard reports of an attack up there, I'm sure. I tell you, quite frankly, such an attack could not have been carried out without inside help. Traitors, if you will, or rebels within the government. We must ascertain the extent of this, this rebellion before we risk the lives of more of our American allies. We really have no idea who the *real* enemy is."

"You must have some idea. Burmese? Communists? Or are we talking about a coup?"

"Let us say, simply, elements which oppose the current government. In any case, my people believe it would be unfortunate if more Americans lost their lives during the crisis on our northern border."

The waitress returned with Tombstone's drink. He accepted it, took a sip, then nodded. "I can understand that. But what now? Are you people looking for Batman—I mean, for Lieutenants Wayne and Blake? It's possible they are alive, but down in the jungle somewhere."

"Commander, everything that can be done is being done, I assure you. And I personally will let you know the moment we learn anything."

Tombstone sat back in his seat. The disappointment was sharp . . . but he knew he could realistically have expected no more. "I can't ask for better than that," he said. He started to slide out from behind the table. "I certainly appreciate your taking the time to talk to me."

"You're not leaving already, surely!" Kriangsak looked surprised. "Stay and have dinner, at least. I would like to discuss modern air tactics with you." He hesitated. "By the way, Commander, are you staying here in the city tonight?"

"No, sir. I expect I'll go back to *Jefferson*."

"Duty?"

"No. Just no particular reason to stay."

Kriangsak pursed his lips. "You know, I could arrange for—"

"Well, well, well!" a slurred voice brayed from close by. "Look who's here! Our own hero of Wonsan!"

Tombstone turned and saw Bayerly, obviously drunk, leaning heavily against an ornamental palm. Several other people in the lounge were looking in his direction.

The man's unexpected appearance was a shock to Tombstone. What in the name of all that was holy was Bayerly doing *here*?

"Thought . . . thought I'd find you here, ol' buddy," Bayerly said. He was wearing his whites, his lieutenant commander's shoulder bars askew, and clutched a glass of ice and amber liquid in one hand. He lurched forward three steps and dropped his free hand on Tombstone's shoulder. He turned and seemed to see the Thai officer for the first time. "Who's your gook friend here? Hey . . . bet y'didn't know my ol' buddy Tombstone here was a genuine American Navy Cross *hero*, did you?"

"You are drunk, Commander," Tombstone said, his voice low and level. "I suggest you get back to the—"

"Uh-uh. No way." Bayerly grabbed an empty chair from a nearby table, slid it up close, and sank into it. "Gotta drink the health of our goddamned *hero* here first, don't we?"

Colonel Kriangsak was watching Bayerly with narrowed eyes. "Sir, I believe Commander Magruder has an excellent idea. I can call some of my men who will escort you back to the *Jefferson*. It appears to me you could use a good night's sleep."

Bayerly ignored the Thai officer. "You know what bein' a hero is, Tombstone Magruder?" He held up his drink and examined it closely. "Bein' . . . bein' a hero is bein' in the right place at the right time. Did you know that?" He turned and smiled at Kriangsak. "You shoulda' seen my buddy Tombstone here at Wonsan. He got the dream duty, let me tell ya! Flyin' lead for an alpha strike over Wonsan, while yours truly flew CAP over the carrier. Hey, CAP's not a hot-shit glamor job, but someone's gotta do it, right? Can't all be aces, right?"

His voice had been getting steadily louder. Tombstone rose. "Colonel, I'm sorry about this. Thanks for seeing me . . . but I'd better get Commander Bayerly back to the *Jefferson*."

"I don't need your help, goddamn it!" Bayerly stood suddenly, knocking the chair over with a crash. The transformation in his face, from drunken amiability to murderous fury, was so abrupt that Tombstone was taken aback. "You've *ruined* me, you bastard! *You've ruined me!*"

"Look, Made It—"

"CAG yanked my flight clearance. Because of *your* report. 'Pending investigation,' the man says . . . but you know how the Navy works, don't you, Magruder? It's all for one and one for all, ain't it? Just as long as you're part of the fuckin' Navy club! As long as you have the right name . . . and an admiral for an uncle to help you over the rough spots!"

"Shut up!" Tombstone snapped, his voice intense. It felt as though every eye in the lounge was on the two of them, and he

saw a couple of Thai waiters hurrying across the room in their direction. "Come on, Bayerly. We're going for a walk!"

"It's fine for the boys in the club! But screw up once . . . just *once*, and if you don't have the right connections, *bam*! You're fucked!"

"Is there a problem, sir?" the headwaiter asked.

"I'm sorry for the trouble," Tombstone said. He started guiding Bayerly away from the table. "My friend here had a little too much to—"

"Damn right I had too much! You *ruined* me, you sanc . . . sanct . . . sanctimonious son of a bitch! How's it feel to be a hero? Hey! Tell me! Why aren't you ballin' your new girl friend, Magruder? You know, that stacked, sexy blond with her own TV show . . . Is that one of the perks of bein' a goddamned *hero* . . . ?"

Tombstone's grip on Bayerly's shoulder tightened. He whirled the man around to face him, his own fury rising. "I've had just about enough of you, Bayerly! Can it, right now!"

"Fuck you!" Bayerly threw a clumsy, roundhouse punch in the general direction of the side of Tombstone's head. Tombstone blocked the punch easily with his left arm, then snapped out with his right, catching Bayerly squarely in the jaw. Bayerly sagged back, landing in Kriangsak's arms.

The two of them lowered the drunken officer onto the seat of the booth. Kriangsak looked across the room, raised one slim hand, and gestured. Tombstone saw two Thais in civilian clothes hurrying across the floor toward them.

Bodyguards? Tombstone gave a mental shrug. Perhaps Thai army colonels never went anywhere without their personal plainclothes guards or aides. He turned to the headwaiter, fishing in his hip pocket for his wallet. "I'm terribly sorry for the disturbance, sir. We'll get him out of here right away." He'd exchanged some of his money at the hotel desk earlier that evening. He produced three of the purple 500-*baht* notes—about sixty American dollars—and pressed them into the frowning waiter's hand.

For a moment, he thought the man was going to refuse. Then the money vanished and the waiter smiled. "No problem, sir.

Permit us to help." Two more waiters materialized to help Kriangsak's men maneuver Bayerly's dead weight toward the lounge entrance.

Tombstone turned to face Kriangsak, who had drawn one of his men aside and was whispering hurried instructions to him. *"Koon krahp!"* the man said, all but saluting before hurrying after the entourage surrounding Bayerly.

"I'm sorry to leave so abruptly, Colonel," Tombstone said. "But I'd better see him back to the *Jefferson*."

"That is not necessary, my friend," Kriangsak said. "Please! Sit down! I have given orders for my men to drive Commander Bayerly back to Sattahip. They will see to it that he gets back to your ship."

"That is very kind of you, Colonel."

"Not at all. Now, please! Sit down!"

"No. Thank you just the same, sir, but I really have to go." The confrontation had left him feeling weak. He needed air . . . a walk and a chance to think.

Kriangsak looked across the room toward the lounge entrance. "Commander, my men have already gone. If I cannot offer you a ride home, I insist that you allow me to find you lodgings here in the city."

"Actually, Colonel, I think I need a walk." He hesitated. Suddenly, he felt the need to see Pamela . . . to talk to her. This hero business, he thought. It's got to stop. Now! "There's someone in town I need to see," he added.

"I will not take no for an answer, Commander." Kriangsak smiled, his teeth flashing white in the dim light. "I'll tell you what. I have some duties to attend to at the Ministry tonight . . . and possibly, just possibly, I can talk to someone about your request." He shrugged. "Who knows? We might find a place for you on one of our planes."

Tombstone's eyes widened. "That's very kind of you, sir."

"It is nothing. Let me talk to some people I know. But please, tell me where you will be. I will arrange for a driver to pick you up there later. Or if you prefer, I will arrange bachelor quarters for you at the air base at Don Muang and call your ship. Is it agreed?"

Tombstone found it hard to resist the man's friendly pressure. He allowed himself a small smile. "Okay, Colonel. You win."

"Excellent! Where can I meet you?"

"Well, my friend is staying at the Dusit Thani. You could reach me there. I can leave my name at the desk."

"Splendid. It's almost eight. In . . . shall we make it two hours then? Is that time enough for your meeting?"

"Two hours will be fine, Colonel. It shouldn't take longer than that."

Kriangsak rose, dropped several *baht* on the table, then extended his hand again. "In that case, Commander, I will see you later."

"Fine. Thanks for the drink."

"Anytime, Commander. We'll talk more later." The smile broadened. "I'm looking forward to it *very* much!"

1955 hours, 18 January
In the Americana Hotel parking lot

Bayerly struggled against the grip of the men supporting him. "I can do it m'sel'!" he mumbled.

The car was already waiting for them, its engine running. One of the colonel's men opened the rear door. "Inside."

"I'm not goin' with you gooks!" Bayerly said, his voice rising once more. "Get your goddamned hands off—" He heard a metallic *snick-snick* behind him. Turning, he found himself staring into the black muzzle of a Colt .45 automatic. "What the hell . . . ?"

"Inside!" the Thai said, his voice a menacing hiss.

"What is this? You can't—"

Something struck Bayerly from behind, a smashing blow to the back of his head which sent him crumpling to the pavement. Dimly, he was aware of hands grabbing his shoulders and legs, of several men stuffing him into the open backseat door of the car.

Then darkness closed in and he was aware of nothing more.

CHAPTER 15

"Washington's on the line, Admiral," the aide said, extending the telephone. "The CNO."

Magruder accepted the handset reluctantly. With no way of knowing how Washington was going to jump on this one, he was not looking forward to the conversation. He glanced at a set of clocks on the bulkhead. Twenty-hundred hours, eight in the evening, was eight in the *morning*, Washington time. "Good morning, Admiral," he said.

"More like good evening where you are, Tom," a voice replied. There was a faint hiss of static over the multiple satellite relay between Thailand and the U.S. east coast.

Admiral Fletcher T. Grimes was the Chief of Naval Operations and, as such, was the Navy's representative on the Joint Chiefs of Staff. In fact, American Congressional law had de-emphasized the CNO's operational responsibilities and he no longer exercised personal command over the country's naval forces. Both the Secretary of Defense and the Secretary of the Navy, however, knew that Magruder and Grimes were old friends, and had directed that the CNO serve as the President's link with his commander in the field this time.

"You have my report, I take it," Magruder said.

"On my desk in front of me. I briefed the President this morning. It looks like you're going to be center stage again, Tom."

"I understand, sir." The Wonsan affair had thrust the *Jefferson* battle group into the public eye three months earlier. Now, the political situation in Thailand was deteriorating rapidly. If the President was to have any hand in protecting America's most important ally in the region, he would have to act quickly . . . and that meant calling on CBG-14 once more.

"The President met with the Thai ambassador yesterday, Tom. Bangkok has formally asked for our assistance over there."

"That doesn't quite square with what we've been getting over here, Admiral. The story we're getting is more along the lines of 'Hands off, we can do it ourselves.' "

"Tom, it is the considered opinion of several of the President's advisors that there may be . . . elements within the Thai military, a faction which could be planning a coup."

"We've certainly heard rumors to that effect here," Magruder said. "I included that in my report."

"Yes, I saw. Tom, the National Security Council has advised the President that a military coup in Thailand at this time could lead to a severe destabilization throughout the area. We can't allow that to happen . . . not unchallenged."

"Understood. What are the President's orders?"

"They'll be coming down through the chain of command later today. I can tell you, though, how they'll read. Provide the legitimate Thai government with full support, air and land."

"That won't help if we can't get local military cooperation."

"We're working on that."

"We also can't help much if we don't have a target."

"We're working on that too. The important thing is to let the good guys know we're backing them. The opposition will be trying to force a wedge between us and the Bangkok government, maybe try to discredit us. It's all laid out in your orders."

"Yes, sir," Magruder said dryly. Orders from the Joint Chiefs generally weighed in like encyclopedias . . . with enough contradictory and generally ass-covering clauses to keep field commanders guessing for months.

But at least Fletcher was on his side.

"Orders have already been transmitted for MEU-6 to join CBG-14 again," Grimes continued. "They were in Singapore on maneuvers, but they're on their way to your position now. Should arrive sometime day after tomorrow, and they'll be in air transport range within eighteen hours."

Magruder pursed his lips. This was being taken seriously indeed in Washington if they were sending in the Marines again. Marine Expeditionary Unit 6, consisting of four ships and almost two thousand Marines, had also been at Wonsan, securing a beachhead to facilitate the evacuation of rescued American seamen. Their primary mission in Bangkok would be to safeguard American lives and property.

"Okay, Admiral," Magruder said after a moment. "What about threats to our people?"

"The people lost near U Feng?"

"Yes, sir. And our AWOLs."

"You still think that incident might be more than it seems?"

"It is a distinct possibility, sir. No hard evidence . . . but it's very suspicious. And it all ties in with what you were just saying . . . with the possibility that someone might be trying to discredit us. What better way than to hit us, hard and unexpectedly?"

"A terrorist attack?"

"Possibly. I'm more concerned about further attacks on our personnel ashore. It's going to be morning before they're all back on board."

"Do you have any suggestions?"

"There's not a hell of a lot we can do, Admiral. Not until we know what they're going to do. I've briefed my officers. We've set readiness condition X-ray Three. We're cancelling further liberty as our people come back aboard tonight. More than that we can't do until we see a definite threat, something we can respond to."

"Understood." There was a long hesitation on the line, as though Grimes was turning possibilities over in his mind. "I'll tell you, Tom. I think our problem is a mole."

"A spy, sir?"

"Someone in the works, gumming them up. Probably in the Bangkok bureaucracy. I'll pass a request on to the DCI to see what can be done. In the meantime, continue as you have been. But be prepared to use your own initiative to render all possible assistance to the legitimate Thai government."

"Does that include sending in the Marines, sir?"

"It means doing whatever you feel is justified to preserve American lives and property, to protect your command . . . and to support our allies in Southeast Asia. I can't be much more specific than that."

"That's specific enough, Admiral." Magruder was already thinking about the possibilities. The Marines from MEU-6 would not be available until midday tomorrow, but he had ninety Marines on board the *Jefferson*. A platoon could be heloed in to the American embassy in Bangkok in order to reinforce security there . . . and possibly to provide a ready mobile force should the three missing seamen be discovered.

Something big was happening in the city, and Admiral Magruder wanted to be ready for it, whatever *it* was.

He only hoped he wasn't already too late.

2045 hours, 18 January
Dusit Thani Hotel, Bangkok

Pamela had been surprised by Tombstone's phone call, but she'd told him to come straight up. She'd been able to sense the strain underlying his words and knew something was wrong.

Since their time together at the Thonburi *klong,* she'd been forced to admit to herself that she felt much more for Matthew Magruder than could be explained by professional interest. It wasn't love—she wasn't ready to go *that* far—but they were certainly friends, and friendship was something which Pamela Drake took very seriously indeed.

"Matt, it's good to see you," she said as she opened the door. "Come in."

He entered, wearing civilian clothes and an expression which could have been hiding almost anything. "Hello, Pam. Sorry to catch you by surprise. Did I interrupt something?"

"Not at all."

"Are you . . . I mean, are the guys in your crew here?"

"We are *quite* alone, Matt! I was going over some script revisions, is all. Can I get you something to drink?" The hotel suite had a small bar and a refrigerator.

"No, thanks."

"Have you eaten? I could call room service. . . ."

"Pamela, I've got to talk to you." It sounded as though he'd been saving the words for a long time, holding them for the moment. "It's about your story . . . the interview."

"What about it?"

"Look, I know this isn't fair, for you or for your show. But I've been having second thoughts about my part in the thing. I was wondering if you had enough that you could do your series without me."

"You're damned right it's not fair. Do you have any idea how much money has been spent on this project already?"

"No."

"Neither do I. That's Accounting's problem. But it *would* be my problem if it all came apart now. So why don't you want me to use your interviews?"

"It's this whole hero bit . . . the way you were building me up. I really don't think I can go through with that."

Pamela felt the anger welling up within, but she held it sternly in check. She'd not reached her current position with the ACN network by losing her temper with recalcitrant subjects.

Or with friends.

She gestured toward the sofa. "Sit down, Matt." He did so, and she watched his face as she joined him. "Look," she said after a moment's uncomfortable silence. "You signed a release form, and that pretty much makes those film clips our property. But maybe if you explained why you wanted them killed . . ."

"It's kind of hard to explain."

"You can be quite persuasive, Matt. That's one of the reasons I wanted to use you. This series could be just another hunt for the dirt under the Pentagon's carpets . . . but you believe in the Navy and the Navy's mission. You believe in that floating airport anchored down at Sattahip, and that comes across in the interviews, so much so that you make a very good case for your side of the argument. And you want me to drop all that?" Something new occurred to her and she frowned. Was there some form of censorship at work here? "Matt, no one's put you up to this, have they? Someone in Washington? Your uncle?"

Tombstone bit off a low, sharp curse. "No, it's not my uncle. I'm here on my own."

"Well *something's* happened to put you into a spin, Matt. Want to tell me what?"

He sighed. "I guess I'm not feeling very much like a hero, right now."

"Hero? That's just a word, Matt. How is a hero supposed to feel?"

"I don't know. Not like he owes everything to his uncle."

"Ahhh," she said. "Maybe we're hitting the root of it now. You think the admiral has been paving the way for you? Making you out to be a hero for promotion and honor, that sort of thing?"

"No, you've been making me out to be the hero." His mouth quirked in a near-smile. "But he may have been making the opportunities."

He began talking about Wonsan, just as he had during several of the interviews. The battle had unfolded with appalling swiftness, with little time to think or act the part of hero. He'd responded according to his training, and only later, when there'd been time to think, had he felt the fear. He'd won the Navy Cross primarily for his refusal to eject when his RIO had been too badly hurt to leave the damaged aircraft.

"But don't you see?" Tombstone said at last. "I was simply doing my job. I was in the right place at the right time." He was not looking at her, but kept his eyes fixed to a framed abstract print hanging on the far wall of the suite. "That damned medal could have been won by anybody."

"But it was you who responded the way you did."

"Bullshit. Any of us could have—*would* have—done the

same." His scowl deepened. "You said the other day that I surprised you by not being a typical arrogant aviator. It's true. I'm not . . . demonstrative. Outgoing. I tend to keep to myself. Half the people on my boat are convinced I have my rank and the choice assignments—because of my uncle."

"That sounds like an exaggeration to me, Matt."

The half-smile played at his lips again. "Maybe. But not by much."

She considered for a moment. "The tape still has to be edited. I could make a note to drop the references to the medal . . . but that's not the real problem, is it?"

"Not really. It's this whole glory-game image."

"Which you are stuck with, no matter what's on the tape." She reached out, impulsively, and laid her hand on his knee. "Ruining my project isn't going to help you, Matt."

He looked away. "I hadn't really thought of it as . . . ruining it."

"What is it, Matt?" She leaned closer, dropping her voice. "Someone giving you trouble about your hero status? About me?" He looked away, uncomfortable, and she had her answer. "You're one hell of a guy, Matt," she said. "I meant what I said the other day. I wouldn't want you to change."

He turned back suddenly, so close now that their lips nearly met. Pamela reached out . . . and then she was in his arms, drawing his head down to hers.

Much later, she disentangled herself enough to murmur, "You'll stay tonight, won't you?"

He looked into her eyes for a time, until she was afraid he would answer no. But he nodded, smiled, and then they kissed again.

After a long time, he pulled back and, rather unromantically, checked his watch. "Can I use your phone?"

"Sure." She got up so that he could move. "Over there, by the window."

He picked up the receiver and spoke briefly to the hotel operator.

"Calling your ship?" she asked.

"I'm square with them," he replied, holding the receiver to

his ear as he waited for the call to go through. "Long as I'm back on board by 0800 tomorrow. No, someone else I saw tonight was going to arrange for a place for me to stay in Bangkok. If I don't let him know, we'll be interrupted by . . . yes? Hello? You speak English? Good. This is Lieutenant Commander Magruder, U.S. Navy. Put me through to Colonel Kriangsak, please. He gave me this number. Yes, I'll wait."

Pamela left Tombstone to finish his phone call and went into the suite's bedroom. She was ready for him by the time he entered.

2325 hours, 18 January
Dusit Thani Hotel, Bangkok

It was the noise that woke him.

At least, he thought it had been a noise, one of those sharp, metallic clicks one hears in a strange room in the middle of the night and can never identify. He lay there in the darkness for a long moment, listening.

Nothing. Or perhaps someone had dropped something, upstairs or in the hallway outside the suite.

No matter. He needed to use the bathroom anyway. Taking care not to waken Pamela, he disentangled his arm from beneath her pillow, then swung his bare legs over the side of the bed. The air in the room, though stirred by the large ceiling fan, still retained the musky scent of their lovemaking.

Pamela. He could just make out her sleeping form on the bed by his side, see the rise and fall of her breasts by the hint of reflected moonlight spilling through the open door from the next room.

Tombstone felt a twinge of guilt as he realized that their relationship had changed again. He'd not told her everything. He *couldn't*. The word that a Navy aviator and his RIO had been lost over northern Thailand was still classified, and any officer leaking *that* tidbit to the news media would be roasted over a slow fire by Admiral Magruder, nephew or no nephew.

And the pain he'd been feeling that evening was due at least as much to the fact that Malibu and Batman were missing as to Bayerly or anything else. If it had just been Bayerly's accusations, well . . . Tombstone could live with those.

But Batman and Malibu had gone down while flying *his* mission . . . while he had been assigned to look pretty for the camera and answer Pamela Drake's questions. He'd never been one to claim that the universe was fair, but this put a new twist to the way God seemed to be running things that left a distinctly bitter taste in his mouth.

Part of the change in his relationship with Pamela was a new desire to tell her about his friends, about his feelings at their loss. It would have made facing that loss . . . easier somehow.

But the secret would have to remain secret.

Swearing under his breath, Tombstone rose from the bed and padded naked across plush carpeting to the bathroom. When he returned, he stopped, staring at the still form of Pamela, masked by shadows. There was something . . . different.

A new smell, a *presence* which hadn't been there before . . .

Before he could piece together his impressions, shadows moved in the darkness, "Who's there . . . !"

Something hit Tombstone a glancing blow across the side of his head. He went down, groping for a shoe, a chair, *anything* he could use as a weapon.

"Rah vang!" a harsh voice barked to his left. Tombstone pivoted in that direction.

Then the room exploded in light.

As his vision cleared, Tombstone was engulfed in a swirl of rapid-fire impressions. There were three men in the bedroom, wearing close-fitting black clothing and carrying silenced automatic pistols. Pamela, sitting up naked in bed, still had one hand on the bedside light switch as she opened her mouth to scream.

A hard, metallic something collided with the back of Tombstone's head and he pitched forward to his hands and knees, the room whirling around him. He tried to rise, to get his legs beneath him.

He was struck again, much harder, from behind. His face ground into the carpet as his vision dimmed in blood and blackness. Desperately, Tombstone fought back against the waves of pain-shot darkness that threatened to engulf him. He fought . . . fought . . .

And failed.

CHAPTER 16

The camp had awakened at four in the morning and begun moving south, traveling through night-shrouded jungle with a confident certainty that Batman found astonishing. It was so dark that he could barely make out the shape of Phya walking a few feet in front of him. Somehow the Karens at the head of the long, snakelike column picked their way along forest trails that were all but invisible, and the rest trailed after, walking in touching distance of the person ahead.

Eventually, the sky grew lighter, but there was no true dawn. By the time Batman could clearly see his surroundings it was raining, a misty, intermittent drizzle that turned the ground to soup and soaked the Americans through to the skin in minutes.

By Batman's calculations, they'd been traveling south long enough that they *must* be in Thailand by now, but there was no sign of a border, no challenge by either Thai or Burmese patrols. For some time he'd been aware of the sounds of jet aircraft overhead, though the planes were hidden by the low overcast. They were passing on what might have been a regular schedule, one following another at intervals of three or four minutes. No doubt the Royal Thai Air Force was up in force searching for the two of them. The engine sounds weren't right for Tomcats or Hornets. Possibly, he decided, they were Thai F-5 Freedom Fighters.

177

At last, the column halted. Batman crouched at Malibu's side just off the trail, as Karen tribesmen moved silently through the thick vegetation on all sides.

Suddenly, all were gone.

Malibu, still lying on his stretcher, propped himself up on his elbows. "What's goin' on, buddy?"

"Beats me," Batman replied. "No one's told me anything." Even Phya had vanished into the bush, and for several long minutes it felt as though the two Americans were completely alone. Insects *keeked* and chirped among the branches as rain continued to drizzle through the leaf canopies overhead and drip to the wet ground. Once more, the wilderness seclusion was shattered by the jet-thunder noise of an airplane flying low overhead, traveling north to south.

Two camo-fatigued shapes materialized at his side so suddenly Batman started. He wasn't yet used to how silently these people could move in the forest and how well they made themselves blend in.

"Phya!" he hissed, recognizing the girl. "What in the hell is—"

She laid one slim hand across his mouth. "No talk," she said, her voice scarcely above a whisper. "Leave friend. You come."

Batman's mouth tightened. "Look, lady. I don't know what the hell your game is. But I'm not going anywhere until you tell me what the score is. And I'm not leaving my RIO. . . ."

Phya shook her head, though whether in exasperation or because she didn't understand, Batman couldn't tell. She plucked at his sleeve. "Come! Colonel Htai want!" She indicated her companion, a heavyset Karen warrior with an M-16. "Van stay friend! You come!"

Impasse. Batman patted Malibu's shoulder. "I'll be back."

"Hey, take your time, dude. I'll just, like, commune with nature."

"Silence, please!" Phya's eyes were on the surrounding jungle.

Leaving Malibu and the soldier called Van, Batman allowed the girl to lead him farther along the path. He followed her up a slope, winding back and forth until they approached a clearing at the top of a broad, flat hill. Other Karens were there, crouched motionless and nearly invisible among the leaves.

Htai acknowledged his arrival with a curt nod. "We've arrived," the Karen leader said.

"But?" Batman said. He'd heard the warning . . . and the uncertainty in Htai's voice, heard the urgency and worry in Phya's. Something was wrong.

For answer, Htai passed Batman a pair of travel-worn German 7x60 binoculars. The American lay on his belly at the edge of the forest and looked into the clearing.

U Feng! They'd made it after all! The relief was palpable as Batman steadied the binoculars in his hands and swept the compound. He could see the tower easily, as well as the rows of low barracks and storage buildings beyond the airstrip. Barbed wire was strung along the perimeter twenty yards from the treeline.

"What's the problem?" Batman asked Htai. "You did it! This is U Feng!"

"Soldiers wrong," Phya said. She was studying the compound without the aid of binoculars. What had she seen . . . ?

Batman brought the field of the binoculars onto a group of men and held it steady. There were twenty or thirty men, more a mob than a military unit, making their way through the drizzle among the barracks buildings.

And then the reality hit Batman like a blow between the eyes. Soldiers wrong indeed! In the whole time he'd been in Thailand, never once had he seen a sloppily dressed or slovenly-looking Thai soldier. The Thais seemed to be universally fastidious about their uniform and equipment. But *these* troops . . .

Their uniforms were as mismatched as those worn by the Karens. A few wore helmets, others straw hats or ball caps, while most preferred boonie hats or berets. Their weapons too were an unlikely mix from various countries, but the AK-47 predominated. Even across five hundred yards, Batman could recognize the Soviet bloc weapon with its curved, thirty-round banana magazine.

Batman blinked as he lowered the binoculars. "Civilians?" he said, half to himself. "Some kind of militia?"

That didn't explain the Soviet equipment.

Thunder boomed in the north.

"Those aren't Thai soldiers," Batman said. "I don't understand."

"Neither do we," Htai said. "But it is not good."

As if on cue, an incoming jet aircraft dropped beneath the clouds half a mile north of the runway. Batman did not need to turn his binoculars on the sleek, delta-winged jet as it descended toward the base, its wheels unfolding for a landing. He'd seen plenty of airplanes like that one . . . though usually the sightings had been made from the cockpit of his Tomcat.

A MiG-21. Through the binoculars, he could make out the silver-gray paint scheme, with red accents on rudders and control surfaces. Strangely, though, the usual red stars or other national emblems were missing. The plane touched down on the runway and slowed, its tiny, circular drogue chute popping and fluttering behind the tail. He had several long seconds to study the aircraft through his binoculars. Yes . . . he could see a spot on the tail where something had been painted out. *Someone* had covered up the markings, making the aircraft anonymous.

Just like the MiGs that had attacked them over the border two days earlier.

Whose were they? MiG-21s were common enough in this part of the world. Vietnam had one hundred fifty of them in her air force, while India flew over seven hundred. Little Bangladesh operated perhaps twelve. The People's Republic of China flew their license-built J-7s. At this range and angle, he couldn't quite see enough detail to be sure which of several possible variants this one might be.

One thing was certain. That MiG was not part of the Western-stocked Royal Thai Air Force. Hell, it wasn't even Burmese; as far as Batman knew, the Burmese Union used

American-made aircraft. He remembered Htai's expression as they'd discussed the United States supplying Burma with arms and equipment, and felt his face flush.

He continued to study the air base. Far across the compound, near the low, flat buildings utilized as hangars, he could make out a number of aircraft parked close together, their outlines broken by layer upon layer of heavy camouflage netting. He studied the group for a long time until he was sure. There were more MiGs there, at least a dozen of them. Moments later, a fresh peal of thunder marked the arrival of another, coming in low from the north.

Who was occupying U Feng . . . and where were these MiGs coming from? Whoever was behind this was no friend of Thailand, that was certain. He wondered if the soldiers he was looking at now had simply stormed out of the jungle and overrun the base, or if some trickery had been involved. Certainly, that mob didn't look disciplined enough to take on the Thais, not on even terms anyway.

"Damn right it's not good, Htai," he said at last. "Who the hell are they?"

"I don't know," Htai said softly. He pointed. "That group over there is wearing Burmese uniforms. So are the sentries in front of the tower. Those over by the barracks might be militia . . . or the army of some warlord."

"What Burmese do here?" Phya said. "This far from nearest Burmese base!"

Batman shook his head. "I don't know what the hell's going on," he said. "But Malibu and I can't go in there."

"Agreed," Htai replied. "You'll have to stay with us awhile longer."

"We kill Burmese?" the girl asked.

"No." Htai was firm. "Our scouts have already counted at least a thousand men in that compound, and others are stationed in the forest around us. But perhaps our American friends would like to go in and give them a good word for us?"

He smiled at his own black humor, but Batman didn't respond. He had just sighted something else, something guaranteed to turn any aviator's heart cold.

At the far southern end of the airfield, nearly a mile away, he could make out a tracked vehicle. Three missiles—three *large* missiles—were resting on launch rails on the vehicle's back. Batman recognized it at once, the mobile launcher for SA-6 missiles, code named "Gainful" by NATO. He could see the incessant circling of a nearby radar tracking dish.

He remembered the tracks he'd seen by the riverbank. Someone was bringing these things into Thailand in numbers, driving them along the river valley, then cross-country through the jungle.

That someone was invading Thailand, and Batman didn't even know who the invader was. And with SAMs, MiGs, and a thousand troops, they were going to be damned hard to stop.

1000 hours, 19 January
A Warehouse, Bangkok

"Awake now, Commander?" a voice asked from behind the light. It was a cultured, educated voice but carried an accent. Thai? Tombstone didn't have enough experience with Oriental languages to be able to tell. "I see you are. I'll give you a moment to . . . adjust to your surroundings, yes?"

The voice added a few sharp words in an Oriental tongue. Tombstone heard water splash, and then something cold and moist rubbed against his face, a wet cloth. He blinked. He could see faces now, several of them a few feet from his own. Several portable lights had been set up, and he was bathed in their glare.

Slowly, Tombstone became aware of a universe of pains and discomforts. The back of his head was throbbing, a crack-skulled agony where he'd been clubbed at least twice by a pistol butt. His arms were stretched above his head and supporting his entire weight. Pain burned in his back, arms, and hands. Looking up, he could see the handcuffs on his wrists, the chain linking them draped across a meat hook suspended from the ceiling. His ankles had been tied, then secured to an iron pin embedded in a steel bucket full of concrete. He could twist against his bonds, but he could move very little.

This was a warehouse of some kind. Stacked crates and boxes created a labyrinth of walls within a large, high-ceilinged storeroom. A clock just visible on the nearest wall read ten o'clock.

He was two hours overdue at the ship, but that didn't mean very much, not here, not now. No one could possibly know where he was.

As Tombstone's head slowly cleared, he was able to focus on the ring of men surrounding him, just inside the circle of light from the tripod-mounted lamps. He was still naked. That and his helplessness contributed to a growing and overwhelming sense of *vulnerability*.

"So! If you are ready, Commander Magruder, we will begin. I fear I am in something of a hurry, so our methods will be, of necessity, somewhat brutal and direct."

The speaker stepped into the circle of light. He looked Chinese. Glasses and gray hair gave him the look of a mild-mannered professor, but there was a hard glitter in those black eyes which chilled. He wore civilian clothing, a flower-print sports shirt and slacks. In his hand he carried a black tube, something like a policeman's billy club, but made of metal and plastic instead of wood.

Tombstone licked his lips. His tongue felt thick and swollen, and his mouth and lips were dry. He had difficulty forcing words out. "Who . . . who th'hell are you?"

"My name is Hsiao Kuoping, though that is not important now. What is important is *this*."

Hsiao's hand snapped up, smacking the end of the club he held into the American's belly. There was a crackling sound, and liquid fire seared between Tombstone's navel and his groin. Muscles spasmed, and he jerked and twisted against the handcuff chain and the rope on his ankles. His knees tried to flex, to curl his body into a tight ball, but the cement-filled bucket kept him stretched rigid against the hook overhead. Tombstone's scream was as completely involuntary as it was unexpected, yanked from his throat in an explosion of raw pain.

Hsiao withdrew the rod, fingering it. Tombstone, blinking back the tears and the red-tinged haze which threatened to cloud his vision, could see the electrodes in the thing's business end, the red button on the other. A cattle prod.

"*Pain*, Commander," Hsiao continued. "Pain is soon going to become the single most important aspect of your existence." With deliberate slowness, Hsiao reached out again, sliding the end of the prod between Tombstone's knees. Tombstone gasped at the touch . . . but the current was off, the head of the prod only slightly warm. His interrogator dragged the rod up . . . up . . . up between his thighs until the electrodes nestled beneath his scrotum.

The terror Tombstone felt at that moment was far worse than anything he'd ever known in his life. He could look into Hsiao's eyes two feet below his own and *know*, without a shadow of a doubt, that the man's thumb was about to come down on that red button set in the prod's plastic base. Anticipation and the searing memory of the pain he'd just experienced made Tombstone's stomach twist, and he was afraid he was about to be sick.

Hsiao smiled at him. "I promise you, Commander, that you will come to know pain very, very well in the next few hours . . . unless you tell me exactly what I wish to know . . ."

By the clock on the wall less than an hour passed, but it was an hour which crawled through an eternity, endless questions punctuated by seemingly random applications of the electric cattle prod. There were five men besides Hsiao, a scarred civilian named Phreng and four others who Tombstone thought might be soldiers, though they did not wear uniforms. Once, Hsiao referred to those four as his "Burmese assistants," which did not explain for Tombstone what they were doing in Bangkok. After the first few minutes, Hsiao turned the merely physical aspects of the interrogation over to the others, standing by only to ask the questions themselves.

Tombstone remembered very little of the details of that hour, but the pain, the sheer horror of being deliberately and methodically *hurt* while being physically helpless, took more of a toll on his mind than on his body.

Hsiao removed his glasses and polished them on a flowered shirttail. "Once again, Commander. We know that *Jefferson* has both antiaircraft missiles and a close-in defense system called Phalanx. What we need to know is if those systems are operational while your ship is in port."

The air stank with the by-products of the interrogation, with the sour-mingled stenches of vomit and feces, urine, blood and burnt hair, and fear.

"Go . . . hell . . ." Tombstone's lips were swollen and bloody, and the words came out cracked and distorted.

Hsiao nodded to Phreng. "Again."

Tombstone watched through swollen, slitted eyes as the grinning Thai extended the prod again. The contacts brushed against the tender skin of his armpit.

When the ragged echo of the scream had died away, Hsiao shook his head sadly. "Don't think you are helping anybody by being so . . . noble, Commander. We have all the information we need, courtesy of three of your seamen." He pulled a notebook from his pocket and flipped through the pages.

"Yes, here we are. Signalman Third Class Charles R. Bentley. Radarman Third Class Frederick K. Paterowski. Seaman Ernesto Rodriguez. These men told us everything we wanted to know. They were quite thorough in their rundown on *Jefferson*'s defensive systems. We know, for instance, the operational parameters for the VPS-2 search and track radar incorporated in the Phalanx CIWS." He read the letters from his notebook, letting each fall like a blow. He flipped the notebook shut. "All we require from you, Commander, is *verification*. You are an aviator. Your life depends on the way your ship's defenses work each time you approach the *Jefferson* for a landing. If you give us this verification, I promise you that you will spare yourself a great deal of unpleasantness!"

Tombstone remained silent.

At this point he wasn't entirely sure why he *was* holding out.

Concepts such as duty and defense of country seemed remote indeed each time Phreng's thumb came down on the cattle prod's firing button.

What was not remote was the purpose behind those questions.

"Shall we talk about aircraft approach procedures, Commander? What if a Thai helicopter wanted to land on *Jefferson*'s flight deck? Who would they call? What would they have to do?"

The silence was broken only by the harsh wheeze of the Tombstone's breathing. So many of Hsiao's questions were like that . . . questions which could be assembled into only one pattern that made any sense at all.

These bastards were planning some sort of attack against the *Jefferson*. Possibly they were terrorists, possibly something else. All Tombstone knew was that the lives of his shipmates might well be riding on whether Hsiao got the verification he demanded.

"You are being needlessly stubborn. You must know we will get what we want sooner or later." Hsiao gestured to Phreng for the cattle prod. Stepping close to Magruder, he slapped the rod against his open palm for effect. "I will have the information I require, Commander. I *will* have it out of you! You can give it to me freely or I can tear it word by word from your broken body, the way a fisherman guts a fish!"

When Tombstone still didn't answer, Hsiao shook his head. "Perhaps, though, we are following the wrong approach. We hold two friends of yours prisoner, you know. Lieutenant Commander Bayerly . . . and your pretty friend, Pamela Drake." He paused and smiled. "You see, we . . . how do you say? Hold the aces. I'm sure you don't want your *lover* subjected to the same sort of treatment that you have been experiencing."

The words were as sharp as the discharge of the prod. Tombstone wrenched wildly against his bonds, summoning all his strength in a useless struggle against them. Hsiao, standing only two feet away, laughed up at him.

His need to strike back drowned everything else. Summoning what moisture he could in his dry mouth, Tombstone snapped his head forward, and a glob of spittle mixed with blood struck Hsiao's face. *"Fuck . . . you . . . !"*

Hsiao darkened. Throughout the past, hellish hour the Chinese interrogator had never lost his temper, but now he whipped the prod up, jamming the tip into Magruder's groin. Tombstone's body twitched and spasmed as fire seared along every nerve, every muscle. His mouth gaped, screaming, but there was no sound. He hung suspended in a deadly dance of snapping, convulsive agony. Hsiao continued pressing the prod's button over and over, again . . . again . . . again . . .

Then the current ceased, and Tombstone sagged from the hook, sinking into the black comfort of oblivion.

CHAPTER 17

1315 hours, 19 January
The Warehouse, Bangkok

Pain. It had become a part of him, a part of his very existence.
Tombstone opened his eyes and his surroundings swam blearily
into focus. He was in a small and empty room, probably a
supply closet of some kind, with a light fixture hanging out of
reach from a high ceiling and a single wooden floor which
looked as solid as the concrete block walls around them.
Tombstone was lying on a cot, wrapped in rough army blankets
with his feet propped up on several pillows. The handcuffs
were gone. His captors, evidently, were taking care to see to it
that he didn't die of shock between sessions.

Memories of the ordeal flooded back, and he squeezed his
eyes shut. Chief among his emotions was shame. He could
remember the taste of his own fear while hanging on that hook,
remember losing control of his bladder and bowels, remember
screaming until his throat went raw.

Finally, at the end, he'd not been able to scream . . . only
jerk and twist under the terrible fire of Hsiao's cattle prod until
blackness had taken him.

Struggling against weakness and the nausea clawing at his
stomach, Tombstone managed to kick free of the blanket and
swing his bare legs over the side of the cot.

Vertigo nearly claimed him, but after a few minutes of
deep breathing, the dizziness receded, leaving him light-

headed . . . but conscious. His injuries, while painful, were not serious. There were angry-looking raw patches encircling his wrist and ankles where his bonds had chewed away at his skin, and inch-long burns everywhere that the cattle prod had arced and sparked instead of making a solid connection. Every muscle in his body felt stiff and sore, as though he'd been methodically worked over with a ball bat, and each movement threatened to overturn the delicate balance of pain and empti-ness in the pit of his stomach.

The *real* injuries, he feared, were in his mind. There were tremors in his knees and hands still, and a fear-born, cramping hollow in the pit of his stomach where the terror threatened to rise again at any moment.

Something which might be a bundle of wet rags in the far corner of the room caught his eye. Shakily, he stood up and took a tentative step toward them. . . .

No . . . !

The overhead light illuminated raw horror, three bodies dumped against the concrete wall as though casually discarded there. Tombstone squeezed his eyes shut, trying to turn away, but that first stark, blood-smeared image remained burned in his eyes and his mind as though branded there. Control over his empty stomach failed and he sank to his knees, retching, trying to rid himself of the sight and unable to do so.

Finally, reluctantly, his heaving stomach quieted.

While the public image of hero had been troubling him, Matthew Magruder was no coward. On the contrary, he was an aviator in the U.S. Navy. The ability to pilot an F-14, to land on an aircraft carrier in conditions ranging from calm seas to stormy pitch-darkness, to face enemy aircraft in one-on-one aerial duels reminiscent of the knightly jousts of another age . . . this set him apart from other men in training, in discipline, in sheer nerve.

But always before when Tombstone had faced death, it had been in the cockpit of an aircraft. There, death was a constant possibility . . . but as a flash, an instant of terror followed by painless nothingness. He stared down at the torn and tortured bodies sprawled on the concrete and for the first time felt the reality of another kind of death, not the clean death of aerial knights, but a filthy, lonely, agony-wracked ending that would go on and on and on. . . .

"Your shipmates," Hsiao said. Tombstone turned. He'd not even heard the door open behind him. "Bentley. Paterowski. And Rodriguez. It took them most of last night to die. Toward the end they were actually begging Phreng to be allowed to tell what they knew. After that, they begged for death."

Tombstone could not take his eyes from the bodies. What had Hsiao said earlier? *I can tear it word by word from your broken body, the way a fisherman guts a fish.* . . .

The comparison was gruesomely realistic.

Hsiao stepped aside, allowing Phreng and one of the Burmese to enter. "Take him."

They half led, half dragged Tombstone from the room, leading him through the maze of stacked packing crates and boxes which filled most of the warehouse floor proper. At the place where the meat hooks were suspended from the ceiling, centered in the glare from the tripod-mounting lights was a table, ominously bare except for lengths of clothesline secured to each leg.

The wood of the tabletop was splotched with brown stains, and Tombstone wondered if that was where the three sailors had died. He shook his head, trying to clear his mind. Horror held his thoughts in a vise.

There were two chairs nearby, and he felt a moment's icy shock. One of the seats was occupied by Bayerly, his wrists handcuffed behind the chair's back, his ankles tied to the front legs. Hsiao had said that Bayerly was a prisoner, but Tombstone hadn't been able to tell whether that had been truth or an attempted bluff. Like Tombstone, Bayerly was nude, and his body showed the savage red burns and welts of an interrogation session with Hsiao's cattle prod. His face looked terrible, puffed and marred with livid bruises where he'd been beaten, and there were streaks of blood around his swollen lips. He was sagging to one side in the chair, held upright only by his manacles, and looking as though he'd been undergoing interrogation for the past hour or two while Tombstone had been unconscious.

Roughly, Tombstone was seated on the other chair, handcuffed and tied.

"This time we will try a different approach," Hsiao said. He gave a signal, and there was a sound of scuffling in the darkness. Then two of the Burmese entered, holding a struggling, naked woman between them.

"Pamela!" Matt called, her name wrenched from him by the shock of seeing her . . . here.

"Matt!" she screamed. Her blond hair, in wild disarray, swirled about her shoulders as she tried to look at him. "Matt! Who are they? What do they want! *Matt!*"

"Put her on the table," Hsiao ordered with a curt gesture. "On her back."

Her captors dragged Pamela to the table and forced her down. As they tied her hands and feet, Hsiao turned to face Tombstone and Bayerly again. "Both of you have had a taste of our hospitality at first hand. Now we will let you *watch* that hospitality demonstrated with another."

"You son of a bitch! Let her go!" Tombstone wanted to beg, to plead . . . knowing at the same time he could do nothing. "She doesn't know anything. . . ."

"I quite agree. But the point, you see, is not to extract information from her . . . but from *you*." He walked over to the table, reached down, and took a handful of golden hair. "You remember what we did to Bentley and the others?" he asked. "How long, do you think, before we reduce this lovely creature to the same condition? How long can we keep her conscious . . . *aware*? How long will you be able to watch us work on her?"

Pamela twisted her head to the side, trying to bite Hsiao's hand. He snatched his hand back and chuckled.

"Her fate is entirely up to you, gentlemen. Tell us what we want to know and we will release her. Either of you can save her, at any time."

Tombstone lunged forward in the chair, feeling the steel of

the handcuffs bite the raw patches circling his wrists. "You bastard! You can't get away with it . . . !"

"I already have, Commander." Hsiao held out one hand and snapped his fingers. Phreng reached across the girl on the table and handed him the cattle prod.

"Matt! Don't tell the bastard anything! Matt! *Matt . . . !*"

Pamela's scream an instant later rang off the warehouse walls, going on and on and burning itself into Tombstone's ears and mind as completely as the sight of the three bodies in his cell. "Stop it! Stop it!"

Hsiao lifted the prod. "Shall we start with the procedures for landing a friendly aircraft on *Jefferson*'s flight deck?"

Tombstone shook his head, helplessly torn between horror and rage. Blood pounded in his temples. He couldn't let them do this to Pamela . . . but to tell them what they wanted to know . . .

"For God's sake stop it!" Bayerly yelled suddenly, as though the words had been torn from him. His voice cracked, little more than a harsh croak. "Ask me! Ask me! I'll tell you! Whatever you want!"

Hsiao looked up, his expression one of mild surprise. "Indeed?" He seemed to be considering Bayerly's offer.

Tombstone turned his head and stared at the other aviator. Bayerly was sagging against the chair, his chest heaving as he gulped hungrily at the air, his eyes bulging with a desperate, consuming terror. His face was as pale as death, glistening under the lamps with a thin sheen of sweat.

"Bayerly, you son of a bitch . . ."

Hsiao gave an order, and one of the Burmese began untying Bayerly's feet. "Come," Hsiao said as he helped the prisoner rise unsteadily to his feet. "We will go someplace where we can talk in comfort."

"What . . . what about them . . . ?"

"Both will remain safe . . . so long as you cooperate." Supporting Bayerly with a hand under the American's elbow, Hsiao turned to the civilians and snapped something at them in Thai.

Phreng replied, the words singsong and incomprehensible.

His hand restlessly stroked Pamela's thigh. Hsiao barked a command. There was resentment in the Thai's face . . . then a curt nod, and he began untying the girl's ankles.

Moments later they were freeing him as well. It looked to Tombstone as though the worst of the horror might be past.

But at what cost? Somehow, the information Hsiao wanted was aimed at the *Jefferson*. What was Hsiao up to . . . terrorism? Holding a U.S. carrier for ransom? Whatever his plan, it might mean the death of hundreds, possibly thousands of his shipmates.

As two Burmese guards led him back to his cell, he knew it was up to him to warn *Jefferson*.

The problem was *how*? There was no way Hsiao and his henchmen were going to let them walk away free, not now.

And Bayerly was spilling his guts. Tombstone felt the desperation rising within his chest and wanted to scream, the torture as bad in a small way as the hour he'd spent that morning hanging from Hsiao's meat hook.

Try as he might, he could see no way out of this mess for any of them.

1624 hours, 19 January
Doi Chiang Dao, Northern Thailand

The Karen party had walked for hour upon hour, stopping rarely, always moving south. Batman lost track of how far they must have come; each forest-shrouded ridge was much like the one before . . . or the one ahead. His legs, especially his knees and thighs, shrieked agony at him throughout the morning. By mid-afternoon he felt a kind of bludgeoned numbness all over, and he had to concentrate with a single-minded fanaticism simply on placing one foot ahead of the next.

There were increasing signs of settlement, however. More than once, the Karens filed out of the jungle and across a road, usually a deep-rutted jeep trail, though occasionally it was pothole-cratered blacktop, a sure sign of civilization. They skirted several villages, and once crossed a large open space with the watery gleam of a rice field off to the left, reflecting the brooding gray of overcast sky and mountains.

The final climb left Batman breathless, and it was so steep that Malibu had to get off his stretcher and hobble along supported by two of the camo-clad natives. By the time the slope leveled off at last, the overcast had begun to break up, allowing intermittent shafts of light to illuminate the green-clad face of the mountain rising above them. The Karens halted at a point where jungle gave way to open ground and a dirt road winding along the face of the mountain.

Htai walked up to Batman. "It is time we parted," he said. "We have brought you as far as we can."

"Now wait a minute," Batman said. "What . . . you're just going to drop us off in the middle of nowhere?"

Htai gestured. "Follow that road. You will be able to find transportation there."

Batman looked up the road. More jeep trail than road, it looked as though it rarely saw traffic. If Htai was expecting the two of them to *hitchhike* back to civilization . . . !

He turned to argue with Htai, and stopped. The jungle was a green wall along the road, leaves and fronds stirring with the breeze. The Karens were gone, vanished.

"Htai!" Batman yelled. "Son of a bitch . . . *Htai!*"

Malibu leaned against his makeshift crutch and eyed the jungle. "Shit, buddy," he said. "I get the feeling they don't care for our company anymore!"

"Looks that way." The way the Karens had disappeared into the forest was eerie. What was it they were afraid of? "C'mon. We can't stay here all day."

Batman was tempted to walk down the road—the going would have been a lot easier—but Htai had pointed in the other direction. Batman didn't know what the Karen colonel's game was, but it would be better to do things his way, at least until this scenario played itself out. They followed the curve of the road along the mountain's flank for perhaps another hundred yards, as Batman's legs threatened to buckle with the unaccustomed strain and Malibu limped along with a grim and stoic silence which said something about his own pain and exhaustion.

The cave opened in front of the two Americans like an unfolding dream. More grotto than cave, it was visible in the side of the mountain like a slash between house-sized limestone boulders. Inside, the afternoon light filtered through a hole in the cavern's roof illuminating the alabaster face of a gigantic, carved stone Buddha.

Other carvings emerged from the dim recesses of the cavern, but Batman was momentarily spellbound by the sight of that largest figure. He took a clumsy step forward. The scene was so remote, so otherworldly it might have been a dream. Already, the light was changing, the carvings receding once more into shadow as the magic of that single shaft of illumination faded.

"Yoot!" The voice carried the whipcrack of authority. *"Yah klihun vahee!"*

They turned slowly and saw the Thai Rangers behind them, M-16s leveled.

"Lieutenants Wayne and Blake, sir," Batman said automatically. If these people didn't speak English, the two of them could be in a lot of trouble. "United States Navy."

One of the Rangers looked puzzled, and then his face creased in a broad smile. "Navy! You long way from ocean!"

The place, it turned out, was Chiang Dao Cave, normally a busy tourist site but deserted since the insurrection began. The only people in the area now were a detachment of Thai Rangers.

Batman looked past the man at the cavern, where the shadows were swallowing the stone Buddha. Nearby, the spires of a *chedi*, or temple, gleamed white against the sky. After days of mud, insects, and nagging uncertainty, the breeze-swept peace of the shrine, of *civilization*, seemed like a breath of heaven.

Within an hour, Batman and Malibu were in the back of a jeep, bouncing down the dirt road toward the town of Chiang Dao, where a government station had been established to assist the hill tribes living on the slopes of the surrounding mountains. An hour after that they were in a Royal Thai Army truck, jolting down Highway 107 toward Chiang Mai.

A telephone call from the government station had already been placed through to Sattahip and the *Jefferson*. By the time they reached the airport west of Thailand's second-largest city several hours after dark, a Navy helicopter was already there, waiting for them with rotors turning.

In another two hours they were back on the ship, and Batman had sworn that he was never dating another stewardess for as long as he lived.

1844 hours, 19 January
The Warehouse, Bangkok

It was dark outside as Hsiao completed work on the last set of operational orders. They were committed now, with *Sheng li* hanging on a single toss of the dice. Leaning forward at his desk, he used the intercom to summon Phreng.

"You sent for me, General?"

"Yes. Get the prisoners."

"Yes, sir." Phreng hesitated, then grinned. "Are we going to start working on them again?"

Hsiao heard the man's not very subtle emphasis on the plural "them." He knew Phreng had been looking forward to working on the girl, and the thought angered him. For Hsiao, torture was a *tool*, not a means for the gratification of twisted personalities.

He was not going to let Phreng enjoy that pleasure . . . not yet, at any rate. The Americans might yet have some value as hostages, and he didn't want them permanently damaged.

There was no need. Bayerly had given him all the information he needed.

"They are not to be hurt. Either of them."

Phreng's expression fell. "Yes, sir."

"Make arrangements for a truck . . . an army truck with a canvas top. We will take them out tonight."

"Yes, sir. Where are we taking them?"

"To U Feng." Hsiao tapped the end of his pen against the

maps spread out on the table before him. "We will want to be clear of the city before the festivities begin."

"Festivities, sir?"

Hsiao allowed himself a shallow smile. "Tonight we begin the final phase of *Sheng li.*"

"Tonight!"

"Yes. Now . . . have my driver bring the car around."

"Yes, sir. And your destination?"

"Lumpini," he said, reaching for the telephone on his desk. That was the name of a large park on Rama Four Road, less than two miles from Klong Toey. He'd used it for meetings with fellow conspirators before. "I have some final arrangements to make."

Phreng made a *wai* and backed out of the office. Minutes later, Hsiao was speaking the innocuous code phrases which would inform Colonel Kriangsak where and when his master would speak with him.

The attack on the *Jefferson* had to be carried off swiftly, before the Americans were aware of their danger.

It would not take long for the helicopters, already prepared for their mission, to reach the carrier from the air base at Sattahip.

CHAPTER 18

Tombstone and Pamela had been returned to the room where he had been held earlier. Mercifully, the bodies of the three seamen were gone, though the coppery stink of fresh blood lingered. Traces of red gore still streaked the concrete floor and pooled about the rusty drain in the center of the room.

Their clothes had been returned to them, though wallets, watches, money, and IDs were missing. Their captors had collected everything they could find back in the hotel room, searching for useful information. That he and Pamela were being allowed to dress was in itself encouraging. Possibly the worst of the ordeal was over.

They were going to be moved, Tombstone guessed. He didn't think Hsiao was going to dispose of his captives, not yet at least. Their Chinese interrogator was planning . . . *something,* something very big. He and Pamela would have hostage value for negotiations if nothing else, and Hsiao did not seem to Tombstone to be the sort of man who would throw away any advantage, however small.

His mind turned to Bayerly. An initial surge of anger died before it more than ruffled his thoughts. It was hard to blame Made It for breaking the way he had; Tombstone himself didn't know if he could have sat there and done nothing while they tortured Pamela.

The question for the moment was not Bayerly's cracking, but what could be done about the situation now.

As he sat down on the edge of the cot next to Pamela, she reached over and took his arm. He was surprised by the strength of her grasp as she leaned close and echoed his own thoughts. "Matt? What are we going to do?"

He glanced around the room without answering, looking at the walls. They might have been put together for eavesdropping purposes. Mikes could be invisibly buried inside the concrete walls. Pamela watched him studying their cell and silently touched her ear, her eyebrows questioningly arched.

She understood. Smart girl.

"I . . . don't know," he said, more for the benefit of any microphones than anything else. Damn it, they needed a *plan*. "All we can do is go along with them. Maybe they're planning to use us as hostages."

Pamela leaned closer, until her matted blond hair brushed his cheek. "Matt?" Her whisper was so low, Tombstone had to strain to hear it. "Matt . . . I know they may be listening. What do they want?"

The question ignited memories . . . waking nightmares of Hsiao demanding answers. Details on *Jefferson*'s defense posture in port. Details of approach procedures by friendly aircraft. The pattern was frighteningly clear.

He turned his head, nuzzling the blond riot of Pamela's hair. "They must be planning an attack on the boat," he whispered.

She shifted position, making Tombstone wince as she rekindled the flame of several injuries. "That's what I thought," she said. "Listen, one of us has got to get away and warn the *Jefferson*!"

"Agreed," he said. "And it's got to be soon. Tonight."

The situation looked helpless. If their captors were planning to move them soon, though, there was a chance, slim but real, for escape.

The hard part would be getting Pamela and Bayerly out. Bayerly might already be beyond his reach, since they hadn't seen the other aviator since Hsiao had led him away.

How to do it, and when? Jumping Hsiao's henchmen when they came to get them here in this room was out. Tombstone still ached in every muscle, and the burns all over his body were small, separate patches of agony where his clothing rubbed them. He would be no match for several opponents, all armed and watchful.

Or rather, he would be a match for them only if he was able to pick the time, the circumstances of his escape. When he moved, he would be able to ignore the pain.

But there would be no second chance.

He turned and let his lips touch Pamela's ear again. "I think they're going to move us soon," he whispered. "We'll try to make a break then. Watch me, follow my cues, and run like hell when I tell you. . . ."

She pulled back, shaking her head.

Silently he mouthed the words, "What's the matter?"

Pamela leaned close again. "Matt, we may not be able to choose. They may not take us together. Look, what I want to say is . . . if you see a chance, take it. Okay? Even if I'm not around. Even if you have to leave me behind."

The idea filled him with fresh horror, with denial, with memories of her stretched out on the table. He started to pull away from her.

Gently, she pulled him back. "*Think*, Matt! You've been through the wringer, and you look like hell! If they believe you're badly hurt, they may not watch you as closely as they will me. If you can get away without me, do it . . . please! *Please!*"

Numbly, Tombstone looked into her eyes for a moment, then nodded. There was no other choice, nothing to be said. He turned his eyes to the locked wooden door, and waited.

1923 hours, 19 January
Government Building, Bangkok

Colonel Kriangsak pounded up the steps to the Government Building, flashed his ID to the soldiers standing guard inside the doorway, then hurried through empty corridors toward his office. The building was almost deserted, save for a few staff personnel working late. That was just as well. He didn't want to have to stop and explain his actions.

It was time . . . *time*! His earlier doubts about Hsiao's ability to pull off *Sheng li* were gone now. Somehow, the former Chinese intelligence officer had extracted the information he needed from his prisoners. And the time to strike was now, before the Americans realized that they were in danger. According to Hsiao, two helicopters were already on their way south from U Feng, would be over Sattahip Bay within two hours.

And his part in the plan had to begin now, before those machines reached their destination.

Hurrying through the empty outer office, he went to his desk and picked up the telephone. *"Savahtdi!"* he said as the switchboard operator came on line. "Colonel Kriangsak Vajiravudh speaking. Give me a line to Sattahip. Major Chani Silapakorn, Army Air Operations. Quickly!"

After a few moments, a voice came over the line. "Colonel Kriangsak? This is Major Chani. What can I—"

"Listen carefully, Major. *The sun sets on two hundred years!*"

"The sun sets. . . ." There was a moment's hesitation from the other end of the line. "Yes, Colonel, I understand."

"Commence operations as planned. Your pilots have received the orders sent over this afternoon?"

"Yes, sir. Everything is ready."

"Excellent. Carry out your instructions, Major."

He hung up the phone. *The sun sets on two hundred years.* A nonsense phrase, actually, one made up by Hsiao as a code signaling the final phase of *Sheng li*. It was apt, however, and Kriangsak wondered whether Hsiao had chosen it deliberately.

Bangkok had become the capital of Thailand in 1782, a little more than two centuries ago, when the first of the Chakri kings, the founder of the current dynasty, had established his seat of power in what was then a fishing village on the Chao Phraya River. And when this night was over, the sun would indeed have set on two centuries of Chakri rule. If King

Bhumibol still ruled, it would be at the sufferance of the leaders of the coup under Kriangsak's command.

And Hsiao, of course . . . though Kriangsak thought it should soon be possible to ease the Chinese general aside from the halls of power in Bangkok . . . or eliminate him entirely. Hsiao Kuoping was more interested in dealing with the drug lords of the Golden Triangle than with controlling Thailand. Many options were open, and soon Kriangsak would only have to choose among them.

There was a delicious irony about the situation. In 1981, Kriangsak's father had died leading the attempted coup which had come to be known as the Young Turks' Rebellion. That rising had failed because the plotters had been unable to enlist the support of the King.

This time, though, it would be different. The King would support the coup, or . . .

Kriangsak made a second call, this time to another major in an army barracks in Bangkok. A third call went to the garrison commander at Don Muang. A fourth to a captain at the Grand Palace.

By the time he was done, men and machines were on the move throughout the Bangkok area.

There would be no failure this time, so long as Hsiao kept his part of the bargain.

The telephone receiver clicked in his hand. He held it to his ear, then smiled. Good. The city's phones had been knocked out on schedule. In the distance, he could hear the crackle of gunfire, and the first, faint wail of a siren.

Now, he thought. Now it begins!

1931 hours, 19 January
The Warehouse, Bangkok

The door banged open. Phreng stood outside the room, between two Burmese holding AK-47s. "On your feet," the Thai said. He too held an assault rifle, and its muzzle was directed squarely at Tombstone's chest. "Now!"

Tombstone stood with exaggerated slowness. "Where are you taking us?"

"Never mind that. Hurry it up!"

"He can't!" Pamela said, flaring. "You hurt him . . . !"

"We'll do a lot more to him if he doesn't move fast." Phreng gave her a leering, gap-toothed grin. "And we're not done with you yet, little *muu*. We were only just getting acquainted when we were rudely interrupted, no?"

They were led at gunpoint through the warehouse, Tombstone walking with a pronounced, halting limp, Pamela supporting him by one arm. A side door opened into an alley between the warehouse and another large, empty-looking building. An army truck filled the road, its motor running.

A bell clanged with an uneven rhythm somewhere in the near distance. Any seafaring man would have recognized the sound, the ringing of a channel marker buoy moving with the lap of the waves. They were near the water, then. The warehouse suggested a dockyard complex. This could well be the Klong Toey district, the rough waterfront area on the river which serviced Bangkok.

Phreng gestured with the AK, directing them toward the back of the truck.

Tombstone was already gauging his chances. There were Phreng and four Burmese, plus the driver, a brawny man who looked like a Thai dockworker. Six men, three with AK assault rifles. The odds were not good.

The Thai barked orders, and two Burmese closed in on Pamela. Standing to either side of her and pinning her arms, they manhandled her toward the truck. "Let go of me!" Pamela demanded. She twisted against their grip.

One of the Burmese bellowed with pain and rage as Pamela's foot caught him squarely in the kneecap. He released her as the girl jerked free, striking wildly at the other guard with her fist.

Phreng turned away from Tombstone. . . .

That was the chance he'd been watching for. Tombstone whipped around, smashing his left elbow into the side of Phreng's head. The Thai slammed back against the side of the truck, and Tombstone grabbed for the AK.

They battled for the weapon in the cramped space between warehouse wall and truck. Tombstone crowded in close, then snapped his knee up hard, aiming for the Thai's groin. Phreng screamed. . . .

And then Tombstone had the AK as the civilian dropped to his hands and knees on the pavement. The two Burmese with AKs stood just beyond, beside the truck's cab, one fumbling with the weapon slung over his arm, the other bringing his assault rifle up to aim at the American. Tombstone's finger closed on the trigger. An ear-splitting chatter of full-auto gunfire exploded in the night, impossibly loud in the tight confines of the alley.

One gunman crashed against the side of the truck, then dropped to the pavement. His partner slammed into the warehouse wall. Tombstone whirled and pounded around to the back of the truck. Where was Pamela? The guard she had kicked was just getting up off the pavement, tugging a revolver from the waistband of his pants. Tombstone smashed him in the face with the AK's stock.

Fresh movement caught his eye . . . Phreng, rising now with one of the dropped AKs in his hand. Tombstone fired, stitching Phreng's torso from groin to throat with bloody explosions.

"Pamela!" he yelled, rounding the back of the truck. Where was she? *"Pam!"*

There she was, on the far side of the truck! Another Burmese guard was holding her from behind, using her body as a shield as he backed away, one hand around her waist and the other clamped over her mouth. Tombstone's eyes met hers, and he saw the terror there.

In the same instant, the canvas curtains screening the back of the truck were thrust aside. Men were jumping out, armed men in uniform. . . .

And behind them, handcuffed to a railing inside the truck's canvas top, he saw Bayerly, staring back at him with eyes as wide and as terrified as Pamela's.

Tombstone jerked the rifle skyward, unable to fire for fear of hitting either of the American captives. A Thai soldier running toward him opened fire, and Tombstone felt something snap past his head.

A *Thai soldier* . . . ?

The alley seemed filled with running men now. More soldiers were arriving from someplace . . . the other side of the alley, from the inside of the warehouse. Tombstone ducked and whirled, seeking cover, but there was no cover in the alley, only trash-cluttered pavement.

He heard a man's yelp of pain, then Pamela's voice shouting in the darkness. "Run, Tombstone. *Run* . . . *!*"

Her scream was drowned by gunfire. Bullets sang from the pavement near his feet and whined off the wall near his head, but he was already running, pounding down the alley toward the open street beyond. Random shots snapped past as he rounded the corner, plunging into a narrow, poorly lit street.

Pamela had given him his chance to escape. If he let himself get caught again, his failure would be like a betrayal.

His lungs burning with the effort, he ran faster.

CHAPTER 19

1945 hours, 19 January
Klong Toey District, Bangkok

Bangkok was in an uproar, a beeping, screeching, milling-crowd panic that exploded on every side of Tombstone as he tried desperately to argue with the wizened driver of one of the three-wheeled taxis called *tuk-tuks*.

He was in trouble. He knew that. The *tuk-tuk* driver spoke almost no English, and he clearly wanted to join the crowd of vehicles and pedestrians surging away from the heart of the city. The unmistakable chatter of automatic weapons fire rattled in the distance, and Tombstone could see a ruddy, spreading glow which might mark the reflection of a large fire on the low-hanging clouds.

It was, Tombstone decided, a coup attempt, a big one, and the presence of those soldiers in the truck outside Hsiao's warehouse headquarters meant that the Chinese general was somehow behind it. It also meant that Tombstone couldn't know who to trust. There were soldiers on the streets. An M-113 personnel carrier was parked at a nearby corner, nervous-looking soldiers manning the Browning .50-caliber machine gun on its roof. Civilians streaming past the vehicle looked at it with expressions ranging from curiosity to fear. Tombstone had considered walking up, identifying himself, and asking to use a radio . . . but he didn't dare. Those troops might very well prove to be working for the wrong side.

He'd thought of and discarded several other options. He could find a public phone but he had no coins. The shops and businesses on the street might have phones, but every establishment he could see was closed and locked, the owner gone or hiding. If he tried breaking in, he could get arrested . . . and the question of whose side the authorities might be on rose again.

His best bet was to reach the American embassy. That was when he'd spotted the *tuk-tuk* and flagged it down.

But the driver didn't seem to understand. *"Tawee lahng bahee!"* he shrieked, gesturing wildly with his arm as Tombstone tried to block his way. *"Blaho! Blaho!"*

Desperate now, Tombstone placed both hands on the front of the tiny vehicle. His laboriously memorized Thai phrases had abandoned him. How did you say "I want to go to the American Embassy?" Damn! If this went on much longer, he was going to attract the very attention from soldiers or other interested parties that he wanted to avoid. He'd thought most taxi drivers in this city understood English. Why did he have to pick the one who didn't?

He searched his memory for the right words. *Sathan thut* . . . that was it. *"Amerighan sathan thut!"* he said. What was the word for *please*? *"Broad! Broad!"*

The driver's face worked for a moment, then he gave a reluctant nod. Tombstone sank into the *tuk-tuk*'s seat with a grateful sigh. *"Kawpkun,"* he said.

With its tiny engine popping, the vehicle wheeled back into traffic, threaded onto a side road, then turned north.

2035 hours, 19 January
Bridge, U.S.S. *Thomas Jefferson*

Commander Stephen Marusko enjoyed standing night watches as Officer of the Deck. It was peaceful, especially when the carrier was in port. So far this evening there'd been only two departures from routine . . . a fight in the crew berthing spaces and a fire and security watch reporting that his relief had not shown up, both incidents best left to the MAA duty watchstanders. There was some continuing activity on deck. The four ships of MEU-6 had steamed into helo range that afternoon, and several big Marine Sea Stallions were parked on the roof. So, too, were two of *Jefferson*'s four KA-6D tanker aircraft. One had just trapped; the other was being readied for launch at 2100 hours to refuel *Jefferson*'s CAP.

A flash of light to the east caught Marusko's eye. He paced to the starboard side of the ship and used his binoculars to scan the shore toward Sattahip.

Odd. The buildings belonging to the naval base were still blacked out. When the lights had gone out a few hours earlier, he'd ordered the incident logged but assumed the Thais were simply suffering from a local power outage. Several minutes later, all phone connections with the shore had been lost when the radio station receiving *Jefferson*'s ship-to-shore radio calls had gone off the air. So far, there'd been no explanation, but most likely it was some sort of technical glitch. Marusko had reported the incident to Captain Fitzgerald—loss of local phone services would mean inconvenience for those of the battle group's crews who were ashore this evening—but there'd been nothing else to do but watch and wait.

That flash could have been gunfire. Marusko thought again of the rumors floating around about a coup attempt ashore. Suppose the loss of phone service, the blackout at the naval base, were part of an attack by rebels?

Marusko had just decided to call Fitzgerald when the bridge batphone rang. The duty bridge watchstander held the headset out to him. "Sir? They want the OOD."

"Thanks." He took the handset. "Officer of the Deck."

"Bridge? This is Chief Paulsen down in CATCC. Are we expecting any VIPs aboard tonight, sir?"

"Negative. What have you got?"

"Two bogies inbound, sir. Range five miles. They say they're Royal Thai Hueys."

Marusko's eyebrows rose. "What do they want?"

"Ah, sir . . . they're requesting clearance to land. They've got the proper frequencies and protocol."

Strange. Some Thai VIP probably needed to talk to the

admiral. Marusko wondered if this had anything to do with the trouble ashore.

"Okay, Chief. Tell 'em to come on in, and pass the word to the Air Boss to give them plenty of room."

"Aye, sir." He heard Paulsen chuckle. "I'm not sure I trust these local drivers."

Marusko hung up the phone, then decided the event was out of the ordinary enough for him to call the Captain.

2036 hours, 19 January
American Embassy, Wireless Road, Bangkok

It had taken nearly an hour to reach their destination, and the *tuk-tuk* driver was not happy about the change in his travel plans. The sounds of the riot were no more than a few blocks away. Worse, Tombstone had no money, Thai or American, and the outraged little man was advancing on him, arms waving angrily and voice shrill when someone came up behind the aviator and put a hand on the his shoulder.

Tombstone started, then turned to see an American Marine in camouflaged helmet and fatigues. "May I help you, sir?" the Marine asked. Tombstone saw that he was a gunnery sergeant, that he was wearing full combat kit and that a magazine was plugged into the receiver of his M-16.

"Lieutenant Commander Magruder, Gunny," Tombstone said. He suddenly felt very tired and was having trouble speaking. "CO of VF-95, U.S.S. *Thomas Jefferson*. I need to talk to the boat."

The Marine grinned. The black skin of his face was glistening with sweat. "Yes, *sir*! I'm Gunnery Sergeant George Johnson. I'm off the *Jeff* too."

Tombstone tried to focus on the Marine. "*Jefferson?* What . . . you doing here?"

He put an arm around Tombstone's shoulders, supporting him. "All hell's bustin' loose all over Bangkok, Commander. And we've got a few thousand American tourists out there caught in the crossfire. C'mon. Let's get you inside." When the Thai driver started to follow them, still shouting what could only be curses and demands for payment, the sergeant bellowed at another Marine standing close by. "Palmer! Pay this man!"

Guided by Johnson, Tombstone stumbled into the brightly lit interior of the embassy. He was suddenly aware of how filthy he looked and felt, the grimy feeling accentuated somehow by the pristine interior of the mansion. Several Thai servants watched wide-eyed from across the marble hall, while two Marines in dress Class-As snapped to rigid attention.

"Looks like you've been through the wringer, sir," Johnson observed.

"Got . . . to call *Jefferson*," Tombstone said. He was so tired he could barely stand. His burns and bruises throbbed and chaffed beneath his clothing making any movement at all an agony.

"Right in here, Commander," the Marine said. He helped Tombstone through a door labeled "Communications." Inside, other Marines and several civilians were manning computer keyboards and radio consoles. "We've been having some trouble with the phones down there, but we can patch in a direct radio hook-up. We'll fix you right up."

Minutes later, Tombstone was talking to a communications officer on board the *Jefferson*.

2038 hours, 19 January
Bridge, U.S.S. *Thomas Jefferson*

"They're hostile!" Marusko barked, hanging up the phone. "Sound General Quarters! All hands to battle stations!"

The shrill rasp of the klaxon blasted from the 5-MC.

"CIC, Bridge!" he snapped. "Are you tracking them?"

"Yes, sir," the CIC watch officer replied. "Two bogies, bearing zero-nine-five, range now four-one-zero-zero yards, speed one-three-five nautical miles per hour."

Marusko thought hard. Those helicopters *could* be what they claimed to be, their refusal to stand off the result of communications failure or misunderstanding. But Tombstone's warning moments earlier still rang in his mind: the coup leaders were planning something against the *Jefferson*, probably an approach by something involving one or more helicopters.

For many years, security had been a major concern of U.S. ship captains and carrier group admirals in every ocean of the world. Aircraft carriers were large, expensive, and extremely tempting as targets. During the Lebanon crisis of the early '80s, serious consideration had been given to the possibility that Syrian-backed terrorists might try to take out an American carrier patrolling off Beirut. Washington had worried about everything from speedboats or Piper Cubs packed with explosives to suicide commandos flying hang gliders, a tactic promptly dubbed "Cruise Druze" by the men forced to stand watch at .50-caliber machine guns mounted along the walkways outboard of the flight deck.

A helicopter loaded with explosives, or bomb-wielding commandos . . . They wouldn't be able to sink the *Jefferson*, but they could cause her a hell of a lot of grief.

2038 hours, 19 January
RTAF Helicopter 163, Sattahip

The UH-1 helicopter bore the red-white-blue-white-red roundel of the Royal Thai Air Force on its tail boom, but only the pilot was Thai, a disaffected officer who had been promised more money than he could expect to make in a lifetime of service to the government. Most of the officers involved in the coup had joined the rebellion because they were angered by what they perceived as inaction and stupidity on the part of the government in its handling of the Communist insurrection in the north. Very few of those mutinous officers, however, could have been induced to attack the American carrier. Ironically, both sides in the conflict still regarded the Americans as powerful and important allies, and a surprise attack on their nuclear-powered aircraft carrier in Sattahip Bay would not exactly endear the new regime to Washington.

But Lieutenant Thran Silatharudah would do anything for money. He'd first met Colonel Kriangsak when he'd been up for a court martial. The Royal Thai Air Force took a dim view of enterprising pilots using military aircraft to smuggle raw opium across the boarder from Laos. Kriangsak had gotten him off by conveniently misplacing some crucial evidence . . . then had recruited him for *Sheng li*.

The co-pilot, Thran knew, was Chinese, one of the battalion of trained pilots Hsiao Kuoping had brought first to Burma, then to Thailand as part of *Sheng li*. Thran had no idea what his reasons for being here were, but it didn't much matter. *Sheng li* had brought a number of wildly disparate elements together, but the plan itself seemed to be working well.

Lieutenant Thran eased the stick forward and let the Huey drift closer to the ground. The helo, Number 163, was an early UH-B transferred to Thailand at the end of the Vietnam War. Mounted on either side of the hull were two weapon pods, each carrying twenty-four 7-cm unguided rockets.

Below, the town and port area of Sattahip were blacked out, but he could see the spark and flare of small arms fire to the north where coup forces were engaging the base's loyal defenders. Ahead, out in the bay, the *Jefferson* was a splendid sight, aglow with lights from stem to stern.

"Arm rockets," he said.

"Rockets armed," the co-pilot replied.

The 7-cm rockets might be unguided, but they were accurate enough over a range of a mile or two, and an aircraft carrier was a very large target.

Thran's briefing, however, had stressed that he was not to simply dump his load of forty-eight rockets at random. Kriangsak's orders had emphasized that foreign national helicopters ought to be able to approach to within a few hundred meters of the ship, and at that range he should have a good shot at a most inviting target . . . the open elevator bay door leading to the carrier's hangar bay. He could see the open bay doors now, two of them on the ship's starboard side, one ahead of the island, the other behind. Yellow light spilled from both flat, oval openings in the carrier's hull. He concentrated on the one toward the *Jefferson*'s stern. Off to his left, the second Huey paced him.

Thran's finger caressed the firing trigger on the stick. If he could just get close enough—say, less than half a mile—some of his rockets were certain to enter the carrier's hull through the open elevator doors.

And the hangar deck, he'd been told, would be crowded with aircraft, with fuel, with explosives . . .

That man-made steel mountain ahead would look spectacular when it exploded.

2038 hours, 19 January
Tomcat 201, on CAP over the Gulf of Thailand

It was the skipper's bird, but Lieutenant "Nightmare" Marinaro had drawn Tomcat 201 for his evening stint on CAP when his own F-14 had shown an electrical fault during the preflight. He was cruising at fifteen thousand feet fifty miles southwest of Sattahip when his RIO, Lieutenant Mike "Sunny" Crampton, called him over the ICS.

"Hey, Nightmare? Sounds like the shit's hitting the fan back on the bird farm. They've just sounded General Quarters."

"They what?" He'd had his radio input off but he snapped it back on now. His earphones picked up the buzz and murmur of voices.

"Cowboy, this is Victor Kilo One-one," a new voice called. "Come in, Cowboy."

Cowboy was the call sign for Marinaro's CAP, while VK 1-1 was the Hawkeye currently coordinating air activities over the battle group. "Victor Kilo, this is Cowboy. Go ahead."

"Cowboy, we have two bogies closing with Homeplate." A rattle-off string of numbers, coordinates and bearings, followed. "Contacts may be hostile. Intercept and identify. Over."

"Rog." Marinaro brought the stick over and kicked the Tomcat's afterburners. "We're moving."

Thunder rolled across the gulf, trailing unheard behind the plane as the Tomcat broke the sound barrier. Hurtling northeast at better than Mach 1.5, it would take less than three minutes to close the range to the *Jefferson*'s unknown attackers.

2039 hours, 19 January
RTAF Helicopter 163, Sattahip

The American ship swelled rapidly to fill the Huey's forward cockpit windshield. The targeting reticle held steady on the after elevator door, now so close that Thran thought he could make out the shadowy silhouettes of men against the yellow glare of the hangar bay. As he watched, the hangar bay light began to contract, and he realized that the massive sliding doors of the elevator openings in the ship were closing.

"Range two thousand meters," the pilot said.

It was close enough, and if he waited any longer the elevator doors would be completely shut. He squeezed the firing trigger, and balls of orange flame flashed past the Huey's cockpit on either side, a rapid-fire spray of rockets in quick succession called ripple fire.

Thran was dead on target.

2039 hours, 19 January
Bridge, U.S.S. *Thomas Jefferson*

Captain Fitzgerald strode onto the bridge, still pulling on his lifejacket. "Situation, Commander Marusko."

"Two bogies, sir, identified as Thai air force helicopters, inbound off the aft starboard quarter." He gestured with the phone, still open to CIC. "They've been warned off but are still approaching. I . . . we just had a call from Commander Magruder, sir."

"Tombstone?"

"Yes, sir. At the American embassy. He said that the coup leaders were planning to attack *Jefferson* with helicopters. On the basis of his warning, I put the boat on GQ, but—"

"They're firing!" The warning from the starboard lookout was echoed by the call from the CIC officer over the telephone in his hand. Marusko turned and saw the rapid-fire, stuttering flashes in the night, the flares of tiny rocket engines streaking like tracer bullets toward the carrier.

"I've got the bridge, Mr. Marusko," Fitzgerald said in a voice as calm as death. He took the phone from CAG's hand and brought it to his ear. "CIC, this is the Captain. We are under attack. You may commence fire."

2039 hours, 19 January
Fantail, U.S.S. Thomas Jefferson

Private First Class Vince Kennedy swung the muzzle of his machine gun toward the approaching threat. He could not make out the helicopters well without lights, but he could see the flashes as they ripple-fired their deadly pods of 2.5-inch rockets.

He heard movement behind him, the high-pitched whine of automated machinery. Looking back over his shoulder, he saw that the squat, white-painted fire-hydrant shape of *Jefferson*'s aft Phalanx CIWS had taken on a life of its own. The six-barreled snout of the 20-mm Gatling gun swung to bear on the attackers, then shifted left, right, up, down in tiny increments as its pulse-doppler radar locked on.

Realizing that he was perilously close to the weapon's line of fire, Kennedy dropped flat on the deck. The Phalanx cannon fired an instant later with a buzzsaw shriek, spitting out fifty depleted uranium bullets each *second*. The radar tracked both target and rounds, adjusting the gun slightly to bring the two into perfect alignment. . . .

Like a string of firecrackers, the incoming rockets began exploding between the ship and the incoming Hueys.

Unfortunately, the range was too close, the rockets too fast for a one hundred percent sweep. An instant later, the first 2.5 inch rockets began slamming into the *Jefferson*.

2040 hours, 19 January
RTAF Helicopter 163, Sattahip

Lieutenant Thran saw the flash of blossoming explosions. A hit! Another . . . but then another, much nearer flash caught his eye. Turning in his seat, he saw Helicopter 179 burst into flame and hurtling debris, even as missiles continued to arrow from its weapons pods.

Instinctively, Thran pulled in on the stick and applied foot pressure to the tail rotor controls on the deck, swinging the Huey away from the fiery eruption to starboard. He was not sure what had happened but suspected that the American ship must have launched a missile of some kind. The night sky around him was filled with falling sea spray, and something heavy slammed into the Huey's tail boom somewhere aft.

Dimly, he was aware that the Chinese beside him was screaming wildly.

2040 hours, 19 January
U.S.S. *Thomas Jefferson*

Eight rockets from that first volley slammed into the *Jefferson* one after another, tearing metal, hurling shrapnel and debris into the sky.

At Elevator Number Three, starboard side aft of the island, the massive steel doors which had begun sliding shut moments after general quarters had sounded were almost closed. One rocket struck the outer door close beside the door frame, buckling steel plate and causing the door mechanism to grind to a halt with the shriek of tortured metal. Had the doors been all the way open when the rocket arrowed in out of the night, the damage might well have been catastrophic.

One rocket made itself felt through sheer bad luck. Coming in blindly, it struck a KA-6D tanker parked just aft of the island. The explosion sent a sheet of flame searing across the deck as crewmen scattered, trying to protect their heads and faces from the sudden heat. An EA-6B Prowler parked within inches of the tanker caught fire and exploded with a hammer-blow concussion, knocking sailors to the deck. Above the roar of flames, alarms shrilled endlessly.

Fire erupted into the night above the U.S.S. *Jefferson*.

2014 hours, 19 January
RTAF Helicopter 163, Sattahip

His Chinese co-pilot was dead. A depleted uranium slug had
passed through the Huey's deck, taken off the man's leg, then
passed through the bulkhead aft, and Thran had not even felt
the shock. Ahead, the night was ablaze as aircraft on the
carrier's aft deck burned.

After breaking off his approach, he'd dropped until his
landing skids were within a meter of the water. Thran didn't
know whether it was his wave-hopping or a lucky hit from one
of the rockets, but the Americans had stopped firing at him.

And he still had twenty rockets remaining in his pods.
His first thought was to break for shore, his mission
accomplished . . . but Thran was close enough to the American carrier now to see that the damage looked worse than it
probably was in fact.

If he could finish the job, the reward might be very rich
indeed. . . .

2041 hours, 19 January
Tomcat 201, on CAP over the Gulf of Thailand

Marinaro's Tomcat roared low across the waters of Sattahip
Bay. He'd seen the flash of rockets firing, the strobing of
explosions, and the dazzling stab of high-speed gunfire from an
aft Phalanx mount. One of the attacking helos had folded up
like crumpled aluminum foil as depleted uranium rounds
smashed through its hull, then erupted in a blazing explosion as
avgas ignited.

Then the aft deck of the carrier had fireballed. *Damn!*

And the second helo had jinked low and circled to the south,
apparently lining up for another shot.

There was no time to coordinate with the *Jefferson*. They
might have a lock on the enemy aircraft . . . or the damage
inflicted by those first rockets might have knocked out the
carrier's defense system. Marinaro knew that he didn't even

have time to get a missile lock on the enemy himself. In seconds he would be past the target . . . and another volley of missiles would have been launched.

But there was something else he could do. . . .

2041 hours, 19 January
RTAF Helicopter 163, Sattahip

He was less than eight hundred meters from the American carrier, which rose in front of his Huey like a gray steel cliff. He could see the aft elevator door, wedged partway open. A full volley into that vital spot might yet cause the fireworks Hsiao had hoped to raise. His finger closed on the trigger. . . .

And then a shock wrenched him violently against his seat harness, and the Huey was spinning wildly as a roar like thunder deafened him. He had a split-second's glimpse of afterburners shining like twin suns, of a cascade of water blasted into the sky by the shockwave of a supersonic jet.

Thran died as the Huey slammed into the water, still trying to bring his stricken ship under control.

CHAPTER 20

Tombstone leaned against the back of the pilot's seat, stooping so that he could look ahead through the helo's canopy. He wore a life jacket and cranial, which made his movements clumsy in the tight confines of the Huey.

He'd been shaken awake by Gunnery Sergeant Johnson at zero-dark-thirty that morning. A small mob armed with rocks and miscellaneous weapons had stormed the front gates of the embassy sometime in the wee hours and had been driven off when the Marines on the perimeter fired warning shots over their heads. One of the rioters had fired back and caught a Marine in the chest with a burst from an AK. Another had caught a bullet fragment in the shoulder. Both were strapped to stretchers in the back of the helo now, two Navy corpsmen in attendance.

And Tombstone, eager to get back to the *Jefferson*, was on the flight as well. He still hurt where his clothing rubbed the burns on his body, but he felt somewhat better for the more than six hours of sleep he'd had on the embassy floor. A battle had been fought outside the front door, and he'd not even heard it.

"This is Hardwire Eight-four-seven requesting clearance for final approach," the pilot said into his helmet microphone. "*Jefferson*, Hardwire Eight-four-seven. We have casualties on board. Please respond."

The Marine helo pilot glanced back at Tombstone after a moment. "We just got clearance, sir," the pilot said. "We'll put you down by the island."

Early morning sunlight gleamed from the surface of the ocean. Tombstone could see the carrier two miles ahead. The vessel was heading south, away from the helicopter, and its wake spread out from its stern like a pale blue arrowhead on the sea. The fires he'd heard about appeared to be extinguished, but there was a very great deal of smoke, a black, greasy stain against the sky above the carrier.

"They're making twelve knots," the copilot said. "Look at that smoke! What the hell happened down there anyhow?"

"Embassy told me a rocket attack," Tombstone said. "I gather they upped-anchor in a hell of a hurry."

"And I thought we had it bad at the embassy," the pilot said. "Okay, sir, hang onto your cookies."

Moments later, the Huey settled to the carrier's middeck, and Tombstone stepped aboard. A sharp wind across *Jefferson*'s bow kept the smoke clear of the flight deck. The 5-MC was blaring, "Now hear this, now hear this. Commence FOD walkdown." FOD stood for Foreign Object Damage, and the walkdown was an evaluation by all flight-deck personnel carried out routinely aboard Navy carriers. He could see the long line of sailors in dungarees or colored jerseys aft, stretched across the flight deck and walking slowly forward side by side, as each man searched for bits of metal, bolts, screws, or anything else which might be sucked into an aircraft's intakes with destructive result. They would be looking for bits of debris left from the explosions and fire the night before, a prerequisite to any air operations planned for the day.

Tombstone wondered what was being planned as he stopped to clear the Huey's turning blades and hurried across the deck toward the island.

"Stoney! Ho . . . Stoney!"

He turned, his eyes widening in surprise at the familiar voice. "Batman! You son of a . . . Where did *you* come from?"

"CATCC. CAG let me come down to play official greeter."

"No, you idiot! When did you get back? Where's Malibu? What happened . . . ?"

Batman grinned. "Malibu and I both got back aboard yesterday evening, courtesy of the Thai army and some . . . some rather remarkable people out in the jungle." He sobered for a moment, then continued. "Malibu's in sick bay. Nothing worse than a sprained ankle. And I think other questions had better wait."

"Why? What's going on?"

"Only about a million people on this tub want to question you, Tombstone. Starting with your uncle and his entire intelligence staff." He jerked his head toward the island. "They're waiting for you topside, in CVIC."

"Then I guess I'd better get up there." He'd been looking forward to a shower and a clean uniform, but it looked like he'd have to settle for a change to his flightsuit. Wearily, he started to climb to the 0-9 level.

0830 hours, 20 January
North of Phitsanuloc, Central Thailand

They'd pulled off the road at first light. Pamela and Bayerly were kept waiting in the truck until Pamela wondered if they were going to be shot. Then their guards bullied them out of the back of the truck and led them at gunpoint along a path to a spot well away from the road. The area was heavily wooded. Pamela saw soldiers everywhere, some resting in small groups underneath the trees along the path, others coming and going along the trail. The main encampment was a group of canvas tents heavily camouflaged with branches and palm fronds.

This, she realized, was a major rebel base. She could only guess at the location, but its presence so far from either Bangkok or the northern border suggested that the communist insurrection was far more widespread and better organized than anyone had realized. The soldiers around her were teenagers for the most part, armed with a motley collection of American weapons and the ubiquitous AK-47s. They did not look particularly formidable. Some swaggered or joked, but most looked simply scared. All, though, possessed an air of grim expectancy.

They were led to a cage, a narrow box of bamboo poles large enough for the two of them to sit side by side, but not large enough for them to stand or move around. A grinning Thai fastened the crude door shut with a length of chain and a padlock, said something incomprehensible with a harsh cackle of laughter, then left them alone. No one in the camp seemed to be paying them any attention, but Pamela was sure that any attempt to escape would bring them plenty of notice.

She was worried about Bayerly. He'd seemed withdrawn, almost shrunken in upon himself since her captors had thrust her in next to him back in Klong Toey. Each attempt to speak with him during the long, bumpy drive had been interrupted by a harsh word or gesture from one of the soldiers in the back with them.

"Commander Bayerly?" she asked when they were alone. What was his running name? She remembered. "Made It? Are you okay?"

The look he gave her was a mingling of horror and some inner pain.

"Listen, Commander," she said when he didn't answer. "Don't you go freaking out on me now. We're in a hell of a jam, and I'd like to think I'm not in it all by myself!"

"There's not much we can do about it," he said. He sounded distant, defeated.

"Maybe not. At least we could discuss our options."

"Options," he repeated. The word was bitter.

"What's with you, anyway?" she asked, exasperated. "Look, we should be trying to figure out how to get out of here while we can."

"Be my guest." He nodded toward the bamboo door with its padlocked chain. "It's not more than a couple hundred miles back to your hotel."

In this mood, Bayerly was going to be useless.

Pamela had a special talent, though, an ability to draw people out in conversation even when they didn't want to talk. She'd used it to good effect for years during her career as a television interviewer. The key was first to get the subject comfortable with the interviewer, feeling that she was on his side, then to get the subject talking about himself. It was simple in theory, but this seemed to be a rather difficult situation in which to test it.

"How long have you known Tombstone?" she asked.

Bayerly shrugged. "Maybe a year." He sounded totally disinterested. "Since I joined the *Jefferson*."

"Is he a friend of yours?"

"That hotdog? No way."

"Hotdog? I heard him use that word once. What's it mean?"

He gave a wan smile, and Pamela knew she'd broken through his outer defenses. "A show-off," he said. "Someone who's always pushing the outside of the envelope . . . and wants people to know it."

"That doesn't sound like the Tombstone I know. He struck me as rather reserved." She smiled. "For a fighter pilot, anyway."

He didn't reply immediately, and for a moment Pamela thought she'd lost him again.

"Yeah, Tombstone's okay, I guess," he said at last. "Some of the guys give him a pretty rough time about his uncle and everything, but he doesn't flaunt it. Not really."

"Why do you dislike him so much then?"

Bayerly studied her for a long moment. "Ah . . . I don't know." He looked away, and appeared to be studying the surrounding forest. "I know this is going to sound pretty damned cruddy, but I guess a lot of it is all the attention he was getting after Wonsan."

"What's cruddy about that?"

"Oh, you know. It's like I'm jealous about his Navy Cross. The hero treatment, and all that."

"Are you?"

"I don't know." He sighed. "Not really jealous, I guess. Tombstone was the one who got the shot at flying CAP for our forces ashore at Wonsan, though. And I was stuck flying CAP over the *Jefferson*."

"He got the glory and you didn't. Is that it?"

"Shit. He didn't do a thing that any other man in the wing couldn't have done."

"Granted. So what's the problem?"

Again, he didn't answer for a long time. "I guess to be honest, the problem is with me, Miss Drake," he said. "Not with him."

"You want to tell me about it?"

He regarded her through narrowed eyes for a long time. He shrugged. "Why not? But if you're looking for a story, I don't think much of your chances for getting it on the air."

She rested one hand on his knee. "I'd like to know, Made It. Really."

"Well . . ." He looked away, as though unable to meet her eyes. He seemed to be having difficulty knowing how to begin. "A year ago I was stationed in Washington, D.C. I'd just finished a tour of sea duty aboard the *America*. CO of one of her Tomacat squadrons." He gave an ironic smile. "Lady, I was on my way up. A tour as squadron skipper . . . and now a hitch at the Pentagon. Know what that means to an aviator?" She shook her head. "It means that the powers that be are grooming him for command. Command! After a tour in Washington, I'd have a crack at a CAG slot. Then another tour in D.C. maybe . . . all leading up to a carrier of my own some day."

"Sounds good."

"It *was* good. I was on Admiral Fitzroy's staff. God, that guy's only about four jumps down the pyramid from the CNO himself!" He gave a wan smile. "My career, to say the least, was off to a promising start."

Pamela read the pain behind the words. "What happened?"

"There was this girl. Sharyl Fitzroy."

"Fitzroy! Not—"

"Yeah. The traditional admiral's daughter. I don't think he cared for having a lowly lieutenant commander date his daughter, but she was the independent type, y'know? Anyway, I was the one with the promising career and all that, right?

"One night I took her to the Kennedy Center. She loved the

opera. There was a performance of *La Bohème*. . . ." He said nothing more for a time. Pamela waited quietly.

After a time, he continued. "Afterwards, we went out for a walk, down by the Potomac. A moonlight stroll, and all that. We were . . . attacked. Punks out joy-riding. Washington . . . Washington's got the highest crime rate in the country, did you know that?" She nodded. "There were three of them. They knocked me down, took my wallet. One of them grabbed her . . . dragged her off. They had a van parked nearby."

Pamela realized with a start that the man was crying. "It doesn't sound like something you could've helped."

He shook his head. "We shouldn't have been off by ourselves. Away from the crowds. Away from the lights. Bad judgment . . . at least that's what the admiral said later." His fists clenched. "*Damn it,* I was there on the ground begging for my life while they . . . while they . . ." He stopped again, and drew a long, ragged breath. "One of them shot me. It just grazed my scalp, but I guess in the dark and with all the blood they thought I was dead. They left me out there on the ground while they took turns with her in the van. Then they shot her, tossed her out. The police found us the next day."

"You were wounded. There was nothing you could have done anyway!"

"Maybe." He sounded bitter. "But I played dead, lay there and didn't make a sound. I thought . . . I thought maybe they'd let her go afterwards, but they killed her.

"So I got branded as a coward."

"I don't understand. Why?"

He looked at her as though trying to decide whether or not she was joking. "Let's just put it down to the Navy's old-boy network," he said, finally. "Admiral Fitzroy had lost his only daughter, and I was the . . . the fucking *wimp* who played dead while she was murdered. I got transferred real fast after that. Probably a good thing. Fitzroy might have shot me himself."

Slowly, he rubbed his mustache. "But the word was out, y'know? This man had gone as far as he can go in the Navy. Oh, nothing official, you understand. I was even assigned a

squadron skipper's slot aboard *Jefferson*. Wouldn't do to have
a former CO get taken down a peg. But it was damn clear I
wasn't going anywhere anymore.

"I suppose the real revelation came during the Wonsan
crisis. My whole squadron was held in reserve, while VF-95
went in to tangle with MiGs. You . . . you've got to understand, Miss Drake. A Navy aviator spends his *whole life*
training for the moment when he can strap on an airplane and
go up against MiGs, one on one. Most men never have that
chance.

"And I didn't either."

"You think Admiral Magruder has it in for you? That he
chose his own nephew instead of you?"

There was a long silence. "I don't know. Maybe not. It
seemed like it at the time. And something . . . something
happened on a flight a few days ago. Up by the Burmese
border. I did something stupid, see. Something I shouldn't
have done. CAG came down on me like a ton of laser-guided
ordnance, and I got relieved. It felt . . . it felt just like the
bastards had been waiting all that time just to see me busted."
He looked at her. "Like I said, pretty cruddy, right?

"The worst of it is, it looks like they were right. All of them.
I . . . broke. Maybe endangered my boat, my shipmates.
I . . . lost it." He looked away towards the woods beyond
the cage. "Maybe I never had it."

She didn't answer for a long moment. "Made It? Back in
that warehouse. When they were questioning you. Was that
why you told them you'd talk?"

"What do you mean?"

She couldn't help feeling that Bayerly must have been
reacting on some level to what was happening to her, compar-
ing it with what had happened to Sharyl Fitzroy. But he looked
so shaken now. Maybe it was best not to dig too deeply.

"Never mind," she said. "Made It . . ." She pressed
herself closer. "Hold me?"

Gently, almost reluctantly, he put his arm around her
shoulders.

She'd thought they were going to stay there at the rebel camp all day, but less than an hour later, uniformed men arrived in jeeps and began shouting orders. Soldiers kicked out fires, others gathered weapons.

And then Pamela and Bayerly were again on their way north.

1012 hours, 20 January
Fantail, U.S.S. *Thomas Jefferson*

Tombstone leaned against the guardrail and looked out to sea. The wake foamed out beneath his feet, spreading astern all the way to the horizon. The sky overhead was a clear and piercing blue, but there was still a dirty, oily tang to the air, the smell of burned rubber, plastic, and paint. He had the fantail to himself. The entire crew, it seemed, had turned to in the cleanup, making *Jefferson* shipshape again after the attack and fire. He could hear the thump and bang of repair crews working in the hangar bay, the sounds echoing down the open machine shop passageway at his back.

His debriefing, the preliminary part of it anyway, was over. It had been routine and automatic, a recounting of what had happened at the hotel, and afterwards, at the Klong Toey warehouse. Made It Bayerly's betrayal had been duly recorded. And it was a betrayal . . . whether the information which had led to the attack on *Jefferson* had come from him or from the three sailors butchered by Hsiao earlier. At the very least, Bayerly had provided Hsiao with the confirmation he'd needed, and quite possibly he'd provided details the sailors could not have known.

They were going to nail Made It if they ever found the guy again. Nail him . . . and why? He'd tried to stop them from hurting Pamela. The thought of what might be happening to the two of them at that moment made him shudder.

It felt as though he'd just reached a new low. He'd abandoned Pamela and Bayerly. And while he'd run in order to warn the carrier, the fact was that he'd *run* . . . leaving Pamela and a brother aviator behind. Hardly the behavior expected of a *hero*.

Slowly, he reached up and unzipped the breast pocket of his

flight suit, where a small lump of metal pressed against his chest. He pulled out the medal which he had retrieved from its case in his cabin only minutes earlier.

The Navy Cross. It lay in his palm, catching the afternoon sun, the blue and white ribbon bright and clean in the light. His fingers closed over it.

He was no hero. Tombstone *knew* that, knew it to his very bones, and all of the medals, all of the television interviews on Earth would not make things different. Heroes were men like his father who had laid their lives on the line trying to drop a bridge in downtown Hanoi.

Tombstone remembered his feelings during the Wonsan op. Half the time he'd been too busy to think, riding on pure training and instinct, and the rest of the time he'd been scared to death. Landing a damaged Tomcat on the carrier with his RIO wounded in the backseat . . . hell, what else could he have done?

He looked at the medal again. If it hadn't been for the hero nonsense, maybe none of this would have happened. Tombstone would have been flying the recon out of U Feng, not Batman. It would have been *him* in the jungle . . . and maybe Pamela would never have been involved.

He opened his fingers and looked at the medal again. Almost . . . *almost* he cocked his arm to hurl the bit of metal and cloth out into the pale blue wake.

Something held him back. Throwing away the medal would change nothing, accomplish nothing.

That, he realized, was what was gnawing at him more even than anything else. Pamela and Bayerly were *gone* and there wasn't a damned thing he could do about it. Tracking the captives through Bangkok's teeming streets was a job for the hard-pressed Thai National Police, not the U.S. Navy.

With a start, he glanced at his watch. Almost a quarter past . . . and an all-departments meeting had been called for 1030 hours. He just had time to make it up to CVIC. He pocketed the medal, then turned away from the railing and plunged back into the machine shop passageway.

CHAPTER 21

"Gentlemen," Admiral Magruder said. "I'm treating this as an act of war. Forces unknown, but possibly operating together with the communist insurrection in Thailand, have attacked this command."

It was silent within the Carrier Intelligence Center, save for the isolated creaks of men moving in the metal folding chairs which had been set up in rows. The chairs gave the large room the feel of an elementary school auditorium. Tension was high, an almost electric sharpness in the air. Every department head, squadron CO, and senior staff officer on the carrier was present. Admiral Magruder leaned against the podium, a large-scale color map of Thailand at his back. There were no TV cameras, but a VCR camcorder was being used to tape the meeting, for the record.

Tombstone leaned back in his chair and considered his uncle. The man had aged. Perhaps he was feeling the strain of his responsibilities, strains that had been on his shoulders since Wonsan. Then and now, it was largely his decisions which would determine peace or war, life or death for the men under his command.

The commanding admiral of CBG-14 surveyed the officers in front of him before speaking again. "The Captain, the Exec, CAG, and the Damage Control Officer gave me their assess-

ment a few minutes ago. In brief, damage to the flight deck is
minimal." He pulled a small notebook from his jacket pocket
and consulted it. "Repairs to the arresting-gear mechanism are
being completed now. Full flight-deck operations should be
possible within two hours. El Three will probably be out of
service until we can return to port, but we can maintain full
service on the remaining three elevators.

"Our total losses during the attack and fire amounted to three
aircraft destroyed, plus a further five aircraft downchecked by
the plane captains for repairs. The most serious losses were two
of our KA-6D tankers, one destroyed, one damaged. This
leaves us with only two tankers functional for air-to-air
refueling ops should we need them.

"Casualties, thank God, were light. Six known dead, four
more missing and presumed lost overboard. Eighteen men are
in sick bay, most from smoke inhalation."

He closed the notebook and looked up. "This is not a formal
briefing, gentlemen. It's a brainstorming session. We've been
hit. Hard. I want ideas, recommendations about what we
should do about it. All of you feel free to chip in. We'll kick
this off with a rundown on the situation from Commander
Neil."

Commander Richard Patrick Neil was an Irish Bostonian,
the Carrier Group Intelligence Officer for Magruder's staff. He
stood and walked to the front of the room, where he took the
admiral's place behind the podium. "Thank you, Admiral,
gentlemen. Well, to start with, our options appear to be strictly
limited." Neil's New England twang was sharply evident in the
way he said "appeah." He looked ill at ease. "After all that has
happened, we still don't know who the enemy really is. We
have a communist insurgency in the north with possible
Burmese involvement, student demonstrators and rioters in
Bangkok, and a military coup breaking out all over the country.
It is tempting to see these separate incidents as somehow
linked, but we cannot yet prove that. As yet, we do not know
who attacked the *Jefferson* last night."

"Shit," someone in the audience muttered. "I thought that

was obvious. We know it was the gook rebels who piloted those helos—"

"No," Neil countered. "We don't. They were RTAF machines and they were based at Sattahip. They may have been piloted by dissident officers, but that doesn't square with what we know about the coup so far."

"What do we know about it?" Admiral Magruder asked.

"That its leaders appear to be Thai army and air force officers who feel that Bangkok is dealing too softly with the communist insurrection. And that is what makes it unlikely that the attack on *Jefferson* was ordered by coup leaders."

He took a step back and unfolded a telescoping metal pointer to indicate areas on the map. "Up here on the Thai-Burmese border, we have a major rebel insurrection . . . probably led by the Communist Party of Thailand." The pointer slid along the border. "We have two separate incidents in this area, encounters with unidentified MiGs, Chinese J-7s, actually. In one of these incidents, one of our aircraft is shot down. Burmese involvement is suspected . . . but the present political situation does not support that theory. Burma had its first democratic elections in thirty years not long ago and is now making the transition from a military dictatorship to a Western-style democracy. There are certainly dissident elements within the Burmese military, but Rangoon denies involvement, and Washington accepts that statement at face value."

The pointer moved again. "Here is U Feng, a Thai military base captured three days ago by forces unknown. The Thais suspect the Burmese, working together with CPT rebels. Again, Rangoon denies involvement. Most of you know by now that two of our people are eyewitnesses to what's going on up there. According to Lieutenant Commander Wayne's debriefing report, there are a number of Shenyang J-7s currently based at U Feng. This solidly links the forces at U Feng with whoever is flying J-7s across the Burmese border but doesn't tell us anything more about who is responsible.

"Down here in Bangkok, and outside the base at Sattahip, we've had demonstrations, even riots, going on now for several weeks. Thai Central Intelligence believes these have been instigated by the CPT. That links them with the rebellion up north, of course . . . but not with the MiGs and the capture of U Feng.

"Finally, we have the military coup. It began at approximately 2100 hours on the 18th. It purportedly involves a number of high-ranking dissident officers who feel the government has been mismanaging the entire campaign against the rebellion in the north. The word is also out that U Feng would never have fallen if Bangkok had taken a stronger line against Burmese involvement in the north. Apparently, the coup leaders insist that the CPT rebellion is being sponsored by the Burmese . . . once again, something Rangoon categorically denies.

"So far, the coup has achieved limited success and appears now to be on the defensive. Apparently, only a few units have mutinied, and most army and air force regiments have remained loyal. According to reports, a large percentage of the Royal Thai Air Force has been crippled by sabotage on the ground, but fighting is light and somewhat sporadic. For the coup to be successful, it would have to win the approval of the King and his ministers. This is a basic factor of Thai politics, and so far that approval seems most unlikely.

"The Thai government has asked for our support through their embassy in Washington. We ourselves have heard very little from the government directly, and we seem to be getting mixed signals here . . . help us on one hand, get out and leave us alone on the other. Part of this may be due to people high in the government who are actually in sympathy with the mutiny and are deliberately confusing things. I should point out, though, that the coup leaders should be trying to cultivate American support, not attacking us. The Thai government has maintained close relations with the United States for many years and is our strongest ally in the region. Washington feels it is unlikely that coup leaders would order an attack on the *Jefferson,* since that would alienate us and isolate them politically.

"So, gentlemen, when it comes to the question of who attacked us last night, we are faced with a contradiction. The leaders of the military coup had the opportunity, using helicopters from the base at Sattahip, but they certainly did not have the motive, at least, not one we understand. The communist rebels have the motive—the anti-American theme of the demonstrations is rather evident—but for the most part they are peasants who wouldn't be able to get access to RTAF helicopters or Chinese J-7s, much less fly them. Finally we have the Burmese, who might possibly acquire J-7s or have pilots who could fly RTAF helos, but who have neither motive nor opportunity. The Thais blame the Burmese, but Rangoon claims they do not want a war with Thailand and are moving away from their Marxist past. They certainly don't want a war with us!"

Neil closed his pointer with a snap. "Where this leaves us, gentlemen, is adrift. *Someone* attacked us last night, but we don't know who. There appears to be no link between the various factions of the fighting in Thailand, certainly nothing which would explain a rocket attack against the *Jefferson.*"

No link, Tombstone thought . . . but there had to be one. He thought about the firefight in the alley in Klong Toey. Those had been Thai soldiers joining Hsiao's men, and Hsiao's questions had been aimed at finding a weakness in *Jefferson*'s defenses just hours before an attack was launched against her. There *had* to be a link between Hsiao and the coup!

Tombstone's debriefing that morning had been cursory, even rushed. He'd described to Neil and the other officers of the admiral's intelligence staff his capture and interrogation, with the emphasis on the man Hsiao and his questions. Tombstone wasn't sure that Neil even believed him, and he had to admit that a lot of what he thought about the Chinese officer was guesswork. He only had Hsiao's word, for example, that several of the other men at the warehouse were Burmese. What if Hsiao had been trying to make it look like the Burmese were involved, for reasons of his own?

"What about the reasoning behind the attack, Commander?" Dick Barnes asked. "I mean, what was the point?"

Neil shook his head. "Unknown. There are possibilities. Someone might be trying to get us involved in a war with

Burma. That is the DIA's guess, based on the attack made by the MiGs. Their theory is that the PRC is secretly ferrying J-7s to a remote base in Burma in order to provoke border incidents . . . and war."

"Maybe someone wants to frighten us off," a voice said.

"Another possibility," Neil agree. "The ultimate in 'Yankee go home' signs. Point is, we don't *know*. And while it's damned tempting to see some vast, international conspiracy behind everything that's going on, the real world doesn't work that way."

"And what is your recommendation, Commander?" Admiral Magruder asked.

"That we pull back and take a longer look, sir. We shouldn't get involved until we know what the real target is."

"What about this . . . this Hsiao Kuoping?" Commander Dick Barnes, the senior CIC officer, said. He was reading a pocket notebook he'd been writing in earlier during Tombstone's debriefing. He looked up. "Mr. Magruder described him as Chinese . . . and definitely in control of certain Burmese elements. That says conspiracy, doesn't it?"

"With all due respect to Commander Magruder," Neil said slowly, "we just don't have enough to go on. Certainly, there is nothing to link this Hsiao character or his Burmese allies with the coup leaders. It is possible, *possible* that Hsiao has something to do with the Chinese MiGs. I've queried the DIA files in Washington, and they report that Hsiao in indeed a high-ranking member of the PRC Intelligence community. A general, in fact."

"My God," Captain Glover said softly. The ship's Exec looked stricken. "Chinese Intelligence? Are you saying the enemy is *China?*"

"Possible, but unlikely." Neil did not sound sure of himself. "The DIA and the CIA are looking into it, but this could well be an independent operation . . . Hsiao setting up in business for himself."

That possibility had not occurred to Tombstone, but it felt right. If Hsiao was a high-ranking Chinese spy, what was he doing running things personally in Bangkok?

"It is possible," Neil continued, "again, only possible, that Hsiao was somehow connected with the attack on *Jefferson* last night. The questions he asked of our people point to that, certainly. But we cannot link Hsiao to the coup, except circumstantially."

Tombstone thought about that. He was certain that Hsiao was tied to the coup somehow because of the Thai soldiers he'd seen. There was a common factor, and it tied Hsiao in with both the communist rebellion and the Thai military coup. Some factor, some *person* . . .

Tombstone's eyes opened wide. The connection had been staring him in the face all along, and he'd not seen it.

Neither had anyone else.

Tombstone raised his hand. Neil nodded toward him. "Commander?"

"This is a little embarrassing, sir," Tombstone said. "But I think I know what the link might be. *Who* the link might be."

There was a buzz of murmured conversation around the room. Tombstone waited for it to die down. He should have seen the link earlier, should have been able to pass it on to Neil and his people that morning. It was obvious, now that he thought about it.

"What do you mean, Tombstone?" Neil asked.

"Bayerly and I were captured and interrogated by this Hsiao character. It only just now occurred to me . . . *how did he know where to find me?*"

Neil frowned. "You told us during your debriefing that you were with the news correspondent, Pamela Drake. In her hotel room . . ."

"And the only other person who knew I was there was Colonel Kriangsak, our liaison with the Thai military command."

There was stunned silence in the room for several seconds.

"You're sure of this, Tombstone?" Admiral Magruder asked. He was standing to one side of the room, his arms folded across his chest. "I think we've been assuming you were picked up at random. Anybody at that hotel could have been an agent for Hsiao."

"Positive, sir. *Kriangsak* called *me*, after I'd been getting a bureaucratic runaround from his office all day. He had me meet him at the Americana." Tombstone felt embarrassment coloring his face, not so much from the admission of where he'd spent the night, but from the realization of how easily he'd been trapped. He'd been as trusting as a sailor on first-time liberty getting rolled for the change in his pocket. "I told him I would be at the Dusit Thani, but I didn't tell anyone else. Later I called him to cancel a car he was sending for me."

Tombstone shook his head. "Now that I think about it, he could have picked up Commander Bayerly at the same time. Some of his people helped the commander out of the Americana. And Colonel Kriangsak was the *only* person who knew where I was . . . who knew I was staying at the Dusit Thani in . . . a certain hotel room." He glanced at Neil. "Sorry, Commander. It just now came together for me. But the pieces fit. It's too much of a coincidence that both Commander Bayerly and I were grabbed at random."

Neil appeared to be digesting the information. "If that's true, Hsiao is playing both sides of the game, helping the rebels and organizing the coup. He's also behind the attack on *Jefferson*, since he could have put that together through Kriangsak, who in turn could have been in on the coup."

"What's the point of organizing both a communist rebellion and a coup which wants to take more effective measures against that rebellion?" Admiral Magruder asked.

"Confusion," Master Chief Buckley volunteered. "Maybe they figure the United States won't intervene if we don't know what's going on."

"That never stopped us before," someone else added, and there was a round of subdued chuckles. The tension in the room seemed to have been broken.

Neil looked hard at Tombstone. "My guess would be that the Burmese incidents, the communist insurrection, the attack at U Feng, all of those were engineered by General Hsiao to create the proper conditions for a military coup. Kriangsak and any other traitors Hsiao was able to recruit with promises of money or power were brought in to organize the coup, to get it rolling. If he could start a war with Burma too, that would just add to Thailand's instability. Now, if Hsiao is behind Kriangsak, it could mean he's planning on toppling the present Thai government and replacing it with one of his own.

"Of course, U.S. intervention would be a problem. Hsiao couldn't afford to have us get involved too deeply helping the legitimate government. By attacking *Jefferson*, he either leaves us in doubt about who the enemy is—and therefore out of the game—or he convinces us that our carrier is vulnerable and forces us to back off. Same result. By God, it *fits*!"

"Okay," Admiral Magruder said. He stepped to the front of the room and took Neil's place. "Thank you, Commander." He waited while Neil took his seat, then addressed the entire group. "Very well, gentlemen. The question is, what can we do about it? Intelligence sharing ought to be our first step. Tell the legitimate rulers what we know . . . help them clean house themselves. We'll need to establish communication directly with the Thai military, bypassing Kriangsak. My impression was that Duong was honest, even if his chief aide wasn't. Commander Neil, check into that, please."

"Aye, sir."

"What else?"

CAG Marusko spoke up. "Admiral, it seems to me if our orders are to support the legitimate Thai government, we could help a lot by flying close support with them. Commander Neil said the Thais had lost a lot of their air force already."

"Close support against what target?" Barnes asked.

"U Feng, for one," CAG replied. "We know it's held by rebel forces. The Thais are going to want to take it back, if only to prove they're strong enough to do so. We could fly close air for them, keep those J-7s grounded while they send in their ground forces."

"We certainly have to provide air support against hostile aircraft," Admiral Magruder said thoughtfully. "At least until we know how many MiGs there are at U Feng. I'm concerned, though, that Hsiao might be working for the Chinese. Washington is going to take a dim view of us starting a war with the

PRC, especially these days, with all the friendly overtures toward Beijing. Dick? Any suggestions?"

Neil smiled. "Considering that the Chinese aren't even supposed to be in Thailand *or* Burma, I'd say we can take any action we feel is justified. If Beijing is in on this mess, they can't very well admit it, can they?"

"Agreed," the admiral said. "We'll wait for a definite word on that from Washington, but I tend to believe they'll go along with it. Anything else?"

"We've got the Marines coming in," Brad Gilmore, Magruder's chief of staff, pointed out. "We'll rendezvous with MEU-6 later today. They can beef up our position at the American embassy and be on hand to protect Americans in the city."

"Yeah. They'd be able to help if it turned out we had to evacuate American nationals," the Exec added.

"Right," CAG said. "And if they're having trouble with air, our helicopter assets aboard *Chosin* and *Little Rock* could help stretch things, at least until we got the word to move our people. If they need airmobile transport into Bangkok, say, the grunts could provide it."

Magruder pulled out his notebook again and wrote something in it. "Good point." He looked up. "Anyone else?"

The room was silent. "Very well. My recommendations to Washington will be as follows." He looked down at his notebook. "First, we share intelligence with the Thai military staff. In particular, we tell them about Hsiao and Kriangsak and what we've uncovered or guessed about the coup.

"Second, we offer close air support to the Thais, filling in for the losses they've suffered to their air force." He looked up. "CAG, start putting together an operational plan for a full alpha strike against U Feng. Catch those MiGs on the ground and leave nothing but debris for the Thai army to mop up. Commander Neil will be able to fill you in on what Lieutenant Wayne saw in the way of defenses up there." Several heads nodded, and there was a scratching of pens on paper as the COs of the carrier's attack squadrons made notes. "We will also look for ways we can help the Thais against rebel forces in Bangkok and Sattahip.

"Third, we'll coordinate with Admiral Simpson when *Chosin* and her consorts join us later today. We will recommend landing Marines in Bangkok to provide security for American citizens ashore. We will suggest providing helo transport for loyal Thai forces." He looked around the room. "Does that cover it all?" He waited for a response. There was none. "Very well. It is now 1110 hours. I want preliminary operational plans on my desk for approval by 1700 hours. That's when I'll pass all of this on to Washington. Department heads, begin working with your people on the assumption that we'll get a go for an alpha strike . . . let's have it ready for 0500 tomorrow. I want all available planes armed and ready for launch at that time. I know this means working around the clock, but tell your crews that this is going to be our chance to hit back!" He searched the faces in front of him. "Where's Commander Murcheson?"

"Here, sir!" A hand went up in the back of the room. Steve Murcheson was the CO for VA-84, the Blue Rangers, one of Jefferson's two A-6 squadrons.

"See me before you start your op plans. I want to talk to you about the mission parameters for a Skipper II strike."

There was a surprised silence. Then, "Aye, sir."

"That's all I have to say. Dismissed."

Tombstone rose and started for the door. He wanted to find Batman before half the air wing got the same idea.

An alpha strike against U Feng! And a Skipper drop as well. This was going to be one hell of an operation.

1430 hours, 20 January
U Feng

It was mid-afternoon when Pamela and Bayerly arrived at U Feng. They were herded off the truck and led to a small shed not far from the fuel storage tanks which were located near the eastern perimeter fence. Lunch was a bowl of rice and assorted bits of meat for them both, more than they'd had to eat in over thirty-six hours.

Pamela noticed that the entire base seemed to be on alert. There were many more soldiers here than there'd been at the rebel camp, and these troops seemed excited, animated, as they talked to one another with gestures and laughter. Through the shed's single small window, she could see the aircraft arrayed underneath the layers of camouflage netting, though she didn't now what kind of planes they were. She also saw something else, a large tracked vehicle of some kind, mounting three large missiles.

She didn't know where they were, couldn't even be sure they were still in Thailand, but the purposeful activity told her this was the heart of Hsiao's plan. So much activity would be impossible to hide from the United States, though. Reconnaissance satellites could be taking pictures of that missile launcher right now.

She wondered what Washington was planning on doing about it.

And in the jungle beyond the U Feng fence, other eyes were noting the activity too, as well as the presence of two white-skinned Westerners.

CHAPTER 22

Tombstone couldn't sleep. Just before midnight he'd gone aloft for some nighttime touch-and-goes on the carrier's flight deck. Every aviator was required to log a certain number of night flybys and traps.

Few enjoyed making deliberate bolters; as one Navy flyer Tombstone had once served with liked to put it, a touch-and-go was like kissing your sister, all the work and risk of setting up the shot, but without the reward of a good, solid trap at the end. For Tombstone, though, the repeated fly-arounds, the drop into the box, the low-speed approach with tailhook raised, the brief jolt as he kissed the deck followed by the full-throttle rush of takeoff were therapeutic. Until that afternoon, he'd not been certain that *Jefferson*'s flight surgeon was going to find him fit for flight duty. The repeated fly-arounds were a way of convincing himself . . . *yes, I'm back!*

Afterward, he'd felt too keyed up for sleep, and despite the knowledge that reveille would be sounding early that morning, he made his way down to the VF-97 Ready Room. Chuck "Slick" Connelly had the Alert Fifteen and was using his time in the ready room to go over his rosters for the next day.

"Hello, Slick."

VF-97's Executive Officer looked up from the paperwork on his desk. "Tombstone! How's it hangin'?"

241

"Fine. Mind if I come in?"

"Grab a chair. Java's hot."

"Thanks." Tombstone helped himself to the Ready Room's coffee mess. Lieutenant Commander Connelly had not been formally named skipper of the War Eagles yet, but as the squadron's XO he'd been running VF-97 since CAG had grounded Bayerly a week before.

"So the Doc gave you a clean bill of health," Connelly said. "Glad to hear it."

"Me too." He sipped the strong, black coffee to cover what he was feeling. Both he and Batman had nearly been down-checked by *Jefferson*'s senior flight surgeon. Batman because of his three-day bout in the jungle, Tombstone because of what the doctor had termed "possible psychological trauma." Tombstone had suffered no serious physical injury, but there was still a very real chance that he'd suffered mental damage, something that might not reveal itself until he was again put under stress.

Stress such as what he might endure during a dogfight in the seat of his F-14.

Well, sure. Go after a guy with a cattle prod and he was going to show definite signs of stress. But the cure wasn't to leave him at home when he had a chance of striking back. The burns still hurt, especially on his underarms, stomach, and groin where his flight suit chafed, but they wouldn't stop him from flying.

He was going on this mission. He owed it to Pamela.

And to Bayerly.

He'd argued the point with the doctor, demanding at last that CAG be brought into it. It had taken some doing, but in the end, and at CAG's urging, the doctor had agreed.

Batman would be flying today too. Malibu Blake had a down chit, of course, and would be in sick bay for another few days with his sprained ankle, but the rest of them would be going. Tombstone checked his watch. In less than four hours now.

"Look. Slick . . ." Tombstone hesitated, unsure how to proceed. "About the assignments for today . . ."

Connelly grinned. "Don't sweat it, hotdog. Sure, I'm jealous as hell . . . but no hard feelings. You've been point on an alpha strike before. That's probably why they picked you."

Tombstone chuckled. "Well, they didn't choose me for my boyish good looks." He tried to make a joke of it. "I figure my uncle has it in for me, is all."

The final details for Bright Lightning had been posted only that evening. VF-95 would be leading the way into U Feng, supporting the Thai air group called Trapdoor. VF-97 would fly CAP over the *Jefferson* . . . just as they had at Wonsan.

Once, Tombstone would have been upset at that. He wasn't certain what had changed. Possibly, he reasoned, he had a more realistic image of himself since his capture and escape. If there was anything *special* about him, it wasn't who he was related to.

And Slick's reaction told him that the other men in the air wing weren't holding his relatives against him either. At this point, though, what the other people thought didn't concern Tombstone. He was going on the mission, and *that* was all that mattered.

That, and the fact that Hsiao still held Pamela and Bayerly out there somewhere.

He would lead the Vipers to U Feng. But God help Hsiao if Tombstone ever met with that bastard again.

0430 hours, 21 January
Americana Hotel, Bangkok

The 1st Special Forces Group (Airborne) of the Royal Thai Army was organized along the same lines as the American Green Berets, concerned primarily with anti-guerrilla ops, intelligence gathering, and missions behind the lines. They trained extensively with their American counterparts, as well as with the elite troops of other nations. Though they normally wore two-piece jungle camouflage uniforms in the field, for special operations they wore the all-black combat suits and balaclavas of other elite units.

The men who rappelled from the hovering Thai UH-1s, then, were almost invisible against the night. They dropped from the helos in teams of four, landed on the roof of the hotel, and made their way quickly to pre-selected vantage points, M-16s and combat shotguns at the ready. For the past several hours, government helicopters had been making low passes over the area, in the hope that the defenders of the hotel's upper floors would become accustomed to the noise. Two bodies lay on the roof, army mutineers on guard cut down by suppressed, nightscope-directed fire from a neighboring rooftop seconds before the Hueys made their final approach.

At the same time that the airmobile force landed on the roof, assault teams entered on the ground level, securing the elevators and stairwells.

As Master Chief Buckley had noted during his closed-circuit TV broadcast the week before, officers in the Thai army were permitted to own their own businesses completely apart from their military careers. A check of government records by the Thai CIA showed that Colonel Kriangsak Vajiravudh was the owner of record of the Americana Hotel in the Yommarat district of Bangkok, as well as the unusual fact that the top two floors of the twenty-story building and the entire basement level below the parking garage had all been reserved for his personal use.

Operating under the tactical principle that it is always better to attack down when clearing a building rather than up, the roof assault teams moved in, splintering the access door with shotgun blasts and bursting into the stairwells. Supported by teams moving up from the eighteenth floor, they broke into the hotel corridors and began breaking into the penthouse suites.

Gunfire stuttered and barked as Kriangsak's bodyguards fought and died. Stun grenades were tossed into hotel rooms seconds before black-garbed Special Forces troops rolled through, M-16s and CAR-15s at the ready. The defenders fought back, but they were disorganized and surprised. One by one, they were cut down.

The survivors began surrendering less than three minutes after the first shotgun blast, and soon the prisoners, disarmed, their wrists secured in plastic restraints, were being led in groups of three to Hueys which waited, hovering, just above the roof.

Fifteen prisoners were taken. Seven army mutineers were killed, at a cost of one commando dead and two wounded. In the basement, the attackers discovered an enormous cache of weapons, including over fifteen hundred Chinese-manufactured AK-47s, thirty RPD machine guns, dozens of RPG rocket launchers, case upon case of apple-green RGD-5 hand grenades, and hundreds of thousands of rounds of ammunition, arms and ammo enough to start a small war . . . which, indeed, they already had. It also provided confirmation that one Kriangsak Vajiravudh was indeed a traitor.

In every way save one, then, Operation *Dahm Baho*, Black Light, was a complete success.

Unfortunately, Colonel Kriangsak was not in the hotel when the attack went down.

0520 hours, 21 January
New Phetchaburi Road, Bangkok

Colonel Kriangsak felt out of place in the commander's hatch of the Cadillac-Gage Stingray as it clattered up the four-lane highway toward Bangkok's central district. His place was on the staff of one of Thailand's senior generals, a world of desks and telephones, of briefing rooms and paperwork, not the clash of steel tracks on pavement or the stink of diesel fumes.

The Stingray light tank was one of six traveling in column toward the cluster of government buildings and royal residences which comprised the heart of the capital. Following the tanks were twenty trucks and over three hundred soldiers loyal to him. Their target was nothing less than the seat of government itself.

Seize the capital. Force the King to see the futility of continued bloodshed within the sacred precincts of Krung Thep. Prove to the armed forces of all Thailand that the army was *strong*, strong enough to stand against the communists and their Burmese hosts.

And with the American battle group gone, it was possible now. Kriangsak regretted his earlier doubts. General Hsiao had been right. The American carrier *was* vulnerable. Kriangsak had been on the shore at Sattahip two nights before, had seen the rocket attack and the volcanic pillar of fire rising from the *Jefferson*'s flight deck. He'd watched as the stricken carrier, still burning, had ignominiously slipped her anchor chain and limped from the harbor, heading south.

The latest reports placed the *Jefferson* almost fifty miles southwest of Sattahip now, still moving away at slow speed. That news would shake the King, and all those who still hoped that American support would come. And it would cheer the CPT revolutionary front now bracing for a Thai army attack at U Feng. At least it would hold them together until the coup could unite the army . . . under the leadership of Kriangsak Vajiravudh.

Everything was unfolding precisely as Hsiao had promised. Kriangsak could only shake his head in wonder.

The tank's radioman tugged at Kriangsak's pants leg, demanding attention. He ducked inside the hatch and accepted the radio headset. "Kriangsak here," he said.

"Colonel! This is Captain Priya!" The voice was rough with static, and nearly lost in the racket from the tank column. "Headquarters has been captured!"

"What? Speak up!"

"I said headquarters has been captured. Special Forces broke into the Americana forty minutes ago!"

The news shook Kriangsak. It was not a fatal blow—there were other arms and supply caches in and near the city—but it meant that the government knew of his part in the coup.

A pair of helicopters roared low overhead, and Kriangsak looked up nervously. It was still too dark to see their markings, but they were flying with lights on. That spoke of arrogance . . . an arrogance born of power.

Suddenly, Colonel Kriangsak felt less confident.

Master Sergeant Phillip Loomis, U.S.M.C., crouched on the
rooftop of a service station with the handful of Thai Special
Forces men. In front of them was a rugged-looking box with
lenses and what looked like a telescopic sight, directed over the
low wall which surrounded the flat roof area and toward a
section of the road some three hundred yards to the east. It was
still dark, but the sky was growing rapidly lighter.

It wouldn't be long now.

"Target area's clear," the Thai lieutenant at his side noted,
lowering his starlight scope. This was a relatively open part of
the city, some three miles east of downtown Bangkok. The
buildings were low and widely spaced, almost like a suburban
neighborhood back home, Loomis thought. South of the
highway was a strip of shops, temples, and patches of trees
running between the highway and the straight-line slash of
Klong Sen Seb.

New Phetchaburi Road was a fairly major artery. Even this
early in the morning it was usually clogged with the beginnings
of Bangkok's business day rush hour.

But the street was deserted now. Many residents had fled the
area during the fighting the day before. Loyal Thai soldiers had
evacuated others, knowing that the fighting would be worse
today. The street was still lined with parked vehicles, but
Loomis could see no movement.

He heard them first, the clash-clank of tracks on pavement,
the rumble of diesels. The lead tank came into view a moment
later, first in a long line of trucks and armored vehicles.

Loomis pressed his eye to the telescope sight, centering it on
the lead vehicle. He flicked a switch from standby to active,
and a bright spot of light appeared on the target, near the top
of the Stingray's turret.

"Firefly, Firefly, this is Zulu Three Kilo," he said. The
pencil mike in front of his lips picked up the words and
transmitted them to a base station a few yards away on the

rooftop. The station relayed the message skyward. "The lamp is lit. I say again, the lamp is lit."

"Roger that, Zulu Three Kilo," a voice said in his ear. "We see the light. Firefly on the way."

The lieutenant at his side was speaking rapidly in Thai into his own microphone, warning friendly forces to keep their heads down. The show was about to begin.

Loomis had been in the Marines for twenty-five years. As a lance corporal, he'd ridden out Tet and fought his way through the shattered streets of Hue. Three months ago he'd been on the beach at Wonsan, working with the Beachmaster to offload AAFV "tuna boats" as rocket and mortar fire dug holes in the sand and Tomcats shrieked overhead. This was the first time he'd ever fought a battle with what was in effect little more than a high-tech flashlight.

The Ground Laser Designator, or GLD, produced a beam of infrared light, invisible to the unaided eye but crystal clear to the proper optics or instrumentation. That intense spot of red light on the Stingray could not be seen by its crew, but somewhere in the night sky, colder, more efficient eyes were already locking onto the light, hunting it . . . and closing in. Elsewhere in the city, he knew, there were other small teams of men, Marine "technical advisors" working with loyalist Thai counterparts, sealing off the city from the rebel attacks they knew must come.

It was, Loomis reflected, one hell of a way to fight a war.

0521 hours, 21 January
Firefly One, twenty miles west of Bangkok

"Victor Bravo Three, this is Firefly One." Commander Steve Murcheson nudged the stick of his A-6 to adjust his course slightly, watching the terrain unfold on his Visual Display Indicator. "We have contact with Zulu Three Kilo and the lamp is lit. Commencing run, over."

"Firefly One, this is Victor Bravo," the voice of a Hawkeye air traffic controller replied. "We have a flight of Marine helos in your area, bearing three-three-niner at forty five hundred, range two-zero. You are clear for your approach, over."

"Roger that. TRAM running and the pickle is hot." The TRAM turret under the Intruder's nose registered the modulated laser light reflected from the target some twenty miles to the east. The Target Recognition and Attack Multisensor fed tracking data to the long, sleek weapon slung from the attack aircraft's starboard inboard weapons station. The bomb was already active, its robot eye following that same distant point of light.

Lieutenant Commander Simms, Firefly One's Bombardier/ Navigator, studied the view of his own VDI, watching a computer graphic image of what the TRAM was seeing, then switching to FLIR to give him an infrared view of the terrain ahead. The A-6's own TRAM could illuminate a target with a laser, but this particular target was in the middle of a city where the slightest error could kill hundreds of noncombatants. It was safer using a Marine spotter on the ground. He locked in the target. "Positive ID," the BN said. "Skipper powered up, release on auto. We're go."

"Rog," Murcheson said. He switched to the tactical frequency. "Firefly Lead, all go and in the game!"

Sunrise was less than an hour off, and the predawn sky was brightening rapidly. Murcheson could see the buildings of central Bangkok rising before him, beyond the silvery curve of the Chao Phraya River. They were approaching from the west, descending now to less than three thousand feet. Off the right wing, the waters of the Gulf of Thailand were a misty blue-violet band touching the sky.

The Intruder's on-board computer continued to monitor the aircraft's course, speed, altitude, the location of the laser-illuminated target, and the input from the BN's console which set its operational parameters. Murcheson kept the Intruder flying on a dead-level course, making minute changes in course as directed by the computer.

"We're getting close," Simms said. "Any moment n—"

The computer's release signal caught them both by surprise. The Skipper II laser-guided air-to-ground missile was fourteen

feet long and weighed over twelve hundred pounds, and as the
AGM kicked free, the Intruder bucked skyward. "Break-
away!" Murcheson snapped. He opened the air-to-ground
channel again. "Zulu Three Kilo, this is Firefly! Package on
the way!"

Murcheson brought the Intruder's stick left and skimmed
north across the city. Buildings flashed past, canyons of
concrete and steel. This close to the ground, the sensation of
speed was breathtaking. "Wheeeoh!" he cried over the open
mike. "Just like Star Wars! Firefly Lead, out of the hunt!"

The missile flashed out of the near darkness, a point of light
on the unreeling white line of a contrail. First introduced in
1985, Skipper II had been created by the Naval Weapons
Center from off-the-shelf components, the solid-fuel motor of
the outdated Shrike missile mated to the warhead of a Mark 83
one-thousand-pound bomb. Its seeker head kept the spot of
infrared laser light centered in its field of view, adjusting the
rocket's fins as the target moved.

At a range of less than six miles, it had a targeting accuracy
measured in inches.

0522 hours, 21 January
New Phetchaburi Road, Bangkok

Colonel Kriangsak propped himself up in the commander's
hatch, his eyes fixed on the line of tanks ahead. With less than
three miles to go before they reached the government building
complex, he'd expected more resistance from the loyalists,
some show of force at least. . . .

There was a thump, as though the tank he was riding in had
hit a pothole, and the predawn semidarkness turned a dazzling
white. There was no sound that he was aware of, but there was
a gut-wrenching sensation of falling . . . then blackness.

0522 hours, 21 January
New Phetchaburi Road, Bangkok

"My God, will you look at that!" Even at better than three
hundred yards, the blast had rocked the service station where

Loomis and the Thais were hiding. Windows shattered, and night turned to day as an orange fireball crawled into the sky on a column of flame-shot smoke.

Loomis used the laser target scope to survey the damage. The lead tank was gone . . . *gone,* along with part of the highway. He couldn't see anything left of the vehicle save for scraps which might have been anything. The second tank in line had dipped nose-first into the crater scooped out of the pavement by the blast and tumbled onto its back. Smoke and flame poured from the wreckage. Tanks three and four lay upended thirty yards from the pit, like discarded toys.

Beyond that, his vision was obscured by the smoke, but he could see at least one truck burning, and make out the shapes of men staggering about on the road or lying motionless on the ground.

"Okay, Lieutenant," he said to the Thai officer at his side. "Looks like we stopped 'em. Now it's up to you."

The lieutenant was already giving orders to his men over the radio.

0528 hours, 21 January
New Phetchaburi Road, Bangkok

Kriangsak opened his eyes. He was lying on his back, his ears ringing painfully, his body bruised and sore. Experimenting gently, he found that he could move, could sit up painfully and look around. Nothing was broken.

He'd been riding in the fourth Stingray in line. At first, he was so disoriented he couldn't find the vehicle. Then he saw it, twenty meters away and lying on its side. He decided he must have been flung clear by the explosion. Several still, broken bodies in army uniforms lay on the street. Blind chance had saved Kriangsak's life. The Stingray's turret had protected him from the worst of the blast, but he'd been thrown clear from the hatch instead of smashed against the interior hull.

Two of the tanks were still intact, but they were motionless, their crews killed or knocked unconscious by the shock wave. Everywhere, soldiers stood or sat or stumbled through the smoky darkness as though drunk. Most wore masks of blood from nosebleeds. Some writhed in agony on the ground and appeared to be screaming, though there was no sound. Only gradually did Kriangsak realize that he was deaf.

He looked up. The weapon which had shattered the column had to have been an air-launched weapon, but there was no sign of aircraft, no hint of where the bolt had come from. Striking a target with such accuracy from so far away that the attacker could not be seen . . . the RTAF didn't have that kind of technology, but Kriangsak knew who did. He had an uncomfortable feeling that the Americans were back in the game.

Shaking his head to clear it, he started moving back toward the line of trucks. Through the high-pitched shrilling in his ears, he could make out the far-off, muffled roar of fires, the screams of wounded men. His hearing was returning.

Several trucks were burning. Others had swerved off the highway and smashed into trees or gone nose-down in a ditch. The trucks toward the end of the column, however, were untouched, though none of the vehicles were moving. Kriangsak had seen the crater in the road ahead. The convoy would not get any further in that direction.

And the Thai loyalists would be closing in at any moment to mop up. Kriangsak knew he had to choose a new target and choose it quickly. Turning, he surveyed the city skyline across the canal toward the southwest. The pyramid-shaped, ultra-modern architecture of one of Bangkok's more modern and luxurious hotels rose beyond the trees of Siam Square, half a mile away.

Perfect.

He reached out and grabbed the sleeve of a soldier nearby, turning him around and getting him moving toward the klong. He found another . . . and another. Within five minutes, Kriangsak had rounded up a small army of fifty armed men and had set them moving across the Wit Thaya Road bridge which spanned Klong Sen Seb. Scattered gunshots and shouted demands for surrender sounded behind them as army troops closed in on the dazed and stumbling survivors of the column.

His fifty men had managed to get clear in the smoky confusion and dim light, though, before the loyalist net closed around them.

The Americans had done this. So be it. If the Americans had seen fit to intervene in the coup, then it would be the Americans who would have to accept the consequences.

Colonel Kriangsak knew he might still be able to bargain from a position of strength.

CHAPTER 23

Tombstone dropped into his ejection seat and accepted his helmet from Chief Smith. The plane captain grinned at him as he went through the motions of strapping on his airplane, and gave him a jaunty thumbs up. "How about bagging another six kills, Commander? For us."

"I'll see what I can do, Chief," Tombstone said, laughing. He settled the helmet over his head and adjusted the lip mike. "I'll see what I can do."

He finished pulling the arming pins for the ejection seat and checking the other necessary preflight details—leg restraints, oxygen and G-suit hoses connected and locked, radio cord snapped into his helmet.

Smith gave his helmet a friendly pat. "Luck! Canopy coming down."

Tombstone could hear Dixie's harsh breathing over the Tomcat's ICS as the RIO went through his own checklist. "Firing up," Tombstone said, and he switched on the powerful Pratt & Whitney turbofans.

"All set back here, Tombstone," Dixie told him.

Outside, the plane captain gave the Tomcat a final quick visual inspection, then signaled his approval. A small army of green shirts began breaking down the aircraft, removing the chocks and chains which had kept it pinned in place on the starboard side of the carrier, just forward of the island. A man in yellow jersey and cranial backed ahead of the F-14, signaling with his hands. Tombstone released the brakes and set the aircraft trundling slowly forward after him.

The launch for the alpha strike code-named Operation Bright Lightning was well under way. *Jefferson* had been hurling aircraft into the sky for the past hour, beginning with the VA-84's A-6 Intruders and VFA-176's Hornets for close support missions over Bangkok.

But the real show today would be in the far north of Thailand, over the airfield at U Feng.

"Eagle Leader, this is Homeplate," a voice crackled in his helmet phones. "Eagle" was the call sign for VF-95 on this strike.

"Homeplate, this is Eagle Leader," Tombstone replied. "I copy. Go ahead."

"Stoney? This is CAG. How are you feeling?"

Tombstone was surprised. CAG did not normally chat with pilots during a launch . . . and he *never* asked after their health.

Still, he understood. CAG had gone to bat for him with the senior medical officer. Marusko had put his own neck on the line, so that Tombstone could risk his.

"Livin' on the edge, CAG," he said. "No problem."

"Take care of yourself, Stoney. Oh . . . and the admiral says, 'Good flying.' "

This last was even more surprising. Admiral Magruder was usually scrupulously careful not to show favoritism for his aviator nephew. A personal message from the CO of the battle group broadcast over the tactical com net could hardly be kept secret.

But Tombstone didn't mind, not anymore. And a little last-second nervousness from CAG over his decision to intervene with the doctors was justifiable, Tombstone decided.

Had he made the right decision? Strange. Tombstone hadn't thought much about it. The hours since his escape had been a mix of frantic activity and exhausted sleep. Was he the same man, with the same reflexes, the same edge? He shook his head, pushing the question aside.

More than anything else in the world right now, he wanted, *needed* to strike back at the man who had kidnapped and tortured him, who had threatened Pamela Drake, who had mutilated and killed three of his shipmates and attacked the *Jefferson* herself, all for the sake of some unknown, twisted power game of his own. For now, that was all that mattered, that and the fact that he was again at the controls of an F-14, ready to ride the cat shuttle into the sky.

Next in line. The water-cooled plate of the Jet Blast Deflector behind Cat One rose in front of him, protecting his aircraft from the engine exhaust of the plane ahead. The color-coded deck crew performed their ritual movements and dances, checking the KA-6D tanker, readying it for launch. The other tanker was already up. *Jefferson*'s Air Ops would have a fine time juggling those two planes today, keeping them aloft with enough fuel to service the entire wing. Later, perhaps, some aircraft could land and refuel at various Thai bases, but that wouldn't be until their safety on the ground could be assured. In the meantime, fuel would be a carefully hoarded resource.

The engines on the KA-6 thundered to full throttle. The cat officer gave his signal, and the tanker thundered forward off the flight deck, leaving a billowing cloud of steam in its wake. Heavily loaded, it dipped beyond the carrier's bow, then rose, sluggish but climbing, its anticollision light strobing brilliantly in the crystal half-light of the early morning.

Tombstone checked his watch. Sunrise was still a few minutes away, but the sky was already day-brilliant, while the surface of the ocean and the carrier herself remained in shadow. The JBD slowly dropped back to the deck, and the yellow shirt guiding his plane motioned him forward. Tombstone eased the Tomcat ahead, bringing the front wheel onto the slot for the catapult's shuttle. Around the aircraft, dozens of deck crewmen hurried about the plane, making their final checks.

A red-shirted ordie stepped close to the cockpit and held up a bundle of wires with red tags on them. Tombstone checked the count and nodded approval. The wires had been pulled from the safety locks on the four AIM-9L Sidewinder and four AIM-7 Sparrow air-to-air missiles under his wings. The decision had been made during the previous day's planning that the far larger and longer-ranged Phoenix missiles would not be used. A Phoenix could lock in and kill an enemy plane over a hundred miles away, but the skies over northern Thailand were going to be a confused swirl of aircraft—Thai, American, and enemy—and it would be necessary to get close enough to see the targets to avoid scoring own goals.

A purple shirt held up a board with 66,000 on it, letting Tombstone verify the Tomcat's launch weight. Green shirts completed hooking the F-14's nose wheel to the cat shuttle.

"Eagle Leader, Homeplate," a voice said. Tombstone recognized it as Commander Dick Wheeler, *Jefferson's* Air Boss. "Trapdoor is now airborne over Don Muang. Victor Four Bravo will give you your vector once you're in the air."

"Eagle copies," Tombstone said. He was feeling tight . . . excitement a living thing twisting in his gut. Victor Four Bravo was the Hawkeye which would coordinate Operation Bright Lightning. Trapdoor was the call sign for an alpha strike of Thai aircraft, F-5s, mostly, and a few of their F-16 Falcons. According to Intelligence, the Thai air force had been badly hurt by bomb-throwing guerrillas at nearly every one of their air bases, and well over half of their modern interceptors and attack planes had been destroyed or damaged. General Duong and other members of the Thai Military Command Staff had been convinced, however, to put their remaining planes in the air, part of a massive air and ground push against U Feng which was already under way.

With so many planes in the air, it was hoped that the presence of *Jefferson's* air wing could be kept a surprise until the last moment.

Tombstone wiped his Tomcat's controls, using the aviator's mnemonic of "Father, Son, Holy Ghost" as he moved the stick back, forward, left, and right. He moved the foot pedals controlling the rudders for the "Amen."

"Eagle Leader, this is Eagle Two. Tombstone, m'man, how're you reading me?"

"Loud and clear, Batman," Tombstone replied. He checked over his left shoulder and saw Tomcat 216 behind him, preparing for a simultaneous launch. Batman had a new RIO in his backseat. Lieutenant Commander Aaron "Ramrod" Kingsly normally flew a Tomcat, but his F-14 had been one of those downchecked after the fire, so he was filling in as RIO this time around.

Tombstone glanced back over his right shoulder at the ready light on the carrier island. It showed green. He could see shadowy figures behind the windscreens, both on the bridge and on the flag bridge. He thought he saw one of the figures salute.

A yellow shirt signaled. Time to crank her up. He eased the throttles forward, bringing the F-14's engines to full power. The plane trembled, yearning to be free of the deck once more.

The squad safety inspector, in green cranial and white jersey, completed his final check and gave a thumbs-up. The Catapult Officer, identified by his yellow jersey and green helmet, looked up at the cockpit. Tombstone saluted. *Ready . . .*

With a graceful twist, the Cat Officer turned, pointed forward, and touched the deck. There was a surge of motion, of power, and Tombstone was flattened into his ejection seat. The acceleration clamped down on his lungs, squeezed his eyeballs back into his head, pressed his spine against the chair as the Tomcat hurtled off the catapult ramp.

"Good shot! Good shot!" he called.

"Tomcat Two-oh-one airborne," Pri-Fly's voice answered in his earphones. "Tomcat Two-one-six airborne." There was a pause. "Good Luck, Stoney. Good hunting!"

"Copy that, Homeplate. Thanks."

Sunlight exploded over the rim of the ocean as he grabbed for altitude. The burst of noise and speed and golden light seemed to break a dam inside Tombstone's soul. He was *alive . . .* and in command of a thirty-three-ton, high-tech fighting machine drilling into the clean, endless blue depths of the sky.

It felt like coming home.

0628 hours, 21 January
Flag plot, U.S.S. *Thomas Jefferson*

Admiral Magruder was leaning over a table on which maps of Thailand and TENCAP photos were piled in seeming disorder. TENCAP—the acronym stood for Tactical Exploitation of National CAPabilities—was one of the most dramatic advances in battlefield management history. For the first time, commanders in the field could call down up-to-the-minute reconnaissance photos from American spy satellites in orbit. Until recently, such high-resolution photos were processed first at the National Photographic Interpretation Center in Washington, D.C., then distributed down the chain of command by the CIA. It had taken weeks, sometimes, for the men who needed the data to get it.

No more. These photos had been taken only hours before. They were in infrared, penetrating the darkness. Individual people were clearly visible. Magruder found himself looking down on two men in ragged uniforms with AK-47s across their shoulders; the glowing tips of their cigarettes registered like tiny, diamond-brilliant stars.

In two hours, Bright Lightning would hit U Feng like a whirlwind. Thai soldiers were already moving into position. They would go in when the bombs stopped falling. The victory had to be clearly theirs, proof to the dissidents and a panicky population that the Royal Army had things well in hand.

Washington had agreed with his assessment. Nothing would discourage the army mutineers or strengthen the legitimate government's resolve faster than a quick, sharp victory at U Feng.

"Admiral Magruder?"

He looked up. His Chief of Staff stood in the door. "Come in, Brad. What do you have?"

"Eagle is airborne, sir. Thunderbird is over the coast now,

on course, on time. Pri-Fly reports that Chickenhawk is ready for launch."

"Thanks, Brad."

Eagle—six aircraft of VF-95—would escort Thunderbird—the Intruders of VA-84—into U Feng. Chickenhawk was the code name for the F/A-18 Hornets of VFA-161. Their job would be flack- and SAM-suppression over the target. Faster, but with smaller fuel reserves, they were being launched last. VF-97, once again, was being held in reserve, providing CAP for the *Jefferson* . . . and reinforcements, should the need arise over Bangkok.

"Uh . . . there's something else, Admiral. Something kind of screwy."

"What is it?"

"This just came through from Bangkok, sir." Gilmore handed the admiral a teletype sheet. "Just been decoded."

He read the message.

UNCONFIRMED REPORT TWO WESTERN PRISONERS, ONE MALE, ONE FEMALE, ARRIVED U FENG MIDDAY YESTERDAY. HELD IN BUILDING NEAR FUEL DUMP.

REPORT BROUGHT TO DOI CHIANG DAO BY KAREN GIRL NAMED PHYA NIN. WOULD DISCOUNT, BUT MESSENGER CLAIMS KNOWLEDGE OF SOMEONE NAMED BATMAN, U.S.S. JEFFERSON, PLEASE ADVISE.

Two prisoners! Magruder knew immediately that it was Bayerly and Pamela Drake.

He felt cold as he scanned the message a second time. Held near the fuel dump . . . and the fuel storage tanks on the east side of the U Feng perimeter would be among the first targets hit by Thunderbird.

Magruder felt as though he were balanced on a knife's edge. *Jefferson* had almost thirty planes in the air or ready for launch, aircraft with a destination five hundred miles north and with fuel in short supply. The alpha strike could not be kept waiting, not for two people who might or might not be Westerners, hostages of General Hsiao.

On the other hand, one of those hostages was a civilian, a well-known American news correspondent.

The other was an officer under his command, Lieutenant Commander Bayerly.

Magruder had heard the stories about Bayerly, about the tragic death of Admiral Fitzroy's daughter and the scandal surrounding the aviator who had been with her when she died. He knew that when a cloud like that attached itself to a Naval officer, that man's career was all but finished.

But Bayerly was a member of *Jefferson*'s air wing, CO of VF-97. More than once in the past, Admiral Magruder had been forced to make difficult decisions regarding *Jefferson* personnel. Not going in to rescue Batman and Malibu the week before had been such a decision, one forced on him by the politics of the situation.

Here was a situation where carrying on with the mission meant killing one of *Jefferson*'s own.

Damn it all! Bright Lightning could not be aborted. The Thais had already been brought in, and to back out now would leave them hanging. To go on . . .

"First," Magruder snapped. "Raise Colonel Caruso on the *Chosin*. I want to get in touch with the Marine Recon team heading for U Feng. Second, get me General Duong, Thai Military Staff Command. Third, I want confirmation on this from Batman Wayne. See if he trusts this woman. Fourth . . ." He hesitated. "Fourth, get down to CIC and have CAG make a signal to ninety-nine aircraft. Bright Lightning is on hold until we get this resolved. Got it?"

"Got it, sir!"

"Then get on it!"

"Aye, aye, sir." Gilmore whirled and rushed out the door.

Magruder couldn't cancel Bright Lightning, but he could delay it . . . a very little. It would mean diverting the alpha strike aircraft to bingo fields in Thailand rather than recovering them aboard the carrier, but that possibility had been considered from the beginning since fuel was such a critical factor.

And the delay might give them a chance to get the Marines in. A twenty-man Marine Recon force was already en route toward U Feng aboard one of *Chosin*'s transport helos. Slower than the aircraft of the alpha strike, the Marine Super Stallion had taken off almost two hours earlier and was over central Thailand by now. The force's mission was to support Thai ground operations and to provide ground spotting and laser designation for the Navy attack aircraft.

But perhaps their mission could be changed to include a rescue.

Magruder hoped so. It was damned chancy tampering with the mission planning at this late hour, but none of the alternatives was attractive.

0634 hours, 21 January
U Feng

General Hsiao stood at the window of his office, hands clasped behind his back, looking out at the jungle as his aide delivered the report. "Go on."

"All radio contact has been lost with Colonel Kriangsak, sir, both with his headquarters at the Americana Hotel and with the troop column tasked with seizing the government complex in Bangkok. There are wild rumors that the Yankees are bombing Bangkok, that their Marines are landing in the city, but nothing confirmed."

Hsiao's finger tightened their grip behind him. "What else?"

"General Kol is waiting outside. He wishes to see you most urgently."

Hsiao turned and smiled. "That I can believe."

"Radar reports unusual air activity between here and Bangkok. There are also rumors of troop movements on the road north of Chiang Mai. Colonel Wu believes that an attack may be imminent and requests a meeting with you at your earliest convenience."

Hsiao sighed. "Very well. Tell Colonel Wu I will see him in ten minutes. At his office."

"Yes, sir."

"That that pig of a Burmese general to come in. I will deal with him now."

The aide made a *wai* and backed out of the room. A moment later, General Kol entered, his chubby face flushed with anger. "I have heard rumors, General," Kol began. "Rumors that the Americans are attacking."

"That is nonsense, Kol."

"You said that there would be no direct confrontation with the Americans. You claimed the damage done to their ship would drive them away." He shook his head stubbornly. "Our agreement never called for armed conflict with the Yankees. I am returning to Burma with my men. Now."

Hsiao laughed. "It is a little late for that now, don't you think, General Kol? Haven't you heard the reports? Thai army forces are closing in on U Feng even as we speak! Your pathetic little army would be trapped and cut down before it got within five kilometers of the border!"

Kol swallowed. "Nonetheless," he said. "My men will not fight the Americans. What do we have to gain from such a confrontation?"

"I'm paying you enough, General. Your men will do what I demand of them."

"We'll see about that." He turned away.

"Have you forgotten General Xiang?" He drew his Type 62 pistol and pointed it at Kol's head. "That, my fat friend, is the price of crossing me!"

Kol turned again, and his eyes bugged out at the sight of the gun. His mouth worked soundlessly for a moment, then he licked his lips. "I didn't mean, General, that . . ."

"The situation is under control, General Kol," Hsiao said. "As planned, the Thais have committed themselves to an attack on our forces here at U Feng. Our aircraft and anti-air missiles will sweep their planes from the sky. When the skies belong to us, we shall rain destruction upon the Thai forces and crush them. You, General Kol, can be a part of the victory, or a casualty. Which shall it be?"

"I . . . I support you, of course, General," Kol said. His eyes were wide as he stared down the pistol's muzzle. "I simply wish to provide counsel . . . to advise caution. Provoking the Americans is a terrible risk."

"I will handle the Americans, if it comes to that," Hsiao said. "You do what I tell you to do."

"Yes, sir."

"Get out of my sight. You make me sick."

The general bobbed his head and departed. Hsiao reholstered the pistol. Kol would have to be killed, of course, and quickly. It would have been foolish to trust the man fully before. Now, afraid and insulted, he was far more dangerous. But the execution would have to be handled carefully, to avoid alienating the expatriate Burmese troops in his command.

Too, the defeat of the Thai assault on U Feng would generate yet more impetus for the mutiny, perhaps even convince the King and his ministers in Bangkok to support the dissident officers' faction. The body of a Burmese general would be a fine, added touch, proof that Burma had been behind the communist rising in the north and the capture of U Feng. That might satisfy the Americans as well, who would still be wondering about the loss of one of their planes in the area and smarting from the attack on their carrier. Burmese involvement would explain so much.

If Kriangsak were still alive, he would pull the whole thing together in Bangkok. Hsiao frowned. Loss of contact with Kriangsak was worrisome. It was possible that the attack in the capital had gone badly, that Colonel Kriangsak was captured or dead.

No matter, really. Hsiao had other contacts among the dissident officers, and the important thing was the destabilization of the Thai government. When the government fell, Hsiao's men would step in. One way or another, Hsiao Kuoping would rule this country before the month was out.

All that remained was to defeat the Thai military forces now closing on this remote and otherwise insignificant air base.

Hsiao picked up a briefcase containing maps and reports and left the office. He had some further surprises to discuss with Colonel Wu.

The Thais thought they had him in a trap. Soon he would show them that it was possible for the trappers themselves to be trapped.

CHAPTER 24

0636 hours, 21 January
Tomcat 216, over Central Thailand

"Eagle Two, this is Homeplate," CAG's voice said over Batman's headset. "The brass has a question for you."

"Uh . . . roger, Homeplate," Batman replied. Now what in the world . . . ?

"Do you know someone named Phya Nin?"

The question startled Batman. "That's affirmative, Homeplate." Hell, he'd told them all about her during his debriefing. What more did they want to know? And why?

"What do you know about her, Two-one-six?"

He thought a moment. "Uh . . . I'm not sure I understand the question, Homeplate. She's a sergeant in the Karen National Army of Liberation. The 12th KNLA Brigade." He'd told them that in his debriefing too.

"Roger that, Two-one-six. Can she be trusted? Over."

Trusted? "Absolutely, Homeplate. Are you in contact with her?"

"Two-one-six, stand by."

He listened to static for a long moment. What the hell was going on?

Below his Tomcat, the land spread out flat and green, a patchwork quilt of rice paddies and farmland. The squadron was about halfway to its destination.

It looked peaceful down there. Indeed the fighting which had

265

torn at Thailand's social fabric for the past weeks had not touched this, the *real* Thailand, where the smoggy sprawl of Bangkok was as alien as the surface of Mars. From ten thousand feet, Batman could see the six-laned intrusion of Route 1 following the Chao Phraya north from the capital, but the countryside itself looked as it must have looked for centuries, remote and untouched.

It reminded him of the jungle in the north and of the girl who claimed that the Karens with God outnumbered their enemies.

"What was that all about, Batman?" Kingsly asked from the back seat, his soft Tennessee drawl pronounced over the ICS.

"Beats me, Ramrod."

Kingsly laughed. "Sounds to me like they want to know more about your gook girlfriend."

"Can that 'gook' shit!" Batman snapped. His anger surprised him. He remembered his own references to gooks a few days before, and the memory burned.

"Well sure, man," Ramrod said, startled at Batman's reaction. "Anything you say."

"Ninety-nine aircraft, ninety-nine aircraft," another voice said over the radio. "This is Victor Four Delta traffic control. Proceed to Point Lima and orbit. Squadron commanders acknowledge, over."

There was a stunned silence, then Batman heard Tombstone responding for Eagle. Then the tactical channel crackled with questions and speculations by other men in the squadron.

"What's gotten into them back there, Nightmare?"

"Damfino, Shooter."

"Another crap-out, guys. Didn't I tell you? Another fuckin' crap-out."

"That's enough, people," Tombstone's voice came over the chatter. "Radio discipline. Keep the channel clear."

Batman couldn't help connecting the questions about Phya with the sudden change in orders, but what did it mean? In the Navy, the gods of Higher Authority rarely told the guys in the trenches what was going on.

He looked out the cockpit again. He could just barely make out the specks of vehicles crawling along the highway. More distinct were the toy-shapes of several helicopters pacing their own shadows as they flew north, parallel to the Tomcats' course but rapidly falling behind. Those were probably troop transports, possibly some of the helos on loan from the Marines to the Thais for the ground attack on U Feng. Possibly, he decided, something had gone wrong with that end of the operation, and the alpha strike was being held up to coordinate with them better.

Batman just hoped that someone remembered that the alpha strike was going to be running a little lean on fuel by the time they reached the skies over U Feng, and the more time they spent circling Point Lima—a marshaling area just north of Chiang Mai, thirty miles south of U Feng—the less time they'd have over the target.

From what he knew of the way command decisions were often made, Batman was not reassured.

0641 hours, 21 January
Thai International Hotel, Bangkok

"Silence! Silence!" Kriangsak shouted in English. His throat was raw with gun smoke and screaming, his head still fuzzy from the blast which had stunned him almost two hours earlier. He pointed the M-16 he'd picked up somewhere at the ceiling and pulled the trigger. The sudden, shocking burst of gunfire cut through the screams and cries of the hostages and brought a sudden, deathly silence to the lobby. "Quiet, everyone!"

Plaster dust and smoke floated in the air of the hotel lobby. Nearly forty civilians, men, women, and a few children, knelt or lay on the expensive red and gold patterned carpet in front of the hotel's registration desk. A half dozen of Kriangsak's men kept their automatic weapons pointed at the crowd, patrolling the outer edge of the group like sheepdogs.

Two bodies lay on the floor nearby, a doorman in a military-looking white uniform and a Thai policeman in khaki, both killed when Kriangsak's men had stormed into the hotel. A third body, a hotel security guard, lay across the room near the front door.

It was a large, long room, lined with shops and opening into a ground-floor restaurant. After fleeing the disaster on New Phetchaburi Road over an hour earlier, Kriangsak's men had broken in and quickly secured the lobby and all of the ground-floor entrances.

Hotel guests in the foyer and the restaurant had been herded into the lobby. Most—all of the Orientals except for the staff—had been freed immediately. Under Kriangsak's orders, the hotel's employees had then begun moving through the hotel, ordering the guests to evacuate the hotel.

As the guests, many of them half-dressed or still wearing night clothes, had exited the elevators and stairwells, Kriangsak's men had sorted them. Orientals had been allowed to leave by the front door, but Westerners had been roughly shoved into the growing crowd in front of the registration desk. One of Kriangsak's men had gone through the hotel's registration book, calling out names. One by one, the Americans in the group of hostages had been identified, the others released.

By now, all of the hotel's rooms had been emptied and checked by Kriangsak's men. Other rebel soldiers stood guard at each window and entrance. It wouldn't be very long before the authorities were forced to act.

"Colonel!" one of the soldiers yelled. He wore a blood-stained bandage around his head, covering a gash where he'd struck his head during the Americans' attack on the tank column. "They're coming, Colonel! Front door!"

Kriangsak walked to the wide windows at the front of the lobby. Outside, the city looked peaceful, not like a city under siege at all. The only signs that anything was wrong were the absence of the usual early morning traffic on the street, and a smudge of smoke hanging above the buildings in the distance.

He saw movement, troops in camo uniforms, moving cautiously among the trees which filled the International's parklike grounds. Soon a white flag appeared above a low mound of earth two hundred meters away.

"Attention!" an amplified voice blared in Thai. There was a squeal of feedback, quickly adjusted. The white flag continued to wave. "Attention in the hotel! We wish to talk with you!"

Kriangsak wiped his face with his hand. The issue, whatever the outcome, was about to be resolved. "Let them come, Dhani," he said to the soldier. "They will have things they wish to discuss with us."

He waited as Dhani showed himself, holding his CAR-15 above his head. The government's negotiators rose from hiding and approached, holding the white flag above their heads.

Kriangsak smiled. The Americans might have thwarted his attempt to seize the government, but in the end, they would still have to come to him, *deal* with him. They would have no choice.

0704 hours, 21 January
Thai International Hotel, Bangkok

Marine Captain Fraser approached the Thai army officer and saluted. "Well, Colonel," he said. "What's it going to be?"

Colonel Vang Chitiburit looked past Fraser toward the low, ultra-modern sprawl of the Thai International. "Do you seriously believe you have a chance, Captain?"

"We have a chance. We sure as hell can't wait this bastard out."

The Thai colonel considered that. "No," he said at last. "You are right."

The colonel had returned from his conversation with the rebel soldiers only minutes before. Their leader, Colonel Kriangsak of the Royal Thai military staff, no less, wanted—demanded—a helicopter to fly him, his men, and a number of American hostages out of the city. He'd not said what his destination was, but U Feng would be the obvious guess.

"Those are Americans that son of a bitch has in there," the Marine officer added quietly, without emotion. "The Marines are here to protect them."

"Your plan has risk. . . ."

"So does giving the bastard what he wants. And damn it, he claims he's going to start *shooting* people in thirty minutes! You want to see if he means it?"

There was a long hesitation. Fraser wondered if the man was

trying to decide whether or not to buck the problem up to a higher command. The problem was, the higher command was busy just now with a coup. At best, the confrontation at the Thai International was a minor distraction.

"Very well, Captain," Vang said stiffly. He sounded relieved, though, rather than reluctant. Probably, Fraser thought, he was happy to have the responsibility for success or disaster riding on someone else's shoulders. "I turn the situation over to you."

"Thank you, sir," he said, saluting.

Vang looked uncertain. "Will there be anything you or your men need, Captain?"

"Yes, Colonel Vang." He smiled. "A small diversion."

"A diversion?"

"When I give the word." And he began to explain what he had in mind.

0730 hours, 21 January
Thai International Hotel, Bangkok

Master Sergeant Phillip Loomis lay flat on the ground, watching the hotel. Captain Fraser had snagged him almost the moment he'd returned to the embassy earlier that morning, explaining that there were Americans being held hostage at the Thai International and ordering Loomis to round up fifty volunteers for a rescue.

The mission, Loomis thought to himself, would have been better suited to a Recon Marine force, but the only Recondos within a thousand miles were north at U Feng, spotting for the Navy A-6s and Hornets.

Very slowly, he raised his head, studying the hotel over the slight, grass-covered rise he and twelve other Marines were hiding behind. The nearest entrance was fifty yards away. He could see one rebel soldier standing guard by the door. There might be others, but if so they were staying out of sight.

Loomis checked his watch. Zero-seven thirty. Where were they? It was time to *go* . . . !

He heard the stuttering drone of an approaching helicopter.

He looked toward the east and saw it approaching low above the buildings in the direction of the embassy.

The captain had explained it to him before they deployed. One of the Marine Sea Stallions, deploying now off the *Jefferson*, was to be flown in and landed directly in front of the hotel's front door. While the rebels were watching the landing—they'd be expecting a trick—Loomis's Marines, Assault One, would storm the side entrance. Assault Two was waiting on the far side of the building, ready to do the same thing.

And there would be still more Marines, code-named Sunday Punch, waiting inside the helicopter as backups.

The Sea Stallion drifted toward the front of the hotel, its rotor wash lashing at the palm trees lining the parking lot. Loomis could hear a singsong barking over a megaphone— Colonel Vang speaking to the rebels in Thai, explaining that their demands were being met and that the helo was coming to take them and their hostages away.

Loomis kept his eye on the sentry beside the side door. The man had a Colt CAR-15 in his hands, was holding it at the ready as he took a few steps in the direction of the helo, trying to see past the corner of the building. A second guard stepped through the door at his back. Loomis waited for a count of ten. No more guards came through the door. He reached out and slapped the helmet of the Marine next to him.

Corporal Halcek was a Marine sniper. He was already taking careful aim with the bolt-action M40A1, a militarized version of the Remington 700 hunting rifle. Halcek took a second more to center the 10-power scope on the target, then squeezed the trigger.

The rifle cracked and one of the guards staggered a step to one side, colliding with the hotel wall. The second guard spun, assault rifle coming up, but Halcek had already worked the bolt, shifted aim, and was squeezing the trigger again. Two shots rang out this time, one from Halcek and the other from a Marine with an M-16, designated as backup.

"Assault One! We're moving!" he said, the words activating the hot mike to the PRC-9 radio strapped to his helmet. The tactical radio would keep Fraser and the others at the HQ designated as Outpost aware of what was going on, but leave his hands free. He scrambled to his feet, shouting to the other Marines, "Go! Go! Go!"

Thirteen men rose as one and ran toward the hotel, booted feet pounding across grass and pavement. With each step that he took, Loomis expected a burst of gunfire from the door which was their objective . . . and then they were at the door and the first men were going through. The two rebel soldiers lay sprawled where they had fallen, blood pooling around them on the sidewalk.

The roar of the helicopter was cut off as Loomis plunged into through the door. There were in a long, narrow hallway now, probably a service entrance. According to the maps they'd studied, the lobby ought to be straight ahead, left, then right.

They left two Marines to watch their rear and kept going, more slowly now to avoid excess noise. Thai civilians who had been escorted out of the hotel had reported that the Americans were all together, in the lobby next to the registration desk.

Two men came around the corner dead ahead, running, AKs in their hands. They skidded to a stop when they saw the Marines, one screaming something in Thai, the other simply staring, mouth open.

Loomis fired his M-16, triggering single shots which slammed into the torso of the shouting rebel. Two other Marines fired at the same moment. The second soldier pitched backward and collided with the first, the two of them sprawling in a heap on the rug. The Marines kept moving.

Rounding the last corner, Loomis almost stumbled into a mass of people sitting on the floor. They all had their hands up or on their heads, and they were staring wide-eyed at a half-dozen rebel soldiers who were covering them with guns. More armed rebels were by the windows at the other end of the lobby . . . lots more. Loomis estimated that there were at least twenty hostiles in that room alone.

The analysis flashed through his head in an instant. He'd already made his decision and was taking action by the time the situation had registered in his mind.

His thumb snicked his assault rifle's selector from single-shot to full-auto. Normally the blindly sprayed devastation of full rock and roll wasn't worth the loss of accuracy . . . but this time he had little choice but to point and spray. The M-16 roared, chopping into rebel soldiers, slamming them down in blood and flailing arms.

"Down! Down!" Loomis was shouting as he cleared the door so the other Marines could come through with a clear line of fire. "U.S. Marines! Everybody down!"

The other Marines joined in, some with carefully placed single shots, some on rock and roll. One rebel threw up his arms and pitched back over the registration desk. One tried to run and was cut down before he'd taken two steps. The hostages were screaming, a wild, eerie sound that drowned out the gunfire.

Another rebel pitched back into the lobby from the foyer near the elevators. More Marines were coming through there, the second assault team from the other side of the hotel. And from the front of the lobby, huge sheets of plate glass exploded inwards, engulfing the rebels clustered there.

"U.S. Marines!" Loomis kept shouting. "U.S. Marines! Everybody down!"

Some of the rebel soldiers were already throwing down their guns and raising their hands.

0732 hours, 21 January
Thai International Hotel, Bangkok

Colonel Kriangsak heard the explosion of gunfire from the lobby. He'd been racing through one of the hotel's shops with two of his men, trying to find a vantage point which would let him see inside the big helicopter's cargo bay when automatic weapons fire began its insistent, full-throated rattling elsewhere in the building.

He knew at once that an assault was underway, that the helo's arrival had been a ruse. He reached a window in time to see two lines of Marines storming down the helo's ramp and rushing the front of the building. There was a loud thump of a grenade, then another. Smoke billowed from beneath the awning over the sidewalk in front of the hotel.

Kriangsak raised his M-16, aiming at the charging Marines through the window . . . then lowered it again. If he opened fire, he could kill three or four, perhaps, but that would not help the coup and it would guarantee Kriangsak's own death.

0733 hours, 21 January
Sea Stallion 936, Thai International Hotel, Bangkok

SA David Howard had volunteered to help load the extra Stokes stretchers onto the big Sea Stallion that morning, never guessing that he was getting a front-row seat to a hostage rescue. The helo's cargo chief had simply asked if he wanted to come along to help with the stretchers at the other end, and handed him a cranial and a life jacket when he agreed.

He wasn't sure why he'd volunteered. He still felt the shock—and the horror—of the deaths of his three friends in Bangkok. There'd been no official announcement yet, but word had already spread through the *Jefferson*'s grapevine. It was horrible.

And that same death had come so close to claiming *him* as well.

Maybe it was a need to lay those particular ghosts to rest . . . or possibly he just needed to be busy. In any case, he'd said yes.

Within minutes of receiving the emergency call from the American embassy, the helo was lifting off from the *Jefferson*. Howard was enthralled by the sight of the carrier—the small city in which he'd been living for the past months—dropping away astern until it looked like a toy, finally vanishing in the distance. The Sea Stallion had touched down at the embassy thirty minutes later and taken aboard at least fifty grim, face-blackened Marines in full combat gear. The flight to the hotel had taken only a minute or two more.

The assault on the Thai International Hotel was over almost as soon as it began, and Howard saw very little of it. The Sea Stallion had dropped to the pavement in front of the hotel and lowered the ramp, but the body of the aircraft was turned so that people inside the hotel could not see into the machine's cavernous cargo bay.

He waited, unable to see, packed in with at least fifty Marines who, save for their garb and weapons, seemed to be men very much like himself. Some chewed gum, others made grim jokes. Most simply stared past the padding covering the inside of the cargo bay and kept their thoughts to themselves.

It occurred to Howard that he was going into combat himself. He heard the sudden crackle of muffled gunfire.

Then the word crackled over an officer's helmet radio loudly enough for Howard to hear it. "Sunday Punch, Outpost! They're in the lobby. Take 'em down!" An order was barked, and the Marines thundered down the Sea Stallion's ramp, the tramp of their feet on metal amplified by the cargo bay walls.

"Marines!" someone yelled, and the cry was taken up and repeated by the others with one thundering voice which drowned out the noise of the rotors. Howard heard the double bang of a pair of grenades, the smash of shattering glass, the crack of gunfire.

When the Marines were clear of the Sea Stallion, the cargo chief talked briefly with the crew through his helmet mike. Gently, the big helo lifted off the ground, rotated, and settled to earth again, this time with the open rear ramp pointed at the hotel entrance.

Smoke gushed from canisters hurled by the Marines as they'd charged. Howard could see through the fog to the gap-toothed ruin of the front windows, could see movement inside the hotel's front lobby, but the smoke obscured his view. Four Marines crouched on the sidewalk outside, mounting guard.

He could hear more shooting over the rotor noise, even distinguish the sharp yells of the Marines, though he couldn't make out the words.

A shape moved through the smoke to one side of the entrance, a shadow in fog . . . followed by another . . . then a third.

Howard was about to shout a warning when one of the shadows opened fire on the Marines by the front door. There was a wild, confused exchange of gunfire. Two of the Marines crumpled to the ground as one of the shadows was sent spinning back against one of the pillars supporting the awning over the sidewalk. Rifle shots cracked from another direction as snipers out beyond the parking lot saw this new threat and opened fire. A ricochet struck the sidewalk, screaming.

A second shadow went down.

The third shadow never stopped, never hesitated. It materialized into a man, a Thai wearing a rumpled officer's uniform and carrying an M-16. His boots clattered up the Sea Stallion's ramp as he stormed the helicopter's cargo bay by himself.

Howard leaped to one side. The M-16 in the intruder's hands spat full-auto noise and flame, and a white hot hammer struck Howard high in the left shoulder, slamming him back against the bulkhead. The crew chief collapsed in a heap. The invader hurried past, ignoring them both.

David Howard did not think of himself as a brave man, but after the first shock his arm didn't hurt. And the Thai officer was heading for the cockpit.

A red-painted CO_2 fire extinguisher hung from its mounting bracket on the bulkhead above Howard's head. He grabbed the cylinder and wrenched it free. At the sound, the invader turned suddenly, the M-16 coming up. . . .

Howard had thought he might spray the intruder's face with cold, high-pressure gas, but there was no more time for thinking, no time to pull the arming pin, no time to do anything but act. Continuing the motion begun when he pulled the fire extinguisher from its rack, he swung the eighteen-inch bottle with all his might. It struck the muzzle of the M-16, knocking the weapon aside just as it fired, sending rounds chewing into the helicopter's bulkhead. Howard swung again, this time catching the invader full in the face.

He struck again . . . and again . . .

The next thing he was aware of was a Marine standing beside him. "It's okay, son," the man said. "You got him."

CHAPTER 25

The Thai UH-1 Hueys touched down in a clearing less than fifteen kilometers from U Feng, as troops of the 1st Special Forces (Airborne) leaped from the landing skids and dispersed across the landing zone. Smoke plumes drifted with the wind, defining the LZ, a scar in the forest left by a recent logging operation.

Super Stallions and twin-rotored Sea Knights bearing the squadron numerals and markings of the U.S. Marines and the 6th Marine Expeditionary Unit were also present, settling to the ground as soldiers unloaded heavy equipment, weapons, and vehicles from their holds. From one grounded Sea Stallion, a line of men with paint-blackened faces and camo fatigues quietly filed down the rear ramp and fell into formation. They wore floppy boonie hats like their Thai counterparts, and carried a variety of weapons, ranging from M-16s to Israeli Uzis to Soviet-made AKMs.

They were Marine Recon, members of the Force Recon company assigned to MEU-6. Their specialty was landing in advance of the main body of Marines during an amphibious operation in order to gain pre-landing intelligence. If Marines considered themselves the best, Marine Recon considered its people the *best* of the best, an elite commando unit as capable as—they themselves would have said *more* capable than—

SEALs, the SAS, or Delta Force. All had been through two
years of special training, making them qualified as combat
swimmers, at HALO insertions, and at combat operations deep
behind enemy lines. They'd been assigned to the U Feng
operation because of their experience as forward air control-
lers, and several of them shouldered the heavy, square cases
which held GLD equipment.

But their training also made them ideal for another type of
mission.

"Listen up, people," the officer in command of the unit said.
Lieutenant Francis Nolan Miller spoke softly but with absolute
authority. "Team assignments stay the same. So do the
operational orders. The only thing different is the initial
objective. Once we have located and freed any American
hostages in the target area, original mission directives are in
force. Our first concern, however, is the safety of Americans
being held in that camp. Questions?"

"Yeah, LT," someone said. "Whose screwup was it this
time?"

Miller allowed himself a tight grin. Last-minute changes to
operations such as this one were detested by the troops. They
never failed to make things more complicated . . . and more
likely to go wrong. Inevitably there was always *someone* who
didn't get the word. "It's ours now, Wojtascek," he said. "It's
in our laps so it's our problem. Right? Move out."

The Marines began separating into the four-man units
favored by Recon. Miller searched the LZ until he saw a Thai
general standing with several of his staff officers nearby. He
walked up to the men and saluted. "General Vinjit?"

"Yes, Lieutenant," the general said in accented English. He
was dressed, like the others, in camouflage fatigues. Only the
star on his baseball cap showed that he was a brigade-level
commander. "Your men are ready?"

"Yes, sir. I just wanted to make sure we're straight on the
plan. You'll keep your forces back and out of sight until you
hear from us."

The general's mouth twitched impatiently. "I and my men

know our duties, Lieutenant. You see to yours." He turned away and continued discussing the map with his staff.

"Yes, sir." Miller returned to where his own team was waiting.

"Trouble, Lieutenant?" Gunnery Hunnicker asked.

"Nah." He glanced back at the Thai officers. "Language barrier."

Miller had an unpleasant feeling about this last-second change in plans. Originally, the Recon Marines were to move in close to the U Feng perimeter and serve as forward observers, first for the Hornets designated as Chickenhawk, then for the Intruders designated Thunderbird. The Marines would then step aside while Vinjit's men took the camp back from whoever had survived the air attack.

Now, though, the presence of American hostages in U Feng had changed things. The air strike was to be delayed until either the Americans were rescued, or until Lieutenant Miller reported that rescue was impossible. Either way, the bombers would not go in until after they'd heard from the Marines.

There was so much which could go wrong. The enemy had to know that several thousand Thai troops were in the vicinity. If the Thais were discovered, getting those Americans out of U Feng might be impossible, and Lieutenant Miller and his men would be left dangling.

If everything went according to plan . . .

Of course, Miller knew better than to expect that. The only question was just what would go wrong . . . and when.

0736 hours, 21 January
U Feng

Hsiao knew the Thais were coming, of course. It was impossible to miss them. Their aircraft, milling about north of Chiang Mai, stood out clearly on radar, and his scouts had reported Thai airmobile forces gathering several kilometers to the southeast.

How best to answer the threat? Hsiao had expected the enemy to begin with a massive air strike. Once certain that the

Thais were committed, he would have ordered his own interceptors airborne, sending them off to the north as if in retreat. When the RTAF pursued, they would cross the Taeng River Valley west of U Feng where he'd arrayed the majority of his hidden SAM batteries. The J-7s would then turn and fall upon the survivors. Meanwhile, his ground-attack aircraft, still based safely across the border at Mong-koi, would stoop on the ground troops, destroying their trucks, their helicopters, their weapons positions, leaving the troops easy marks for his own soldiers.

But the operation already was not going according to plan. For some reason, the Thai air elements had stopped short of U Feng and were circling uselessly some fifty kilometers to the south.

Did that mean they were launching a ground assault first? Possibly the Thai Special Forces were planning a sneak raid aimed at destroying the J-7s on the ground. That was a chilling thought. The same strategy he'd already applied against the RTAF might be turned against him.

Hsiao had heard the American adage "Use it or lose it" and knew its meaning. The aphorism was appropriate here. He picked up a telephone.

"Get me Colonel Wu," he said. A moment passed. "Colonel? This is Hsiao. We are through waiting. Launch your aircraft."

Seconds later, a siren began wailing across the compound. If the Thais did not come to him, he would go to the Thais . . . and *Sheng li* would be complete.

The first of the silver-gray Shenyang J-7s screamed into the morning sky three minutes later.

**0740 hours, 21 January
Tomcat 201, Point Lima**

"Eagle Leader, this is Victor Four Delta." The voice of the Hawkeye CIC officer circling over Bangkok crackled in Tombstone's ears. "We have multiple bogies at U Feng, your bearing three-five-zero. Do you copy, over?"

"Got 'em, Mr. Magruder," Dixie reported from the back-seat. "I make it eight bogies . . . correction. Make that ten bogies. Looks like they're taking off two by two."

"Victor Four Delta, this is Eagle Leader. We have your bogies."

"Eagle, be advised that Thunderbird is closing with bogies."

"Copy, Victor Four. We're tailing."

The Thai aircraft, some sixteen of them, were already peeling out of the wheel of aircraft above Chiang Mai and streaking toward the north. Someone, Tombstone thought, should teach them some patience. Or some *discipline* . . .

But then, this was their country, invaded by an unknown enemy. Yeah, he'd be impatient too.

"Eagle Leader to Eagles," he radioed. "Let's go, but keep the throttles light. Follow them in." He didn't know what those MiG drivers had planned, but it couldn't be good.

"Ninety-nine aircraft, Victor Four Delta," the Hawkeye controller called. "Bogies appear to be withdrawing, bearing three-three-zero. Estimate two-zero bogies, now making for the green line."

Withdrawing? Without a fight? Tombstone considered the possibilities and grimaced beneath his helmet visor. His hours as General Hsiao's guest in Klong Toey had taught him a thing or two about the man. He was utterly ruthless, and he was methodical. Smuggling MiGs to a captured air base, mounting a complex operation in both northern Thailand and in Bangkok . . .

Hsiao would have foreseen this assault on his position, and he would have planned for it.

"Eagle Leader to all units," Tombstone snapped. "The people we're up against are tricky. Watch for snakes." He was thinking of the vehicle-mounted SAMs Batman had reported seeing at U Feng . . . SA-6 Gainfuls. Hsiao had certainly had time to bring in a number of those monsters from Burma or elsewhere. Those tracks Batman had seen suggested Hsiao had run them south along the riverbank and across the border into Thailand. The jungle below was probably crawling with men sporting shoulder-launched anti-air missiles too.

Tombstone eased the stick forward, letting the F-14 descend to eight thousand feet. Jungle-carpeted hills flowed beneath the keel of his aircraft. Dixie reported that the Thai formation was still pursuing the fleeing bogies and was now approaching U Feng. He gave the other aircraft of Eagle a quick check, looking left and right. The Vipers of VF-95 numbered ten F-14s, but only six had been assigned to the alpha strike. The others were destroyed or under repair, back on the *Jefferson*'s hangar deck.

"Hey, Tombstone?" Dixie called over the ICS. "We're picking up some new radar. Have a listen."

Dixie piped the radar tone to Tombstone's headset. He heard it, a mournful thrum like a plucked cello string. "Long Track," he said. "Batman's Gainfuls."

"Long Track" was NATO's code name for the radar used for early warning and to acquire preliminary target data for the SA-6. Guidance during lock-on and boost was called "Straight Flush."

Tombstone opened a new radio channel. "Snow White, Snow White, this is Eagle Leader. Do you read me, over?"

"Eagle, Snow White. Loud and clear. Go ahead."

"Snow White, we have a Long Track paint. Time to sing them your song."

"Copy that, Eagle Leader. You guys prefer blues or the hard stuff?"

"Sing 'em the blues, Snow White."

"Snow White's jamming, Tombstone," Dixie said. Somewhere miles to the south, an EA-6B Prowler of VAQ-143 designated Snow White circled at altitude, transmitting on frequencies designed to jam enemy radar. The jamming would break down at close range, but it would shield the alpha strike from long-ranged attacks and keep the enemy guessing about Thai and American numbers and intentions.

"Chickenhawk, Chickenhawk, this is Eagle Leader," Tombstone called. "Where are you, Smiley?"

"Eagle, Chickenhawk Lead," Lieutenant Commander John "Smilin' Jack" Van Dorn replied. The former XO of VFA-161 had moved into the skipper's slot after the tragic death of Marty

French at Wonsan. "We're one hundred fifty miles out and catching up."

"Chickenhawk, Gainfuls are confirmed. You guys are going to be busy."

"Roger that, Eagle. Warm 'em up a little for us, will you?"

"We'll see what we can do."

"Tombstone!" Dixie shouted. "Trapdoor is under fire!"

"Right," Tombstone snapped. "What's going down?"

"I'm getting missile indicators." Dixie paused, reading his scope. "SAM launch, Tombstone! SAMs!"

And Tombstone knew that Hsiao had sprung his trap.

0742 hours, 21 January
Falcon 992, over the Nam Mae Taeng Valley

Lieutenant Colonel Vasti Nithanivituk pulled back on his Falcon's stick and kicked in the afterburner. Green-clad mountains wheeled past his canopy as he stood the nimble aircraft on its tail and boosted for altitude. A veteran of six months in the United States training on F-16s at Nevis AFB, he was proud of his aircraft, fiercely proud of what he could make it do. The Falcon shrieked into the sky, inverting as it twisted out to an Immelmann.

The red warning light for a SAM lock still flashed on his console, next to the glowing computer symbols of his HUD. Upside down now, pressed into his ejection seat by the G-force of his loop, he looked "up" through the canopy, searching the greenery and valley folds overhead.

There!

He'd seen films at Nevis, but never the real thing. Just as the American pilots always described the thing, the SAM *did* look like a telephone pole as it rose from the jungle, balanced on a tongue of white flame. "Trapdoor! Trapdoor!" he shouted in Thai. "Launch! I have a launch! Nam Mae Taeng Valley, sector three!" The missile was accelerating rapidly, arrowing toward him.

Lieutenant Colonel Vasti was the leader of Trapdoor, the Thai force assigned to secure air superiority over U Feng. He'd flown over twelve hundred hours in modern interceptors and was widely regarded as the best of Thailand's elite fighter pilot corps.

He was scared now. The SAM was less than a mile off now, still accelerating as its radar held its lock on his ship. This was the worst part of evading a SAM launch, as his American instructors had warned him, those long, long seconds when he had to keep his aircraft flying straight and level until the SAM was committed. He kept his eye on the missile, now visible only as a bright pinpoint of light, a flare in the sky rapidly growing brighter.

Now! Vasti stabbed at the chaff button and rolled his aircraft into a hard right turn. The idea was to twist out of the way before the missile could react and change course. Once its solid fuel motor burned out, it would pursue a ballistic trajectory into the ground and explode.

The skin on his face stretched back from his eyes and mouths with the force of his 7-G turn. He kept hitting the chaff dispenser, spewing packets of metallic foil along the Falcon's path in a cloud which would distract the SAM's radar and let him slip away.

Recovering from the break, he chanced a look back over his right shoulder. The enemy missile should . . .

He had only a second's glimpse of the missile as it arrowed up toward his plane. Twenty feet long and over a foot thick, the Gainful had an eighty-kilogram warhead which could explode on impact or by proximity fuse.

The missile exploded less than five meters from the Falcon, sending jagged chunks of metal tearing through the fighter's thin skin like rocks through tissue. The concussion slammed Vasti's helmeted head against the left side of his canopy. His instrument panel lit up with warning and failure lights. A harsh buzz and a brightly pulsing red light warned of a fire in his starboard engine. Numbly, he struggled to adjust the Falcon's trim.

No good. He was losing it. "Trapdoor, Trapdoor, this is Trapdoor Leader! I'm hit! I'm hit! Major Kraisri, take command!"

"Eject, Colonel!" He heard Major Kraisri's voice say. "Eject!"

He was reaching for the ejection handle when his stabilizer tore free with a jolt that felt like a second explosion, and Vasti was slammed into the right side of the cockpit. Stunned, he tried to focus on the view forward through his windscreen, a swirl of green rushing up to meet him. . . .

Spinning wildly, the Falcon slammed into the side of a mountain. The explosion tore a fifty-foot gap in the jungle and sent a fireball uncoiling into the morning sky.

Then the sky seemed to catch fire as more SAMs rose from hiding.

0743 hours, 21 January
Tomcat 201, Point Lima

"Victor Four Delta, this is Eagle Leader," Tombstone radioed. "From here it looks like Trapdoor is falling apart. Can you confirm the situation, over?"

"Ah, roger, Eagle Leader," the Hawkeye CIC officer replied. "Looks to us like they've stepped in a snake's nest."

It took less than two seconds for Tombstone to arrive at a decision. The revised plan called for all aircraft, Thai and American, to hold at Point Lima until Victor Four Delta gave them the go-ahead. But Trapdoor had gone in alone, chasing the bogies which had appeared over the captured airfield.

Operation Bright Lightning's whole reason for being was to support the Thais. He couldn't stand back and watch the less experienced Thai pilots get cut to pieces by whatever it was that Hsiao had waiting for them up there.

"Let's hit it." He keyed the tactical frequency. "Eagle Leader to Eagles. Let's give our Thai friends some help. Lead in."

"Eagle Two," Batman echoed. "We're in."

One by one the other Eagles called in.

"Eagle Three, in." Army Garrison in Tomcat 204.

"Eagle Four, us too." Price Taggart in 203.

"Five, yo!" Shooter Rostenkowski in 248.

"Eagle Six, count us in." Nightmare Marinaro in 244.

Six pale gray arrowheads, wings swept back against their flanks, streaked toward the north.

As they closed, Tombstone's RIO described the trap's closing as it unfolded on his Tactical Information Display. "Looks like a heavy SAM concentration in the Taeng Valley," Dixie said. "Trapdoor is reporting casualties . . . at least three planes down. And the bogies are turning."

"How many bogies you got, Dixie?"

"Hard to tell, Tombstone." Distance and friendly jamming would be confusing the picture. "At least twenty . . . maybe more."

"Okay." He keyed his mike to squadron tactical. "Eagle Leader to Eagles. We'll go in low over the airstrip. If you catch any MiGs, on the ground or taking off, nail them." It would be easier to whittle down the odds if they could hit the enemy planes before they were airborne. Not as sporting, perhaps . . . but despite the popular concept of winged warriors and man-to-man combat, there was little room for chivalry in war. "Stick together for the first pass," he continued. "Tight deuce."

While the Navy's loose-deuce tactics provided the greatest flexibility in air combat maneuvers, Tombstone wanted the formation to stay close together until they knew for sure what they were up against. There would be so many planes in the air over U Feng that it would be easy for the American Eagles to become widely scattered, unable to support one another.

"I'm counting twenty-two bogies now, Tombstone," Dixie reported. "Looks like they just splashed another Trapdoor."

"Rog." The odds were not good. Trapdoor had gone in with sixteen aircraft. Four, so far, had been shot down. Eagle numbered six. The Hornets of VFA-161 numbered eight more, but they were still a long way off and dedicated to SAM suppression, though they would take on the fighter role once again after they'd dropped their ordnance. The Intruders of Thunderbird didn't count since they were strictly ground-attack aircraft and mounted neither machine guns nor air-to-air missiles.

So that made it eighteen friendlies against twenty-two

hostiles . . . twenty-two *known* hostiles, Tombstone added to himself.

And a hell of a lot worse than that if the Thai formation fell apart. Tombstone didn't like relying on the unknown quality of the Thai pilots. He didn't know how they would stand up to the killing stress of ACM. He knew how his people would react . . . but the Thais were untested, hence unreliable. They might prove themselves yet, but Tombstone couldn't count on them until they did.

So until the Hornets of Chickenhawk arrived on the scene, Tombstone could count on six Tomcats against no less than twenty-two MiGs.

"We're closing, Tombstone," Dixie said. "Closing fast. Bogies now inbound, bearing three-one-zero, range five miles. They're closing on Trapdoor, coming fast. . . ."

"This is Eagle Leader," Tombstone said. "Let's go down on the deck." He nosed the Tomcat over, dropping toward the jungle. The tactic was called terrain masking, hiding the aircraft in the ground clutter of ridges and hills. It might give them some precious time before someone started loosing SA-6s at them.

Of course it also put them within range of the small and highly portable SA-7s, like the one that had nailed Batman.

Trees and ground flashed past the cockpit of his aircraft, a green blur. With startling suddenness, jungle gave way to a broad, open clearing littered with buildings and the dark-gray slash of an airstrip. U Feng! The runway appeared clear. Perhaps all of the MiGs were airborne.

As quickly as it had appeared, U Feng vanished behind the hurtling aircraft. Sunlight flashed from the surface of a river dead ahead . . . in the Taeng Valley.

"Watch it now, people," Tombstone said. "Watch for snakes in the grass."

"Looks like they're turning and burning with the Thais," Price Taggart said. "We've got some major ACM up there."

"Bandits!" Tombstone's RIO called. "Six . . . correction, eight bandits, inbound, range three miles! Bearing three-four-zero!"

"Tally ho!" Batman called. "I've got visual on the bandits."

MiG-21s. The sky over the Taeng Valley appeared to be filled with aircraft, Thai F-5s and MiGs, turning and burning in a twisting, far-flung dogfight.

"Two-four-four confirms," Nightmare added. "We're picking up Jay Bird here—"

Jay Bird was the code name for the MiG-21 J-band radar used to illuminate targets for the Atoll AAM.

"Arm missiles!" Tombstone brought the Tomcat up, turning to meet the new threat. "Here we go!"

0744 hours, 21 January
U Feng

Hsiao held the radio microphone to his mouth. Before him on the table was a map, vectors and sighting tracks plotted on it in grease pencil.

"Area four-seven," he said. "Fifteen kilometers southeast of U Feng. A number of enemy radar tracks converge there, and we believe it may be a helicopter staging area for a airmobile assault, almost certainly. Get the Q-5s airborne at once."

"They are armed, fueled, and ready to go, General," the voice on the radio replied. "But what of the enemy fighters?"

"Colonel Wu has them at bay, Group Commander. You should have a clear run to the target."

"We go." He could hear Dao Zhu Qingtong's confident grin over the radio link. *"Sheng li!"*

"Victory, Group Commander Dao!" Hsiao repeated. "U Feng out!"

Hsiao had been holding Dao's ten Nanchang Q-5 ground attack planes in reserve at Mong-koi, the final part of his trap for the Thai forces. Launching from the Burmese air base now, they could be over the Thai assembly point within five minutes.

CHAPTER 26

The walls of the shed trembled under the deafening onslaught of noise. For one moment, Pamela thought that someone had planted a bomb squarely on the fuel pump nearby. As she lowered her hands from her ears and looked up toward the shed's small window, though, she realized that the sound had been caused by jets flying low overhead. She could still hear them, engines shrieking, as they pulled over the airstrip and corkscrewed into the sky.

They'd come! The Thai army had come . . . possibly the Navy as well. She moved over to the corner of the shed, where Bayerly sat on the dirt floor, a strange expression on his face. "I think it's a battle," she said.

"F-14s," he said, listening. "Tomcats. They're ours."

Pamela felt a sudden thrill which jolted through her. Tombstone! If there were Tomcats overhead, one of them might be Tombstone!

Bayerly was looking toward the door now. "We'd better get ready," he said. "If they're buzzing the airstrip, ground troops can't be far behind. And I don't think our new friends are going to want us to get rescued."

"But what can we do?"

He gave her a tight smile, a mirthless stretching of his lips. "We'll manage something," he said.

0746 hours, 21 January
Near U Feng

Lieutenant Miller peered up through the jungle canopy as the
six Tomcats thundered into the sky. There was a thump,
followed by a slithering hiss, and a line of white smoke
scrawled its way across the blue. Someone on the ground had
just loosed a SA-7 Grail . . . but far too late. The Navy
planes were already nearly out of sight by the time the missile
was loosed.

Miller noted the launcher's position in his mind. Part of the
close-in perimeter defenses, no doubt.

Lieutenant Miller lay on his belly at the edge of the clearing,
studying the compound through his binoculars, taking care not
to turn the lenses toward the sun and give away their position
with a flash. The Marines had moved silently to this location,
staying off the trails, slipping like shadows among the trees.
Security elements were posted, guarding flanks and rear.

They were directly on the U Feng perimeter now, looking
into the camp across a cleared fire zone a hundred meters wide.
Behind barbed wire and sandbags, the enemy camp was in an
uproar. Large groups of armed men were running among the
barracks, apparently deploying along the perimeter defenses to
the south. A pair of tracked SA-6 chassis were parked by one
end of the runway, each mounting three Gainfuls side by side,
probing the sky.

Miller cursed. Those Gainfuls meant big problems. They'd
have to be taken out before the Thais could assault the camp,
or they'd play hell with the Thai-American grab for air
superiority. The leader of that flock of Tomcats that had just
gone over had played it smart, Miller decided, coming in low
so the Gainfuls couldn't nail them with their Long Track
radars. As he watched, though, a missile on one of the
launchers spat flame, and a billowing white cloud of smoke
engulfed the vehicle. The missile rose into the air, an ungainly,
finned pencil shape balancing atop a column of fire.

He looked up. The Tomcats were almost out of sight

already . . . but the SAM radars would have them locked in hard.

A second missile slid clear of the launch rail with a hissing roar.

God, Miller thought. This can't go on much longer. Someone would have to take out those SAMs, or this whole operation would be blown.

He turned his attention back to the compound. The word was that the prisoners were being held in a shed or small building close to the fuel tanks. He could see the tanks, not far from his present position, but there were several buildings which could be the one the Karen scouts had meant.

Damn! Which one?

0747 hours, 21 January
Tomcat 201

"Stand by to break, people," Tombstone ordered. The Tomcats were climbing now, the enemy just coming into visual range. He could see the mingled contrails of dogfighting aircraft two miles ahead and ten thousand feet above. "On my mark . . . *break!*"

The tight cluster of F-14s opened like the blossoming of a flower, a maneuver called the bomb burst at Top Gun school. Three pairs of sleek gray aircraft separated from one another, the pairs themselves slipping apart as the formation went from welded wing to loose deuce.

"Eagle Leader, Eagle Two!" Batman called. "We're being painted by Straight Flush. They're trying for a lock!"

Tombstone rolled his Tomcat into an inverted position so he could see the ground. There could be hundreds of SAMs lurking down there. "Keep your eyes open, Batman," he said. "I don't—SAM launch! SAM launch on your six!"

0747 hours, 21 January
Tomcat 216

Batman turned in his seat as Tombstone yelled the warning. He searched the jungle behind them, saw the telephone pole shape rising from the direction of U Feng. "Launch! Launch!" he called.

"Oh, *shit*," Ramrod added from the back seat. "He's locked onto us, Batman! He's got a lock!"

Batman heard the warbling chirp of the Gainful's Straight Flush radar. A warning light labeled SAM flashed red next to his HUD.

The Gainful climbed above the treetops, accelerating at a sky-burning twenty Gs. Then the solid booster burned out. Looking back again, Batman saw the spent booster falling away. The missile was now moving toward him at Mach 1.5. With the booster gone, the rocket converted to a ramjet, gulping air through four ducts as it continued to accelerate. Top speed for the SA-6, Batman knew, was Mach 2.8, well above the best the Tomcat could do.

Batman brought the F-14 into a sharp turn. "I'm breaking, Eagle Leader," he said. "I need some maneuvering room."

"Roger that," Tombstone replied. "Get clear."

He held the break, grunting against the increasing G forces. "Keep it coming," he said, more to the aircraft than to Ramrod or anyone else. "Keep it coming. . . ." His compass reading dropped as he turned through a full 180 degrees, until he was heading straight toward the oncoming SAM. He couldn't outrun the thing, but having seen its launch, he had a chance to outsmart it.

He checked his altitude. Six thousand feet . . . that was going to make it damned tight. The missile was angling over now, flying almost on the same level as Batman's aircraft. Still hurtling toward the SAM, Batman rolled the Tomcat right until he was canopy down, then brought the stick back and headed for the ground.

The Gs built as Batman held the inverted dive. "Good night . . . Ramrod!" he grunted against the crushing pressure. There was no answer from the backseat, and Batman knew his RIO was either unconscious, or too busy breathing to reply. He stabbed the chaff release again and again, scattering false targets in the F-14's wake.

Green jungle filled the forward half of his canopy as his

altimeter spooled rapidly toward zero. The G-pressure was gone now, replaced by the dropping-elevator sensation of free fall. He chanced a look over his shoulder, saw the SAM arrowing toward the ground now, hard on his tail and getting closer. His first chaff release hadn't fooled it, and it was now a race to see whether the plunging Tomcat would be destroyed first by the missile or the uprushing ground.

Now . . . !

He pulled back on the stick, watching the ground swoop away beneath the Tomcat. The G-forces returned with a vengeance, crushing his chest, dragging at the skin of his face, on his guts. He slammed the throttles full forward past the detents and into afterburner. The Tomcat's twin engines shrieked fury as he started to climb again, leaving the ground behind. The plane was shuddering with the terrible stress. A number on his HUD showed that he was pushing nine Gs, and he was aware of blackness closing in at the periphery of his vision, a sure sign that he was about to lose consciousness.

Then the F-14 shrieked into clear sky. He looked back and saw a boiling mushroom of white smoke where the SAM had smashed into the jungle.

Made it! Batman let out a long, unsteady breath. That one had been a hell of a lot closer than he really wanted to admit.

0747 hours, 21 January
Tomcat 201

Tombstone kept his heading dead on for the approaching MiGs.

"This is Eagle Three!" Garrison called over the radio. "They've locked on to me!"

"Say again, Eagle Three. . . ."

"Tracking lock! Tracking lock—correction, launch! I have missile launch. . . ."

"Eagle Six confirms. Bandit launch."

"Looks like they want to play," Tombstone said. He shifted frequencies. "Victor Four Delta. Victor Four Delta, this is

Eagle Leader. We have SAM and air-to-air launches on American planes. Engaging."

That answered any question about the ROEs. The bad guys had fired first, and the Navy was responding with appropriate action.

At least, that was how the official after-action reports would read. Somehow the follow-up reports never managed to carry the exultation of air-to-air combat.

Or the terror.

"Break left, Army!" Taggart called.

"Roger. Left."

"Watch out, Tombstone!" Dixie called. "Twelve o'clock! We got two taking us head-to-head!"

Tombstone saw the MiGs streaking toward his plane dead ahead. "Rog! Let 'em come!" In an instant they swelled from specks in the distance to aircraft flashing past. The combined speeds of MiGs and Tomcat amounted to better than Mach 2.

One of the strange effects of combat which Tombstone had noted before was the almost surreal slowing of time. At Mach 2 there was no way for an aviator to see any detail at all in the other aircraft . . . yet as he turned his head to follow the passing MiGs it felt as though he could count every rivet. He could see the J-7s' mid-fuselage delta wings, could see the arrow-slim heads of their Aphid and Atoll missile loads, could actually see into the cockpits and see two red-helmeted heads with the black sun visors canted up, looking back at him.

Then they were gone, vanishing into the blue distance behind him.

"Eagle Leader," he called. He pulled back on the stick and the Tomcat climbed. "I'm on them. Going for a vertical reverse."

"You want to let me off at the next stop?" Dixie asked.

"Just keep your eye on those MiGs," Tombstone replied. The F-14 was climbing straight up now, but Tombstone kept the afterburners off. The plane was losing speed. "Where are they?"

"Going into a turn, Tombstone. Range one mile . . ."

The vertical reverse was the modern equivalent of the stall

turn sometimes employed by fighter pilots in the age of prop planes. The aircraft climbed straight up, losing speed until it threatened to stall out completely, then turned toward the ground. The plane's low speed made it possible to turn in an extremely tight radius, but there was a very large risk that the fighter would lose control.

Tombstone brought the Tomcat's swept-back wings forward and engaged the flaps. The F-14 bucked, stress vibrating through the hull, but the airspeed indicator showed less than one hundred and forty knots as he kicked in the rudder and brought the stick over. For one shuddering moment, the F-14 fought and bucked, and the stall warning light on his caution/advisory panel flashed once.

Then they were arrowing toward the ground once more. Tombstone cut the flaps and brought the wings back to full sweep, trading altitude for speed in an all-out dive for the deck. Two miles away, the MiGs were halfway into their turn, barely visible as a pair of black specks almost touching one another as they broke left in unison.

He pulled the F-14 out of its dive and hurtled toward the MiGs at almost five hundred knots. He selected the targeting display for his HUD and saw the small box symbols appear over the specks as the plane's computer identified potential targets. "We'll go for a Sidewinder launch," he told his RIO. He brought the targeting pipper on his HUD across one of the specks, saw the square flash into a circle with the computer graphic "M" for missile displayed.

His fingers closed on the firing button, and an AIM-9J Sidewinder slid clear of its rail. "Fox two!" Tombstone called, warning of a heat-seeker launch. "Fox two!"

The MiGs held their turn as the all-aspect heat-seeker arrowed toward the left-hand target. Both J-7s began popping flares, bright orange pinpoints of light which arced away from their hulls like Roman candles, trailing smoke.

"Two more bandits," Dixie warned. "Coming on our six. Range three miles."

"Let 'em come." Tombstone pulled the stick left, turning

inside the MiGs ahead, hoping to line up a shot at the second plane. He saw the contrail brush the MiG. There was a flash, and the J-7's wings folded toward one another, the fuselage disintegrating in white flame. Secondary explosions ate their way through the burning wreckage as fuel and munitions exploded. Burning debris scattered smoking trails into the jungle below.

"Splash one MiG!" Dixie called. "Chalk one for Tombstone!"

Tombstone began lining up for his second shot. The target was weaving and jinking now, aware that the American was closing fast inside his turn.

"Two bandits on our six," Dixie said. "Two miles. They're trying for a shot."

"Almost there," Tombstone said. "Almost there—"

A warbling tone sounded in his ear. "Stoney! They have lock! They have lock!"

"*Damn!*" Tombstone snapped the stick back to the right, throwing the Tomcat into a sudden split-S. The warble was the tone of an Atoll missile, the radar-guided Soviet and Chinese equivalent of the American Sparrow.

"They're still comin'," Dixie shouted. Tombstone could hear the RIO shifting back and forth in his seat, trying to keep his eyes on the approaching MiGs. "They're breaking right!"

"Hold your stomach, Dixie!"

"Launch! Launch!"

Tombstone hauled the Tomcat's nose up and rammed the throttles forward, past full military power to afterburner. His F-14 shrieked toward heaven.

0748 hours, 21 January
One mile south of U Feng

The Thai army column had deployed on either side of the trail and was well-hidden. The men were under orders not to fire, but the nearness of the enemy, the ear-piercing low pass by jet aircraft, the hiss and roar of launching SAMs had an unnerving effect. One soldier in particular, a private named Pang Rajathasithuk, found himself trembling as he lay in the jungle, watching a raggedly dressed column of troops walk south along the path.

It was a patrol, one of several sent out by the invaders to search for the leading elements of the Royal Thai Army, which was known to be in the area. Until this moment, Pang had not seen the enemy, had heard only stories and rumors about the coup, about the attack on U Feng, about pitched battles fought here and in Bangkok.

There were so *many* of them, some in Burmese uniforms, most in mismatched bits and pieces of uniform which suggested they were members of some private militia rather than an established army. Pang watched the line passing his position and wondered how large this invading army at U Feng really was. Could General Vinjit match such a force?

One of the ragged-looking soldiers on the path broke away from the rest of the column, his hands fumbling with the buttons of his trousers as he searched for a place to relieve himself. Chance put him squarely in front of Pang, and only a little below the level of the slope on which the Thai private lay. He looked up. . . .

Pang never knew whether the soldier saw him or not. To the Thai private, it seemed that the man was looking straight at him through the leaves. His finger closed on the trigger of his M-16, and the roar of the weapon on full auto echoed along the trail.

Burmese and rebel soldiers dove for cover. The other hidden Thai troops opened up, and the jungle trail became a bloody killing ground at the nexus of a deadly crossfire. Gunshots crashed and boomed among the leaves, and the steady, hammering thunder of an M-60 added to the racket. A Burmese soldier pitched to the ground, shrieking as he clutched his shattered knee. A rebel threw up his arms and toppled forward as bloody guts erupted from his side and back.

Long seconds passed before the ambushed troops recovered from their surprise enough to begin firing back, and by the time they did dozens of their number had crumpled to the ground or were already fleeing north as fast as their legs could carry

them. The heavy crump of grenades and 40-mm explosive
rounds joined in.

And from the control tower of U Feng, less than a mile to the
north, Hsiao heard the gunfire and knew the base was under
attack.

0748 hours, 21 January
Near U Feng

Shit! Lieutenant Miller's fist hit the ground in front of him with
frustration. He'd heard the sudden eruption of gunfire to the
south, knew the element of surprise was gone before the first
of the ambush survivors began streaming out of the forest
and onto the airstrip. From his hiding place, he could see their
wild gestures, hear their shouted warnings as they spread the
alarm.

Well, it couldn't have lasted long, not with several thousand
men wandering around loose in these woods. He gestured for
the radio, took the handset from the commo operator.

"Green Throne, Green Throne," he said. "This is Alligator.
Do you read, over?"

"Alligator, Green Throne. We read you. Go ahead."

"No joy on primary," he said. The words hurt as he said
them. But there was no way now to find any American
prisoners in that camp. "Repeat, no joy. Crocodile is engaging." Crocodile referred to the Thai contingent, and he wanted
Green Throne to know that it was the locals who'd screwed the
pooch.

"Understood, Alligator," the voice on the handset said.
"Green Throne" was Colonel John Caruso, monitoring the
action from his CIC back on board the *Chosin*. Communications were being relayed through a circling Navy Hawkeye
somewhere over central Thailand. "Revert to original op plan.
We will direct Chickenhawk and Thunderbird to move in."

"Roger that, Green Throne. Wilco. Alligator, out." He
handed the radio handset back to the commo operator. "Okay,
Sciaparelli. Hoburn. Break out the GLDs. Move it! Move it!

We don't have all day." In fact, he knew, they had very little time now at all.

It was too damned bad about those Western prisoners the Karens had reported seeing. But there was nothing more that could be done for them now.

0748 hours, 21 January
U Feng

Hsiao was gathering his maps and papers when an aide entered his office. "Hua! Get my pilot. Have him ready my helicopter. And send some men to get the Americans and bring them here."

"You are leaving, General?"

Hsiao nodded. "It is perhaps best if I take the Americans to Mong-koi."

"It could be dangerous. The air battle . . ."

"I shall be traveling at treetop level, and the border is only a few minutes away. The Americans will not pursue me into Burma."

"Yes, sir."

"A precautionary measure only, Hua. I think it best that I and my prisoners stay out of the line of fire until after the Q-5s destroy the Thai forces."

"As you command, General."

The aide hurried out, and Hsiao began gathering his maps and papers. This was more than precaution, he admitted to himself. The arrival of the American carrier planes had been a complete surprise. Wu might be holding them at bay, but at last word he'd lost five aircraft doing it, with no American kills reported yet. The Yankees' technology and their skill might yet turn the battle against his forces. If Wu was defeated, Dao's Q-5s, now on the way across the border from Burma, would be easy prey. And if the Q-5 attack was stopped, the Thai assault would come, possibly within minutes.

He did not wish to be in the area if that happened.

From Burma, Hsiao could retain control of his forces whatever happened, and the American prisoners would give him considerable bargaining power, both with the Thais and the Burmese. He might even be able to make a deal with the Americans, if they thought highly enough of their female news reporter.

He collected the last of his papers and strode unhurriedly from the room.

CHAPTER 27

"Made It!" Pamela said. "What's that? Shooting?"

She'd heard the sound before in the streets of Bangkok, a distant rattling sound. It was hard to associate that fireworks snapping with gunfire and death.

"Sure as hell is," Bayerly said, listening. "We'd better get ready to didi."

"Pardon?"

"*Di di mau*. Move out!"

"Move?" she asked, confused. "Where?"

Bayerly jerked his head toward the door. "Gunfire means someone's closing in. Probably a pretty big op if it's supported by Tomcats off the *Jeff*. These bozos here can't afford to let us go or get rescued. They'll either move us, maybe try to use us for bargaining later . . . or they'll shoot us."

"Oh, God . . ."

He gave her a tight-lipped smile. He seemed calmer now than he had earlier, calmer and more self-possessed. "Something tells me our friend Hsiao isn't going to want witnesses around talking about his part in things. Like kidnapping, torture, and murder for a start. Or revolution." He stood next to the shed's door, stooped slightly as though listening. "Okay. Stand back."

"What are you doing?" she asked.

301

He didn't answer but took several steps back to the far end of the shed, then threw himself at the door, smashing against the wood with his shoulder. There was a loud crash, but the door held. "Made It! What are you doing? The guards will hear!"

"Shit," he said, rubbing his shoulder. "It always works in the movies!" He backed up again, paused, then took another run at the door. The crash was so loud that Pamela thought the sound must be carrying all over the base.

"They'll *hear* . . . !"

"I think our guards took off the first time those Tomcats buzzed us," Bayerly said. He slammed his shoulder against the door again . . . and again. "By now they're halfway back to Burma."

He hit the door once more, this time with a splintering crash which tore the door from its hinges. Bayerly plunged through, landing on his hands and knees on the wreckage of the door.

Bayerly grinned. "Let's get out of here."

"Yin kin! Yin kin!" The soldier appeared out of nowhere, an AK-47 raised to his shoulder, the muzzle thrusting at Bayerly's face. Pamela didn't know if he'd been there all along or had just arrived to investigate the noise. His face twisted in fury. *"Reho kaho!"*

"Okay, okay!" Bayerly said, holding up one hand. He started to rise. "Keep your shirt on—"

He sprang forward and up, getting under the soldier's AK and knocking its muzzle toward the sky just as the man's finger jerked at the trigger. A burst of full-auto fire rattled the walls of the shed.

The rebel soldier went down on his back, Bayerly on top of him, both men wrestling for the AK between them. The American outweighed his opponent by at least fifty pounds and had the advantage of having one knee on the man's chest. Bayerly tugged hard at the weapon . . . then changed tactics and pushed down as hard as he could. Caught off guard, the enemy soldier took the full force of the blow across his chest. Bayerly pulled again, and this time broke the AK free of the soldier's grasp. Pamela saw the assault rifle rise in the air, butt down . . . then descend sharply. There was a crack, and the guard lay motionless on the ground, his forehead oddly misshapen.

Bayerly racked back the bolt on the AK, checking the chamber. A gold cartridge spun through the air. "Let's go."

They hurried around the corner of the shed, then sprinted for the fuel tanks.

Beyond, a hundred-yard clear stretch separated them from the jungle.

0750 hours, 21 January
Tomcat 201

Tombstone kept the Tomcat in a vertical climb, afterburners howling. At thirty-five thousand feet he put the aircraft into a half-twist, then cut the burners and let the plane fall on its back, canopy down, as his fingers stabbed at the chaff-release button. Looking "up," Tombstone could see the dark green folds of mountains and valleys, the silver twistings of the Taeng River.

The contrail of the Atoll AAM arrowed toward him from the Earth.

Still pumping chaff, Tombstone let the Tomcat slide into an inverted dive. The trick was to create a large enough radar target for the oncoming missile that its microchip brain would believe that the target's center lay somewhere behind the aircraft . . . instead of squarely between the stabilizers and the cockpit.

He held his breath as the missile closed . . .

. . . and flashed past the tail of his aircraft just as he cut in the afterburners once more.

The Atoll exploded somewhere astern, and the Tomcat shuddered with the blast. Tombstone heard a loud *ping*, metal striking metal, but the lights on his warning panel remained blissfully unlit.

Falling now, Tombstone righted the F-14 and throttled down to eighty percent. His eyes went to his fuel gauge. Not good.

They'd been in the dogfight for less than three minutes, but using the afterburner had burned a hell of a lot of fuel.

He was on top of the dogfight now. Looking down, he could see aircraft and contrails everywhere he looked, spread out between him and the jungle, silvery specks moving against dark green. South he could see the scar of U Feng; west the sun flashed from the Taeng River.

"Eagle Three, this is Eagle Six! I've got two on my tail! Get 'em off! Shit, they're going for lock! They've got lock!"

"Hold on, Nightmare!" Garrison's voice called. "I'm on them!"

Still diving, Tombstone plunged back into the aerial melee. Pulling up, he saw a Tomcat in a hard turn a mile ahead, closely pursued by a MiG, which in turn was being pursued by another F-14. He was too far to read the numbers, but he knew the Tomcats were Nightmare Marinaro and Army Garrison.

"Break right, Nightmare!" Army called. "Break right!"

The lead Tomcat cut hard to the right just as Garrison fired. "Fox two! Fox two!"

One of the MiGs exploded seconds later, a burst of jagged, flaming fragments spilling from the sky. Army's Tomcat overshot the second MiG before he could get a shot, however, and the enemy plane stuck to Nightmare's tail.

Tombstone saw that he was in a good position to cut across the arc of Nightmare's turn. He pushed the throttle to full military power, lining up his target pipper on the second MiG.

"Army!" Nightmare called. "Where are you, man?"

"Steady, Nightmare," Tombstone said. "I'm on him."

"He's still got lock!" Nightmare yelled. "Hurry, Stoney!"

The two planes were leading Tombstone now. The pipper on his HUD trailed the MiG, but he couldn't turn hard enough to catch up. "Nightmare!" he called. "When I tell you, break left. That'll give me a clear shot at his six!"

"Rog!"

"On my mark . . . three . . . two . . . one . . . *break*!"

Nightmare snapped left in a sharp split-S, and the MiG followed. This guy is good, Tombstone thought. But he'd known in advance where Nightmare would be going and had been able to anticipate the MiG's move and be ready. His HUD showed a target lock and a tone growled in his ear. "Lock! Fox two! Fox two!"

The missile sped from its rail, slipped up the J-7's tailpipe and exploded. The MiG's wings closed together like folding hands.

0750 hours, 21 January
MiG 612

Colonel Wu pulled his J-7 around in a hard, left-hand turn, following the F-5 toward the jungle. He watched as his Aphid heat-seeker AAM slammed into the Thai Freedom Fighter's tailpipe. A blossom of orange flame engulfed the target's tail, blasting away bits of whirling metal, and the F-5 began plummeting toward the jungle.

That made five kills scored against the enemy, two of them downed by Wu himself. The Thai aircraft were relatively easy targets. The American-made F-5s were as good as his squadron's J-7s, but the superiority of the Chinese pilots' training was making itself felt.

"Wu t'uan chang! Wu t'uan chang!" an excited voice yelled over his headset. In Chinese military usage he was "Regimental Commander Wu" rather than "Colonel."

"Who calls?" he snapped. The other pilot's voice betrayed growing panic, and Wu could not allow that to continue.

"The American planes, Regimental Commander! They are turning the battle against us!"

Wu looked up through his canopy. Contrails snarled and twisted above him. He saw the black streak of an aircraft burning as it fell and realized it was one of his own.

He'd lost track of the numbers on either side. There was no way to follow the battle in any detail now, not with so many combatants involved. But the Thais seemed scattered . . . and between the onslaught from Wu's J-7s and the SAMs at U Feng and along the river, they'd taken heavy casualties. There seemed to be six American aircraft . . . and he still had eighteen J-7s in his squadron.

Discounting the Thais, that made the odds three to one in his favor.

Wu made a snap decision. "All Dragons," he called. "This is Dragon Leader. Ignore the Thais. Concentrate on the Americans! Repeat, concentrate on the Americans!"

It was the only way to stop the deadly attrition of his own forces.

0751 hours, 21 January
Tomcat 201

Airplanes fell from the sky. Tombstone watched another Thai F-5 explode, victim of a MiG-launched Aphid. Seconds later, Price Taggart loosed a radar-guided Sparrow from almost ten miles away, tracking a MiG which dove for the jungle. The Chinese pilot tried to lose the Mach 4 hunter by weaving in close among the forested ridges . . . and failed in a spectacularly blazing fireball.

Garrison and Marinaro both reported kills as well. The MiGs were frantic now, and Tombstone thought he detected a new pattern to their movements. Though spread now across twenty miles of sky, all the way from U Feng to the green line, they appeared to be trying to close with the American planes, forcing them into close combat.

"This is Eagle Two, Eagle Two!" Batman called. "I've got two on my tail. Correction . . . four on my tail! Four on me! Jeez, where're they coming from?"

Under that kind of pressure, the Americans' luck wouldn't hold for long. There were at least eight Thai aircraft still in the area, but they were not understanding—or responding to—Victor Four Delta's calls, and the battle was quickly collapsing into a slugfest, eighteen MiG-21s ganging up on six Tomcats.

Tombstone saw Batman ahead, a black speck pursued by four smaller specks, weaving and twisting back and forth, working to shake his pursuers.

Tombstone checked his position, then swung left, positioning himself so that the morning sun was squarely behind his Tomcat. "Eagle Two, Eagle One," he called. "Coming in on your four, right out of the sun. Give 'em a high speed yo-yo!"

"Copy, Tombstone," Batman replied. "Give the word."

"Ready . . ." Tombstone studied the rapidly swelling MiGs. They showed no sign that they were aware of the Tomcat stooping on them out of the sun's glare. *"Do it!"*

Batman's plane started to turn left, then pulled up sharply just as three of the four J-7s on his tail were committed to the turn. They shot past him as he went high, inverted, then dropped again, pulling in behind the former hunters.

The fourth MiG had been lagging behind and countered Batman's maneuver, sticking to the American's tail.

But Tombstone had assumed that the tail-end charlie would be the one to cause trouble . . . and had already locked on with a Sparrow radar homer. "Fox one! Fox one!" The heavy missile slid out from under the Tomcat's wing.

Tombstone was already concentrating on his next target, a J-7 which was now turning sharply across his line of fire, still in a tight break after passing Batman.

"Target lock!" Batman yelled. "Fox two!"

Tombstone locked onto his target and triggered a slim, heat-seeking package of death. The Sidewinder arrowed away. . . .

The Sparrow caught its target behind the cockpit. Eighty-eight pounds of high explosive shredded the MiG's starboard wing. Fuel in the wing tanks ignited.

Seconds later, Batman's AIM-9 made its kill, followed by the flash and billowing debris cloud of Tombstone's Sidewinder. The surviving MiG was already fleeing, throttled up to full afterburner and lunging for the far side of the green line.

Tombstone dropped onto Batman's wing. "Good to have you back," he radioed.

"Good to be back. Watch it! Three more, nine o'clock!"

"Let's take 'em. Break left."

"Eagle Two in!"

The Tomcats stood on their port wings, turning toward the new targets. The MiGs, aware that they were being stalked, abruptly broke off and fled north.

"This is Eagle Four!" Taggart called suddenly. "I'm in trouble!"

"Eagle Four! Where are you?"

"On the deck! Two bandits on my six. I've taken a hit. . . ."

Tombstone looked down, saw Taggart's 203 aircraft streaming smoke low above the treetops. VF-95's luck had just run dry. The MiGs on his tail were too close to use missiles. Tombstone could see the puffs of smoke from their cannons dotting a pair of long, straight lines behind them.

"Let's go, Batman!"

"With you, Boss."

Tombstone brought his Tomcat over, plunging toward the ground. He let the lead MiG slide into his targeting pipper as he switched his selector switch to radar homing. Target lock! He heard the familiar growl in his headset and fired. A Sparrow homer *shooshed* toward the enemy plane.

"Fox one! Fox one! I'm on him, Price! Hold on!"

"Hear you . . . Stoney . . ." Taggart's voice was straining against the G-forces as he pulled up. The J-7s followed. . . .

Tombstone's Sparrow started to follow . . . then swerved erratically and slammed into a jungle-covered ridge.

"God damn it . . . !" Either the Sparrow had accidentally locked onto the ground . . . or the MiG had decoyed it with chaff. He opened the F-14's throttle wider, closing the gap.

The lead MiG was firing again. Tombstone saw bits of metal flaking away from the twin stabilizers of Taggart's F-14. The smoke from his engine was heavier now. Taggart was still climbing, but his plane was reacting sluggishly. Tombstone dropped down on the two MiGs less than a quarter of a mile behind them.

"Got the one on the right," Batman yelled. "Lock! Fox two!"

"I've got the left!" Tombstone decided to stay with the Sparrow missiles. He had two of them left, and only one heat-seeker. "Fox one!"

The hunted Tomcat seemed to stagger. Tombstone could tell

that Taggart was fighting to keep the wounded turkey under control.

"Eagle Four, Eagle Leader," he called. "Punch out, Price!"

"I can hold it, Stoney!" His Tomcat was dropping again, skimming the trees as the MiGs weaved back and forth on his tail.

Taggart's aircraft exploded with stunning suddenness, bursting into flame, then tumbling over and over and over again until the wreckage sheared through the uppermost branches of the forest canopy.

"Tomcat down, Tomcat down!" Batman called. Tombstone could hear pain in his wingman's voice. "Eagle Four down three miles east of Taeng River, five miles south of the green line . . ."

The MiGs were climbing on full burners. Tombstone's second Sparrow followed, zeroing in on the lead MiG. He could see the number 612 on the MiG's nose. Tombstone found himself willing the missile to detonate. . . .

A miss! *Damn!* The Sparrow had passed fifty feet behind the jinking MiG, decoyed this time, Tombstone was certain, by a timely burst of chaff.

His attitude and position were wrong to pursue. "Two-oh-one breaking, Batman! Going high!" He pulled the F-14 clear of the trees.

"I'm with you, Stoney," Batman replied. He sounded shaken.

Behind them, black smoke curled into the sky, grave marker for Lieutenant Ronald Taggart and his RIO, Lieutenant Charles Ziegler.

0752 hours, 21 January
U Feng

Their flight was an all-out run away from the shed, past the neatly aligned fuel tanks, and into the open space beyond. The camp was in complete chaos. Pamela could hear the rising whine of the planes she'd seen being started earlier. Once she chanced a look back over her shoulder and saw two heavy-bodied aircraft lifting from the runway with a thundering roar. Other planes seemed to be milling about at one end of the runway, readying for takeoff.

Where were the Navy planes? She could hear a distant rumble of jet aircraft, but outside of wisps and streaks of white high in the sky, she could not see them, couldn't tell if they were engaged in battle or not.

She could see soldiers in the camp, but none were close by, and none appeared to notice the two fugitives. "Run!" Bayerly yelled, and she ran, her legs pumping away. Memories of Hsiao and the warehouse drove her on.

The clearing around U Feng was a hundred yards across, but the ground was soft and broken, making each step treacherous. She quickly found herself slowing. She'd eaten little more than a bowlful of rice in two days, had slept no more than a few hours. In minutes, her lungs were burning with the effort, her breath coming in gasps. She clutched at her side as a stitch hobbled her. She couldn't run much farther. . . .

They were halfway across the clearing when someone saw them. Pamela heard a burst of gunfire behind her, much closer than the rattlings off in the jungle, and something went *snap-snap-snap* just above her head, making her duck involuntarily. She started to recover . . . and then her foot turned and she went sprawling to the ground.

"C'mon! C'mon!" Bayerly yelled. He stood above her, breathing hard, the AK-47 raised to his shoulder and pointed back toward the base. "Run!"

But Pamela was on her hands and knees, unable to get up. Her knees, her legs were trembling with the effort which had brought her this far. "I . . . can't . . ."

"*Move, damn you . . . !*" Bayerly's scream was like a physical blow. She found her balance and got her feet under her. Still shaking, she lurched forward.

"*Yoot!*" a shrill voice yelled behind them. "*Yawm pa!*"

Bayerly's AK fired, a short burst that assaulted Pamela's ears. She turned in time to see three Thais less than fifty yards away. Two of them staggered and fell with the burst. The third turned and ran back the way he'd come.

She looked back toward the camp. More of those heavy-looking aircraft Bayerly had called Q-5s were climbing into the sky. Her attention was drawn by a loud roar . . . not the thunder of jet engines but a chattering, propeller sound. Something was rising above the fuel storage tanks. . . .

A helicopter. She recognized the distinctive shape, an American-made Huey, probably a relic of Vietnam.

And it was skimming low across the fuel tanks, coming directly toward them.

CHAPTER 28

0752 hours, 21 January
Tomcat 201, near the Thai-Burmese border

Tombstone's oxygen mask was slick with sweat, and he had to keep blinking his eyes to clear them. This ACM encounter had lasted longer than the usual dogfight already and showed no sign of letting up.

"Victor Four Delta, Eagle. Where's Chickenhawk, over?"

"Eagle Leader, Chickenhawk is inbound at primary target, on final approach. ETA two minutes, over. Thunderbird is five minutes behind them."

"Tell 'em to hurry," Tombstone replied. "We can't hold much longer."

"We copy, Eagle. Homeplate advises that the ground attack is under way at U Feng. Hang tight a few more minutes, fellas."

U Feng under attack? That wasn't supposed to go down until after the place was hit by the Hornets and the Intruders. Well, enough had gone wrong already. Maybe the ground assault had gone by the board as well.

"Eagle, Victor Four Delta," Tombstone heard on his radio. "Come in, Eagle."

"Eagle copies, Victor Four Delta. Go ahead."

"We have new targets," the Hawkeye CIC officer said. "Estimate eight to ten bogies, low altitude, originating Mongkoi. They're on a vector that will take them toward Tango LZ."

312

Tango LZ . . . the Thai helicopter staging area.

"Don't see 'em, Stoney," Dixie said. "I think we're too low." The Hawkeye, circling at a much higher altitude and using ECM tricks to look past Snow White's jamming, was in a better position to see what was going on over U Feng than the Tomcats, even though they were much closer.

"Victor Four Delta, Eagle Leader. No joy on your bogies. Vector us in, over."

"Roger, Eagle Leader. Come to one-seven-three. That will put you on the bogies in approximately two minutes."

"Copy that, Victor. Wilco."

"Watch it, Tombstone," his RIO warned. "Check our fuel."

"I see it, Dixie. We can go for a while yet."

"Tombstone . . . fuel's gonna be a problem! We've got maybe fifteen minutes . . . assuming you don't go to burner anymore!"

"I said I see it, Dix!" Tombstone put the Tomcat into a gentle roll, searching the sky below as they inverted. The dogfight had scattered the combatants for tens of miles in every direction. Dixie's VDI showed plenty of bogies but they were no longer within close combat range of one another. Long-range missiles like Sparrow were useless now. No one was squawking IFF; without Identification Friend or Foe, there was no way to tell who was friendly and who the enemy.

Dixie was right, though. They were down to one Sidewinder and one Sparrow left, plus the 675-round drum for his Tomcat's M61A-1 20-mm cannon. Ten more minutes and they'd be on bingo fuel; fifteen minutes and it would be joker.

But the local sky was clear of MiGs, while large numbers of aircraft were reported taking off from U Feng. If they didn't want to fight their way all the way back to Point Lima, it would be better to catch the newcomers before they got organized.

"Eagle Leader to all Eagles," he radioed. "Muster over U Feng. We're going to investigate those bogies."

"Roger, Eagle Leader," Batman said. The other VF-95 aviators checked in one after another.

Five Tomcats began closing the range toward U Feng.

0752 hours, 21 January
U Feng

Pamela watched the Huey dropping toward them, slewing
sideways until she could see the RTAF markings on the tail
rotor boom, until she could see into the open cargo hatch.
There were men there, soldiers . . . and a professorial-
looking man with gray hair and glasses.

Hsiao.

A soldier on the cargo deck next to Hsiao raised his AK to
his shoulder. Pamela couldn't hear the shots, drowned in the
thunder of the rotors, but she saw the flicker of muzzle flash
against the shadows of the Huey's interior. Ten feet in front of
her, Bayerly staggered and almost fell.

Her paralysis of mind was gone, replaced by raw fear. Hsiao
was coming for them, coming for her! She ran to Bayerly,
grabbing at his arm. "Come on!" She had to scream to be heard
over the helicopter's roar.

He shook her off.

"Please, Made It!" Tears streamed down her cheeks. "Run!
Please!"

He turned, almost reluctantly, and then he was running with
her . . . but he'd only taken a dozen steps before he stopped
again. She saw the red stain spreading across his shirt, just
beneath his left arm.

"I'll help—"

"No, damn it!" He planted his hand on her shoulder and
shoved her roughly toward the treeline. "Get the fuck out of
here! I'll hold them here!"

She felt torn between the need to run and the need to stay.
She reached out again but he turned away, dropping to one
knee and raising the captured AK.

The helicopter was hovering just above the earth less than
seventy yards away. Soldiers were jumping out and advancing
across the clearing toward them.

Bayerly's assault rifle hammered off a volley. The enemy

soldiers dropped to their bellies and started firing back, but Bayerly was not firing at them, she realized.

He was aiming at the helo.

She heard the change in the pitch of the Huey's rotors. It was lifting again, nose high. Bayerly fired again, holding the trigger down and describing a small circle with the muzzle of his weapon, spraying the helo with lead. Smoke burst from the machine's engine, a small puff at first . . . and then an expanding, billowing white cloud which was caught by the rotor wash and swirled about. Pamela could hear an ominous clanking mingled with the rotor noise now. The Huey turned sharply, trying to gain altitude, but the pilot seemed to be in trouble.

One spinning rotor blade caught the earth. . . .

The helicopter seemed to leap skyward, nose high, but its tail boom slammed into the ground. There was an explosion. Orange flame engulfed the convulsing machine and the shock wave struck her like a hot slap across her face. Pamela had the impressions of an instant seared into her brain, the sight of a snapped-off rotor blade cartwheeling across the sky, of men on the ground wreathed in flame as the ammo in their belts cooked off.

She lay face down on the ground for a long time, not remembering falling, not knowing anything but the hell of noise and the piercing stink of aviation fuel. When she looked up, the Huey, still burning, was reduced to a twisted, blackened skeleton. The soldiers who had been on it were dead.

Hsiao . . . She didn't see him, but he'd been aboard. He must be dead as well.

Bayerly was lying a few yards away, his sightless eyes staring up at her. A bullet had drilled through his right cheekbone and entered his brain.

She sank to her knees, taking Bayerly's head in her lap. She cradled him for long moments, as the sounds of gunfire, the crump of explosions grew closer.

"Miss? Miss!" A hand touched her shoulder. "He's dead, miss. And we have to go!"

She looked up. Several Marines were there. She'd not even heard their approach.

"Are you all right?"

She nodded.

"You're Miss Drake?"

"Yes . . ."

"Come on, please, ma'am. This place is about to get dumped on."

She didn't want to leave Bayerly, but strong hands pulled her to her feet and guided her away. "Lieutenant Miller, ma'am," the Marine said. "Marine Recon. We've got to get to cover, fast!"

Blood stained the front of her blouse. Not hers, she realized numbly. His. "Wha . . . what?"

"We've got to get under cover. We've got Hornets and Intruders coming down on this place like a ton of bricks, and we don't want to be here when they do!"

She looked up as Tomcats screeched overhead, their thunder deafening as they headed south.

0753 hours, 21 January
MiG 612, near U Feng

Colonel Wu watched as five of the blips on his radar converged, moving south toward U Feng. Those would be the Americans . . . and it was easy to guess at their target. The radar returns from Dao's Q-5 attack Squadron were also clear, now passing some five miles south of U Feng as they readied for their bombing run.

It was too late to help the bombers, but a tactical opportunity was opening up for a decisive blow against the Yankee fighters.

"This is Dragon Leader," he radioed. "All Dragons on me. I'm going in!" He lined up his J-7 on the American formation and cut in his afterburner. While they were concentrating on the bombers, he would strike from behind.

0753 hours, 21 January
Tomcat 201, over U Feng

Tombstone saw U Feng flash beneath his Tomcat, but he was more interested in the jungle-hopping aircraft five miles ahead.

"I've got them, Tombstone!" Dixie called. "Bearing one-eight-three. They're crossing in front of us, right to left."

"Let's get a lock on 'em," Tombstone said. They had one Sparrow left. He let the F-14's AWG-9 radar pick out one of the planes in the tight enemy formation, transferred the lock to the Sparrow, and pressed the trigger. "Fox one!"

"Fox one, fox one!" Batman echoed.

"I'm in," Garrison called. "With one for Price Tag. Fox one!"

0753 hours, 21 January
Nanchang Q-5 No. 70813, five miles south of U Feng

Group Commander Dao Zhu Qingtong saw the Thai staging area first, a broad clearing several miles ahead. As he drew closer, he could see the RTAF helos, dozens of them, arrayed in orderly ranks with their rotors turning.

He flipped the arming switches for his payload and opened his bomb bay doors. Each Q-5 carried four Chinese FAB-250 general-purpose bombs in its internal bay, plus four more on wing and fuselage pylons. Eighty bombs . . . each weighing two hundred fifty kilograms . . . that helicopter assembly area was about to become a slaughter pen. . . .

There was a flash to Dao's left. He snapped his head around in time to see Aircraft 70816 crumple like paper in a blaze of white flame, as fragments splashed across the sky. Two tons of high explosives detonated in a shattering secondary blast that rocked Dao's aircraft wildly, forcing him to grip the stick with both hands.

They were under attack! The Q-5 had no passive warning receivers, and the attack was literally coming in out of the blue. Another plane exploded . . . and a third.

"Break off! Break off!" Dao shouted into his radio. Duty to the People and to the Party was well and good . . . but death in support of a minor military rebellion in this barbarous jungle country held no appeal for the pilot. People and Party could be better served by intact aircraft . . . and living pilots.

The seven surviving Q-5s swung toward the northeast, still flying at treetop level as they raced for home at Mach 1.

Unfortunately, the Sparrow missiles already launched could not tell that Dao had broken off the engagement. Two more planes died in fiery eruptions.

Dao Zhu Qingtong never felt the blast which killed him.

0754 hours, 21 January
MiG 612

At better than Mach 1, Wu's J-7 closed with the American planes from behind. He'd already targeted the one he assumed was the leader.

The other MiGs of Dragon were scattered, but closing. If Wu could take out the enemy leader, he might be able to break their formation.

0755 hours, 21 January
Tomcat 201, over U Feng

"Watch it, Stoney," Dixie warned. "Bandit comin' onto our six!"

"Right." His last Sparrow gone and one Sidewinder in reserve, Tombstone knew he would not be effective against the Q-5s ahead. But he could run interference for the rest of the pack.

"Batman!" he called. "Stay on the bogies! I'll block this clown."

"Copy, Tombstone. Be careful."

"Rog." He pulled the Tomcat up, breaking clear of the F-14 formation. The MiG closed.

"Still coming," Dixie said. "He's dropping onto our six, range two miles."

Tombstone glanced back over his shoulder. "I see him. Hang on and we'll take him for a ride."

He put the F-14 into a left turn, waiting for the MiG to follow him into the break. Once the enemy pilot was committed, he slammed the stick back to the right, at the same time pulling back on the throttles and cutting in the flaps. The maneuver, a split-S, was designed to force the pursuing plane to overshoot.

"No good, Stoney!" Dixie said. "He's still back there!"

Tombstone brought the stick back left again, waited for the MiG to commit . . . then boosted to full military power and pulled into a climb, rolling inverted at the top of a short climb, then dropping toward where the bandit should have overshot. . . .

"No good again! He's still comin'!"

Damn! This guy was too good. . . .

"He's got lock!" Dixie called. "He's going for launch!"

Tombstone heard the tone of a radar lock. He went into another climb and kept pushing. "Hit the chaff, Dixie!" he yelled.

"Launch! Launch!"

"Keep punching out chaff!" He held the Tomcat's climb, then dropped into inverted level flight. "Where is it?"

"Still coming! There it goes!"

He saw the missile pass astern of the Tomcat, a white streak scratched vertically into the sky. He caught only a glimpse of the missile itself, a pencil balanced on orange flame. Quickly, Tombstone pulled a half roll, then started climbing again. The MiG was still climbing, sticking to his six with a grim and deadly determination.

"Keep an eye on him, Dixie," Tombstone said. He eased the throttles back, cutting power. The Tomcat slowed, still climbing. At one hundred fifty knots the wings slid forward and the plane began shimmying, threatening a stall.

"Gettin' close, Tombstone! Range one thousand . . ."

"A little more . . ."

"Shit, I think he's goin' for guns, Stoney!"

"A little more . . ."

The Tomcat hung at the peak of the climb. The port engine coughed and the stall warning light flared. Tombstone let the Tomcat fall onto its side, kicking in rudders and flaps as the F-14 fell sideways, then slid into a tight vertical reverse.

The MiG pilot was good . . . no question there. But Tombstone was capitalizing on the advantages in maneuverability the F-14 had over the MiG-21. His pursuer *couldn't* match that turn in a MiG-21, not without stalling out or falling out of control.

The Tomcat was plunging earthward now. Tombstone watched the MiG swell until it filled his HUD. He flashed past head to head, picking up speed rapidly. In that frozen-instant of passage, Tombstone saw the MiG climbing past him, the number 612 prominent in red on the nose.

The MiG that had eluded him earlier . . . and downed Price and Zig-Zag.

As soon as he was past, he brought the stick back and cut in his afterburners. G-forces pressed him down in his ejection seat, draining the blood from his brain and threatening him with unconsciousness. Then he was hard into a right break, twisting his head back in an attempt to locate his opponent.

"Where is he, Dixie? Do you see him?"

"One-two-zero, Stoney. Three o'clock high . . ."

There he was. Tombstone held the turn, climbing slightly now, rising under the other plane. The MiG driver was trying to turn inside Tombstone's break, but the Tomcat's position was perfect.

One Sidewinder left. Tombstone got the lock and triggered the launch. "Fox two!"

The missile arced away toward the enemy plane, drawing closer . . . closer . . . *No!* The MiG was twisting away, scattering dazzling pinpoints of light in its wake. Tombstone watched as his last Sidewinder curved away, uselessly following a flare.

"Let him go, Tombstone! We're almost bingo fuel, man! We don't have the gas!"

"Just a moment more!" At full military power he closed the gap between the Tomcat and the MiG.

"We're out of missiles, Tombstone."

"Switching to guns." He thumbed the selector switch on his stick. The concentric rings of the M61 target reticle appeared on his HUD. The MiG was turning again, trying to break right. Tombstone anticipated the turn, leading the MiG by a generous margin. They crowded in closer . . . closer. . . .

He brought his thumb down on the firing switch. The F-14's four-barreled Gatling cut loose with a buzzsaw shriek, pumping out 20-mm shells at the rate of one hundred per second. The MiG was jinking, the pilot throwing the delta-winged aircraft back and forth, up and down, trying to break Tombstone's aim.

Puffs of smoke appeared on the tail section, and bits and pieces of metal began falling away. Tombstone kept the trigger depressed, firing round after round after high-velocity round into the stricken aircraft.

The MiG fell. . . .

0755 hours, 21 January
MiG 612, south of U Feng

Colonel Wu knew the aircraft was lost when he pulled back on the stick and felt no response in the controls at all. The ground was twisting crazily as his MiG began tumbling, and still the American's cannon shells were crashing into the plane, shredding hull metal and control surfaces and electronic circuitry. His control console was lit with a dozen systems-failure lights, and the fire warning light was on.

"Dragon, Dragon," he called over the radio. "This is Dragon Leader. Break off the attack. Regroup, then make for Fuhsingchen. Repeat, make for Fuhsingchen."

It was useless to continue. Half of his unit was destroyed or would never fly again, and the Americans were on their guard. By ordering his people to break off, perhaps some would

322 Keith Douglass

survive. Perhaps General Hsiao would be able to reorganize the
unit back in the People's Republic.

He felt a savage bitterness at the failure of Hsiao's plan. It
was the American carrier planes that had broken the operation.
The coup, he thought, might yet succeed.

But it would fail or succeed without the help of his Dragons.

The American had stopped firing, whether because he was
out of ammo or because he'd lost a workable firing angle, Wu
couldn't tell. His surviving pilots began acknowledging his
last transmission as his MiG fell toward the ground, now
some eight thousand feet below. It was time to abandon the
aircraft.

He hit the canopy release, bracing himself for the blast of
wind which buffeted him full force as soon as the cockpit was
open. Then he grabbed the ejection handle and pulled.

The ejection seat's rockets fired, rocketing him clear of the
aircraft.

It was unfortunate for Colonel Wu that the canopy had not
separated completely from the aircraft, a defect in the original
Soviet design which had never been corrected by the Chinese
engineers who'd reworked the J-7.

Wu's body slammed into the cockpit at two hundred miles
per hour. His chute opened and lowered him gently to the floor
of the Taeng Valley, but he was dead long before he hit the
ground.

0755 hours, 21 January
Tomcat 201, over U Feng

Tombstone watched the stricken MiG fall into the jungle and
wondered who he'd just been facing. That guy had not been
Thai, had certainly not been Burmese. Chinese?

"He's gone, Tombstone," Dixie said. "And it looks like the
other bandits are breaking off."

Tombstone didn't answer. At Wonsan he'd led his men into
combat, knowing who the enemy was, knowing that they
fought to save American hostages held by the North Koreans.
But this . . . this was different.

He found that, like millions of military men before him, he wasn't entirely sure what he was fighting for . . . or why.

"Tombstone? We're bingo fuel. We've gotta get this bitch to a Texaco."

"Right, Dix. Whistle 'em up and let's get a drink."

There would be time for analysis later.

0800 hours, 21 January
U Feng

Once the remaining Q-5s turned away from the Thai LZ, the rest of the battle was anticlimax. The RTAF Hueys and the Marine helos on loan to the Thai airmobile forces lifted from the jungle clearing at almost the same moment that the American Hornets were hitting SAM sites at U Feng and along the Taeng River Valley. Ten surviving RTAF planes regrouped at Chiang Mai as the last of the enemy aircraft vanished across the border, and control of Thailand's skies returned to the Thais.

Within moments, the A-6F Intruders of VA-84, the Blue Rangers, call sign Thunderbird, roared out of the south, scattering antipersonnel bomblets. On the airstrip and among the barracks at U Feng, Burmese soldiers, Thai rebels, and drug lord militiamen died by the tens . . . by the hundreds, cut down by shrapnel like wheat before a scythe. Orange flames leaped into the sky, and a pall of smoke hung above U Feng like a shroud.

The helicopters skimmed in above the treetops, door gunners ready to fight for the U Feng LZ, but only isolated and scattered gunfire met them. Thai Rangers and Special Forces dropped from the helos while they were still airborne, dispersing throughout the compound. The defenders began surrendering. A ponderously fat general named Kol ordered all of the Burmese troops remaining at U Feng to lay down their arms and give up. Within moments, the rest of the defenders were following the example of the Burmese, surrendering en masse.

The battle was over by 0830, when members of the Thai
First Division (Airborne) raised the national flag of Thailand
over the traffic control tower.

0841 hours, 21 January
U Feng

It had been a near thing for the Tomcats of VF-95. Fuel almost
gone, each aircraft had received only enough from one of the
two orbiting KA-6 tankers to get them safely to the ground.
Aircraft with enough fuel remaining in their tanks bingoed to
Chiang Mai or all the way to Don Muong. Others, like
Tombstone and Batman, set down at U Feng, dropping onto a
runway partly masked by drifting smoke.

He saw her waiting by the runway as he climbed out of his
Tomcat.

"Pamela!" Then she was in his arms as his flight helmet
clattered on the tarmac. He embraced her for a long time.
"Pam, it's so *good* to see you. . . ."

After a long moment, he pulled back. "Where's Made It?"

A shadow passed behind her eyes, and he knew Bayerly was
dead. "Show me."

She took him to the place beyond the burned-out skeleton of
an old Huey Slick. He lay where she said she'd left him,
staring up at the sky. "Tombstone . . . he died saving my
life," she said. "He thought he was a coward, but he died
saving my life."

Tombstone squatted next to the body and gently closed the
man's eyes. He wanted to do something . . . something more
for the man who'd saved Pamela.

He became aware of a weight in the shoulder pocket of his
flight suit. Wondering what it was, he reached in and pulled
something out.

The medal . . . his Navy Cross. Tombstone remembered
stuffing it there, back on the fantail of the *Jefferson*. He'd
never had the chance to transfer it back to the safe in his
quarters. Damn. . . . He'd almost thrown the thing over-

board, convinced that his own presumed heroism was a fake.

Impulsively, he reached down and pinned the blue and white ribbon to the front of Bayerly's shirt. When he stood, Pamela took his arm and squeezed.

"It's not the medal, you know," she said. "It's the *man*."

EPILOGUE

The ceremony took place in the outer courtyard of the Grand Palace, directly adjoining the gold-spired magnificence of Wat Phra Keo, the Temple of the Emerald Buddha. The crowd had begun assembling there hours before, old women with cropped hair and betel-stained lips, students in school uniforms, businessmen in suits, society matrons in pastel-hued silk, office workers, soldiers in full dress whites.

A separate block of white-clad men in ranks stood in a position of special honor, before the throne set under the temporary awning before the temple gates. They were a contingent of officers and men from the U.S.S. *Jefferson*, resplendent in their full dress whites, standing at attention as one official succeeded another at the speaker's podium in front of the throne.

On the throne was King Bhumibol Adulyadej, also in white, with a gold sash across his chest.

The current speaker was the American ambassador, who was thanking the American Navy and Marines for their timely defense of American interests in Thailand. The speech had been going on now for nearly twenty minutes, and Tombstone wondered just how thankful a diplomat had any right to be.

At least, Tombstone thought, he knew now what he's been fighting for . . . and what he'd been fighting *against*.

The coup was over. Without the support of the King or the people, with American Marines and aircraft openly siding with

326

the loyalists, with the *Jefferson*, her consorts, and her air wing on station between Bangkok and Sattahip, the rebellion had collapsed as quickly as it had begun. The rebel officers were under arrest. The soldiers, most of them, had been disarmed and allowed to return to their barracks. There was talk of a general amnesty for all save those who had directly threatened civilian lives.

The ambassador was talking now of heroes.

Heroes? Yes, there had been plenty of those. Bayerly . . . killed defending Pamela. Taggart and Ziegler, shot down in the dogfight over U Feng. And there was that sailor, young David Howard, just promoted to Seaman and awarded the Silver Star for his part in the hostage rescue at the Thai International.

An *unlikelier* hero Tombstone could not imagine, a five-foot-six eighteen-year-old who had beaten a rebel colonel unconscious. Kriangsak was still in the hospital and under guard. His conversations with Thai and American interrogators had already filled in most of the missing pieces, and the Burmese general captured at U Feng had told them the rest.

Evidently, the whole operation called *Sheng li* had been put together and run by Hsiao Kuoping, the former Chinese intelligence officer, a man with underworld and revolutionary contacts throughout Southeast Asia. It was incredible that the entire plot had been assembled without sanction, without help from Beijing . . . but stranger things had happened. As the halls of power crumbled in communist capitals around the world, it seemed, more and more of the occupants of those halls were trying to carve new and secure niches for themselves elsewhere.

Hsiao had been one such . . . his ally General Kol of Burma another. Their plan had been to topple the Thai government and install their own, probably with Kriangsak as the new leader and with themselves as the powers behind the throne. Hsiao and his organization would then have been in a position to control much of the opium and heroin trade coming down from the Golden Triangle . . . a control which would

have been worth tens of billions of dollars and made Kriangsak, Kol, and Hsiao three of the wealthiest and most powerful
men on Earth.

The ambassador concluded his remarks and stepped away
from the podium, to general applause from the audience. An
expectant hush fell over the crowd as the King rose from his
throne and took several steps forward.

General Duong stood behind the podium, adjusting the
microphone. "Lieutenant Commander Matthew Magruder," he
said. "Front and center!"

Tombstone gripped the hilt of his dress sword with his
gloved left hand and strode forward. He'd rehearsed this
maneuver time and time again . . . always with the secret
dread that he would trip over the unaccustomed obstacle of his
scabbard and fall facedown in the grass.

Bhumibol made a short speech in Thai, then turned and held
out his hand. General Duong opened a wooden box, revealing
the medal.

The *Ramathepbodi,* the King's Coin of Courage—Thai
equivalent of the Medal of Honor. The King removed it from
its red velvet resting place, unfolded the ribbon, and draped it
over Tombstone's neck.

"Thank you, my friend," the King said in English, his
clipped and slightly Bostonian accent reminding Tombstone of
Commander Neil. He remembered reading someplace that
Bhumibol had actually been born in Cambridge, Massachu-
setts, while his father was studying medicine at Harvard.
"Your leadership in the battle over U Feng saved a number of
our fighters . . . as well as the helicopters of the airmobile
forces. We owe you . . . and your men . . . a debt which
can never be repaid."

Tombstone snapped a rigidly correct salute. "Thank you,
Your Majesty."

The King returned the salute. Mindful again of his sword,
Tombstone wheeled an about-face and marched back to the
ranks. His uncle stood in the front row, beaming, and Tombstone knew that *this* award had nothing to do with Admiral

Thomas J. Magruder. Another Magruder—Sam Magruder of the Doumer Bridge in Hanoi—would have been proud.

So was Tombstone. He saw Pamela standing in the front rank of civilians, caught her eye, and grinned.

She smiled back, radiant. He knew now that he loved her. And that was more important than any medal.

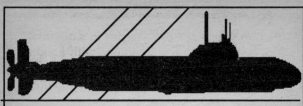

Tom Clancy's

#1 *New York Times* Bestsellers

___THE HUNT FOR RED OCTOBER 0-425-12027-9/$5.95
"Flawless authenticity, frighteningly genuine."
—*The Wall Street Journal*

___RED STORM RISING 0-425-10107-X/$5.99
"Brilliant . . . Staccato suspense."—*Newsweek*

___PATRIOT GAMES 0-425-10972-0/$5.99
"Marvelously tense . . . He is a master of the genre he seems
to have created."—*Publishers Weekly*

___THE CARDINAL OF THE KREMLIN 0-425-11684-0/$5.99
"The best of the Jack Ryan series!"—*New York Times*

___CLEAR AND PRESENT DANGER 0-425-12212-3/$5.99
"Clancy's best work since *The Hunt For Red October*."
—*Publishers Weekly*